The station had been blessedly quiet for hours. Most of the guys were in front of the tube, watching the pre-pre-pregame shows for the All-Star game. Her cell phone went off. She glanced at it. Mom. Huh, odd, this was the time their shift started. Usually she and Dad were hot on some project at Alienville at this point in the day. She answered it. "Hi Mom, what—"

The sounds coming over the phone stopped her heart. Screaming. Explosions. Someone—it sounded like Dad—yelling. "In the shelter! Now! *Go, go, go!*"

And her Mom's voice, shaking, saying only "Red alert. Lockdown."

Then the phone went dead.

Then the klaxons in the station went off.

All hell broke loose outside.

Inside the fire station, no one paid attention to the klaxons signaling the callout of all possible personnel. It didn't matter. They couldn't have gotten there anyway. Bella crouched in the door and stared in horror.

There were nine-foot-tall suits of chrome-plated armor, hosing down the street outside with the energy cannons built into their arms.

It looked like there were about twenty of them; one of them was all black, but the rest of them gleamed in the harsh Vegas sunlight like something right out of one of the city's stage shows. Except that things out of stage shows didn't explode cars and chase screaming civilians and—

Oh hell no—

Those cannons were swiveling to point at the station!

INVASION

Book One of the
SECRET WORLD CHRONICLE

Created by Mercedes Lackey & Steve Libbey

Written by
MERCEDES LACKEY
with Steve Libbey, Cody Martin & Dennis Lee

Edited by Larry Dixon

BAEN

INVASION: BOOK ONE OF THE SECRET WORLD CHRONICLE

Copyright © 2011 by Mercedes Lackey, Steve Libbey, Cody Martin, and Dennis Lee

A Baen Books Original

Baen Publishing Enterprises
P.O. Box 1403
Riverdale, NY 10471
www.baen.com

ISBN: 978-1-4516-3772-4

Cover art by Larry Dixon

First Baen paperback printing, January 2012

Library of Congress Control Number: 2010052022

Distributed by Simon & Schuster
1230 Avenue of the Americas
New York, NY 10020

Pages by Joy Freeman (www.pagesbyjoy.com)
Printed in the United States of America

Jonathan Hickman, Sean McKeever, Dale Eaglesham, Nicola Scott, Howard Porter, Carlo Pagulayan, J.H. Williams III, Harry & Jay Knowles & AICN, Spider Jerusalem, Cracked.com, BoingBoing.net, Wizard's Asylum, Zeus Comics and our amazing friends at Comic Book Resources, YABS, and Comics Alliance, The Cities of Claremore, Las Vegas, Atlanta and Tulsa, The Ventures, The Aquabats, Tom Waits, Nick Cave, Mark Mancina, SomaFM, Radio Rivendell,Scott Shaw!, Unscrewed!, Gayla, Dalton, Tiyada, Awbrey, Mr. Mike, Dale, Keith, Rob, all of our RPG and gamer buddies, Curt, Tammy, Alex, Paul & Tor, Joe Phillips, Adult Swim, Ken Mitchroney, Seanbaby, Chris Sims, Tony Bedard, Peter David, Scott McCloud, Dan Slott, Tamora Pierce, Barb & Karl Kesel, Jodi Picoult, Paul Gulacy, Doug Moench, Brian Stelfreeze, Peter & Gary, AtlasOK, Heather Reddy, David Libbey, Charity Heller Hogge, Wm Thoma, Bengt Halvorson, Austin Wright, Jon Christopher Hughes, Gene Wolfe, Stanislaw Lem, Thomas Pynchon, The Gentlemen at Centaur Guitar, Leo Fender, Champ & Violent.

For everybody who ever bagged & boarded a comic book, picked up a d20, and ever wanted to fly.

And the biggest

best

Thank You

goes to the fans of the ongoing podcast series voiced by Veronica Giguere at www.secretworldchronicle.com for their continuing enthusiasm and support.
We could never have gotten this far without you.

ACKNOWLEDGEMENTS

But above all:

. We owe this story to City of Heroes/City of Villains/ Going Rogue, the MMORPG by NCsoft and Paragon Studios where all these characters first were born. They evolved, grew, and changed from their original concepts, but much of that development took place in the world of Paragon City. If you would like to play in our favorite addiction, go to www.cityofheroes.com and give it a try. Who knows? One day you might meet up with one of us.

PART ONE

The Way the World Ends

The blue-skinned, blue-haired woman known by the callsign "Belladonna Blue" leaned into the oval hatch of the captain's cubby. She was already suited up in her white, full-body nanoarmor, with only her head exposed. Her helmet was under her arm. "You've got about two hours, Vic. Make the most of it."

Victoria Victrix nodded. She hoped someone was going to be around to read the file when all this was over.

She began to type, hesitantly at first, but picked up speed as she went to make the most of what little time there was left.

Whoever you are that's reading this, you might not know that the real genesis of where we are now was back in 1935.

That was when the first metahumans first started showing up in Nazi Germany, paraded before screaming crowds at Hitler's rallies. The very first to appear were Vaterland, *and his sidekick,* Hitlerjungend. *Then came the one the rest were named for—Ubermensch. And honestly, nobody thought they were anything but propaganda blow-ups using stage magic and fakery until the Blitzkrieg started pounding across Europe. But there* were more of these Ubermenschen, and all by themselves they were the equivalent of entire battalions and tank corps. For a while they had it all their own way, too.

That changed during the Battle of Britain; the waves of fighter-bombers were being led by a Nazi who had reflexes like nobody's business and hardly needed a plane at all.

The Black Baron.

Bullets literally bounced off him. His "plane" was a frame with eight machine guns and an armored engine. He could pull maneuvers that would easily have sent anyone else into full blackout. He was an unstoppable one-man fighter squadron. And he was cutting the RAF down at the coastline.

One of those RAF pilots was Lieutenant Commander Nigel Patterson, whose plane burst into flames and disintegrated around him under the Baron's guns.

Except "Nige" didn't die, because something happened to him in that instant. Out of the explosion burst a fireball that was a man, who proceeded to punch holes with his body into every Nazi fighter-bomber in that formation. Then he landed on the frame of the Black Baron's craft, ripped the control cables and fuel lines out, and punched the Baron square in the nose for good measure, knocking him out. The Baron's "plane" folded up and plummeted. Maybe the Baron could survive bullets, but he couldn't survive a terminal-velocity fall with an armored V-16 engine crushing him. He turned into a red smear on the ground.

Spitfire, the first of the Allied supers, was born.

Time after time, again and again, it happened during the War. Nazi, Italian Fascist and Japanese metas would show up and kick butt for a while, and then something bizarre would happen on the battlefield. Suddenly they were facing someone that could take them. That changed the way the war was fought. The metas battled it out one on one, gladiator style, leaving conventional forces to win or lose the battles. And after the war was over, the metas that didn't much cotton to law and order just moved on to crime. Which was where Echo came in, funded by the eccentric but charismatic nephew of Nikola Tesla who had a boatload of his uncle's inventions and the savvy to make them pay off handsomely. Echo organized the old metas from former WWII vets and recruited new ones, bundling them all into a single organization. And for a while, well, things in the world looked a lot like the comic book writers from before the war used to picture them. Every city had its Echo HQ, and you'd see the occasional metavillain pulling off something extreme and your local Echo OpTwo or Three would take him out, either alone or with a team. People got used to it, and couldn't remember a time without metas, actually. They collected trading cards and action figures, and wore buttons with their favorites on them, like they did with ball players. Metas got legislated, with the Extreme Force laws and the Control Officer mandate. Echo built special containment prisons for metavillains. It was a lot less scary than the threat of the A-bomb, and then the H-bomb. And a lot more marketable.

Echo's main HQ was in Atlanta, because Yankee Doodle and Dixie Belle got married right after the end of WWII and settled there, and they were the pride of the US Metahuman Corps. Atlanta was pretty central, fairly modern, and had access to just about anything, but was not Washington, DC, or NYC.

Andro Tesla wanted to keep Echo away from the US centers of politics.

Then came the day that everything changed. My friends and I were right in the middle of it.

Who am I? I'm Victoria Victrix Nagy, magician, metahuman, romance writer, and hacker, at your service. I'll try to chronicle what happened. I'm not a reporter—I'm trying to pull together notes and stories, write this all down as best I can and I hope I don't screw it up. I'll give you the truth, as far as we know it. You'll know the mistakes we made, and hopefully someone will have a record of who was a hero, who gave all, and just how much we lost. And for us, for me, this is how it began.

Welcome to our nightmare.

CHAPTER ONE

Before The Storm

MERCEDES LACKEY, STEVE LIBBEY,
CODY MARTIN & DENNIS LEE

Atlanta, Georgia, USA: Callsign Eisenfaust
I Minus 24:00:00 and Counting

Eisenfaust hunkered in the shadows of an alleyway outside a bar. At the end of the block, a stark white wall terminated the nighttime darkness like a false horizon, surrounding a brightly lit tower with windows as slender as a man's arm: the Echo Security Facility, one of the most heavily guarded buildings in the United States of America.

He had survived the plane crash—as Germany's greatest pilot, he knew how to ditch a plane—but he hadn't counted on the flimsiness of twenty-first century aircraft; his broken arm throbbed, not quite healed yet.

Better than the fate his pursuers had encountered in the Andes. He almost wished he was back in the jungle stronghold, just long enough to mock the Commandant who had stolen his beautiful Valkyria from him.

Ah, Effi. Your betrayal cut deep.

7

He would not fall prey to the foolishness that won Valkyria. Eisenfaust had fought for the Fatherland, for his fellow Deutschlander, for the freedom his people deserved. But this...this was madness.

And in keeping with his *nom de guerre*, he'd crush it under his fist. But he needed allies, and he needed time to plan.

Slowly, he made his way down the dim street to the Echo compound. These American *Ubermenschen* would surely be surprised by the identity of their uninvited guest.

The guard at the gate eyed him. "The campus is closed, sir."

"I wish to speak to your commanding officer," Eisenfaust said. "Fetch him at once."

"Ah...right. You'll have to come back tomorrow. We open at nine A.M."

"I have no intention of waiting." Eisenfaust scowled at the enlisted man. "Your commander—bring him."

A second guard stepped out of the booth, wary of the increasing tension in the air. "We can't do that, sir. Please step away from the gate."

Eisenfaust cursed under his breath. Even the Allied Aces had shown him more deference than these flunkies. He pointed at the security tower. "That is my destination. If you cannot assist me, step aside."

Both guards reached for their sidearms. Moving with the inhuman speed that made him Germany's greatest aerial ace, he swatted the guns out of their hands before they could level them in his direction. The two men gasped.

With his good arm, he flattened the first guard with a blow to the chin. "I will find him myself!" he exclaimed furiously. The second guard knelt to seize his gun; Eisenfaust booted the man in the side, hurling him back into the booth.

With a contemptuous sniff, he kicked the guns aside and walked to the door of the detention facility.

In wartime Eisenfaust would never have been so careless as to simply leave the guards unconscious, but his goal was not to kill these men. He was here to make his presence known. Eisenfaust opened the glass doors, approving of their weight; the bulletproof glass was two inches thick and obscured the lobby.

"Stop right there, mister." The speaker was a fine example of American manhood: tall, wide-shouldered, a face with mongrel features, topped with a swath of light brown hair. His black Echo uniform sported epaulets decorated with the Stars and Stripes. A thick metal gauntlet on his right hand glowed with plasma energy—and was directed at Eisenfaust.

"*Guten nacht*, my friend. I am told you have rooms for rent."

A score of Echo guards with rifles lined up behind the meta. "We have plenty of room for punks who smack our people around. Don't make me use force."

"Good. I was hoping to speak to someone with authority." He drew himself up into a salute. "I wish to turn myself in."

"Now that was easy." The meta motioned the guards forward, who circled Eisenfaust. "Take him in, boys. Watch those hands."

Eisenfaust gestured to his broken arm. "You have nothing to fear from me, young man. I am a colleague of your father's." A guard handcuffed his wrists, eliciting a wince of pain.

"I doubt that. Pop died over twenty years ago, and I don't think he ever managed to buddy up to a German after the war."

A tinge of doubt crossed Eisenfaust's mind. "I... I am sorry to hear this. He was a fine warrior, the best I ever faced."

"Huh?" The metahuman looked at him closely. "Now you're messing with me. You can't be a day over thirty."

"You are correct, in a sense." The shackles clanked as he offered his hand. "I am Oberst Heinrich Eisenhauer of the Uberluftwaffe of the Third Reich." He paused, enjoying the look on the young man's face. "Your father, Yankee Doodle, knew me as Eisenfaust."

The meta looked from the hand to Eisenfaust's face. "Bull," he said at last. "He died fighting the Allied Aces. In 1945."

"Then your father told you about me. Clearly you carry on his legacy."

A succession of expressions passed over the American's face so quickly that anyone lacking Eisenfaust's metahuman perceptions would not have registered anything but a frown: first surprise, then reflection, then the cold, strategic calculation of a man used to secrets. His bluff bravado returned in less than a heartbeat.

"As Yankee Pride, yeah. And we're a little too savvy to let some Nazi fetishist get his rocks off by pretending to be a dead Nazi war criminal. Did you leave Hitler's brain in your Panzer tank out front?" Yankee Pride backed off as Echo guards seized Eisenfaust's arms, wrenching his broken arm. "Put him in a holding cell under suicide watch until we can ID this wingnut."

The guards began to drag Eisenfaust down the hallway towards the cell block. He called out: "Ask your mother! Or Liberty Torch! Or Worker's Champion! They knew me. They *feared* me! They will recognize me!"

"Save it for the shrink, Fritz," Yankee Pride replied. He tapped at controls on his gauntlet, gesturing oddly at Eisenfaust for a moment.

Eisenfaust calmed himself. He assumed the Americans would be suspicious of a man claiming to be one of their country's greatest foes. He would overcome their doubts.

"You're taking me to a cell?" he asked a guard. "Is it secure?"

"No one's ever gotten out of Echo," the man sneered.

"That's admirable." Eisenfaust gave the man a prophetic smile. "But it's who will try to get *in* that concerns me."

Las Vegas, Nevada, USA: Callsign Belladonna Blue I Minus 6:37:22 and Counting

The name on her badge said "Bella Dawn Parker," but Bella's Las Vegas Fire Department callsign was "Blues." Not because she sang them, but because she *was* blue—blue-haired, blue-skinned, a metahuman.

Metahumans didn't stand out in a city like Lost Wages, where you could stand waiting for the bus next to a Russian acrobat, a seven-foot-tall transvestite in Cleopatra drag, a guy with an albino anaconda wrapped around his shoulders, and five Elvii, and all anyone wanted to talk about was the Rebels' football scores.

She was the rookie in Station 7 of the Las Vegas Fire Department, alternate driver of Rescue 2, Paramedic

Parker, EMT-4, the highest EMT rank there was, and not so coincidentally, a registered OpOne with Echo Rescue.

There'd been a huge dump fire earlier that had taken hours to put out and had occasioned a three-station roll-out, so everyone was starving. They all rolled back about 2 A.M., oh-dark-hundred, and it was her turn to cook, which mean they were getting spaghetti, easy to reheat. Rarely did anyone in a firehouse get to finish a sit-down meal.

She lounged back and watched the guys trundle in, mostly still wet from showers. They still stank a little of burnt rubber.

"Hey, Blues?" One of the other rookies looked over at her as he was dishing himself out red sauce. "How'd you get to be EMT-4 so fast? You're only what—19? 20?"

"I slept with the instructor," she smirked. "Naw, it's actually a lot less dirty than that. I started taking the EMT courses while I was still in school. They needed me at ball games and stuff, and they wanted me legal. I got the jumpstart 'cause Echo Rescue tapped me for the touch-healing when I was twelve."

"Damn, there goes my bet..."

New York, New York, USA: Callsign John Murdock I Minus 6:22:17 and Counting

John Murdock sat on a bench in an out-of-the-way corner of Central Park with his face buried in his hands, laden down with a feeling that could only be described as "soul-weary," assuming there were such things as souls. Since he'd found this spot, he'd never seen anyone else use it. Possibly because it was a frequent target for pigeons. With his eyes closed, he tried to shut out the happy ruckus of ordinary folks having a cheap good time.

In the middle distance, he could hear a street preacher sounding off. And then, from somewhere behind him, the sirens of three cop cars wailed as they gave chase. He'd stopped looking for somewhere to hide whenever he heard sirens about a year ago, but the sound still made his nerves twitch.

Whoever they were chasing wasn't giving up without a fight.

Probably there was no one in this park who could hear what he was picking up: the sounds of gunshots under the sirens. Single shots, all semi-auto. Handguns, then.

Then he picked up something else. Microjets, tearing through the concrete canyons, on a vector that would converge with that of the sirens.

Echo jet pack. Whatever the perps had done, it had to be bad to earn them metahuman attention. *Tough luck, chumps. Cavalry is comin'.* He leaned back, sighing heavily. *Like you're one to talk, chump.* Every time he heard something like this, ten years of training to protect the innocent warred with five years of paranoia, but as ever, survival instinct and the paranoia won. The sounds ended with no way of telling the outcome—other than that the meta with the jets had clearly triumphed, since they spun down a minute after the shots ended.

He shook his head. Things, little things, really hit home for him when it was bright and sunny out, like it was today. There were days when he wondered why he had ever been born. They were happening a lot more often lately, and this was one of them. And "never been born" all too easily morphed into "better off dead." He was close, close to that point of no return, but he'd kept on living so far and damned if he was going to give up now. Sheer stubbornness maybe, or just the bargain-basement revenge of outliving the bastards that had put him in this position in the first place.

He stood up, tired of feeling sorry for himself. He started walking away from the park, skirting on the periphery of the tree line, and kept going for several blocks, letting his mind go blank. Funny how people thought of New York as a terribly dangerous place to live. In fact, it was more like a series of vertical villages: people knew each other, went to the same little snack shops, bought milk at the same bodegas. The fact that he didn't belong in any of those little enclaves made the gloom wrap around his soul even tighter.

Eventually, he found a bar; a real Irish neighborhood joint that must have been there for a century, the sort of place that firefighters and steel workers went to after putting in their shifts. Alcohol wasn't really a cure, but it sure worked wonders for the short term. Six A.M. might be early to start drinking by most people's standards but nobody in this bar was keeping track.

But he wasn't going to get any trouble here as long as he didn't start any himself. At six feet even and 200 pounds, he wasn't huge, not by the standards nowadays, where you saw Echo metas that were the size of park statues, but he wasn't a pipsqueak either.

Mostly, though, it was the way he moved and held himself that made trouble avoid him, recognizing him for a fellow predator.

Inside the door, he looked up. There was a patina of hard use and age on everything. He strode up to the bar, spying a whiteboard listing the drink prices. *Cheap.* It was the first bit of good news he'd had all day. Money was running out. It went fast in this town, even when you were sleeping rough and making do with the showers at the Salvation Army. Be time to find a job soon, under-the-counter pay, shady construction work, janitor...he hoped he wouldn't have to go on the gray side of the law. Still, he figured that he had enough to get drunk with, and maybe even some money left over for half of a decent meal. Or one full meal at a soup kitchen and a real bed at a flophouse.

John sat down hard on the wooden stool, resting his elbows on the worn counter in front of him. The barkeep was busy having a conversation with a middle-aged couple at the right end of the bar. John knew what the barkeep saw: a customer maybe, but one that wasn't going to spend a lot of money, even by the standards of this place. Clothing nondescript. Jean jacket, white shirt, and cargo pants; clean, but they had seen too many hard wearings and washings. His brown hair, a little too long and uneven, hadn't seen a barber for a long time. Compact muscles and expressionless gray-green eyes, like two cold pebbles, also said he might be trouble, as did the callused knuckles. Fingerless gloves. Fistfighters tended to wear those. John rapped his knuckles against the counter a few times until the bartender tore himself away; he was an older man, with shock-white hair and a day-old stubble shading his chin. "What'll it be?" he asked, his tone shaded with impatience as well as wariness.

John looked up wearily, meeting the bartender's

eyes, and shoved a ten spot toward him. "Whatever's the house special."

"House rye, dollar a shot, coming up." The barkeep really *was* in a hurry to get back to the conversation. He shoved a half-full bottle—John's eagle eye measured the contents as just about ten shots' worth—and a shot glass across the counter at John, and turned back to the couple. He resumed his banter, stopping short to eye John up. "We'll be having you pay as you go, too."

Echo Headquarters, Atlanta, Georgia, USA:
Callsign Eisenfaust
I Minus 02:32:15 and Counting

By day, the Echo detention facility hummed with energy. Metahuman prisoners could not be afforded the same liberties as conventional convicts: no exercise yard, no recreation room, no library. Even the classic prison pose, leaning against the bars with hands useless and dangling, was denied them. The reinforced steel doors contained grills that afforded a limited view of the corridor.

Some deemed it cruel. Most considered it necessary due to the unique nature of the metahumans. Ordinary criminals could be disarmed, metas couldn't. Metapowers were, by law, lethal weapons that had to be registered with local law enforcement and the government.

Eisenfaust paced his cell. After his death-defying escape from the clutches of the Thule Society, confinement was maddening. These imprisoned men and women were scum, and to be interred with them, even by choice, grated on his nerves.

The grill at the foot of his door slid open to admit a tray with his lunch. "Guard," he said. "I have waited for your commanders to speak to me for far too long. Where is Yankee Pride?"

"Out doing his job," the guard answered abruptly.

"Why has he not contacted me? I told him I have critical information, a matter of national security." Hand pressed against the door, he perversely longed for the typical iron bars of a jail.

"Sure you do."

The guard tapped a button with his foot. The serving grill slid shut with a final clatter. He stepped back behind the food cart.

"You're all in terrible danger," Eisenfaust said, his voice becoming strident with urgency. "Please, you cannot ignore this threat for long."

The guard sighed. He leaned against the door. "Listen, pal," he said. "If it'll shut you up, I can tell you this: they're sending an Echo Support detective down here to interview you after lunch. Save it for her, okay?"

Without another word the man wheeled out of sight. Eisenfaust stepped back, mind racing. A detective? Hardly an official, but at least someone who was trusted to report on matters of consequence.

He felt momentarily giddy. "*Danke*," he called down the hall.

"Dankay? What kinda nonsense you spouting?" The rough voice came from the cell directly across his. The face behind the grill was black; blacker than a human should be.

"*Deutsch, mein freund.* German. It means 'thanks.'"

"You ain't been here long if you're thanking the

COs," the black shape said. "You probably think you're in here by mistake."

"*Nein*. I asked to be here."

The voice laughed, a coarse bark. "Didn't know stupidity was illegal."

Eisenfaust scowled. "I suppose you're incarcerated for rudeness."

Again, the staccato laugh. "Not me. Robbery with metahuman powers. Aggravated assault. Resisting arrest."

"You're lucky Echo is so permissive. I'd have killed you on the spot."

"Oh ho ho, big man. You're scaring me. What're you in for?"

Eisenfaust thought for a moment. "I killed one hundred and twelve men that I know of."

Silence fell upon the corridor around them.

"Yeah?" The black shape moved away from the grill, his voice smaller.

"Yes. Shooting. Bombing. By plane, by pistol . . . two with a knife. One with my bare hands." All necessary deaths in wartime, he told himself, though in this den of thieves he took some relish in trumping their claims. No criminal can exceed the sins of a man at war.

"Damn."

"So in my eyes, you're all mere amateurs. Worse, your crimes were committed for selfish reasons. I fought for my country."

Every ear seemed to be turned to their conversation. Eisenfaust flushed. His story wasn't for these lowlifes; only Echo and their metas were his peers, regardless of what cause they served.

A high-pitched voice sang out from his right: "He shut you up good, Slycke!"

"Go to hell," Slycke rumbled. "My daddy served in 'Nam. Killed him a dozen gooks and brought back their fingers on a string. This guy ain't no different, except..." His voiced trailed off. "Who'd you serve under?"

"Haven't you guessed?" Eisenfaust paused for effect. "Adolf Hitler."

The corridor erupted with angry shouting. The guards came through in squads, banging on the cell doors with energized prods and calling for order. Eisenfaust took his meal to his seat and smiled as he picked at the cornbread and ham. Soon he'd meet with the detective and give her enough tidbits to earn him an audience with the master of the house.

Alex Tesla.

Atlanta, Georgia, USA: Callsign Victoria Victrix
I Minus 02:23:56 and Counting

Victoria Victrix Nagy stood in her cozy living room, surrounded by the sandalwood scent of her candles, by the armor of her shelves of books and music and movies, and stared at the closed door of her apartment, gathering her strength and her courage. She was about to do battle, as she did about every two weeks, and the fight was going to require every resource she could muster. She checked, once again, to make sure that her protections were in place, that she was covered from chin to toes with not so much as a millimeter of skin exposed. The battle she faced was inside herself, and she faced it every time she had to leave her apartment.

And it wasn't getting any easier for standing there.

She took a shuddering breath, felt her throat closing, her heart racing, heard the blood pounding in her ears. And the fear, the terrible, blinding, paralyzing fear spread through her, making her knees weak, her hands shake.

But there was no choice. She had to eat. It was time to do the grocery shopping, panic attacks or no panic attacks.

<Come on, Vic,> she heard her cat, her familiar Greymalkin, say in her mind. <You can do this. Do it for me. I'm out of tuna, and the kibbles are almost gone.>

That did it. That broke the hold for a moment, as Grey had probably figured it would.

"Selfish beast," she said aloud, with a shaky laugh.

<What did you expect? I'm a cat, not Mahatma Gandhi.>

On the strength of that laugh, she got to the door, and opened it. There was no one in the hallway, with its worn brown carpet and forty-watt lighting. It was people that triggered her panic attacks, not places.

She chose her time and day carefully. It was early afternoon, the day of the All-Star game. Those who were not at the game, or the pregame events, or thronging to glamorous parties in hopes of getting a glimpse or even an autograph of some movie star, or on the streets hawking cheesy giant foam hands and sun visors, were either at work, or at home. No one sane went anywhere, unless you could do so without resorting to any major streets or, god forbid, the Interstates. The traffic reports said that within a mile of some of the Star Parties it was taking an hour to go three blocks. The grocery stores would be deserted. Earlier this morning there would have been a last-minute run on the staples of the day: beer, hot dogs and buns, beer, ice, beer, soda and beer. Now, bored employees would be bowling in the empty aisles with frozen turkeys. Fortunately, the neighborhood of Peachtree Park would be spared most of the horror of the day. It was a blue-collar, working-class neighborhood, but the workers had, for the most part, long since retired to their thirties-era bungalows. There wouldn't be many barbecues here today; the residents were inside to watch the game, sensibly isolated from the unseasonable heat (ninety degrees in February!) and the bugs, and especially from the "Georgia State Bird," the mosquito. So the streets should be as deserted as if it was four A.M. on a Sunday.

She made it down the hall to the elevator, an ancient model complete with brass grill inner doors. She pushed the button for the first floor, and the old cage shuddered and made its slow descent. There was no one in the lobby. Her sneaker-shod feet made barely a whisper against the worn-out gray linoleum as she crossed the lobby and let herself out through the front door.

The parking lot was full. This was, after all, a fifteen-story apartment building constructed in an era when people took buses and streetcars to work. The parking lot was always full, and those few residents who didn't own a car could command a nice little monthly fee for the use of their assigned space. Vickie's was as far from the building as physically possible, because the super knew that she only moved her little econobox when she absolutely had to.

It looked as if there wouldn't be much in the way of cloud cover today, and cars would turn into ovens, even with the air conditioning on. It was only around nine A.M., but this was going to take her...a while. Her little light blue, nondescript basic-mobile was parked under a giant live oak, which could be a nuisance in acorn season, but its shade was nice now. She could actually hold the steering wheel without using oven mitts.

Once in the car, she let out a sigh of relief, and waited for the trembling in her arms to stop. The first hurdle was cleared.

Actually driving was not a problem, even when there were other cars on the street. It wasn't rational, but her gut regarded the car as a safe little shell, and the panic eased back to jitters as she negotiated the narrow, thirties-era streets. Peachtree Park wasn't a trendy neighborhood, and it certainly had seen better days, but it wasn't a slum. Cracking and peeling paint, and aging roofs, stood in contrast to the immaculate yards.

At the border of Peachtree Park and the next neighborhood of Four Corners, things were changing. There was an Interstate exit that fed Four Corners. There had been demolition and rebuilding in the fifties, then the seventies, and now again. Here was the chain grocery Vickie made her pilgrimage of fear to whenever the supplies got too low. As she rounded the corner, she prayed that she would find the parking lot empty.

It was, and again she breathed a sigh of relief. There was nothing there but five identical semi-truck trailers—odd, but...

Well, it was the day of the All-Star game, and it

was entirely possible the drivers had realized they were never going to get anywhere today and had rendezvoused here to watch the TVs in the cabs and have an impromptu party of their own.

This was the least of her worries. In a moment, she would park the car. She would have to get out of the car, and walk to the entrance of the grocery. Only a few feet but—there would be people there. People who would stare at her, the way they had looked at her—after. With revulsion. With loathing. With hatred—

Get a grip. This is now, not then. They're just people. People here for groceries, nothing more.

But her palms were sweating now, and her short hair was damp with sweat, her mouth was dry, and as she turned off the ignition, her hands and arms were shaking and she had to force herself to reach for the door handle and then pop the door open. She was hot and cold by turns, her stomach so knotted that she was getting sick and regretting that cup of coffee and morning toast...

It would probably take her two hours to convince herself to leave the car.

Atlanta, Georgia, USA: Callsign Red Djinni
I Minus 01:58:27 and Counting

In a perfect world—well, in *my* perfect world—things would still be chaotic. I know I'm in the minority here. If you're one of those people who strive for that great secure job with regular cash showers in your ten-acre estate, I'm sorry, I just don't get you. I can't think of any place more boring than the common perception of paradise. To have everything you want when you want it, when would you ever feel your blood rushing through your veins with the bit caught in your teeth, riding the razor's edge with a wind of flames at your back, or any other dozen clichés for the extreme life?

See, I need the rush, but I wouldn't say I'm a thrill-seeker. It's a trait that gets a lot of people killed. I've seen it happen, believe me. Heh, I once knew this crazy bastard called Gash. *Big* guy! Loved movies with midgets, dainty blondes he could pick up with one arm, and he had this weird thing for... badgers.

Don't ask.

But what Gash loved most was *speed*. He'd get into anything with propulsion just to see how fast he could go. This one time, he got some booster rockets, right? Don't ask me how, but he did, and then he...

Wait, sorry. That's a long story, and the stuff about the badgers will haunt you.

So... thrill-seeking. I don't think it applies, not to me, not entirely anyway. Risking your neck for nothing more than thrills can get real old real fast. There has to be more, there has to be... well, yeah, there has to be *women*. And pardon me for saying it, as women make up a good part of why I'm alive, but even that's not enough. Fame? Yes, that works for some. Money? Definite bonuses there.

Beating the other guy? Oh man, nothing gets it done like competition.

So that's where you'll find me—high risk, high stakes. It brings out the Masters and I am a Master, if I do say so myself. I never got caught, not until that day. And I don't even think that day *counts*. I know, a Master doesn't let his surroundings or the situation get to him. He stays on the job, he keeps focus, and he wins his prize. But you have to understand, that day was the worst day. Ever.

Who am I? Red Djinni at your service. Chameleon, acrobat, mercenary and lover.

Let me paint you a mental picture. Three men and a woman get out of a dark, sporty sedan. Something has their attention. They are watching a group of masked idiots with guns running into a bank.

Notice the four people are wincing.

They're not wincing in fear. Together, these four have run gauntlets of jagged metal rain and poison gas. Combat, while avoided when possible, is second nature to them. The last time they were here in Atlanta, they were forced into an open .street battle with an OpTwo and her flunkies. It cost them months because it forced a retreat into the labyrinths of America's metahuman underground.

They're not wincing in disbelief. The idea of robbers holding up a bank in broad daylight, and in one of the most Echo-populated cities in the world, might seem absurd—but let's remember something. In every demographic, from world leaders to the criminal element, you're going to find some really stupid people.

So no, not fear and not disbelief. These people are wincing in anger. For about a month now they'd been planning a job of their own. A heist like this in Atlanta had to be done carefully. You had to get in, grab the goods, get out, and get away without anyone even knowing you were there. If so much as a brief physical description got out, Echo would be on you within a day, a week, tops. Say what you want about the showmanship and flash of Echo agents, they were damned good at their jobs. Countermeasures had to be taken. This crew had learned that lesson once the hard way. To do this job, they had to be invisible.

And that's where I come in. If you haven't already guessed, I'm one of the four. Not the short man drowning in muscles, and not the man who's as thin as a rail and sporting a long beak nose, and obviously not the gorgeous brunette with legs that go up to her neck. I'm the elderly driver with the withered, beaten-down-by-life expression, with the beer gut hanging over a cheap imitation-leather belt, and sporting a worn polyester security guard uniform bearing a cracked plastic name tag for a "Walter Semsdale." Not what you expected, huh? Well, that's the point. If you know how, you can be invisible in plain sight.

We had planned and trained and waited for the day of the All-Star game, the day the majority of security forces in the city would be concentrated on the other end of town. We had charted rapid routes of escape, memorized the full layout of the bank, and more importantly, of the secret bunker underneath where items of immeasurable wealth and importance were often kept. Simply nicknamed the Vault, this was the most secure facility in the city after the main Echo headquarters, hidden beneath a façade of a medium security investment group and banking outlet, and we knew the place cold now. We had studied this job from every angle, and we realized it could only be done one way, just the one, if we were going to get out with no fuss.

This had to be an inside job.

Like most high-security places, the design is to keep people out and not so much in. Study any blueprint of a vault or fortress and you'll see it. A group starting at the heart of the place can work their way out, disabling alarms, taking out cameras and incapacitating armed resistance with just a little coordination. But the worst-case scenario, whether you're heading in or out, is an alarm being triggered. Once the entire place is up in arms, the odds of surviving, let alone reaching your prize, are slim. Hey, I love a challenge, but I hate suicidal runs. The object is to live to tell the tale, you know? So we needed an inside man, but the last thing we needed was another person to siphon off a split of the take.

Enter Walter Semsdale.

Walter's one of the senior security staff at the Vault, and while he doesn't hold top-level clearance, he can walk in through the front door, descend from the public bank above and into the Vault's inner sanctum. He has access to the main monitor room. He's also a 49-year-old divorcé who suffers from regular bouts of gout, indigestion, and epic levels of halitosis. His sense of humor matches his diligence to personal hygiene. I know all this because I just spent the last two weeks getting to know Walter at his favorite watering hole. Didn't take much. A few stories about loose women, buying the first few rounds, and I became Walter's new best friend. I even got to like him a little. Pathos, I guess. Walter is a world-class loser, and I tend to root for the underdogs. Studying Walter—his mannerisms, his own bawdy stories and taking in one whore joke after another—I found him an easy mask. Walter proved to be one of the simpler people I've studied to impersonate. Probably the hardest part of this job was learning to grow Walter's face. He has that look of a beagle, with folds that droop from his eyes and mouth like his skin is trying to escape. Growing that much skin is a pretty tedious task, even for me...

Guess I should have mentioned it before. I'm a meta. Don't need to get into all the details right now, but let's just say I'm closer to my skin than anyone else alive.

So...Walter. Right now we've got Walter strung up in his home. I'm wearing his uniform, sporting his less-than-dapper looks and I gotta tell you, this fake beer gut I've got strapped on is hotter than hell.

The inside job is the easiest, the safest and the stealthiest job you can perform. Still, when your mark is a fortress like the Vault it requires a lot of time and energy to plan out. So when we watched these rank amateurs, toting some cheap-ass, dime-store-bought hardware, rush into the bank, we knew what would happen next. They would get the people cowering on the floor, they would take out what superficial security there was in the bankfront, and by doing this, they would trigger the alarm that would put the whole facility, including the Vault, on alert. The Walter guise was now useless. I wouldn't be able to get where I needed to, to knock out surveillance and communications, and while we had contingency plans, the one thing we absolutely needed was for me to get in undetected. A whole month of preparation, wiped out just like that.

Still got that picture of the four of us, mouths open, watching our plans go up in flames? Good, hold onto it for a second, it gets kind of funny.

I've had maybe four perfect jobs in my life. The rest can range from "we're twenty seconds behind schedule" to "where did that OpTwo come from?" In each case, we've dealt with it. At times, I admit we've been damned lucky. But this . . . *this* was beyond a mere glitch. This was every god in the heavens looking down and saying: "We're sorry, but today we will make you our bitches."

The beak-nosed man is Duff Sanction, probably my best and oldest friend. In this game, you need people you can trust, and Duff has pulled more jobs with me than anyone else. He is simply the best safecracker and demolitionist I have ever met. Oddly enough, he's also a craftsman who makes the most delicate works of crystal and glass. So yes, here we have a man who has the patience and meticulous touch of an artist, but loves to blow things up for his day job. He has an odd, hot-and-cold temper to match. A moment before, I'm sure he had been calculating oxygen balance percentages and composition priorities in his head. These sorts of jobs often called for on-the-fly explosions. Unbelievably, Duff preferred to make some bombs on the spot. To do that, you need to think fast and with complete certainty, two feats that require a level head. On the other hand, when his temper did go off, the results could be spectacular. I once watched him collapse a building using forty sticks of dynamite, rigged in under ten minutes, really!

It was awesome, and all over a pet peeve.

Wait, sorry. That's a long story. Let's just say that those pigeons will never poop on anyone ever again.

By comparison, I'd say Duff took this setback rather well. He wasn't blowing anything up, just smashing his fist repetitively against the side of the car.

"When I catch up to these jerk-offs, I'm going to

make them choose between deep-throating TNT or getting bunged up with nitro enemas!"

He's so gosh-darned cute when he's angry.

The leggy brunette leaning against the car is Jon Bead. It might look like she's nodding enthusiastically with Duff's harsh and colorful words, but really she's just trying not to scream. Too bad, this girl is a great screamer. No, I'm not going to tell you what that means, you already know. Jon is our artillery unit. I've lost count of how many times we've just stood back and let her go to work. A one-woman army when situations get tight, you want someone like Jon on a rooftop providing cover fire.

The short, muscular man sporting the tan duster and lighting a cigarette is Jack. That's the only name he seems to have, and *we* gave it to him. Jack and I handle information gathering, and we both plan the jobs, but in the field he calls the shots. I've never seen him angry, or frustrated, or even crack a smile. He's ice, and always knows what to do. God knows how many of our jobs have needed some weird exotic skillset, and wouldn't you know it, Jack always seemed to have the know-how. Hence his nickname: Jack of all Trades.

"Back in the car." Jack's voice was as gruff as he was short. "Red, drive us around, we'll find some cover and park. Once there we'll suit up."

I wasn't looking. I was still watching the bank, but I could feel Jon and Duff stare at Jack in disbelief. He was proposing to hit the Vault head on, not by the easier route of guile through the bank front, but a full frontal assault on the heavily guarded rear-access blast doors, the one thing all of our scheming and preparation had worked to avoid. Maximum security, and even if the place wasn't now on high alert, getting in would be tantamount to a defiant act of suicide.

"He's right," I remember saying, cutting off any protests they would have. All of them reasonable, I might add. But this time, we had dug ourselves in as deep as we could go. "We're committed; we have to do this. Get in the damned car."

A pause, with just a moment of temerity, but all Duff did was mutter and climb back into the rear seat. Jon did the same, but she did it with *sass*. It had taken them a moment, but it was dawning on them. Jack and I were not asking them to go all Butch and Sundance. We were proceeding with the only course of action that allowed a hope of survival.

You see, we were on Mr. Tonda's dime.

You've heard of Tonda, you must have. He'd gotten so successful as a crime kingpin that his name had escaped the whispered, frightened tones of the underground and into modern pop culture. There were songs written about him, and at the time the latest craze in TV villains were barely concealed imitations of his rumored existence. Most consider him an urban myth, but trust me, he's real. Echo knew about him too, but this man had managed to stay out of their reach for over a decade. He was just that good. If you happened to be good enough to land a job for him, your reputation was made. He had his favorites and didn't hire new blood that often. Still, every once in a while, one of his favorites would screw the pooch, and Tonda's got this zero-tolerance policy. You don't mess up. Fail and you're dead. It was just that simple: one of the secrets to his success. Fail in a *spectacular* fashion and he would see you live just

a little bit longer. You just wouldn't want to. Keep
in mind, his assassins and torturers were under the
zero-tolerance policy too.

I was the one who pushed for this job. Working for
Tonda was only for those at the top of their game.
I had been working up to this for ten years, and I
knew we were good, maybe even the best. Still, it
took a lot of fast talking to get Jack and the others
to agree to it. Tonda's rep is about as unsavory as you
can get. We approached Tonda, and that wasn't easy
either, I can tell you. He seemed impressed that we
had found him, and landed us this job.

So here we were. The brass ring had been dangling
in front of us for a month, and wouldn't you know
it, just as our fingers were almost on it, the ring had
grown some pretty scary looking teeth.

I shared a brief look with Jack. "Told ya," was all
he said. So much for fun. The game had turned into
the ultimate contest, our lives on the line, and with
little hope for success.

"All right," I said, guiding the sedan around the
facility. "Let's get to work."

Moscow, Russia: Callsign Red Saviour
I Minus 01:18:05 and Counting

Drenched in the crimson rays of a setting sun, the
crowd of Muscovites roared for blood in Red Square.
Militsya in riot gear corralled the protesters. The largest
of the signs they hoisted into the warm evening air
were legible to the sharp eyes of Natalya Nikolaevna
Shostakovich from the window in the hallway of Block
14, the Presidium.

WE DON'T NEED A SAVIOUR, one read. *Spasskaya*
for "Saviour" was written and underlined in the red
of the Soviet flag.

The *Spasskaya* Gate, Saviour's Gate into the Kremlin,
had been shut to the crowd, a sign that the *militsya*
expected trouble. That was because Ivor Triganov was
popular, and Natalya Shostakovich, Red Saviour . . .
was not.

Ivor Triganov was a glorified thug, a rich oligarch
who flaunted his wealth, yet contributed to charities
and cavorted with celebrities while his empire played
fast and loose with the tissue-thin laws of the new
capitalist economy.

Triganov armored himself with lawyers and powerful friends. When Natalya kicked down his door, he
only laughed at her as though she were the evening's
entertainment.

"Come to beg for opera tickets, Red Saviour?"
He asked with a smirk, making his fellow partygoers
titter like characters at a Tolstoy ball. "I would offer
you balcony, but I think you'd prefer my private box.
Wouldn't you, my dear?"

A broken arm and bloody nose later, Triganov had
stopped laughing. His eyes promised equally bloody
revenge, in his own way. Now the smoke of two
packs' worth of her *Proletarskie* cigarettes wafted in
the hallway outside the council chamber where Director Yvegeniy Murov and the rest of the leadership of
the FSO—the Federal Protective Service—grilled the
militsya detective who accompanied her on the bust.

"You're like an American rock star," a deep voice
said behind her. "Your fans await you."

She didn't turn around. Supernaut had removed his

immense helmet. He stood too close to her. The man was seven feet tall without the bulky scarlet armor that made him into a giant walking flamethrower. Natalya was used to being taller than most men she met; with Supernaut she was reminded of her childhood . . . and the bullies she used to plot revenge on.

Turning only enough to blow smoke at his face, she said: "Shut up, Vassily Georgiyevich." Supernaut narrowed his scarred eyes.

"*Da*, leave your Commissar alone." Molotok—the Hammer—nearly two feet shorter than the giant, chimed in as he walked up at Red Saviour's left. He craned his neck to meet the huge man's gaze. "Right now the last thing she needs is your insubordination."

"Fine. *Horosho*. I'll just keep my mouth shut until a vacancy in CCCP leadership appears." He smirked at Molotok. "That mob is as ready to kick out the Communists as I am."

Red Saviour waved off Molotok's angry retort. "Enough, *tovarisch*. If you ignore him, he wanders off to find somewhere else to boast."

The Moscow contingent of the CCCP—*Super-Sobratiye Sovetskikh Revolutzionerov*, or Super-Brotherhood of Soviet Revolutionaries—had come out in force to support her during this hearing to determine her future as Commissar. Her father, the original Red Saviour, had led the team in the 1950s during the early stages of the Cold War. Everyone had thought that the beautiful, charismatic daughter of the famous war hero would surely lead the CCCP back into the hearts and minds of the Russian people.

Yet her tenure had been a litany of one public relations disaster after another. Breathless news stories of the lovely new Commissar were supplanted by news bulletins of brutal raids on drug labs, accusations of backroom interrogations, and finally the arrest of the popular billionaire Triganov. Many hardliners lauded her heavy-handed methods; many more politicians cried out for censure. Some questioned the need for a metahuman branch of the Federal Protective Service at all.

Their garish dress uniforms could not have looked more out of place in the elegant neoclassical corridors of the Presidium. Supernaut resembled a red fire engine tipped onto its end; Molotok contrasted him with a crisp black suit with red piping. Petrograd's armor had been styled after the MiG fighter plane; trapped inside it because of the clumsy machinations of 1940s Soviet superscience, he sat like an awkward, isolated teen on a divan. Soviette, as elegant as ever, read from a children's book to the stony Chug, who came up to her shoulder but seemed to fill the space with his squat bulk.

Legs crossed in a lotus position, Natalya's friend and mentor Fei Li, whose callsign was Meng Dao Ye—People's Blade—seemed at ease in the alien environment. The diminutive Chinese girl housed the two-thousand-year-old spirit of a legendary general, Shen Xue, and wielded his deadly sword as well. The serene smile on her face diffused some of Natalya's anxiety. Beyond her the rest waited, in varying poses of unease.

My troops, Red Saviour thought. *My people. Have I lost their respect as well? They do not look me in the eye.*

As she gazed at the anxious members of CCCP,

those furthest down the corridor sprang to attention, saluting a new arrival. Boryets himself: Worker's Champion, Hero of the Russian People.

He'd marched in the October Revolution, fought in the Great Patriotic War, counseled Lenin, enforced Stalin's directives, founded CCCP itself, and watched the birth and death of the Soviet Union. "Natalya Nikolaevna," he said, discarding her honorific. "I have been summoned to appear before the FSO to deliver my opinion on your competency. Is this how you repay my advocacy?"

Years receded as she braced against his withering glare. She was a child again, intimidated beyond words by "Uncle Boryets."

She straightened her back. "Did you read my report?"

"Of course. You write with the impatience of a schoolgirl. Perhaps if you took more than five minutes to explain your evidence against Triganov, the council wouldn't jump to assumptions."

"They jump when Batov says jump," she said, glancing back at the protesters.

"They jump"—anger clouded his already dour countenance—"when you rampage through the countryside like a Cossack!"

Natalya winced. Her fearlessness dwindled in the face of this man, as always. "Comrade, Triganov looted government funds for his own purposes! I followed the trail of bribes right to his front door. My contacts—"

"Your contacts are not material witnesses. We are no longer Soviets, you foolish girl."

She flushed. "But, sir, if I'd waited for—"

He cut her off with a curt wave. "Save it for the

Director." He turned away to look out the window at the square full of angry Muscovites.

The double doors of the council chamber swung open. Lieutenant Cestimir Romanov ducked his head unconsciously as he slumped out of the chamber, followed by several of the council. He shook his head, avoiding her eyes. "I'm sorry," he murmured, pushing past her.

"Sorry for what?" she said to his retreating back.

"He is sorry for telling us the truth," a voice dripping with assurance said at her side. Arkady Levich Korovin, Undersecretary of Intelligence for FSO, favored Red Saviour with a patronizing smile. "Your friend tried to paint as pretty a picture as he could of your antics, but facts are facts."

"Triganov is a criminal," she said. "*That* is a fact."

"Perhaps, but the facts can interfere with the truth." Korovin was a few inches shorter than Natalya, but he spoke with a confidence won from years of bureaucratic battles. "We're taking a brief recess. May I have a word with you?" Without waiting for a response, he lightly took her by the arm and guided her to a foyer away from the gathered metas.

"I have little stomach for this nonsense, Arkady Levich. I am a soldier, not a politician. How many speeches must I tolerate?"

Korovin sighed, still holding her arm. "How did we become so antagonistic towards each other? We both serve the FSO, Natalya Nikolaevna. Our duties are clear-cut."

"Your duty is to boss around a staff of train conductors to evacuate Kremlin officials," she said with scorn. "CCCP shouldn't even be under your purview."

"We shouldn't argue, my friend." He paused, daring her to question the familiarity. "You and I both know Triganov belongs in prison."

"*Da!*" Red Saviour grinned at him. "Finally, someone sees reason."

"But this is not 1980. We are no longer a totalitarian state. Triganov is a powerful—and very popular—figure in Russia right now. We must tread very carefully with the likes of him."

"You can smooth out the ruffled feathers, Arkady Levich. Talk to Molotok. He has many friends in GRU."

"I will of course do my best. But how will we save you?"

"I need no saving. I am doing my job." She pursed her lips. "The council will lecture me about due process then let me go."

"Not this time." Korovin moved closer. "You've stepped on too many toes. Triganov has allies throughout the government, and they're all screaming for blood. The council may sacrifice you to save CCCP."

Atlanta, Georgia, USA
I Minus 00:32:15 and Counting

Detective Ramona Ferrari and the girls hushed when Mercurye strolled into the Echo cafeteria. "He walks like he really *is* a god," Sheryl the researcher whispered with a smirk—but Ramona's thoughts were strictly in the gutter. How could they not be? Staring at his broad shoulders and muscular chest—on display because he notoriously spurned shirts—one would have guessed him to be taller than his actual height. Blond curls peeked out from under a winged helmet straight out of an FTD florist logo. To complete the picture, a steel caduceus hung from his hand. His pants, however, were standard issue Echo nanoweave, as was the Echo caseless round pistol strapped around his waist.

Way, way, way out of my league, even if he wasn't a meta, Ramona lamented.

"Mmm, those pecs," Sheryl said, licking her lips. Ramona and the others giggled. Ramona relished her weekly lunches with her friends on the Echo campus. Although they stared and giggled like schoolgirls, their jobs were anything but whimsical. Sheryl studied psychopathic behavior among metahumans. Denise worked in the infirmary, though her skillset would have placed her in any emergency room in the country. Midori worked in weapons tech.

To accommodate all their schedules, they met in midafternoon. Many lunches ended prematurely when a cell phone rang.

"If my husband knew how many of these metas were studs, he'd make me resign," Midori said.

"And lose that paycheck?" Denise snorted. "Not likely. Just buy him a cape and a mask for a 'fantasy night.'" The table erupted in laughter, drawing a glance from Mercurye himself. That got them laughing even harder.

"Oh, Jesus," Sheryl said, wiping tears from her eyes. "I needed that. So, Ramona: got any good cases right now?"

"Hmm." Ramona poured more sugar in her coffee. "We just wrapped up that kidnapping case, the three kids. Turns out the perp was just a kook in a mask. I had Shahkti set up to drill him, but Atlanta PD took over." She shrugged.

"Well, she missed having to fill out hundred-page reports about the incident, to steer clear of the Extreme Force law." Sheryl made a face. "Then again, she could just tie him up in spider webbing... splat!" The other girls snickered.

"Webbing?" Ramona furrowed her brow. "She can do that?"

Sheryl waved her arms like a giant bug. "Probably. Doesn't she creep you out?"

"Her extra arms? You get used to it." Ramona thought back to the cases she'd worked with the four-armed Indian metahuman. "What's creepy is how dour she is. Does she even know how to smile?"

A man wearing a pair of elaborate metal gauntlets and Stars-and-Stripes epaulets entered the cafeteria. Yankee Pride spotted Ramona's table and strode towards them purposefully. Ramona stared at him blankly for a moment, then her stomach lurched. She'd forgotten the prisoner interview he'd scheduled. She scrambled to dig through her briefcase for the paperwork.

"Ladies," he drawled, inclining his head with a polite smile. The son of war heroes Yankee Doodle and Dixie Belle was said to power his energy gauntlet through a reservoir of internal energy. Somehow he didn't have the aura of intimidation that most meta-humans gave off unintentionally.

"Well hello, tall, dark and patriotic," she said, still fishing for the paperwork. "I was just reviewing the file on that perp..."

"Were you?" He grinned at her.

She came up empty-handed. "No. I spaced it."

Yankee Pride pulled up a chair to the table. "We have a minute now. You gonna eat that pickle?" He pointed to Midori's plate. She chuckled and pushed it towards him.

Ramona brought her briefcase up to her lap to leaf through the papers. The file was buried by reports, dossiers, faxes and notepads.

"'Heinrich Eisenhauer.' Any relation to Dwight D.? I'm kidding."

"He referred to himself as 'Eisenfaust.' German for 'The Iron Fist.'" He shrugged. "I looked it up in Pop's old papers, then online. Plenty of material on this guy from the historical sites."

Ramona found the printout of the online article. "Nice detective work. What do you need me for?"

"Look at the dates, Detective."

She bristled for a moment until she realized he used her title with respect, not sarcasm. "Hey." She blinked at the printout. "This says he died over the Atlantic. The Bermuda triangle."

"Fighting the Allied Aces, right. Which makes our friend over in the security facility a liar or a science fiction novel come to life."

"Occam's Razor," she said, making a cutting motion with one hand. "The simplest explanation is probably the best."

"Sure, but the man's a meta. I watched the security tapes. He moves like greased lightning." Yankee Pride favored the women at the table with a meaningful look. "That changes everything."

"You bet," Sheryl said, nodding gravely. "Can I see?"

Ramona handed her the file. Sheryl moved her lips silently as she read the dossier, incident report and Yankee Pride's research. Her shoulders hunched as if she were trying to force herself into the pages.

"He certainly believes he's Eisenfaust," she said in a small voice. The rest of the table leaned forward to hear her. "Bring a shrink."

"Already reserved a slot in Doc Bootstrap's schedule." Yankee Pride winked at her. "Good to know I can still research."

"Oh, please." She returned the file to him, but he passed it right to Ramona.

"She's got a little reading to do. Thirty minutes, Detective." The seriousness returned to his demeanor. Did he think Ramona would find something he and Sheryl had missed?

Ramona sighed. "I'll be ready," she said, giving in to her own weaknesses and lighting up another cigarette, despite the cafeteria signs.

"He was my great-uncle," Alex Tesla said with infinite patience. "My father knew him as a teenager."

Framed by the gigantic plasma TV screen, the CEO of Computrex had reverted to giggling adolescence. "He *knew* Nikola Tesla? Are the stories true? He was building a death ray for the Army?"

"Uncle—er, Great-Uncle Tesla experimented on a wide variety of inventions, peaceful and otherwise. Some do lend themselves to lurid speculation. The Pentagon never provided him funding for any of his wartime projects."

The man was undaunted. "So there is a Tesla death ray?"

"Yes."

"Really?" The CEO, a mousy man with an ill-advised goatee grown to hide a double chin, lit up in excitement. "Does Echo have the prototype?"

"I'm teasing you, Mr. Faber. Echo Industries focuses on the peaceful applications of my great-uncle's work in broadcast energy." He smiled into the video camera. "Wouldn't you say there are enough weapons in the world already?"

"I suppose." Faber was unappeased. "What about antigravity? They say that—"

"Trust me, if we had antigravity technology, you and I would not be discussing broadcast power sourcing to server farms. I'd be selling flying cars and floating cities to Arab sheiks."

Faber laughed thinly at the quip. *Reality never fails to disappoint*, Tesla thought.

Yet ever since Echo was founded in the 1950s by his father, Andro Tesla, Echo had used their metahuman law enforcement contractors—what amounted to a private army—to maintain public goodwill towards the alternate energy source that had made Nikola Tesla famous.

When Alex took over in the 1980s, he hoped that the oil shortages would spur acceptance of broadcast energy for automobiles. Yet the oil companies would not be beaten easily; their network of purchased politicians pushed laws to limit the uses of broadcast energy sources "pending further study."

Ultimately the legend surrounding Nikola Tesla caught the imagination of technology industry entrepreneurs who sought any shortcut to market saturation. Restrictions were loosened, awkward young multimillionaires like Gerald Faber requested meetings with Alex, and inroads were made.

"In all seriousness, though, you might be interested in our Industry Leader Retreats, which we offer to our best customers. A week touring Echo facilities, viewing the latest research, meeting the operatives—"

"I can hang out with the superpowered metas?"

Alex hoped his smile hid the hunter's sense of triumph he felt. "The Echo Ops are common at any Echo campus. You'll surely become accustomed to them, as we have."

"What's that cost?" Faber's face loomed in the plasma screen, eager as an amateur porn actor.

"It's provided as a courtesy to our *elite* customers. Why don't we review the prospectus—"

A gentle buzz tickled his wrist in an alternating sequence of short and long bursts. He jerked erect.

"Mr. Faber, I fear something has come up that requires my immediate attention." He paused. "Something urgent involving our Atlanta metas. Can we continue this conversation at your earliest convenience?"

Without waiting for a confirmation, he waved his assistant forward. Planner in hand, the young man took Alex's seat as he raced out of the room.

Alex all but ran back to his office. Kim held up a sheaf of faxes and letters but he cut her off with a gesture. "Hold my calls," he said, disappearing into his office. He ignored his desk, walking up to the bookcase and tugging at *Bullfinch's Mythology*. The book tilted forward with a click. The bookcase swung into the wall to reveal a narrow, dark spiral staircase. He gripped the rail as he vaulted down the stairs three at a time, descending ten stories and down into the ground.

The small room at the foot of the stairs was lit only by the glow emanating from the panels of sleek machinery attached to the walls. In the center of the room, four coils mounted on posts sparked and hummed. Before the square they formed was a wooden chair; a helmet bristling with wires and antennae hung from the seatback.

Alex flipped a few switches: the coils came to life, coruscating electricity between them, a four-cornered Tesla coil of a design unknown to the outside world. The tangy taste of ozone permeated the dank room.

Alex scooted the chair back a foot and sat. The helmet flattened his electrically excited hair. When he closed a circuit on the helmet, the intermittent shapes filled the air and took on a recognizable form.

"I'm here, Uncle," Alex said.

His soul contained in a matrix of neutrons, the entity that had been Nikola Tesla took a moment to process the visual data fed to him by the machines in the tiny, hidden room. A speaker converted electrical impulses into sound.

"Alex. We must talk, you and I, about your guest, this Eisenfaust."

The bookcase opened and shut behind him. Head bowed, Alex mused on his great-uncle's words. For Nikola to call so abruptly could only mean that the man—if he could still be called that—regarded the matter of Eisenfaust with enormous concern. He needed to talk to Yankee Pride, whose suspicions had been triggered enough to send a message to Metis, to Uncle Tesla—

"Oops, chief. Didn't mean to interrupt."

Alex started. Doc Bootstrap stood by his desk, arranging a set of syringes, as casual as a bartender.

Alex glanced back at the bookcase. "I thought I'd locked the office door."

"You did. Kim let me in." Doc Bootstrap nodded at the closed door. "Nice bookcase. When do I get one?"

"Ah . . ." Alex hesitated. "Executive washroom. Left-over from my father's time." He waved a hand in front of his nose. "You don't want to go in there right now."

Doc held a syringe up to the light. "I hoped to catch you before I had to sit in on the Eisenfaust interview." An odd expression crossed the man's face—half worry, half triumph.

"Eisenfaust. Yes. Um . . . Yankee Pride gave me a quick rundown. What do you think? Is he the real thing?"

Doc Bootstrap shrugged. "Are you asking me if a man who disappeared in 1945 can waltz into our laps as if sixty years hadn't passed?"

"I guess," Alex said, chuckling.

The psychiatrist patted his syringes. "We'll find out his side of the story in a few minutes. I can tell you this, though." A grin widened on his face until it was a rictus.

He lunged forward and jabbed the syringe into Alex's neck.

Alex staggered back. He hadn't even seen the man move. Numbness spread from the injection through his throat, so that he couldn't speak. His hands clawed at the syringe; he fell across his desk. Paperwork fluttered to the floor.

Doc Bootstrap loomed over him. The room began to spin, and it seemed to Alex that the doctor's features softened as though his bones shifted.

"You hold our old friend, the real Eisenfaust, in your pathetic cellblock, *Amerikaner*." Doc Bootstrap's accent had shifted from a gruff Midwestern twang to a clipped Germanic. "I could kill him myself, but it is not my place. My superiors will be here shortly to exact revenge on the traitor." He patted Alex's cheek. "Nor will I kill you. Better for you to live as we burn your little army and your city in a ring of cleansing fire. The Thule Society wants you to live on to experience your humiliation in the eyes of the world."

The doctor rolled up his syringes. "Now, I have an appointment to keep. I would ask Kim to look in on you, but I had to snap her neck to get your key."

He rolled up his sleeve. A small metal device on his arm blinked red and green. Doc Bootstrap pressed it: the red vanished, leaving the green light.

"We'll meet again, Alex Tesla. I can become anyone, male or female. Your mother, your lover, your best friend, your doctor. You'll never know it's me until you feel my breath on your neck. I love—absolutely love—that moment of realization. It is the thing I treasure most in this world. You will live long enough to see my face change. Then, and only then, will the Doppelgaenger take your life."

Alex's eyes rolled up into his head and he slumped over.

CHAPTER TWO

Ignition

MERCEDES LACKEY, STEVE LIBBY,
CODY MARTIN, DENNIS LEE

Such an ordinary day. All over the world, literally, people who would never have reason to know each other, much less end up as tight as we were, were going about their lives, some of them on opposite sides of the law. Then at eleven-thirty Eastern Standard Time, the world as we knew it changed forever.

Las Vegas, Nevada, USA: Callsign Belladonna Blue

The station had been blessedly quiet for hours. Most of the guys were in front of the tube, watching the pre-pre-pregame shows for the All-Star game. Her cell phone went off. She glanced at it. Mom. Huh, odd, this was the time their shift started. Usually she and Dad were hot on some project at Alienville at this point in the day. She answered it. "Hi Mom, what—"

The sounds coming over the phone stopped her heart. Screaming. Explosions. Someone—it sounded like Dad—yelling. "In the shelter! Now! *Go, go, go!*"

And her Mom's voice, shaking, saying only "Red alert. Lockdown."

Then the phone went dead.

Then the klaxons in the station went off.

All hell broke loose right outside.

Inside the fire station, no one paid any attention to the frantic klaxons signaling the callout of all possible personnel. It didn't matter. They couldn't have gotten there anyway. Bella crouched in the door that had opened automatically for the engines to move out, and stared in horror.

There were nine-foot-tall suits of chrome-plated armor, hosing down the street outside with the energy cannons built into their arms.

It looked like there were about twenty of them; one of them was all black, but the rest of them gleamed in the harsh Vegas sunlight like something right out of one of the city's stage shows. Except that things out of stage shows didn't explode cars and chase screaming civvies and—

Oh hell no—

Those cannons were swiveling to point at the station!

Just as that fact registered on her brain, she felt someone grab her shoulder and fling her backwards, just out of the path of the first swath of energy pulses. She scrambled the rest of the way out under her own power as the blue-white light engulfed the front of the engines. She followed the others out the back and down into the dry wash behind the station, just as the station itself went up in a fireball. She ducked her head and the wash of superheated air scorched over her.

Instinctively she looked up as soon as it had passed and did a headcount.

Shit. Three short. Gadgets, Long John and the other rookie. *Shitshitshit*—

"*Incoming!*" screamed the captain before she could more than register the fact that there were probably three men down in what was left of the station, and she ducked her head in automatic response to the roar from behind—

The sonic boom was enough to flatten her into the desert sand, yet somehow she looked up, dazed, just in time to see the entire line of armored monstrosities swept off their feet and engulfed in rocket-fueled explosions so white-hot it was like looking into the sun—

—as the Air Force *Thunderbird* team pulled up and out and rolled over and came back for a second sweep, traveling at mach one at the very least.

She and the others were on their feet, cheering, even though they couldn't hear themselves cheer, pumping their fists in the air, as the aerobatic team came back on their second pass and raked the war machines with another set of wing-fired rockets. Despite the similar paint job, these weren't their display planes, oh no. These were specialized warbirds. The *Thunderbird* pilots were the elite of the Air Force elite, and like anyone else really in the know, Bella knew that part of what went on at Groom Lake was that once a week, the show team made the hour flight out and practiced live-fire exercises, exercises with weapons and skills designed to take out rogue metahumans. Just to keep their hands in. Because the Boy Scouts weren't the only group whose motto was "Be prepared."

Whatever those powered suits had been built to withstand, it wasn't what was in the rockets fired by these fighter jets. They were down. And they weren't moving.

The *Thunderbirds* pulled around for a third pass, but it wasn't needed. The suits were down, and stayed down. The *Thunderbird* team didn't slow down; they peeled off and headed east, where more smoke and fire and the flash of an energy cannon betrayed another point of attack.

Bella staggered up out of the wash before the jets had cleared the area. Three men missing . . . screaming told her there were civvies hurt. If there was anything left of her kit in the station—people needed her. Even without the kit, she had her touch-healing, she could hold them stable until—

"*Incoming!*" the captain screamed again, and she hit the ground as something roared in overhead, and she heard—

Her comm unit made a noise she'd never heard it make before, a kind of warble, just as the thing overhead, too small to be a jet but moving at least that fast, did a kind of wingover and plunged straight down towards her and blasted to a landing, backpack jet unit whining as it ramped down.

A meta—

A hand in powered armor reached down and hauled her effortlessly to her feet.

The other hand pulled up the visor of a red, white and blue helmet, and a pair of absurdly young eyes stared at her.

A meta—one on our side—

"Bella Dawn Parker?" asked a voice amplified into a hollow audibility that cut through the ringing of her ears.

She nodded numbly, half of her mind still on the remains of the station, the injured civvies, the missing members of her own crew.

"You're activated. This is a full Code Red emergency. I am directed to take you—"

That part registered, and she stared at him in outrage. "Take me? You're taking me *nowhere*, mister! My job is here! I don—"

"Parker!" the young man barked with surprising authority. "You're *activated*. Groom Lake's being hit this second and we're assembling a meta team to go in—"

That was when it hit her with the force of a blow to the gut.

Groom Lake.

Mom and Dad—

New York, New York, USA: Callsign John Murdock

John had what he wanted, though probably not enough of it to make much difference. He was nursing the bottle to make it last, to justify his occupation of a bar stool. The stuff smelled like diesel, but it didn't matter. *To the past,* he thought, upending the shot glass—

—and about the same time that the booze hit his stomach, the front of the pub exploded inwards.

It felt, and it sounded, like the end of the world. The pressure wave from the blast hit him about the same time as what felt like half the contents of the front of the place, and he somersaulted over the bar. He slammed into the backbar and the entire contents of that came down on top of him. Glass, wood, and concrete blasted into the bar patrons like grapeshot, shrapnel tearing into flesh and ancient tabletops with equal indifference. Pain lanced through John's back as the world went white.

A final impact meant he'd landed. He knew he was on the floor, so he tried to stand up, and with a surge of panic, discovered he couldn't. His vision cleared a moment later, and he found himself behind the counter, wedged between the aged marble slab of the top of the backbar, which was now tilting crazily against the wall, and a busted cabinet; and as if that wasn't bad enough, he was upside down on broken glass.

Incongruously, he was peripherally aware that he was cold—the alcohol he'd been drenched with evaporating away—and that he smelled like an alkie's idea of heaven.

John toppled over, coming down on his right side on more debris and glass. His head was swimming, his sensitive ears ringing, and he could barely make out the shrieks and crying of the other people trapped in here with him. *Terrorist bomb? Gas line exploding?* His head cleared as he pushed himself upright, resting his back against the shattered cabinet he'd been thrown into by the blast. What was left of the barkeep was embedded in the wall where a bar-length mirror had been. *What the hell—what kind of an explosion did* that?

Swaying slightly, he stood up. As soon as his frame cleared the top of the ruined counter, he felt the immense heat of the fire engulfing the front of the building, which was starting to spread into the main room. Through eyes that were still trying to focus, he frantically surveyed the rest of the pub. He was the only one standing. People had been tossed around the interior, still lying where they'd landed, broken and bleeding, most of them thrown against the back wall.

A lot of them were tangled with furniture and—his stomach churned—body parts. A shocking number of the victims that appeared mostly intact were moving. If they didn't get out of there soon, they wouldn't be moving for long.

The sprinkler system went off, misting down the room and dropping the temperature. It wasn't doing much about the fire, but it *was* going to buy him some time. He coughed through the smoke, which was starting to get thicker near the ceiling. Flashover was a real possibility here, especially with so much alcohol vapor.

Once again, training warred with survival, but this time the training won.

"Everyone still able to move, we need to get everybody out of here!" he shouted, using his "command" voice. A few folks were trying to stand up, looking about dazedly or staring in shock at their own wounds. Through a gap in the smoke, John spotted the hallway that led to the bathrooms, with an exit sign at the very end of it. Stumbling, he started hustling people into the hallway, even carrying a few until they moved on their own. Those that were ambulatory, whether they wanted it or not, found themselves with a victim draped over their shoulders. John was the first through the rear entrance, kicking it open as more alarms wailed from buildings all around, burdened by an elderly man with a huge gash on his forehead. Another fire alarm went off as soon as the door bar was shoved down. John had done a good bit more than just shove—it was bowed in the middle.

It took a few minutes, and a hell of a lot of shouting and acting like a drill sergeant on steroids, but after two more trips into a room that was looking more and more like a blast furnace, he was satisfied that the pub was cleared of anyone still living.

Hunched over in the alleyway, he took inventory of his own wounds. Blood trickled down his arms from his back. He had plenty of lacerations, puncture wounds, and scrapes. His shirt was sopping wet, torn in several places, and was more red than white now.

"What the hell happened? Was it a bomb?" shouted someone. John looked to his right; it was the man from the couple that the late barkeep had been talking with. He was holding his right arm; the wrist was bent at an odd angle, in addition to minor cuts and bruises.

"Stay here; wait for the cops or the paramedics to get here. Don't move unless the fire spreads out here." John stood up gingerly, not wanting to hurt his back more than it was already.

Not a chance They could have found him, was there? Dammit, would They take out a whole pub full of innocent bystanders to get him?

He already knew the answer, of course. It was "yes." Either way, he wasn't ready to stick around for the police or anyone else to show up; he'd done more than his fair share already.

Smoke billowed out of the emergency exit, bringing with it a rank taste of burning plastic, so that way was out. He sprinted for the end of the alley, dodging and vaulting dumpsters, aiming for the patch of light shining off a bright red car parked across the street from the end.

That is, he *was* aiming for that bright red car... until it vanished in a wash of actinic energy.

What the hell? He focused, and could hear the

clomp of metal on asphalt. He immediately flattened himself against the alley wall to his left, trying to cut down his profile to whatever was coming up the street. He edged his way to the corner, peering slowly around the wall. What he saw nearly took his breath away.

He'd seen more than his share of metas before, but the suits marching down the street looked like art deco illustrations of some future master race. Which was not so farfetched a concept, considering what was enameled on their upper arms where a regimental patch would have been.

A black crook-armed cross on a white circle on a red field. The Nazi swastika.

Three of them were marching abreast down the street, sweeping anything and anyone in their path with some sort of energy cannon mounted to their arms. Cars, people, *buildings*—they were destroying everything around them almost effortlessly.

John didn't waste another moment. He turned in place and sprinted with everything he had back to the group of pub survivors. He crossed the distance in seconds. Panic tinged his voice as he shouted at the crowd. "We're movin', now! Everyone up, let's go! Go, go, go!"

"But you said to wait for help—"

"Help ain't comin'! We need to get the hell outta here, now!" The survivors were frightened and startled by the fear in his voice, and started to respond, albeit sluggishly. John dragged people to their feet, forcing others to help those who couldn't move on their own. The sounds of explosions, about a million car alarms and fire alarms going off, and people screaming were starting to get close; those . . . things couldn't be too far off. John started off at a trot, leading the way for his band of burned and lacerated survivors. He tried his best to keep off the streets heading away from the Nazis, or whatever they were. After a few minutes that seemed to stretch into hours, he turned a corner only to come up short in an open street. People were milling about, coming outdoors to see what was happening. The armored supersoldiers hadn't made it this far, yet. John looked about wildly, hoping for some refuge.

Then he saw it. Sanctuary. In the form of a subway entrance. That armor was too tall for the entrance; chances were the Nazis would stick to the streets for now. He immediately started shoving people towards it. "Everyone, down into the subway! Get outta the streets! Move!" The explosions were getting closer, with smoke obscuring the sky behind him. The citizens on the street started moving; some ran for the subway entrance, but most of them went back into the buildings they had first ventured out of. *Dammit, stone or brick walls won't stop these things!*

But it was impossible to save everybody. He just had to try and save as many as he could. He was going to have a hard enough time keeping himself alive, much less any of the clueless wandering around him. Even with his advantages, there was precious little he could do against something that had the power of a damned tank. Still...

He could...

No. He couldn't. Not even now would he...not after...

Screw it. He would do the best he could, get as many people as safe as he could. Then he would get the hell out of Dodge if he had to steal a car to do it.

Atlanta, Georgia, USA: Callsign Victoria Victrix

Vickie had moved to Atlanta in the first place to join Echo, except after what had happened to her, she couldn't. Her crippling panic attacks kept her from doing more than getting the registration papers from Echo. She'd filled them out, but after being unable to even do the interview, she had been rejected. After all, what good was a metahuman sorceress who couldn't even stop shaking long enough to crumble a pebble? Never mind she was trained to a fare-thee-well as a warrior Geomancer. Never mind that those in the know were aware she was that rarest of birds, a techno-shaman. Echo needed people they could count on.

It had, indeed, taken her two hours to wind herself up enough to open the car door into the people-populated outside world. She stared at the asphalt, and goaded herself with the memory of a mostly empty bag of cat food and what Grey would do to avenge himself on her if she got back in the car and went back home. And she was just about to put her weight on her feet when—

A tremendous metallic crash made her freeze. Perhaps most people would have leapt in startlement and whacked their heads against the door frame, but the panic attacks made her freeze whenever anything unexpected happened. And then she looked up in the direction of the noise.

The five tractor trailers had come apart at the seams. That was the sound she'd heard, the trailer walls falling to either side and crashing down onto the pavement. And now she stared at—

At first her mind registered only metas.

Then she saw the swastikas. And the guns. And the five spheroid war machines rising up into the air with a hum that made the fillings in her teeth ache. They were larger in all dimensions than the trailers they'd been hidden inside, expanding from an unfolding array that looked for all the world like the insides of a toaster, but inside those rails, space seemed *bent*. And now, Vickie's anxiety panic attack was replaced by panic of another sort altogether.

She didn't remember getting out of the car. She didn't remember running, or screaming. But she must have done both, because when she came to herself again, she was cowering behind a dumpster outside an apartment block, dripping with sweat, throat raw.

What did I do? Whatever it was, she'd gotten out of the grocery store lot—without her car.

Her teeth began to ache again, and she glanced up reflexively, to see one of those shining spheroids floating easily above the level of the rooftops about a block away. It was dotted with baleful orange windows or ports, and the bottom tenth or so glowed the same angry orange. Except for the humming, it looked innocent enough—

A heavy *chuff-chuff-chuff* from behind her made her crouch further down and glance to the rear, as a Blackhawk chopper in National Guard colors moved purposefully towards the sphere. The sight would have reassured a normal civilian . . .

But Vickie was not a normal civilian, and the sight of a National Guard chopper heading towards what was clearly a metahuman-guided supercraft made her want to stand up, wave her arms and scream at them to retreat as fast as they could.

But of course, she didn't do that; she just crouched there like a scared rat, cowering and shaking as it passed overhead. Not that anyone was going to be looking down, or would pay attention to one lone woman screaming and waving at them if they did. And there was nothing overtly threatening in that serenely floating chromed sphere . . .

Or at least, there wasn't, until a dozen segmented metal tentacles whipped out from hidden ports on its sides. Like a nest of cobras, they struck, half of them seizing the chopper, half impaling it.

It exploded in a massive fireball that hurled debris in all directions.

Her throat closing with fear and anger, under cover of the smoke and flames, she ran.

She wasn't sure where she was when her luck ran out. It wasn't Peachtree Park, that much she knew. It must have been Four Corners. The streets were wider, and she could hear the screaming, see the black smoke from the fires on the Interstate, in the distance. It was at that point she tried to duck across the street that she found herself looking up at the chromed armor of a Nazi metatrooper, flanked by two more just like him.

The helmets featured aggressive blast shields covering the eye area, a mouth shield like the grill on a '57 Chevy. Twin, swept-back antennae projected from the helmets, one over each temple. There were extremely stylized designs incised into the chest plates.

The armor looked *angry*. No telling what the people

inside the armor were like, but the armor itself was over eight feet tall. There was one not-so-subtle exception to the shining chrome theme. That was the black swastika set inside a white circle on a field of red enameled on the right bicep of every suit of armor.

There were five more closing in behind her.

As she stared, part of her brain noted that there was one among the chromed supersoldiers who wore black armor instead of silver. This one had stylized eagle wings on its helmet instead of antennae. Or maybe these were still antennae, just decorative as well as functional. If the other armor looked angry, this looked lethal.

SS, said her brain. *That's SS. The SS wore black uniforms—*

As she stood there, numb, frozen, waiting to die—a rabbit caught in a circle of wolves—she almost closed her eyes so she wouldn't see it coming. But she didn't. So she did see the panicking, crying ribbon of children that streamed in between two of the buildings, and stopped, the kids stumbling to a halt, clutching each other, and falling silent as they realized that they were trapped.

The Nazi metatroopers raised their weapon-arms.

A decade and more of training, practice, and discipline, coupled with rage, overcame Vickie's fear, smashed through her paralysis, and took over.

"You hateful *bastards!*" she shrieked, as the power rose up into her, from the Earth Her Mother, into her hands, building as quick as thought into the weapon she had wielded for most of her life.

The Earth rose up in answer.

When the Tuatha da Danaan fought, it was said, the

Earth itself ran like water and crested like the ocean waves. That power was Vickie's: the skill, knowledge, and the magic of the Geomancer. The Earth thrust upwards in a blindingly fast wave between the Nazi troopers and the children, a wall of broken asphalt and dirt and stone that caught and absorbed the terrible power of their arm cannons. Nor was that all, for like the wave, it crested and crashed down on them, half burying them in debris. A second wave began as they struggled to their feet. The Earth's magic power flooded through Vickie in a molten torrent, and she stood there with her arms outstretched to it, surrounded by a golden glow.

"Run!" she screamed to the children, intercepting a second, more scattered barrage of blue-white energy with her Earth-wave. "Run, you little rats!"

And she sent a secondary wave, bulging the asphalt, to shove them on their way.

They ran. And the Nazis staggered to their feet again, this time turning their attention towards her, exclusively.

Energy beams concussed the pavement to either side of her as she changed her tactics, calling on the Earth to heave up right under their feet, knocking them down and back. *Can't aim if you can't stand...*

But she hadn't forgotten the spheres. She began backing away from the Nazis, alternating upheavals with Earth-waves, one eye on the sky. Because these guys were going to call for help eventually—

Where the hell is Echo? Where are the metas? she thought frantically.

But she knew where they were. She could see the black smoke of fires, hear the explosions, and in the distance, the screaming. The metahumans of Echo were all around, doing what she was doing. As the sweat of exertion and fear ran into her eyes and clumped her hair, she called on the Earth to deflect and protect her. As she ran low on stamina and her control over the magic faltered, she heard the sound of a heavy truck motor behind her. Incredibly, it was accelerating towards her and the Nazi metatroopers. Vickie heard the truck skid to a halt with screaming tires and shrieking brakes and she heard people pile out of it.

And then she heard the barrage of gunfire.

They're nuts! she thought incredulously. *They can't—* and the knee joint of the Nazi metatrooper nearest her, only just steadying himself and bracing to fire at her again, disintegrated.

He toppled over. Another barrage erupted, and the knee joint of another trooper vanished in fire concentrated with pinpoint accuracy, as only a sniper could muster.

But the remaining troopers aimed—and Vickie's rage returned. She slammed into them with another upthrust of broken concrete and dirt.

"Keep it up, miss!" came a voice from behind, cracking with strain. "I'm gonna run out of bullets before we run out of bad guys!"

Moscow, Russia: Callsign Red Saviour

"Commissar," Stokov said. "Please pay attention to our discussion."

"I am listening," she said, disgruntled. She'd lost any momentum she might have had.

Korovin stepped back in. "FSO has spent money and

time to defuse the negative publicity stemming from your zeal. You're living in the past. We don't brutalize rich men because we're jealous of their success."

Outside, at the edge of the Square, a Delex truck pulled up close behind another, drawing her eye. "I don't follow."

"That's been obvious for months." Korovin shook his head. "The council has discussed a reorganization of CCCP."

"You can't do that," she said. "Boryets—Worker's Champion—is here. He'd never agree to it. He founded CCCP before you were even born."

"It is our responsibility now, and for your information, we have already discussed the matter with him. He has agreed to come out of retirement to lead—Commissar, I must insist that you pay attention to the proceedings!"

Natalya had been staring at the third Delex truck, parking on the heels of the second. The space between the trucks wasn't enough to squeeze a body through. Something was not right; a knot grew in her stomach.

"*Da*," she said, eyes glued to the window.

"You're being demoted, Natalya Nikolaevna," the Chief Director said in a soft voice. "You'll be given the rank of Associate Commissar, under Worker's Champion's direction."

"Associate, *da*," she agreed. A fourth, fifth and six truck were completing a semicircle around the protest. They couldn't possibly unload their cargo while parked so close together.

"Commissar!" The Chief Director pounded his coffee cup on the table, splashing coffee. "I will not be ignored!"

Her anxiety had reached her chest. She stood. "Something is wrong," she said.

"Natalya, sit down," Korovin said.

"Shut up, *svinya*," she said, moving towards the window as if in a trance.

As she touched the cold glass, the metal sides of the trucks shredded. Metal figures burst out of the trucks, dozens, hundreds, as if packed in the trailers like sardines. Their chrome armor reflected the artificial light in hyperreal starbursts. Arm guns the size of bazookas pointed at the crowd; the figures towered over the protesters at nearly three meters.

Behind her, Korovin was the first to process what she'd seen. "Terrorists!" he shouted.

Natalya sprinted for the door. The Chief Director called her name. "Where are you going? This building is full of officials who need to be evacuated!"

"Do it yourself," she said, pushing a guard out of the way. In the hallway, members of the CCCP had gathered at the window. Red Saviour didn't stop running. "Fall in!" she shouted. The metas fell into step behind her.

"Natalya," Worker's Champion said, matching her stride. "What are you doing?"

"Leading my troops," she said. "You can fire me afterwards."

Molotok sped up to her side, getting in Worker's Champion's way. "You have a plan, *sestra*?"

The window at the end of the hallway loomed before them.

"*Da.*" She raised her voice. "Follow me down! Spread out and confront the terrorists! Protect the workers first!"

Energy coruscated around her hands. Five feet away from the window, she threw it forward in an enormous blast. French windows that had been assiduously cleaned and painted for a century exploded outward.

"*Davay, davay, davay!*" She yelled. "Come on!"

By ones and twos, the heroes of the CCCP burst through the hole in Block 14 of the Kremlin, either taking flight as Red Saviour did on a plume of meta energy, leaping with metahuman muscles like Molotok and Chug, or sliding down the ice ramp that Father Winter formed from the moisture in the air.

The walls of the Kremlin stood at twenty meters, forcing Winter to maintain the elevation of the ice ramp. The ice creaked and roared as it formed unnaturally fast. As quickly as they moved over the wall near the Saviour's Gate, she knew they were seconds away from a massacre.

The terrorists, moving with military precision, leveled their guns on the crowd. Blue-white light passed, and left death behind.

They were already too late.

"Squad *Odeen*, engage! Squad *Dva,* right flank. Provide diversion! The rest of you, crowd control!" She gathered her energy at her feet to follow Squad *Odeen* into battle.

Beneath her, Chug had paused on the ice ramp, clenching and unclenching his fists. Tears fell from his eyes.

"Chug not unnerstand," he rumbled. "Why are silver men mad at shouting peepuls?"

"They are bad men, Chug," she said. "Go make them mad at you instead."

Chug unleashed a primal roar, his whole body

shaking, sending mineral-laden tears to freeze in a misty halo around his head. His legs tensed and he leapt from the ice ramp into the nearest line of—were they terrorists?

The *militsya* themselves had recovered first from the shock of the attack. Those nearest the attack opened fire on the armored figures with pistols. The terrorists as one then directed their fire at the *militsya*, cutting them down without effort.

Petrograd and Netopyr had reached the front lines. Their own armored forms were dwarfed by the giants surrounding the square. They'd understood Red Saviour's orders perfectly: draw fire away from the civilians.

Petrograd unleashed his arm cannons in a wide spray. Something had jammed their microcomm units, so she only heard his howl of rage as a word she'd heard her father utter with venom during his war stories: *"Fashista!"*

She swooped in towards the line of terrorists, and saw an emblem that awakened horror in the Russian collective memory. A black swastika in a white circle, on a flag of blood red.

"Nasrat," she cursed. "They're Nazis, real Nazis!"

Red Saviour accelerated towards her target, letting her meta energy crescendo in her body until she felt as though she'd burst. The Nazi trooper's helmeted head turned up to watch her approach. Metal joints groaned as he elevated his gun to fire upon her.

Two seconds, she gauged, *for him to lock on to me*. She twisted her body in anticipation of the blast. It came—a second earlier than she expected. The beam blazed across her back, missing by an inch but burning her nerves regardless. She focused her rage from the sudden agony towards the trooper. Her fist glowed with energy. One hit should shatter his helmet—in the past she'd knocked over a car with a well-placed, energy-augmented punch.

The trooper was an easy target, slow and lumbering. She braked just enough to add her velocity to her punch and swung her fist at his head. The release of her energy would coincide with impact.

Energy exploded in a shower of sparks; the Nazi's helmet rang like a bell. He swayed for a moment, then hefted a gauntlet the size of her head to retaliate.

"*Shto?*" Red Saviour couldn't believe it. The armor had absorbed the punch as if it were a sandbag. She darted away from the trooper's clumsy swing and hit him with both fists on the top of his head. Again, no effect. The unnatural hum around the trooper intensified.

Remembering her *Systema* training, she let loose with a series of blows to his head and torso, expending quantities of energy that should have leveled a house. The more she hit him, the better a target she became. She knew she had to move before they opened fire.

"Commissar!" The muffled shout was Netopyr's. The walking tank planted himself next to her and blasted at the troopers with his own energy cannon, which glanced off their armor as harmlessly as her blows. They switched targets to the large, slow moving, armored Russian; a volley of beams lashed out at him, tearing his armor off in chunks, crushing the man inside.

She howled as he crumbled to the ground like a bag of bones. The moment of distraction was all her opponent needed to connect. His metal fist caught her in the ribs and hurled her back into the panicking crowd.

Stars erupted before her eyes. She spat blood and scrambled to her feet. Three *militsya* fired hopelessly at the Nazis. A captain helped steady her.

"Commissar! We can't hurt them!"

"Then stop trying." She pointed at the walls of the Kremlin: one of the ceremonial guards at the Saviour's Gate, dressed in a colorful medieval uniform, was trying to attract the protesters' attention by swinging his dulled halberd in the air and shouting. Over the tumult, no one paid attention. "Saviour's Gate," she told the *militsya* captain. The legend of the gate was that it had protected Moscow from invasion. "Get them through the gate. Now!"

The captain nodded and shouted orders to his men. They turned their backs on the Nazi soldiers to herd the crowd towards the gate.

Atlanta, Georgia, USA: Callsign Red Djinni

In times of uncertainty we have abandoned jobs, split up, and vanished. Whether in the initial stages of planning a heist, or minutes away from our mark, if things looked too dicey, we booked. That's the nature of the game. When we felt the law, we dropped everything and left, and we disappeared for a while. And I mean *disappeared*, brother. We never underestimated the detectives, especially ones with access to metahuman talents. They had ways to pick up on anything, no matter how insignificant, so time was the only thing we could leave in our wake.

What we were about to do was in direct violation

of all we had learned, counter to every method of guile and misdirection we had honed in our five years together.

This was an all-out assault, and it demanded flawless execution. There was no time for subtlety. Just getting to the goods now meant a quick death to anyone who got in our way. This sort of "kick-in-the-door" approach guaranteed us being made. Made, and linked to multiple homicides. We might as well have faxed our vitals to Echo headquarters, we were so screwed. Our previous record of a few thefts and a minor brawl with an Echo Ops training team had kept our perceived threat level low. Infiltration of the Vault and the massacre of security personnel rated astronomically higher. You didn't just walk away from something like that; this time, we would have to go into hiding for years.

We each had our own way of dealing with that knowledge.

Jon had started taking deep breaths. Trust me when I say that's bad. It meant she was building up a thirst for some messy violence. She dealt with problems the only way she could; in her mind, any conflict or argument could be resolved with her guns. Sudden ambush? Spray down a little cover fire. Victim's getting away? Clip him in the legs a few times. Red wants to give S&M a try? A clean shot through his shoulder should shut him up. She was still taking deep breaths when she left for a final reconnaissance.

When agitated, Duff would usually babble in a constant stream of descriptive cursing, often involving an adversary's mother in various states of humiliation and affliction. As I watched him strap on his gear, I couldn't help but notice that this time, he was strangely quiet. And he was shaking.

That was a first.

Was he scared? Well, I'm sure he was. We were all scared. Don't let the calm exterior fool you, I get scared a lot. You learn to use fear, though. That shot of adrenaline tends to fire up all five senses, six in my case. Being in tune with my skin carried a lot of advantages, including a radial awareness. The more skin I had exposed, the more I could sense from my immediate surroundings.

I caught a quick, furtive look from Duff. He blanched as I watched and quickly turned back to his guns. Another first, and a bad sign. We needed him at his best, and I was beginning to wonder if we should turn back after all.

Jack was obviously thinking the same. As he climbed into his flak suit, his eyes were buzzing like he had hit REM sleep. It was one of Jack's few tells. His mind must have been absolutely racing to deal with our current predicament. Did we have any alternatives left to us? It came down to who we were most afraid of—Echo or Tonda. Both had formidable resources and drive, but there were extremes the law-abiding Echo people wouldn't go to. Jack, who persisted in his belief that there were always options, was pondering the angles and looking for loopholes. For once, he wasn't seeing any. For Jack, that must have been torture.

I was going through my own brand of hell. Unless your nerve endings have been rewired to perceive pain as pleasure, self-mutilation is not fun. Still, it was an emergency, so I took my pocketknife and slit my face along the hairline, sides, under the chin and around my eyes. Reaching up, I took several deep breaths and tore my face off.

Nothing like immediate, searing pain to take your mind off a dismal future.

Did it hurt? Of *course* it hurt! Hello! I tore my face off! My face! Off! It always hurts! Under normal circumstances, I like to grow a new face slowly, usually takes about a day. It's relatively painless and I can start and stop as I choose to slough off the old look and get the base foundation going, followed up by attention to fine details. In emergencies I can grow a new look within a few minutes, but I have to start from scratch and build it up. I'm incapacitated during this time, forced to stare in a mirror at my blood-soaked, skinless face as it regenerates epidermal layers. It takes a lot of concentration. It's a struggle to keep a careful watch on where and how the new layers are forming and to not vomit at the same time. Also, there's the screaming. It takes a lot to keep from screaming.

The face was just about done, a young man's face with dumpy features, when I started pulling on an imitation Echo uniform from one of my mish kits. The suit was made of a tough polyester double-knit blend, and wouldn't fool the guards up close. From a distance, however, it would pass for nanoweave. I selected a trim blond wig from the dozen in the kit, stripped the plastic seal from it, tore off the wax paper on the glue pads, donned it, then went to work pasting on the eyebrows. While I could regenerate skin quickly enough, hair was another matter. Keeping a shaved scalp helped. Wigs were easy enough to switch out.

Jon returned. She was still breathing heavily, and was now sporting a disgusted scowl.

"We've got a potential problem," Jon reported. "I saw an Echo bike pull up to the bank."

"For the other robbery?" Jack asked.

"Don't think so; he didn't have the usual backup. Maybe he's just here by chance?"

"Lot of that happening today," I muttered, pulling on my visor. "We might have to deal with a meta now. This change anything?"

"No," Jack said. "We proceed as planned. If we do this right, we might not even see him. If he shows, perforate him. Use everything you have. We've got one shot at this, with just one thing going for us—no one's ever tried this before."

"No one's been stupid enough," I grunted, pulling on my boots.

"Yup. But that gives us the element of surprise. We've done jobs with less. Let's go; we're losing our window."

As the others got into position, I started a deliberate march to the guardhouses, my hands behind me, my fingers starting to elongate into pointed claws. More than anything, I didn't want to be here. After the initial strike, my disguises would be worthless. This wasn't artful infiltration, it was intentional slaughter. And for the first time, right when the rush should have been kicking in, I hated my job. This wasn't what I did. Jon got off on killing; I'm a different kind of pro. Killing is the last resort. The very last resort. Not that I hadn't done it, but not often. And not like this.

"Hey, you're not an Echo Op...!"

I had tried to look relaxed, difficult when your entire body was a coiled spring. The guard's cry was the signal. I tackled the desk guard, thrust up his chin with one hand and drove my claws into his throat with the other. He wouldn't be able to trigger the main alarm. I felt dirty.

Jack started the clock, and in the corner of my visor I watched the heads-up display come on and the first countdown begin. With one guard down we had given ourselves a ten-second window to eliminate the other two.

Shattered glass and gurgling told me Jon had sniped the man in the other guardhouse. Jack moved in with silenced pistols, and a stream of lead slammed into the last, the roving sentry, with the muffled *chuffs* characteristic of silencers. We hauled the bodies from sight while Duff pulled up in the sedan.

Checkpoint One was clear. But this exterior guard post, like the bank front, was largely a façade. The real obstacle was inside, and the numerous cameras painting the area had surely alerted Checkpoint Two of our presence.

On his mark, Jack and I both hit the synched release buttons in the two guardhouses, and while the tunnel doors opened, we all dove into the car. From above, at street level, we heard a tremendous explosion, then more explosions in the distance. We didn't really have time to consider what this meant. If anything, we were thankful for whatever diversion that other robbery was bringing to the mix. Jack reset the clock.

Twenty seconds.

At the base of the one-hundred-foot tunnel and flanking the heavy blast door, twin-mounted mini guns encased within swiveling metal spheres provided the main defense for this checkpoint. Able to deliver over a thousand rounds a minute, these guns packed enough punch to bring down anything from an armored car to a light tank, either of which could handily fit in the tunnel. The mini guns made this a well-fortified choke point, enough to hold off any major offensive. However, the ball turrets weren't remote-controlled, and they weren't kept manned. These guys had a union, and a turret chair made a lousy duty station. So we figured twenty seconds was what they needed to man the guns and secure the blast door.

We had run a few simulations in case this happened. Jack wasn't wrong about the element of surprise. We had gone over the schematics of this place until we saw the layout in our sleep. While the Vault looked impenetrable on paper, it had never been battle-tested. They ran drills, we were sure of that, but a real assault is a scary thing. We were banking it all on their inexperience, in hope of a few moments of hesitation.

Duff hit the accelerator and we flew down the tunnel. Jon and Jack took a moment to switch their guns with the rifles that lay on the rear seats. The large blast door was closing and two figures appeared, one in each turret. Dammit. We had underestimated them. There was no hesitation on their part. As we hit the lower fringe of the ramp, they opened fire.

We were saved by momentum. The stream of bullets disintegrated the front grill and bit into the engine. The force was enough to slow us down, but not quite enough. Jack had run the numbers to prove that, so far as it could be proved. Our acceleration should have been just enough to clear the closing blast door. But numbers were one thing, reality another. Now, fighting against the stopping power of the mini guns, we were just shy of a photo finish.

"Down!" Jack yelled. We all pressed ourselves as low as we could and braced for impact.

The base of the blast door slammed into the windshield, shearing the top off the car above our heads, and our momentum did the rest. As the blast door dropped down into its slot behind us, we continued through and smashed into the far wall of the admitting bay.

We had done it. It was less than perfect, but we were in. No strict need for timers now, but we still had to move fast.

"Wait for it," Duff hissed as he chucked two volleys of grenades in opposite directions. We covered our eyes and, over the startled shouts of guards, heard the telltale *phoomph* of the flash bombs, followed momentarily by explosions.

Duff Sanction's signature "Blind Man, Exploding Man" maneuver. Despite the god-awful name, it was a ploy the rest of us had come to respect. There was more shouting, accompanied by screams of pain.

Jon was up next. She rose from the back seat, a warrior goddess, and began laying down cover fire. The two guards manning the turrets were wide open. The turrets may have had superior shielding to the tunnel, but here on the inside, the gunmen were sitting ducks. They fell quickly enough to Jon's attack. The rest of the guards, the ones that were still breathing, were scrambling for cover and returning fire in wild bursts.

Jack emerged, now toting his own rifle, and with his back to Jon's, they scoured the room with a rain of bullets. Taking position behind them, Duff watched as the guards, clearly on the defensive, took cover behind whatever they could find. He targeted them, signaled us to drop back into the car, and lobbed grenades their way. We like grenades. We always carry lots of grenades. *Lots*. Dropping down, Jack and Jon reloaded, waited for the blast, then were right back up and firing. Deafening, blinding, disorienting and deadly. After a few repetitions of that maneuver, Jack called for a cease-fire.

"Thirteen down," he reported. "One unaccounted for. If he's alive, Plan A is still a go."

Duff was looking around furiously, wildly scanning the admitting bay. "Well, where the hell *is* he then? If you don't see him, I'm setting up to blast our way in right now."

"Quiet!" I hissed. "Be still!"

Standing up, I tore away my Echo costume to expose my arms and torso. I felt the radial awareness return. Hopping out of the car, I took a few steps and closed my eyes to get the lay of the room. I sensed the others behind me, the heat signatures of the mini guns, and of the numerous bodies, and a few body parts that were strewn about.

One heat signature was shaking. Contact.

I scrambled over a massive desk and tackled the last guard, who was crouched in fear. First raking him across the face with my claws, I closed in. He dropped his gun, whimpering, and began to plead for his life. I tore his armored vest away and as I drove my claws into his stomach, I watched his eyes widen, then bulge in anguish. He started to scream. For a moment, everything stopped.

He was just a boy.

He couldn't have been older than twenty. A new recruit then—I would have bet this was his first assignment out of training. Sure, why not. Show him the ropes at the Vault. Nothing ever happens at the Vault.

I felt my stomach heave. This was all wrong. I should have been trading jokes with this kid, getting to know him the way I had gotten to know Walter and using him, not erasing him. I should have been a ghost in his life, not his butcher.

"Red!" Jack barked. "Get the codes!"

This boy, this *pup*, wasn't a fighter. Not yet, anyway. He was...new. And he was dying. My claws had gone deep and were slowly tearing the life out of him. The smell of cordite and the metallic tinge of blood hung heavy in the air, bombarding my senses, bombarding my skin. It was something I had trained myself to ignore. Now, I couldn't block it out.

Jack, Jon and Duff were now screaming in unison. "RED!"

I felt myself tighten up. Right. The *job*. Through clenched teeth I hissed at the trembling boy, hating myself.

"Give us the codes, and I'll end it." Closing my eyes, I forced my claws to spread wider.

He gave us the codes. No, he screamed us the codes. Jack punched them feverishly into the console. A second set of blast doors opened to the inner sanctum. With a quick slash, I withdrew my claws, and slit the kid's throat.

Jon couldn't keep her eyes off me. I didn't look at her, I couldn't. It all seemed different now. I could taste the boy's blood on my hands. I shed the claws away, grimacing from the pain of it. It wasn't enough, everything still tasted like ashes; this was not what I was supposed to be. As we hustled to the short, wide corridor that led to the main Vault room, I paused only to reach into the destroyed sedan to pull out my scarf. The mask I was wearing, a simple generic face I had picked up over the years, didn't seem to suffice. Trotting down the corridor with the others, I wrapped the scarf around my head. It was only cloth, but for the years when I had problems controlling my skin, it had kept the world out. It had felt like armor. It still did, like a security blanket made of Kevlar.

"Security cameras weren't picking up any movement in the building above," Duff reported as we entered the massive vault room. "We should be alone now."

"Bank heist upstairs must have cleared people out," Jack muttered.

"How long before reinforcements show?" Jon asked.

"Hard to say," Jack said. "Estimate ten to twenty minutes. We should have enough time, but it'll be metas."

That was good enough to convince me to rush it. I wanted this job done, I wanted to get out of this place, to just get *out*, get the goods to Tonda and leave town. The fact that we'd be forced to flee into hiding no longer mattered. I *wanted* it. Forget the training, I was on the verge of panic. I heard this happened to a lot of professionals, that it was inevitable. I had never considered the possibility that it could happen to me.

"I really don't feel like dancing with metas today," I muttered. "Hard part's done, let's just get the damned thing and go."

Most buildings like this might have held a parking garage beneath it. Here, the basement levels were taken up by one huge room, three stories tall with massive columns of concrete and steel. Here, you could find all manner of high-tech goodies. We passed by racks of weapons, tall caches of ammunition and rows of armor before we came to a storage dome with a circular vault door. Jack and Duff immediately went to work, and in five minutes we scrambled for cover as Duff blew the lock. A staccato of small explosions, and we heard the clatter of pins as the door's seal was broken. In my haste, I rushed the dome and sped inside. The shelves were lined with odd devices. Some looked to be guns, others were shaped like futuristic jet packs, and others . . . well, I couldn't say. A few objects were so exotic in their design they could have been high-tech sex toys for all I knew. The one thing everything in this dome shared was that each object was unique, a prototype.

Our mark for this job was a modern marvel, a testament to man's ingenuity to make really big explosions come in really small packages. Don't ask me for the technical babble about this bomb, but it was enough to make men like Duff soil their shorts and drool just thinking about it. In short, some genius out there had devised a way to condense an explosive's critical mass. Another genius had taken it a step further and had separated the explosive into stable components, which exponentially increased the bang you got for your buck. Yet another genius had invented a novel carrier system, which used capillary action engraved into small computer chips to directly mix these components. The result? You could carry a small device the size of a wallet, and with a simple timer attachment, obliterate an area the size of a football field. The initial explosion would be enough to pulverize everything in the blast radius, but a second incendiary effect would raze the area with white-hot plasma. A bomb, a very high-tech and special bomb, named the Inferno.

It wasn't hard to guess why Tonda wanted this. He had his own guys, his own geniuses who tinkered with doodads, and having this kind of technology would make his life much simpler. At that moment, I didn't care what Tonda wanted it for. I just wanted out. I saw something that matched the description, and picking it up I was surprised how heavy the device was. Turning, I was about to pocket the bomb in a belt pouch when I noticed Jack had his pistols trained on me.

"Sorry, Red." He seemed truly apologetic. "This is Tonda's call."

Jon and Duff appeared next to Jack. They didn't look very happy about this. Careful not to make any sudden gestures, I held up the Inferno, and tossed it to Duff. He caught it deftly and turned away. Jon closed her eyes, and followed him.

Jack and I stared at each other for what felt like minutes. Then I asked the only thing I could.

"Why?"

Jack shrugged. "Tonda can't trust you. He can't trust most metas, but especially one that can morph his face. Killing you is part of this job for us. That's just how it is, that's just the game."

Right. The game. The goddamned game.

"See you in the next life," Jack growled, as he emptied his pistol's magazines into me.

Echo Headquarters, Atlanta, Georgia, USA

Yankee Pride glanced at his watch. "It's not like Doc to be late."

"He's probably berating an OpOne for feelings of inadequacy. Can I smoke in here?" Ramona lit the cigarette before the CO could object. The smoke soothed her nerves. She hated prisons.

In other countries, Echo housed metahuman criminals in state-run facilities, contributing money and know-how to the special issues of detaining metahumans. Only in America was the entire operation farmed out to Echo. She'd heard talk of privatizing the federal prison system; if it were run as tightly as Echo's was, it could only be an improvement. She and Yankee Pride had gone through four security checks set up at killpoints with alert snipers concealed behind blast plates. For the sake of convenience, she'd left her sidearm in her locker. They didn't confiscate Yankee Pride's power gauntlets, though.

"This guy's been dying to meet you, Detective," the CO said with a smirk. "He thinks you're going to save him."

"So he's having a midlife crisis?"

"Could be." The CO shrugged. "Or delusions of grandeur."

"That's what I'm banking on. Still, it beats being on a stakeout. He just turned himself in?"

The man scowled. "Took out three of our guys first. Hardly turning yourself in."

"According to the report, he asked to talk to their commanding officer. Maybe he's just a snob." She winked at him.

The gate behind them clattered open. Doc Bootstrap bustled through, looking flustered. "You'd think they'd know me by now." He pushed past them. "Let's get started. We're behind schedule thanks to me."

The CO made a stubbing motion at Ramona. Frowning, she ground the cigarette underfoot. "No skin off my back," she told the psychiatrist. She brandished the file at him. "Want to read this?"

"No need. I'll know everything I need to know the moment this loser opens his mouth."

"I bet you're missed at Harvard."

He hesitated. "Harvard?"

"I'm kidding, Doc. After you."

They accompanied the CO down the corridor. The hubbub began: insults, taunts, catcalls. Ramona tried to ignore them. The CO spoke into his comm unit when they reached Eisenfaust's cell.

"Let me tell you the drill, Eisenhauer," the CO said to the prisoner. "No funny business. No sudden moves. We have sonics directed at your head at all times. Any aggressive behavior will result in incapacitation. Be nice to the lady."

"Oh, he will," said a coarse voice behind them. "The Kraut been waiting for his girlfriend all day. Maybe he shut up now."

"Please ignore him, *fräulein*. His kind lack manners." Eisenfaust spoke through the grill in his door.

The dark form cackled behind his own grill. "There he go with that Nazi talk again."

The door slid open. Eisenfaust stood at attention, his broken arm tucked neatly into a sling. "Oberst Heinrich Eisenhauer, at your service." His ice-blue eyes looked directly into hers.

Ramona swallowed. The man had a powerful presence. She cleared her throat. "Detective Ramona Ferrari. This here's Yankee Pride."

Eisenfaust nodded to the OpOne. "We've met. A pleasure to see you again, young man."

"Hrumph." Yankee Pride looked down his nose at the Nazi.

"And Doc Bootstrap, our psychiatrist."

Eisenfaust furrowed his brow. "You think I'm insane?"

"No, we think you're a time traveler. We brought the shrink in case you had lingering issues with your mother." She opened his file. "Don't waste my time, buddy."

"Certainly not." Eisenfaust indicated the bunk with a sweep of his hand. "Would the *fräulein* care to sit?"

Everything about the man's body language seemed to come from another time. This interview would take a while. "Sure, why not?" She and Yankee Pride entered the cell. He leaned against the wall as she arranged herself on the stiff mattress.

Doc Bootstrap edged into the cell, never taking his eyes off Eisenfaust.

Ramona looked from the Doc to Yankee Pride, who raised his eyebrows. "Your lead," he said.

"All right." She fastened her gaze on Eisenfaust and his blue, unblinking eyes. "We all know why you're here—"

"Forgive me, but you don't have the first clue why I am truly here. And I won't tell *you* everything. My story is for Alex Tesla's ears alone."

Yankee Pride guffawed. "Listen to this guy. You're not so eager to get out of jail, are you?"

Eisenfaust paused. "I'll tell you enough to confirm my identity. Then you will convey my request to speak to Mr. Tesla in person, *ja*? You may take any precautions you wish to protect your commander."

"Our *boss* doesn't make a habit of chatting with prisoners." Ramona pinched the bridge of her nose. "Fine, fine. Make your pitch."

Eisenfaust cleared his throat. "We knew it was the final days of the Reich; our forces had been spread too thin over too many theaters. My Uberluftwaffe had engaged the Allied Aces over the Atlantic Ocean, in the region near *die* Bermudas. My best pilots were dead. My—" A look of pain crossed his face. "My second-in-command and I fled the battle with the Aces in hot pursuit."

Ramona knew all this from Yankee Pride's printouts. The prisoner's story could have come from any history book. Yet she registered his unconscious movements as he spoke: the twitching of his hand as though it still held a yoke, the alert posture. Whoever he was, he was military, possibly a pilot.

Yankee Pride opened his mouth to speak but Ramona silenced him with a raised hand. "Go on," she said.

"We commenced evasive maneuvers, Effi and I, but the Aces smelled blood. Corsair, the American, and La Faucon Blanc, the Frenchwoman, took turns shooting holes in my tail. Brumby and Gyrefalcon closed in on Effi's plane. I veered into their path to take the bullets intended for her. A fuel line was punctured. I would have to bail out over the open sea. I would not be a prisoner of the damned Allies. Eisenfaust would die a hero, and perhaps Effi would live on. I saw my chance and steered for Gyrefalcon's fuselage. Even a skilled pilot such as he could not evade so suicidal a charge.

"But he surprised me. Instead of turning away, he turned towards me. Our wings clipped and sheared off, but we were both alive—albeit in planes spiraling towards the ocean. I fought against the acceleration to eject. Then a green light suffused the cockpit. I thought I had hit a green flare, but the light intensified. I hit eject and pulled the ripcord at once. Outside the plane, all was green. I could no longer see the water, the clouds, or Gyrefalcon. The parachute deployed badly. I braced myself.

"Moments before I hit, I saw in the thick green light that the water was gone. I was over land! My reflexes allowed me to adjust my position in hopes of cushioning the impact somewhat, but when I crashed through the canopy and hit the ground, the pain was immense. I blacked out."

"That's where you broke your arm, then?" Ramona pointed to his cast with her pen.

"*Nein*. That comes later, a story for your commander. I awoke to horrible bruises and a headache, but I was alive. I lay on the ground, struggling to breathe, for an eternity. When I opened my eyes, the green light had gone. In its place were a devilish red sky and the stench of rotting foliage.

"I had never seen so sinister a jungle as this. All red and black trees and vines, like the exposed intestines of a giant. I heard a groan nearby. When I found the source, I wanted to believe I was hallucinating.

"Gyrefalcon's parachute had caught in the drooping branches of the trees. The vines..." He shuddered. "They moved! Like the tentacles of an octopus. One had laid open his leg. The tree was consuming him. He was too weak to fight it.

"The man had tried to kill me, yet I could not let a good soldier die like that. I used my knife to hack him free from the vines."

Eisenfaust paused for a breath. Ramona and Yankee Pride exchanged looks. She was surprised to see the veneer of skepticism had peeled away from the meta's face. In its place was a deep seriousness.

"Interesting," he said, still bluff. "Keep going."

"Gyrefalcon faded in and out of consciousness. As slow as the vines were, I felt threatened by the jungle itself, and I had the growing sense that we did not belong there. Then I heard an engine roar above: Corsair's Hellcat, trailing smoke. Pursuing it was a craft unlike any I'd ever seen—"

Doc Bootstrap stepped forward with a syringe dripping blue liquid in hand. "I've heard enough."

"*Nein, Doktor.* Hear me out."

Doc Bootstrap swung his fist at the German's face. In spite of his metahuman reflexes, Eisenfaust was too surprised to duck. He staggered back from the force of the blow. The doctor lunged at him with the syringe brandished like a dagger.

"Whoa! *Whoa!* Doc, fer crissakes..." Ramona interposed herself between the doctor and the German. She tried to intercept the arm holding the syringe, but the doctor fended her off with his free hand. Yankee Pride wrapped his arms around the doctor from behind.

Eisenfaust stood stock-still, face upraised to the ceiling. "Something is wrong," he said.

In one fluid motion, Doc Bootstrap elbowed Yankee Pride in the stomach, knocking the wind out of him, and then punched Ramona in the face. She saw stars.

The syringe darted towards Eisenfaust. He took his eyes off the ceiling for a moment. Without changing his posture, he stepped nimbly out of the way of the oncoming needle. "Too slow, *Herr Doktor,*" he said. His hand snaked out, seized the syringe, and stuck it into Doc Bootstrap's chest. The doctor's eyes bulged.

Ramona and Yankee Pride gaped at their impaled colleague.

"You are not who you claim to be," Eisenfaust said in German. "They have come for me, haven't they?"

"*Ja*, traitor." Doppelgaenger answered in equally fluent German. His face twisted in contempt. "If it weren't for your boundless ego, Echo would have learned everything by now."

"Doc speaks awful good German all of a sudden." Ramona held her bloody nose.

Yankee Pride flipped a switch on his gauntlet. Energy coursed through the circuitry. "Too good, if you ask me." He aimed at Doppelgaenger, who had gone limp on his feet. "You gonna stay awake long enough to enlighten us as to who the hell you are?"

The doctor's face relaxed. His expression softened... then his face softened, as if the bones themselves flowed like putty. His coarse features became flat and masklike.

"Oh, *ja*," he said in a wet voice. "I would not want to miss your deaths." His inhuman countenance tightened for a moment. Blue moisture colored the front of his jacket around the syringe.

"Call Security," Yankee Pride ordered the guard.

"I've been trying, sir. Nothing but static."

The shapeshifter laughed as they checked their comm units. No one could get a signal.

"What about the sonics?" Ramona edged away from the doctor. "Hello? Anyone? The fail-safe containment system?"

"Offline for hours," Doppelgaenger said. He spread his hands in triumph. "I have brought the end of your precious Echo."

"You and what army?" Ramona said. A deep explosion shook the building. The shock wave of the blast shivered through her legs. "Don't answer that."

The prisoners erupted in a chorus of fear, followed by the whoops of the alarm system. Yankee Pride bit his lip. His gauntlet wavered.

"Damn it. I should be out there."

"Then clobber this guy first, for Pete's sake." At that moment, Ramona craved her sidearm more than nicotine, sex or money. "Don't leave us here with him."

"Oh, right." The gauntlet flashed and a burst of energy threw Doppelgaenger against the concrete walls. He collapsed in a smoking heap. "That should keep him. Kick him if he wakes up. Hell, kick him now."

"I'm coming with you," Ramona said. "Eisenfaust is the least of our worries right now."

Yankee Pride paused to study the German. He tilted his head to one side. "You're a tough one to read, mister. I had you pegged as a nutcase. Now I almost believe your crackpot story."

"I wish to my heart it was fabrication. Now I have brought the wrath of the Thule Society down on you. I hope you can withstand them, or my story will come to an abrupt end."

The distant groan of concrete crumbling interrupted them. "A breach," Ramona said. "Whatever they're using, they broke through the perimeter."

"The armory isn't far," the guard said.

"Go," Yankee Pride said. He turned to Eisenfaust. "Stay put. You'll be safest right here. Remember, you're still our prisoner."

"I hope to remain so," Eisenfaust said, bowing. "Good luck, *mein freunden*."

Ramona and Yankee Pride followed the guard back down the corridor. The prisoners shouted questions as they passed their doors.

"Stay calm," the guard answered. "The situation is under control."

Whose control? Ramona wondered. *Ours, I hope.*

The guard reached the cellblock door first. As he reached out to tap in the security code, a blue glow shone through the peephole.

"Down!" Yankee Pride lunged at the man. The door disintegrated into pieces under a barrage of azure energy beams. The concussion was terrific; it shredded the clothing and skin off the guard, who died instantly. It threw Yankee Pride into Ramona. They tumbled back down the corridor in a heap. Ramona's ears rang.

"You should buy me a drink first," she said, trying to push him off her. He shook his head to clear it. "Get up, YP, damn it. They're coming."

They were kicking out the remaining chunks of steel-reinforced concrete with metal-shod boots. Any doubts she had about Eisenfaust vanished.

A dozen armored troopers stepped into the cellblock. The chorus of howls from the prisoners was that of trapped animals. Yankee Pride rolled to a crouch and aimed his gauntlet. Energy lashed out at the lead trooper, toppling him. One trooper stopped his advance to lift his comrade back to his feet, seemingly unharmed. The rest moved towards them.

Ramona decided to obey her urge to run for it. She levered herself to her feet. Ahead of her, Eisenfaust had come out of his cell. He had pressed his face against the grill of the cell door across from his and was whispering fiercely. Despite her fear, the detective inside her wanted to know what he was saying.

"We have come for Eisenfaust," a voice boomed. "Ah, there he is now."

The voice summoned images of evil, cruelty, and a weary, jaded impatience with the uncooperative world. The man possessing it wore jet-black armor with no blast helmet. Long blond hair cascaded down to his shoulders, like an Aryan warrior of old.

"He's made new friends, I see." The tall woman who stepped forward was dwarfed by the armored giants around her. Her black leather outfit evoked a fetishist's version of a Nazi uniform, complete with cape and fishnets. "Heinrich," she cooed in a mocking singsong.

Yankee Pride dodged back as the troopers grabbed for him. Their long strides carried them past him. Surrounded, he yelled and struck out with his gauntlet. Their own metal fists rose and fell with wet impacts until he stopped moving.

Ramona, alone, stood between the Nazis and their quarry.

The troopers raised their weapons. *I deserve one last cigarette,* she thought wildly.

"Allow me," the Nazi woman said, drawing a wicked-looking pistol. A classic pistol: a Luger, in fact.

"Effi, *nein!*" Eisenfaust shouted.

Valkyria fired at Ramona's heart with deadly accuracy. Ramona crumpled. She lay still as the metahuman woman stood over her to gloat. "America has grown fat and complacent," Valkyria said. "You should have chosen your allies more carefully, darling."

The nanoweave vest Ramona wore under her blouse had absorbed most of the bullet's force. Her rib cage had taken the rest, and from the shards of pain when she took a shallow breath, she guessed she had a cracked rib.

Eisenfaust turned again to the cell door. Ramona

thought she heard him say, "You must tell them." Valkyria and the Commandant bellowed at him in harsh German, calling his name. He ignored them and spoke rapidly to the occupant of the cell.

The Commandant barked a command. The troopers directed their cannons at Eisenfaust and powered up with a cacophony of whines. As one, a dozen energy beams filled the air.

The blue beams tore up the walls, the cell door and the floor around Eisenfaust. Several hit him straight on; he made no effort to dodge. The force sent his broken form skittering across the floor. Ramona had a vision of his striking blue eyes and earnestness.

Valkyria cursed in German. Then the Commandant laid a familiar hand around her shoulders and pulled her close. She folded into him, leaving no question about her new choice of man.

The stray beams had destroyed a few cell doors. The prisoners peeped out, unsure whether they had a chance at escape. The troopers opened fire on the prisoners. One was too slow; his head vanished in a blue cloud. On the Commandant's orders, the troopers went from cell to cell, blasting down the doors and shooting or pummeling the occupants.

The Commandant led a detachment of troopers to the cell of the prisoner to which Eisenfaust uttered his last words. Ramona tensed as the armored giants stepped over her still form.

"Come out," the Commandant ordered the prisoner.

"The hell with that," the man said. "You come in here and get me, sucker."

Valkyria had reached the pulverized cell door. "*Ach*! Disgusting. What *is* that thing?"

A black, shadowy form slipped through them with a strangely casual motion, as if excusing himself from a crowd. Ramona recognized the prisoner, a petty thief who called himself Slycke.

He had chosen his nickname well; the troopers grasped at his frictionless, inky black skin without success. He paused before the Commandant, who goggled at him in surprise.

"Ain't it funny that I get sprung from Echo by punk-ass Nazis?" He laughed in the Commandant's face. "Echo's gonna slap you sideways for this crap. Me, I'm outta here!" He spun on a heel and slid down the corridor like an ice skater. Within seconds he was gone.

"Stop him!" the Commandant bellowed. Blue beams followed the jet-black metahuman out the door.

Ramona kept still and prayed they wouldn't check their handiwork. *If I get out of this alive,* she swore, *I'm going to find that Slycke and have a nice long conversation with him.*

CHAPTER THREE

A Nightmare On Main Street

MERCEDES LACKEY, STEVE LIBBEY,
CODY MARTIN, DENNIS LEE

We know now that the Nazis figured their "Neue Blitzkrieg" was going to paralyze us and let them roll over the top of us.

They completely forgot to plan for one simple thing.

Being wrong.

Las Vegas, Nevada: Callsign Belladonna Blue

Bella crouched in the shelter of a blast door, fear putting a metallic taste in her mouth. The door was of Cold War–era vintage, as thick as her arm was long, and it was hanging askew, blown partly out of its track by something. Were the arm cannons on those Nazi monstrosities powerful enough to do that?

Or was there something worse in there now?

She glanced over at Iron Hawk, the Navaho meta who'd been the code-talker for the Air Force metas on the German front. He was the leader for their ill-assorted bunch of babies and retirees.

He could not have been young when he'd signed up for the job back in the day, and he was old now. When her grandfather had been working alongside Oppie, he had been driving the Nazis nuts, trying to figure out what he was saying. No wonder he was here. He remembered the first go-around against them.

"This is not the time for subtle," he was saying, looking over them all. "You all got the briefing. The weak points on that armor are the joints, the visor if they haven't got the blast shield down, and that spot *here*—" He pointed at the same place in his throat where Bella would do a trach, if she had to. "The rest of the armor is too tough for anything but plasma-hot fire. So tell me, what you got? Left to right."

Farthest left was Bella's own high-school classmate, Fred Saltzberger. "I've got a pretty blast-proof hide; I'm strong and tough," he said, the red of his blush mostly hidden by his red complexion. "I can bench-press a car easy enough. Not strong or tough enough to punch through them though—"

Iron Hawk shook his head. "Not necessary. Just throw things, the bigger, the better. Aim for the knee. I need a name for you; I won't remember Fred."

"Red Rock," Fred replied instantly.

Iron Hawk nodded brusquely. "Next."

"Top Gun. I got your plasma cannon right here." This was the young guy who was half jump jet that had pulled Bella off her Fire Department crew. He patted one forearm. "Well, lasers, but they get plasma-hot."

"How long a burn?" Iron Hawk demanded.

"Ten seconds. Computer-assisted targeting."

"Visor primary, knee joint secondary target. And

keep your head down, you don't look like you've got enough armor to stop a pea-shooter. Next."

That was her. "Blues, LVFD Paramedic, psychic healing." Her jump bag was at her feet. Bag, not box. She wanted her box. Every paramedic had his or her own box, and his or her own way of organizing it. But her box was somewhere back in the ruins of the station, and this was what they had given her.

"Stay down, like you would on a SWAT assist. Next?"

"Sparky. Electrical arcs." That was Violet, one of Bella's best friends, engaged to Fred. "I'm guessing nothing short of a lightning bolt is going to get past the armor?"

"You'd be guessing right. Stay out of range and try and screw up their knees." He looked around at the rest in the group. "That goes for all of you. The armor can take a direct hit from a Stinger missile. If you can't punch through something like that, don't try. SWAT team fire has taken out knee joints so go for those, or try and hit them with large, heavy objects." He resumed his roll call. Bella again took inventory of her bag. She had to know where everything was, be able to put her hand on what she needed without looking.

This was going to be hell.

Within seconds of their first engagement, when Top Gun was shot right out of the air to fall headless at her feet, she knew it was going to be worse than that.

Heal and patch up. Heal and patch up. Forget even looking at minor injuries, this was combat triage—

Her supplies were long gone, and she was working off what she found in the emergency medical kits that were bolted to the wall of each room. Working for the Vegas FD inured you to a lot of things, but not to having someone decapitated in front of you.

They were about halfway through the underground complex, which didn't bode well, seeing as they'd already taken three casualties. Top Gun, Fred, and Vi. The energy cannons were devastatingly effective. Vi had gone into hysterics when Fred went down, and arced her useless bolts of electricity at the Nazis, only to be hit by three cannons at once. There wasn't enough left of them now to fill a single casket.

Bella could feel hysterics of her own boiling just under the surface. If she survived this, her breakdown was going to be spectacular.

There was something else building inside her too; it felt like pressure, like a migraine or the way some people could feel a seizure coming.

She had scant time to think about what that could mean though, not with people dropping and the fire from energy cannons taking divots out of floor, walls, ceiling.

Half the lights were out, and they were fighting from room to room in a crazy quilt of fluorescent brightness and shadow, crawling through holes where doors used to be. The complex had been built to Cold War standards, meant to take direct hits from nuke-armed ICBMs, so what was load-bearing was still standing, but the cinder block and Sheetrock internal walls were no match for what had invaded.

And the noise . . . the whine of weapons powering up, explosions, the howl of the alarm system—screams—

There were bodies, some dead, some still alive, everywhere. Mostly bodies in military uniform; some few in suits and lab coats, a couple in coveralls. She stopped to check each one, which tended to drop her behind the rest. That was where most of her supplies had gone: to the injured and unconscious here in the complex.

Because members of her team didn't need her supplies. They needed her psychic ability to push cells into replicating and healing so fast you could see the wounds closing. Nothing less would do, because anything less wouldn't get them back in the fight.

You didn't get something for nothing, not even with a psychic power. The energy for that came from her; she burned herself up to heal them. In the ambulance she gulped pure glucose. Here...

Here she was on her own.

"Blues!" Another shout from up ahead and she hurried to catch up, scrambling over a tumble of cinder blocks and across the wrecked desk, coughing on the smoke from something on fire at the other end of the room. Even as she coughed, the sprinkler system went off, and she swept wet hair back as she scuttled around another cubicle wall to where she "felt" someone in agony. A guy calling himself "Turbine." Speedrunner; not all that useful until about six rooms ago he'd figured out he could spin like a top and knock the suits over. When they were knocked on their asses, they couldn't shoot at anyone.

Except someone must have gotten off a shot at him, indirect or he wouldn't be alive. Maiden America, one of the war vets, was holding him. Bella put her bare hands against his bare flesh, and immersed herself.

It was a gestalt sort of thing, somehow she "knew" where to send her psychic energy, what to heal first—

First off, block off consciousness. He didn't need to be here for this. He stopped screaming and she didn't have to look at him to know his eyes were closed.

—tear in the pericardium—

She sent the heart cells into a frenzy of replication, being "in there" was like being in a mosh pit, except that she had a modicum of control in there.

—broken ribs—

Bones were harder, they didn't heal as fast. She bolstered them with cartilage as she lifted the pieces into place, gluing the bits together with the flexible stuff, better for her purposes than bone, really.

Finally—*chest muscles*—

Turbine's chest looked like hamburger, but that didn't matter. Beneath her hands, rivers of cells flowed into place, the muscles were rebuilt, strand by strand, fiber by fiber. Veins and arteries, nerves rejoined. And the last step, the easiest, skin crept across the muscles that had once been open wounds.

Then a jolt to his head, to bring him out of it. He came awake all at once, his mouth opened to scream when he suddenly realized he wasn't in pain. Maiden America heaved him up. "Get back with the others, and be more careful," she growled, as the kid—younger than Bella for sure—felt his chest.

She felt him turn, felt the thanks welling up in him, but she was already gone, following the next thread of agony, the next call of "Blues!"

They were dropping faster now, and she felt lives ebb away before she could even get to them.

She was crying, crying now, and she couldn't stop. She ran out of energy just as Iron Hawk went down. She put both her hands on him and tried to squeeze out something, anything, but there wasn't anything left to give.

She lifted her head, about to howl with anger and grief, and looked straight up into the visor of a Nazi.

And something inside her *snapped*.

She did what she had sworn never to do, from the moment she knew she was telempathic. Ruthlessly, coldly, she reached inside his head—

Brain scrambled, he went down, twitching. Two of the team fell on him, and cut arms and legs off at the joints. The occupant of the suit didn't even register the pain as his life bled out and Bella did nothing to stop it.

Still holding the lifeless body of Iron Hawk, feeling like a bundle of sticks in her arms, she sent out her mind three more times, invading the minds of the Nazis, to paralyze one with fear, throw the second into a mire of confusion, and the third—oh, the third—*him* she gifted with his own paranoia, a fear that all of those around him were traitors and would kill him, and made that fear real. The best-armed of the lot, he began strafing his own men until, finally, one of them brought him down.

And then her rage ran out, leaving her holding onto the verge of consciousness with the tips of her fingernails.

But it was enough. That turned the tide. And as soon as she knew they didn't need her anymore, she let go of consciousness and slid down into a place where, for a little while, there were no tears, no grief.

And no guilt.

At least, for now.

Atlanta, Georgia, USA: Callsign Victoria Victrix

The gunman behind her sent another volley of automatic fire past her, into the fray. This time the barrage took out the elbow joint of the first metatrooper target. The bottom half of the arm, the half with the energy cannon in it, flailed uselessly.

Vickie backed up, one slow step at a time, until she fell in with the line of Atlanta SWAT cops that the armored vehicle had disgorged. By the time she reached them, she and they had fallen into rhythm. Where they missed the joints, bullets pinged and whined away, but where they hit the joints...that was the vulnerable spot. Vickie kept the active Nazis off their feet, while the SWAT team concentrated on rendering one Nazi helpless at a time.

When one went down for good, all four limbs rendered useless, she buried him. That might not kill them, but maybe they'd bleed to death, or their oxygen would give out, or an OpTwo or Three would show up to give them the *coup de grace*.

"This is..." she panted, "...frickin' brilliant..."

One of the snipers next to her grunted. "Lost six SWAT teams workin' it out."

Six? *Six?* Atlanta PD didn't lose more than one SWAT member over the course of a year, and they'd lost *six teams?* Atlanta SWAT had Echo OpOnes on it...

How many of these things were there?

And if this was what was tearing up a blue-collar neighborhood, what was going after the important targets?

What was going after Echo HQ?

Suddenly a shadow fell over them, and one of the SWAT guys in the process of reloading looked up.

"Mary, frickin' Mother of God..."

Vickie whirled.

All that came out of her throat was a whimper.

It was one of the spheres, bristling with tentacles, bearing down on them with horrible slowness. Half the SWAT team turned and started firing on it, but there were no vulnerable places on this thing, not to bullets, anyway.

They were dead.

She heard energy cannon behind her start to ramp up. She saw ports for more cannon open on the side of the sphere.

And then—

"I bring you Fire and the Sword!"

The voice was a trumpet call from above, a clarion cry that both elated and terrified, filled the ears and the soul, and suddenly the sky was awash with flames.

Vickie had seen metas before. OpThrees and even once, at a distance when she was with her parents, one of the near-legendary OpFours, Amphitrite, who might or might not have been the real, genuine goddess, the wife of Neptune of myth.

This was no metahuman.

She hovered in the midst of fire, was clothed in fire, bore a flaming sword in one hand and a flaming spear in the other. Her hair was living flames, and her wings, easily thirty feet across, blazed like those of the phoenix.

There was a reason why, in the truly old texts, the first thing out of an angel's mouth when it manifested were the words, "Fear not." It was because the first sight of an angel should turn your knees to jelly and your guts to water, and throw you down onto your face with sheer Glory-induced terror.

Half the SWAT team did fall down; Vickie would have, but terror locked all her limbs and she couldn't have moved now. All she could do was look. Look on the face of a creature that lived to look fearlessly into the face of God.

The angelic warrior darted straight up, avoiding all the grasping tentacles as easily as if they were waving blades of grass. She alighted on the top of the sphere, paused for a heartbeat, then drove the spearpoint home, slamming the spear down until her fist hit the top of the sphere with a hollow *boom.*

For a moment, nothing happened. Then the sphere started to wobble, then kite sideways. The tentacles thrashed, entangling, two hanging limply.

The angel leapt off, landing on one knee on the ground before Vickie, as the sphere struggled to rise, but canted over, reeling drunkenly over the housetops until it was obscured by trees—

—the angel engaged the first of the two remaining Nazis, flinging up her hand as she passed it. A wash of flame engulfed the visor—

—she spun in an impossible backward move, slashing that blade of fire through both knee joints of the second without even looking at what she was doing, ending up on the other knee, head bowed—

Both Nazis crumpled and fell over backwards, into the mounds of dirt and rocks and torn-up asphalt left by Vickie's magic.

A crystalline sphere of silence surrounded them. Outside that sphere, sirens and car alarms wailing, distant screaming, the sounds of gunfire, rockets, energy weapons and explosions.

Inside that sphere—the sound of a single rock clattering down the mound echoed like an avalanche.

The angel looked up. Her eyes were a solid blaze of gold.

She Looked into Vickie's eyes. Saw everything. Vickie *felt* it. Every mistake and fear, every fault and hope, every secret, the smallest memory, were all laid bare in one white-hot instant.

There was a flash of unbearable pain across the angel's face. It was there for only an instant, and then it was gone again, leaving no trace behind—

—or was there?

One tear slid down the perfect cheek, across the serene and glorious, unhuman face.

The angel opened her lips.

"*Run*," she said.

One word that filled Vickie's ears and heart and soul and left no room for anything else. Her body reacted while her mind still reeled, stunned.

She ran.

She did not stop running until she reached Cold-water Apartments, somehow untouched. Her apartment was as she had left it. She snatched up Grey and locked them both in the closet. She shook and cried and curled into a fetal ball and did not come out again until the last of the noise of combat was over and the night was heavy with cordite and smoke and utter, utter silence.

New York, New York, USA: Callsign John Murdock

John was in the middle of helping a mother and her child over to the subway entrance when the bottom of the world fell out. A short brick wall back in the direction he had fled from came tumbling down. Through the dust, he could make out the silhouette of one of the armored troopers; it had already started scanning for targets of opportunity. He wasn't more than fifty feet away from the trooper, by far one of the closest people. Those that were still out on the streets finally recognized that there was imminent danger, and predictably panicked. The armored monstrosity stepped through the brick rubble, raising its arm cannons to fire.

It took John a few moments, but he remembered that he still had a gun on him: a battered 1911 .45, GI issue. Practically an antique, but he'd bought it cheap and under the table from a shady gun dealer. He felt an all-too-familiar twinge, an urge to do something...drastic. *No, no powers.* The normal gun, on a normal man: nothing else was safe. Five years on the run had proved that.

John unholstered the pistol in a smooth motion from the holdout holster in the small of his back, taking aim at the trooper's center of mass. He squeezed off four shots in rapid succession; the .45 had some kick to it, but he hardly felt it. The heavy slugs pinged off of the trooper's chest plate. John had placed the rounds in a tight group, but there wasn't even a dent in the armor. He advanced, taking up an aggressive stance as he set his sights on the front grill in the armor's blast helmet. Four more shots, all direct hits save for one that merely glanced off of an antenna. This last bullet got the trooper's attention; his cannons relaxed at his sides as he stomped up to John. One man with a pistol wasn't a threat to such an unholy terror.

John performed a tactical reload with a fresh pistol magazine, letting the spent magazine fall to the ground. He slowly backpedaled, firing in measured intervals at his opponent. A flash of red to the left of John's peripheral vision caught his attention; a red-headed and freckled teenager was standing on a stoop, frozen in place.

"Kid, run! Go!"

The teen just stood there, eyes fixed wide with terror at the oncoming figure. John gritted his teeth, reloading his last magazine.

The trooper decided that it was time to quit fooling around; it took two large steps towards John, who was still firing at its head, putting him within reach of its massive arms. John finished off the last of his ammunition; the Nazi hadn't even paused, not after being shot a total of twenty-two times. *Well, now what?* he thought, dropping his pistol onto the asphalt. The skull helmet of the trooper's armor canted downward, malicious red eyes staring holes into John. Tinny speech came through a grill in the helmet—it sounded German—followed by a guttural laugh. Lacking a meaningful response, John flipped the trooper off. The Nazi raised his arm cannon, leveling it at John's head. An ultrasonic whine—audible to him, but probably too high a frequency for anyone else to hear—issued from the raygun as it powered up, about to turn him into a smoldering corpse. John's only thought before the explosion was of concern for his parents; he really hoped that this wasn't going on where they were.

Again the twinge, the—automatic reaction—*do it!*

No. Not here. He couldn't take the chance——

Better he die than——

John's thoughts ground to a halt, violently interrupted. There was a flash and heat, and the next thing John knew, he was crumpled in the gutter on the other side of the street. Stars exploded in front of his eyes as he sat up gingerly; his ribs creaked in protest. *I'm really getting tired of things exploding.*

He felt warm, as if the temperature outside had risen 20 degrees when he wasn't paying attention.

Where he had been standing was the Nazi—only its entire right side lay unevenly melted, the suit locked upright despite the fact that the right arm, torso, and part of the head were missing. John's head swam. *Weapon backfire? What—?*

It didn't make any sense, though. Asphalt, brick, metal railings on the stoops: they were all melting and combusting. It took John a few moments to notice a human figure in the flames, and that's when it clicked—the red-headed kid.

The teen, his features completely obscured by the fires that seemed to now *comprise* his form, walked past the gruesome statue that the Nazi had become.

He paused, and through the veil of plasmatic fire, John watched as he raised his hands and bent his head to look at them, marveling at his arms and body.

A voice came out of the fires, curiously, still the voice of a kid.

"Oh my god—dude! I'm a meta!" John didn't respond, but the kid didn't seem to be talking to anyone but himself.

The teen walked up to the dead trooper, and then placed his hand on the trooper's waist, the only spot he could reach; the metal of the armor glowed red, split and cracked, then started to melt and pool at his feet. The rest of the armor immolated after a few seconds, sending a foul cloud of black smoke into the air.

"Holy crap!" The kid sounded as if someone had just given him a Ferrari for his birthday. Surely this hadn't sunk home with him yet. He was still in some kind of video-game world where none of this carnage was real and it could all be restored with a reboot. "This is *awesome!* I'm a meta!" He turned his head towards John. "Did you *see* that? I melted him!"

John finally stood up; his sopping wet shirt and jacket were now covered with equal parts water, blood, and grime. Holding a hand against his ribs, he walked to retrieve his empty and useless pistol. "Yeah, I was there, kid." It hurt to speak; hell, it hurt to do anything. John had to raise his hand to shield his face against the heat emanating off of the teen.

"Dude! We gotta find more of these guys!" The kid was practically jogging in place. "Come on! Time to kick ass! What're you standing there for? Let's go!"

"Whoa! These bastards mean business. You can't just go chargin' off after 'em; you don't know how many there are, what kind of weapons they're using, anything. And what about the people around here? They're the one's that're gonna get killed if you get into some sort of fire fight." He looked the kid up and down quickly, taking stock of the blazing teen. "No pun intended." He stripped off the rags of what had been his jacket, torn to the point of being useless and ruined, and never mind the grime. John took a few steps back, noticing steam rising from his wet clothing; the fires the kid was putting off were getting hotter.

"Oh come on, dude, I *melted* the jerk!" the kid scoffed. "Like what's gonna be able to stop me?" John only managed to shake his head, looking down at the puddled essence of what used to be part of the trooper.

Then something blotted out the sun from above.

They looked up simultaneously.

He'd thought the trooper was bad news. This was nightmare. The floating sphere looked like something straight out of a 1950s science fiction magazine. It looked *mean*.

A moment later his assumption that the round orange holes were gunports was confirmed when it vaporized the top three stories of a couple of buildings just so it could pass. John and the teen both ducked as small bits of debris rained down into the street around them. He envisaged what would happen if a flying meta tried to approach it. If the guns didn't find their target, the tentacles surely would.

"What could stop you? How 'bout one of those?" The sphere passed over the street without further incident; apparently, it had more important things to destroy than some residential buildings. "We have to get the hell outta this city, and fast. There's no tellin' what other sorta choice horrors those things brought with 'em."

The kid balled both his fists at his side. "You *chickenshit!* We gotta *do* something! If you won't, I will!" He whirled and headed off at a run back in the direction the Nazi had come, flames streaming out behind him, like the tail of a comet.

John cursed everything under the sun, spitting on the ground. *Dammit! Stupid kid! He's just gonna get himself killed...* John watched as the kid's blazing form ran down the street, superheating the asphalt under his every step. The smart thing to do would be to run in the opposite direction of where the kid was. Stay away from the main roads, make his way back to his bolt-hole in the woods, or make a new one for that matter. With this going on, he didn't much reckon there'd be a lot of priority on chasing squatters out of national parks. But...

But . . .

The screaming in the distance . . . men, women, children. People like his own folks. And not a damned one of them stood a chance without some outside help. Without some *meta* help.

John cursed again. Cinching up his belt, John took off at a sprint after the teen.

The kid's trail wasn't all that hard to follow; John just had to look for the spot fires of rubbish or molten footprints in the asphalt. He could hear the troopers, or at least the end results of their destructive spree. Explosions, screams cut short, the screech of metal being shorn off by concussive blasts: John knew he was getting close. His stomach tightened, and he felt himself break out into a cold sweat. *This is going to suck.*

Going to? It already sucked. This was just going to suck personally.

John rounded a corner into a passage between two brownstones, barely wide enough for him to squeeze his shoulders through. He emerged into a narrow alley just big enough for some dumpsters. Turning right, he saw a small crowd of civilians running and hobbling away; to his left, the kid, crouched down partially behind a dumpster. As he neared the boy, the alley started to feel like a kiln. Keeping his voice down to a whisper, John got as close as he cared to to the fiery teen. "All right, Ace. What's the plan now?"

"Get the jump on 'em," the kid replied, sounding not at all surprised that John had shown up after all. Well, that was how it happened in movies, right? The meta makes a speech and the reluctant old coot comes along.

Of course, usually the reluctant old coot ended up the dead old coot.

"Fine." John paused for a moment, gauging where the troopers were along the street by the sound of their steps. "Wait until they're past us about 30 feet, then lay into 'em. Any way you can shut your fire off?"

"I dunno how I turned it on, and you want me to shut it off?" the kid asked crossly.

"All right, all right. Just try to stay behind the dumpster as much as possible; if they spot us in here, though, we're dead." Besides the dumpster, there wasn't any cover, and there wouldn't be any chance for them to retreat. It was a kill-chute. A rotten place to stage an ambush. If it had been John alone—or John's choice—

Well, he wouldn't have been here.

Before he could give any more instructions to the kid, the troopers came into view. One, two, three— five of them in all. They were walking abreast, just marching down the street and destroying anything that struck their fancy. They acted as if they didn't have a care in the world, and in those suits, they probably didn't. He held his breath as they passed, wondering if they'd spot the kid's flames. Luckily, they didn't; probably just ignored it, thinking it was another of the spot fires their attack had caused.

It didn't take the armored soldiers long to move down the street; a few strides, and they were in just the right position—

The kid burst out from behind the dumpster, dashing into the street. "All right, you bastards!" the kid yelled, his voice breaking. "Eat fire!" He grappled with the one nearest him, and his flames went white-hot.

This was it. Maybe it was seeing the sphere that had changed everything. Maybe it was just seeing the kid...

I can do this. I can keep the lid on it. And... He had to be honest with himself, finally... *I have to. Nothing less is going to stop them.*

John emerged more cautiously, sticking close to the wall. He took a deep breath, concentrating for a moment, remembering his training from years ago—

A feeling inside of something lurching awake, and a nanosecond of pain, a worse moment of uncertainty, of teetering right on the brink of control and there it was. Fire cascaded down his hands. It'd been a long time since he'd used his powers; getting them started was the hard part, the worst was to try to control them. Now, all he needed to do was...relax. The fire coalesced at his palm, concentrating and building upon itself; a moment later, it leapt from his outstretched hand, lancing out at the centermost Nazi. The fire washed over his armor, turning it red-hot after mere seconds. Before John could get off another wave of flame, one of the troopers on the outside of their skirmish line raised his arm cannon, and fired.

The shot went wide and down; not very well aimed. Concrete erupted where the beam struck, jagged holes gouged out of the street.

John dodged anyway, as the kid screamed something his mother would have blanched to hear and lunged for the trooper's arm, letting go of the one he'd grappled with.

Or, more precisely, letting go of what was left of the one he'd grappled with. The rest abruptly realized they had something more immediate to worry about than John.

John displaced, running in a diagonal arc to the skirmish line; the human eye followed horizontal and straight-line movement best, so this move would give him an extra half second, hopefully. He relaxed his internal guard more; the fire collecting at his hands surged, setting the elements in the air around it ablaze. A twitch, and a solid beam of fire cut into his original target. The trooper staggered, then fell backwards. His chest had been melted through, almost to the back of his armor. The man inside was instantly cooked. Three troopers were left; the kid was dealing with the one that had shot at John, and the other two were just now coordinating. Both were leveling their weapons at the kid.

Reflexively, John snapped off a wave of plasma; it blazed forth at phenomenal speed, glancing off of the asphalt a meter in front of the two unoccupied troopers. It arced up at just the right angle to catch both of them at one knee each. The plasma wave sheared through metal and flesh, instantly throwing both of them off-balance even before their brains registered the pain. They both toppled in a heap, their weapons discharging harmlessly into the air. *At least I hope it was harmless.* They were still threats though, even with their mobility gone. John rushed them, gouts of flame shooting forth ahead of him. The downed troopers both writhed as their armor turned into twin furnaces, immolating them. The one furthest to the left managed to fire off a shot of actinic energy before he succumbed to the fire; the bolt of blue-white energy struck a car that John was running by, crushing it and detonating its fuel tank. The blast threw John to the ground, skidding him across the street.

Once again, as his head hit the ground, John saw stars. This was getting old.

When his vision cleared, he looked up in time to see the kid shoving his burning hand through the chest of the trooper he'd grappled with, fire now so hot there was only the faintest hint of yellow at the edges of his flames. The hand emerged out the back of the armor. The kid pulled his fist back then. All the joints in the armor must have fused; it still stood upright.

John picked himself up off of the ground, almost dragging himself up. He could feel a few new cuts, as well as a nice bit of road rash on his right arm. By all rights, he should have been numb by now, but... no. No such luck. This was just pain on top of earlier pain, even as his own metahuman body started the recovery and healing process. Resting his scraped and bruised palms on his knees, he looked up to see the carnage that he and the kid had wrought: four troopers lay smoldering on the asphalt, with one still upright in a caricature of life. A long time ago, he might have felt sick to his stomach. But that was—before. When he was just a little older than this kid. When he was plain old John Murdock, and no one wanted to kill him. The kid was taking a step back from the last trooper that he had killed. It was getting hard to look at him straight on.

"Kid," John managed to wheeze between his teeth. "You gotta shut it off."

"I—can't—" came the voice from the core of the fire. Then, more panicked, as the core went from white to blue-white, "I can't! I can't! How do you turn this off? You got fire. Tell me how to turn it off!"

Damn it. John looked around, trying to find something that might be able to put the kid out. Something, anything—there! John snapped his hand up, pointing to a fire hydrant. "There! Snap that off, douse yourself!" John jogged over, staying a safe distance away from the new meta.

The kid lurched for the hydrant, and his hand scarcely touched it before the cap had melted, then the body of the hydrant, then water geysered up out of the stump.

And turned to steam, flash-boiled before it even touched him.

The kid was his own fuel somehow. Maybe he was burning the very air. Nothing around here was going to touch the heat—

"We have to get you clear, get you away from these buildings. Can you fly?" he shouted over the gushing hydrant, the howl of the kid's own flames, and the noises in the distance.

"I—don't—" the kid began, and then shot into the air like a rocket. "Make it stop! Shut it off!" was the last thing John heard before he got too far away to hear his screaming over the cacophony around him.

The kid became nothing more than a flicker of light in the sky, which quickly changed into a second sun, not because the kid was falling, but because he was, somehow, getting brighter and hotter. His fires were blazing too hot, ramping up too fast—now they really were consuming the very air around him.

Ah hell! He's going crit—

There was another flash, followed by a too-loud

subsonic boom. John was blinded for a moment, falling backwards onto the ground; everything seemed to blur around him again. There was a blossom of fire in the sky, right where the kid had last been.

His heart stopped. *Damn it...goddamn it all.* His vision swam again, his eyes focusing and unfocusing. He *wouldn't* look away, though. He didn't even know the kid's name...

—then—

Bursting through the heart of the fire flower, another creature of flame.

Wings of fire that spread across a quarter of the visible sky, human—if a human could be clothed in fire—

It cradled a still form in its arms as tenderly as a mother would cradle a child.

It? No—not "it." He.

He Looked down at John for one heart-stopping moment. John felt like a bug impaled on a needle. Felt as if his whole life had just been read. Felt—

He wasn't sure what he felt. Grief too great to bear, fear, awe—portent?

But there was no doubt he *heard* something. A voice, a voice that cut through everything, even though it was only a whisper. It was a whisper that shook him to his roots.

Live.

As quickly as the emotions and the whisper came, they were gone. The figure vanished in an instant, almost as if it had never been there. John collapsed backwards again, panting. It was all just too much for him, too much in one day and too fast. Passing out was a relief. Even...a reprieve.

Moscow, Russia: Callsign Red Saviour

The troopers clustered in squads of five, coordinating their fire against CCCP metas or the crowd. Each of the CCCP metas had attracted their own squad. The armor of the troopers withstood their attacks; only Chug and Worker's Champion appeared to be holding their own against the Nazis, toppling them with mighty blows. Yet the troopers climbed back to their feet and grappled with the ultrastrong metahumans again. Red Saviour couldn't understand it. Worker's Champion had gained a reputation for tearing apart Panzer tanks in the Great Patriotic War. Either the elder meta's powers had waned as her father's had, or this Nazi armor was more than just a metal suit. She glimpsed his eyes, wild with a freshly recalled hatred from beneath his disheveled hair.

People's Blade seemed no more than a child amongst the giant Nazis. She leapt from one to the next, drawing sparks when her purportedly magical sword glanced off their armored shells. Energy beams licked out at her and off into the sky. Natalya realized that she was using the sword only as a distraction, to engage as many troops as possible, drawing their attention away from the innocents. She would reach a critical mass of adversaries though, an energy weapon would find its target, and tiny Fei Li would die.

Molotok zoomed from one trooper to another, his terrible strength allowing him to uproot the giants before they could slay more civilians.

That was all she saw in the brief moment of respite before the five troopers reoriented on her. Desperate for an escape route, the crowd had followed the *militsya's* commands towards Saviour's Gate, clearing spaces in the square like ripples from thrown pebbles in a pond. The troopers didn't track the fleeing protesters: she had succeeded in her immediate goal, to her own great peril.

Energy weapons had eaten away at the fringes of the crowd, creating a wall of bodies five or six deep. Natalya looked for CCCP where the Nazis had clustered. Her strategy had worked too well: the troopers had closed in on individual metas.

The mortar they'd spotted had fired, its report unheard in the chaos. A wicked yellow cloud formed over the crowd massing at Saviour's Gate, stinking of rotten garlic. The wind died just as the plume began to descend onto the square.

She'd only read about the smell of nerve gas. Yet she knew at once what it was. Their efforts to protect the civilians had only delayed their deaths.

The square grew silent all at once, as the troopers waited for the gas to descend, unafraid in their sealed suits. The exhausted CCCP metas stared at the cloud in helplessness. Upturned faces of protesters watched death fall upon them.

She gasped with the inspiration. She looked frantically for Petrograd. His perpetually aloft silver form had come to a halt above a squad of troopers.

"Petrograd!" Her voice seemed tiny in the silent square. "Petro!"

He turned his dented helmet head towards her.

"Mach one!" she called to him, pointing to the cloud. "Now!"

Petrograd's armor had been optimized for supersonic

flight, but he needed to build up momentum to achieve those speeds. He hesitated; they both knew the limits of his rocket pack. Then, with a crisp salute, he launched into the sky on a plume of exhaust. He banked hard over the Kremlin, trailing white smoke. Flames spat from his rocket pack. Angling upwards, his form shrank to a speck then grew in size as he strafed the cloud of nerve gas.

A sonic boom could exceed one hundred pounds per square-foot pressure, the equivalent of a sonic vacuum cleaner. Petrograd burned hotter and brighter as he blasted across the square. He was gone in the blink of an eye, too fast for the Nazis to fire upon. The nerve gas followed him up into the atmosphere, dispersing in the sonic boom that battered their ears. It was the loudest sound Red Saviour had ever heard, and it swallowed the lesser sound of Petrograd's rocket pack exploding and burning him alive. Black debris fell at the end of his vapor trail. She bit back the wail of grief inside her.

A moment passed as the crowd digested what had happened, then a single cry of relief swelled into a chorus, then an uproar. Supernaut took the moment to unleash his fire. It heated their armor bright red. The asphalt puddled around their feet. But a stray bullet from a rifle—could it have been Korovin's?—struck the shoulder of a Nazi; he flinched and blood spurted from the wound.

Supernaut had exposed the Nazi armor's weakness.

"Comrades!" She rose into the sky. "Comrades! We won't run any more. Burn these *fashistas* out of the Motherland!" She pointed at Supernaut. "Vassily! You want to lead? Start now! Melt their armor!"

Supernaut loosened the nozzles on his backup tanks.

Flames billowed out from his gloves, his arms, in wide tongues of fire, shaping his wild outpouring into a curving bank of fire that cut the Nazis off from the crowd.

"Spread it out!" Red Saviour flew near them. The heat from the wall brought sweat out on her forehead.

Bleeding from a dozen wounds, Svetoch stepped up next to the two flamethrowers. He, too, could ignite materials at a thought, and he added burning asphalt to the wall of fire. The flames licked twenty feet into the air.

The CCCP regrouped, those that remained: Worker's Champion, his dress suit in tatters; Molotok, breathing hard; People's Blade, her serenity replaced by cold determination; Soviet Bear and Soviette; Chug, his stone face a mask of childlike rage.

The metas seemed dispirited, shoulders hunching forward, steeling themselves for another attack on the Nazi horde. The roaring wall of fire painted their faces orange like a Dark Ages fresco of Hell.

"We must evacuate these people," Worker's Champion said with a tone that brooked no argument. "There is little time before the next wave."

"Nyet," Natalya heard herself tell the greatest meta the Russian people had ever produced, and then she knew why. "Nyet, Comrade Boryets, because we are the next wave. The fire weakens their armor enough for us to defeat them. This we must do."

Worker's Champion drew himself up. "And what about the civilians, Natalya Nikolaevna?"

"They are not civilians." She turned to face the crowd waiting to see what their protectors would do to save them. "They are my army." She expended some energy to hover before the onlookers.

"*Tovarischii,*" she declared. "These *fashistas* think they can herd Russians like sheep. Have they not forgotten what we taught them before? That Russians are wolves!" Energy coruscated around her upraised fists. "They think they can use you as bait to separate us and kill us one at a time. Instead, we'll show them the collective strength of the Russian people!"

Director Korovin, bleeding from the forehead, stepped forward with the antique rifle. "Tell us what to do, Commissar."

Natalya showed them her teeth in a feral grin. "Find a weapon. We're going to mix our spilled blood with some of theirs. These flames soften their armor."

"For Mother Russia!" someone in the crowd cried out. The words spread through the crowd as fists pumped the air, many holding pieces of rubble or metal pipes. Protest signs with her name had been reduced to clubs. Outrage and anger had replaced the panic in their eyes.

She surveyed the crowd of pale Russian faces, intermixed with tourists of all nationalities. *The face of international brotherhood,* she thought, *but only when we come under attack does it show.*

Red Saviour rewarded Worker's Champion's glare with a smile tinged with madness. She took up the chant with the crowd: "For Mother Russia!" Then she flew close to the trio of flamethrowing metas.

"Push that wall out through their ranks. Give them a taste of the flames of revolution."

"Ha!" Supernaut wagged his helmeted head in exaggerated bravado. "You heard our Commissar, comrades. Follow me!"

Nazi troopers cringed as the flames heated their armor to a crimson glow.

"Forward the proletariat!" Red Saviour bellowed. She let loose a blast of energy at the first trooper revealed; the energy exploded in a splash around him. Armor shards flensed off the Nazis.

The crowd roared and surged forward. They hurled rocks, fired recovered police firearms, and screamed for blood. The CCCP metas dashed ahead of them, combining their attacks on the troopers. The flame and the charge took the Nazis by surprise. A pitiful handful of energy bolts shot out, missing metas and civilians wildly.

People's Blade propelled herself through the air, her ancient blade, Jade Emperor's Whisper, held behind her shoulder blades in both hands. Using her momentum, she swung in a vicious arc at the head of a red-hot Nazi trooper. The blade sliced through overheated metal, flesh and bone. His head toppled to the ground and bounced with a hollow sound.

"They bleed like any man!" she cried in accented Russian.

The troopers' hesitation ended. They were vulnerable at last. The next volley of energy bolts found their marks, and dozens of protesters screamed in furious agony. The bolts cut a swath through the crowd, yet they stepped over their fallen neighbors, stopping only to pick up more rocks.

Red Saviour's army of the people advanced on their enemies.

Atlanta, Georgia, USA: Callsign Red Djinni

What a day.

Unlikely events bordering on divine intervention, befuddled by a sudden, creepy reawakening of morality, and now betrayed by the crew who had watched my back for five years. The booming thunder from Jack's greased pistols was a wake-up call. I felt the barrage pound into me and the steel shelves of the strong room bite into my back. I clutched at my chest and toppled forward. A curtain of red and black pain hazed everything.

Jack turned away. Was he in such a rush to book? Enough to walk away without even checking for a pulse? Or did he just trust that sixteen bullets finding their mark in a man's chest was a pretty conclusive end? In either case, he was on the move and I was dead to him.

Get up, Red. It can't end like this, it can't...

The blood was flowing, I knew it, just as I knew I could fix it. I had kept a secret from all of them, and it was that I could fix this; I just needed to get past the pain. I could barely move, I could barely think, and I needed to concentrate, to fix this...

Startled yells came from a distance. I heard Jack in there, shouting a warning. And another voice. A female voice. A *familiar* voice. A voice that had once purred in my ear all the love one man could stand. My wounds forgotten, I strained to listen and to slowly crawl through a pool of my own blood to the door, to see what was going on.

"We don't have time for this! I don't care if they're Echo metas, take them!"

"Captain, we can *take* them! We need to reach the armory and get back *out* there! The people...!"

"Get that gun out of my face, asshat! Didn't you hear that? They're right behind us!"

"It's four on three, Jack! And they've got that god-damned Echo armor..."

"Shut up! Shut up! Shut up! None of this matters right now! They're coming down here and they're going to kill us all!"

I managed to peek out the door, and for a moment the pain went away, replaced by shock. A group of Echo operatives, OpOnes by the look of them. And in front, screaming at my crew, was Victoria Summers, callsign Amethist, Echo OpTwo. The same Echo OpTwo we had run into last time in Atlanta.

It was a Mexican standoff. Everyone had their weapons trained on each other, shouting to be heard over the din. But over them all, Amethist commanded attention, and screamed the words that brought Jack, Jon and Duff to a puzzled halt. As for me, they were a painful reminder of the surreal, dreamlike quality of that day.

This day just can't get any worse...

"Look, you morons, we're under attack by Nazi metatroopers! We're *all* under attack! You help us—help us help *you*—or we're *all* dead!"

Okay, I stand corrected.

Jack hesitated, and that was all she needed: Amethist took control immediately, and commanded everyone to arm themselves from the weapons depot.

"Anything big and meaty that looks like it can punch through a tank! Grab it, arm it, aim it at the blast doors!"

Jack was done looking startled. He realized that Amethist had meant him, Jon and Duff as well. He signaled the others to follow her. Dumbly, Jon and Duff scrambled for what looked like high-tech rocket launchers.

The look on their faces...if I hadn't been swimming in my own blood, I might have laughed.

They took a defensive position behind a short ledge,

waist-high, lined with riot shields, and trained their hastily armed weapons at the tunnel.

"Where's Red Djinni?" Amethist demanded.

"Dead," Jack answered. "Back in the vault."

Amethist just looked at him, started to say something, but her attention was drawn back to the tunnel. There came a steady thumping of steel slamming into stone, a march of metallic feet crashing down in unison. Whoever they were, I muttered a curse at them. If they hadn't distracted her, Amethist might have looked back, might have seen me lying in the strong room, weakly waving at her.

She would have seen I was alive.

Would she have rushed to my side? I'd like to think so. I mean, it'd be dramatic. Our lives had gone in such different directions, it was sometimes hard to imagine us as those crazy kids. Still, there was a time when nothing could have kept us apart, when nothing else mattered.

Does that surprise you? Does it confuse you that I had a history with the OpTwo that had sent us scurrying into hiding a couple of years back? It shouldn't. Like I said before, this was the worst day, ever. The love of your life always plays a pivotal role on your worst day.

"Fire!" Amethist bellowed.

As one, the seven defenders unleashed hell on the advancing troopers. Just moments before, they had been ready to kill each other. Now, they fought side by side against a metal-clad death squad.

Nothing like a Nazi invasion to bring people together.

And I, watching my world accelerate into a delirious cosmic opera of crazy, chuckled a maniacal laugh of confusion, continued to bleed, and felt myself black out.

❖   ❖   ❖

How long I was out, I couldn't really say. It couldn't have been that long, but in those moments I saw my life—the parts I wanted to see.

I wanted to see Victoria.

Soft light streaming through white silk curtains, making her features burn as her eyes fluttered open, and her first smile of the day warming me with a fiery glee that I could feel creeping through my whole body. Despite how it ended, how she had left it, I chose to remember her that way.

Vic had grown up in Manhattan, in the small neighborhood known as Hell's Kitchen. She was the youngest of three daughters of a simple shopkeeper and his wife. A bright, fair-skinned, blond beauty, she believed in the tired old ideals of justice and honor and was raised to believe that people, at their core, were good. She fought for the underdog, hated bullies, and had a pretty solid left hook to back that up.

Do you remember that July evening, years back, when a freak snowstorm ravaged the state of New York? That was the night we met. The coast took the brunt of the storm. It made my life pretty miserable, I can tell you. I was a street urchin at the time. No, seriously, I lived in alleys, on deserted rooftops and when the weather got cold, in steam tunnels. Those days, I always wore the mask. My control over my skin was, shall we say, lacking finesse? Still a teenager, I was constantly fighting growth spurts and the mask would hide the ropes of skin that would sometimes erupt from my head. To survive, I had made theft my trade and the compact urban jungle of Manhattan my routes of escape. Up to that point, I had kept it simple and stole from unattended homes or small-time

stores with no security. But that night I was caught
in the sudden turn of weather. I was without shelter,
in nothing but my mask, worn cut-off jeans and a
ragged shirt, and I was freezing to death. So I tried
to mug someone.

Vic had been walking home late from a jazz competition. In the open solo competition, her saxophone
set had landed her second place. She had shown up
her critics, the ones who had beaten her down with
their caustic comments for months. That night, she
had stepped away from the musical theory, from the
tightly regimented rehearsals, and had just bared her
soul for all to hear. She felt wonderful, and despite the
cold, she felt truly warm and alive. Part of that, I'm
sure, was from the thick parka she was wearing. And
for a young, freezing and desperate Red Djinni, that
parka offered a warmth that was impossible to resist.

I had never tried to mug anyone before. This was
made painfully obvious from my awkward efforts to
drag her into an alley. The girl didn't even have the
decency to be scared. She shrieked insults at me,
which led to a pretty childish argument. Hey, we were
kids. By the end, I remember letting my claws extend
in disgust tinged with petulant anger. Her eyes grew
wide, at first with astonishment and, finally, register-
ing some fear. And then, inspired by true stupidity,
I demanded she hand over the saxophone too. Her
eyes narrowed into feral slits. There was just no way,
not that night. She began pelting me with ice. That
confused the hell out of me. I didn't know where she
was *getting* this ice. Jagged chunks of it just seemed
to appear in her hands.

That was the night Vic Summers discovered her

own metapowers, which she used to make Red Djinni scream like a little girl while running for his life.

By our next meeting, I had made a name for myself as a ghost, a spook of the neighborhood. The soiled red scarf I always wore as a mask had branded me for life. "Get in before dark!" mothers would lecture their children, "or the Red Djinni will getcha!" My game had improved. I had learned to control my skin, to hug the shadows and to dance across rooftops in nightly raids. Doors that had seemed impenetrable before began opening up to me. That was the night of my first big job, a local club on the cusp of a successful run. The plan was simple, but it was the scariest thing I had ever tried. Grab the money as Red Djinni, disappear into the crowd and leave.

That was also the night that a new, cold-powered meta named Amethist made her debut in Hell's Kitchen. I'll spare myself the more embarrassing details, and just say that the job was a major flop. I didn't get the money. I didn't even make it into the club. That night, all I got for my troubles was a clumsy escape, a new nemesis and a mild case of hypothermia.

The next couple of years started out rough. Amethist was *everywhere*. I couldn't pull even simple jobs without her lurking about. We did the dance, had any number of street fights, complete with premeditated insults and witty remarks, and continued to be thorns in each other's paws.

But after a while it became . . . fun.

We fought constantly, but I never beat her in a straight fight and she never managed to capture me. The dance continued, and I couldn't have asked for a better partner.

I don't think either of us wanted a clear victory. We wouldn't admit it, but we defined each other. We needed each other, each forcing the other to be faster, smarter, tougher, to be *better*. I learned so much from sparring with her—how to fight, how to plan and how to judge your opponents.

That was an important lesson. Know everyone. Be they your enemies, your friends or your victims, you controlled your destiny by predicting the greatest variable there was—the actions of people. After a few tussles with Vic, I had made it my job to read people, to get under their skin. If I couldn't deal with her in a straight fight, I figured I could get to her another way—by understanding her drive, by observing those she cared about, all to predict her actions, her reactions, and ultimately, her.

This accomplished two things.

First, I learned how to generalize people, classify them, and imitate them. I learned how to read people as open books.

Second, I came to the startling conclusion that I was in love with Amethist.

I hadn't seen that coming. I should have. Did I mention she was beautiful? Well, it turned out it wasn't skin deep. This girl was *beautiful*. She always fell for my traps, each one, and why? Because I put people in danger and she couldn't let people get hurt, even if she knew it was just a diversion so I could pull some fast job on the other end of the city. And every time she saved them, *every* time. A few times she even managed to catch up with me to foil whatever petty job I had planned. And she did all that because it was the right thing to do. How do you not fall in love with someone like that?

And even after all my careful planning, my vigilant observations of her, there was still a lot I couldn't figure out. I did my homework. I learned her secret identity. That Amethist was a poor Kitchen girl named Victoria Summers only deepened what love I had for her. She had these remarkable abilities, and she didn't use them for herself, or even to give her family a better life! She used them for any poor Joe who was victim to jerks like me.

But the greatest mystery was about her feelings for me. Somewhere, somehow as our paths continued to bump and bang against one another, she had fallen in love with a jackass like me. She told me later that she'd known, from the first night we met, that I wasn't hopeless. She said she knew there was something in me worth her effort and patience.

That did it. It had been so long since I'd heard anyone say those words to me.

"I believe in you, Red."

So I tried it. I tried being like her, a hero. I ran with Amethist for months, and we stopped some pretty sick individuals. Before long, I had bared my soul to her. In return, she told me things that made me marvel at her curiosity, at her naïvety. How did someone who faced the worst of humanity stay this unblemished, this *pristine*, even after all the horrors she had witnessed? I didn't know, or care. I just wanted to protect that innocence, to protect *her*. I had to laugh at myself. The plan had backfired. Learn to read people, predict what they'll do and they're yours, right? Funny how that works out. When you draw someone close like that, you forget that it's a two-way street. As you're digging around inside them, they're sinking their claws inside you.

By the fall of 1991, six months after we had confessed our love for each other, she wanted out.

No. I don't want to see this. Please . . .

She had tried to talk herself into staying, because she did love me. I knew that. But it wasn't enough, and in the end I couldn't be the hero she needed me to be. There were extremes that I would go to, to fight the bastards that ran organized crime. And I'm not talking about bravery. I'm talking about brutality. We had been fighting a losing war with the local mobs. Anytime we felt we were close to busting them, to exposing them, someone we needed would die. An informant, or a witness, the mob saw them dead by morning. I was determined to stop it. So I targeted the bosses. I made their lives hell. When that didn't work, I resorted to beating them senseless. In a few cases, I overdid it a little. The last boss I killed, Vic caught me in the act. It didn't matter that he had committed murders a hundred times worse. When Vic walked in on that, she saw me as one of them. A murderer. She was scared of me.

No . . . no . . .

But leaving me was complicated. We were expecting, the two of us. We had just learned of it. A child. Our child. But on that day, she came to me, deathly pale, and told me she couldn't do it. She knew how I felt, that I would never consent, could never stay away from my own child, and so she had made the decision alone. The abortion clinic . . .

That's ENOUGH!

Enough? No, not enough. Not *nearly* enough. I still blamed her, a big part of me hated her, wanted to hurt her. *You see it, Red? You see what you did?*

You did it. Everything you tried to protect her from, you did it to her yourself.

Now go tell her, and pray it isn't too late.

Amidst shouts and the exchange of energy blasts and explosions, I came to. Rolling over, I looked down and saw the riddled holes in my chest and the blood seeping out. But Jack's bullets, designed to puncture skin and tear through flesh, hadn't quite done their job. Like I said, I'd kept it secret even from my team. My skin wasn't just skin-deep. It made sense to wear a bulletproof vest, sure. But Jack and the rest knew that I wouldn't, because I needed my skin under no more than, say, a shirt, to use my extra senses. So I pulled a trick they never suspected: I grew my body armor *under* my skin.

Out of some deep reservoir I didn't know I had, I shoved the pain aside, concentrated, focused in a way I had only tried once or twice and with an intensity I'd never felt before. Because this was new. While my skin had kept the entry wounds shallow, I was still in real danger from bleeding out.

I started growing the tissue that would push the bullets out ahead of it. Skin, but...well, it was my skin. My skin, whatever the hell it is. I stopped bleeding, and one by one, sixteen bullets squeezed out of my torso like a kid popping zits, to clatter down onto the concrete. All the while, *out there,* explosions, the whine of energy weapons, screaming and shouting and cursing, the metallic taste of blood and the smell of hot metal and burning plastic.

I lay there for just a second. I was *tired* in a way you just can't imagine, but I didn't have time to be

tired. *You can rest when you're dead. Oh. Too late.*
Out there the woman I had loved, the woman I still
loved, was fighting for her life. I knew it had to be
that dire, or she would never, ever have joined forces
with my crew.

. I grabbed the first thing that looked big, mean, and
nasty, flipped a switch on the butt of it, and as it powered up, dashed out the door and threw myself down
between Vic and Jack behind what was left of the barrier.

"We gotta stop meetin' like this, darlin'," I said, as
Vic's eyes jerked over to her right, saw me, widened
with shock, and then went alight with joy. Even now
I couldn't resist a smart-ass quip.

Jack's eyes flickered to me, and back to the fight.
"I should have known," he muttered.

Everyone you ask is going to tell you that they just
weren't prepared for their first sight of those Nazi
armored troopers. Everyone is right. Nothing could
have prepared us for this: Hitler's wet dream. Serious.
Everything that crazed housepainter could have thought
up, everything any of his mad scientists could have
thought up, all packaged into chromed and enameled,
unstoppable death machines. Now, after terabytes of
video and millions of photographs, hours of analysis
and a phalanx of eminent experts, people are used to
seeing them. But that first sight? It was more than
a jolt to the gut. It was a kidney punch, a brick to
the head and a karate kick to the face, all at once.

This is Evil and it has come to kill us all.

And damned if I was going to let it.

I aimed whatever it was that I was carrying at the
Nazis, and pulled the trigger.

And nothing happened. I mean, it made a *whoompf*

noise like a dragon farting—and yeah, I *do* know what that sounds like—but that was about it.

I cursed and was about to throw it away, when my skin told me that whatever my eyes said, there was something going on. Something...building. Pressure. There was a pressure wave, out in front of us. And the Nazis started to take a step.

And couldn't.

It was like an obscene version of a street mime in the classic "walking against the wind." They tried to move, and it was in slow motion, shoving against something, a wind that wasn't there. They even leaned into it, as Vic and the rest sent a hell of incendiary and explosive rockets into their midst.

But my toy was only slowing *them* down. It wasn't doing a thing about their arm cannons. And they let loose with those, forcing us to duck behind an increasingly smaller barrier, forcing me to move my gun out of harm's way.

They got Duff; he was just a fraction of a second too late. One of the energy blasts took his head right off, vaporized it, and the headless body flopped down next to Jon.

I tried to get Vic's attention, then—this might be the last time, the only time I'd be able to tell her how sorry I was, how sorry for everything, but there wasn't any time, and she couldn't have heard me over the blasts, the scream of the energy cannons, and Jon's stream of curses.

We weren't stopping them. We could slow them, but we couldn't stop them. And if they hadn't known about the Vault before, if they had only followed Vic and her crew in by accident, they surely knew what it was by now. They'd have everything that was in the Vault, of which the Inferno was only one part, and probably not even the most important.

The Inferno—

That was when I knew, I *knew* that the Inferno bomb was the key. We needed to let them in, let them past us, and blow the Vault with the Inferno—

I made a dive for Duff's body, scrambling through his clothing, his pockets, trying to find the damn thing. My hand felt it in his vest and I looked up to see every Nazi trooper had his energy cannon trained on me. They'd blasted away the last of the barrier over Duff's body, and now I was in the open. I heard the whine as the weapons all ramped up.

My skin wasn't going to stop that.

You know how they say, in moments like this, everything moves in slow motion? It does. Just like some cheesy special effect—I watched as Vic launched herself at me. I felt myself falling over as she hit me. I slid sideways, behind more of the barrier, out of harm's way.

I watched her glow white, then vanish in the crossfire of a dozen energy beams, taking the blasts meant for me.

The world stopped. She was gone. Forty-five heists, thirty-two meaningless trysts, six Nazi troopers and fifteen years too late, I had finally found peace with us, but I would never get to tell her. I would never get to hold her again, or see that winsome smile meant just for me. All the good that was Victoria Summers was gone in a flash of light, and my world crumbled in the wake of that blast.

I lost it.

I didn't care anymore. I know I must have been

screaming something, and it must have been coherent, because Jack, Jon, and the three OpOnes went wide and around, letting the troopers shoot their way past us and into the Vault itself, dodging blasts as they ran. I screamed at them, taunting them, moving, always moving, getting them to chase me deeper in. I saw Jon go down, then two of the OpOnes. I didn't care. All I cared about was living long enough, just long enough, to take those bastards out. Once they were well into the Vault, I turned and dove for the tunnel, somersaulting and rolling, coming to my feet and dropping the Inferno to the ground.

Jack and the last OpOne and I ran up the tunnel, through the delivery bay, and made for the outside. The troopers were a lot slower. They turned as one, and started their slow march toward us. And I waited until they were right on top of that bomb.

"Ignition!" I screamed. And I hit the remote trigger and turned to watch as the other two hit the dirt.

They were right to call it "Inferno." The Vault glowed a magnesium-flare white. The columns holding up the ceiling collapsed, and the whole building above fell down, down onto the troopers. An enormous cloud of rubble spewed out of the tunnel doors, slamming into us, throwing us back to land in battered heaps on the ground.

I blacked out again.

It couldn't have been long.

When I came to, and crawled to my feet, the only sounds were the ticking bits of falling rubble, explosions in the far distance, and Jack's feet hitting the pavement as he booked out of there.

Vic's last OpOne and I stared at each other through

the settling dust. I could tell what was on his mind. This was the infamous Red Djinni. And any other day, if I hadn't been on the Ten Most Wanted List before, after blowing into the Vault I would have been.

On the other hand, compared to what had been in here with us, and what was plainly still out there now, I was a pretty pitiful minnow among the piranha. The world as we both knew it had just done a complete one-eighty. And I knew what Vic would have done . . . would have asked me to do.

"Look," I said hoarsely. "Let me help you save whoever we can. Arrest me after. Okay?"

Wordlessly, he nodded, got to his feet, and offered me a hand up.

CHAPTER FOUR

The End Of The Beginning

MERCEDES LACKEY, STEVE LIBBEY,
CODY·MARTIN, DENNIS LEE

Everywhere it was the same. The Nazis had miscalculated. We weren't sheep. We weren't going to bare our necks to the knife. If we went down, we would go down fighting.

Mind you, I say "we" in the larger sense, because I personally was groveling and shaking in a closet, too afraid to crack the door. I'm not proud of that. But in the larger sense . . . we were far from out for the count.

Echo Headquarters, Atlanta, Georgia, USA

Dull explosions cut through the roaring in Alex Tesla's ears. Under the influence of Doppelgaenger's injection, he lapsed in and out of a dreamlike torpor, but beneath the disorientation, his mind raced and tossed ideas into his addled consciousness.

Uncle Nikola. Echo. A ring of fire. His dead secretary. Eisenfaust. Doppelgaenger's shifting features.

Lying on his side, facing the window, he watched

a figure with a winged helmet dash through the sky, twisting and turning to avoid stabbing blue beams of destruction.

Mercurye: a part of his mind recognized the OpOne. Mercurye, the messenger.

A ring of fire, dissected by a Y. It seemed so familiar to him. He rubbed his eyes to wake himself.

Surprised, Alex stared at his hands. He could move! He levered himself up to sit in his chair. From the vantage point, he could see armored men spread in squads across the lawn of the Echo campus, directing their weapons at buildings and scattered flying metahumans. Mercurye drew a large part of the fire; he danced between the beams as if running through a forest.

He forced his hand to move across the desk and tap the buttons of the intercom for a line out. Static hissed out of the speaker. He thought he'd pressed the wrong button, but no channel gave him a signal. Mercurye zoomed past his window, a spry blur. The beams followed him; they tore at the masonry of the building. The window exploded inwards. Shards of glass rained on Alex. Adrenaline overcame his paralysis: he dove under the desk.

The sounds of battle were no longer muted. Cries, screams, gunfire and detonations reached his ears. Papers littered the floor from his earlier fall. A letter on Echo stationary lay inches from his face. *Echo Corporate Headquarters*, it read. 100 Echo Way, Atlanta, Georgia.

Atlanta. The intersection of I-75 and I-85 formed the Y in the ring: I-285, the Perimeter. His unconscious mind had already processed what Doppelgaenger hinted at: *Better for you to live as we burn your little army and your city in a ring of cleansing fire.*

It wasn't merely an attack on the Echo facility. The Nazis had far greater designs.

He needed a messenger.

The last of the Nazi troopers had vanished through the hole in the cellblock wall, in pursuit of the prisoner who called himself Slycke. The Commandant and Valkyria had taken their squad—and the unconscious Doppelgaenger—back the way they came, towards the administrative wing of the facility. Ramona counted ten painful breaths and rose to her feet.

In order for the Commandant to stroll in as casually as a red-carpet celebrity, he must have brought a massive force to engage the Echo metahumans.

The guards around her were dead. Yankee Pride still had a weak pulse but looked like the ingredients for sausage. He would be of no use to her.

Her options were not encouraging: follow Slycke and his hunters out of the building, or trail the Commandant and that evil bitch.

This is where we earn our hazard pay, she concluded, making for the cellblock door.

The armored Nazi contingent was easy to follow. Ramona could have kicked over a table without being heard over the din of metal-shod feet and cannon shots.

Once they had cleared the cellblock and the checkpoints—each one a gruesome scene of bloody, broken guards—they turned to the left, the direction of the administration building. The majority of the metahumans present on the Echo campus would be in that building, filling out paperwork in their offices, researching leads, or eating a late lunch.

The only reason to march an army towards a metahuman center, Ramona thought grimly, *is if you're looking for a knock-down, drag-out fight.* She stooped to retrieve a pistol and her ribs sang a song of pain. She gritted her teeth against it.

The sounds of battle grew in volume until they drowned out the stomping soldiers. Peeking around the corner, she saw that the Commandant's party had joined up with a contingent of troopers. Dozens. Her stomach flopped. She ducked back behind the corner and tried to calm herself.

A few stray bullets hit the wall behind the Commandant. The troopers returned fire with their shrieking arm cannons. The air shuddered with the blasts. Ramona forced herself to remember the layout of the administration building. The gunfire could only have come from one direction: south. Thus there had to be a group of Echo personnel in that direction. She could bypass the main corridor by cutting through the secretary pool.

But to do so, she would have to cross the corridor in plain sight of the Commandant and Valkyria.

There's no hope for it, she decided. She screwed up her courage—what little she had left—and bolted for the door.

It stood half open, a relief. She slowed herself so that she could push it without making noise . . . and heard a woman's voice bark at her in German.

"Aw, hell." She dove into the roomful of cubicles.

Discarding stealth for speed, she sprinted between the cubicles and their Post-it notes, Dilbert cartoons and memos. Valkyria flung the door open behind her and unleashed a barrage of bullets over the cubes. The maze of cubes led Ramona into a dead end filled with copy machines and printers.

"Come back, damn you!" the German shouted.

She could hear the creak of leather as the woman drew close. Ramona unplugged the Ethernet cable from the printer. It would have made a good garrote... but she couldn't find the terminus; it passed into the wall. She settled for the AC power cord and hid in a nook created by an overlong divider.

Valkyria entered the printing cubicle, pistol first. "Come out, *liebchen*," she said. "I will make it painless."

Ramona lunged at her with the power cord in her fists. Valkyria squeezed off a shot so close to Ramona's ear that it deafened her—but she got the cord around Valkyria's neck.

Wrestling was where Ramona's extra pounds worked to her advantage. She put a knee in the German's back and leaned away. The woman tried to wedge her fingers under the rubber cord while flailing with her pistol. Ramona slammed her against the divider and then against the wall, but the metahuman bucked like a bronco.

"Hold still, damn you," Ramona panted. The effort to keep the cord taut made her ribs feel as though they were cracking further.

Valkyria found her footing and lashed out at Ramona. Her strength broke and she staggered back. The metahuman clawed at her throat, gasping for air, but her eyes promised death to the detective.

Ramona grabbed the laser printer—a nice, heavy, outdated model—and threw it at Valkyria's head with an enormous crash. The impact knocked the metahuman down. Ramona ran for it, digging the gun out of her pocket.

A wide, thin-fingered hand threw the door open in front of her. Her face collided with someone's stomach.

Panic took over. She snatched the gun up to fire at the giant. The gun floated out of her hand and hovered in the air.

"Easy there," a voice said above her. Ramona craned her neck. The speaker, whose stomach was in her face, was Southwind, one of the freakishly tall metahuman Four Winds. His large eyes with their oversized pupils made her feel as though the flying saucers had landed.

"Get her," she managed to say.

With flawless timing, Valkyria leapt onto the top of a cubicle, pistol in hand. Ramona had a priceless glimpse of the German's look of shock before Southwind sent forth a blast of telekinetic force that dashed her up into the dropped ceiling. Her legs dangled from the punctured drywall, twitching.

"You make it look so simple," Ramona said.

"It's not, believe me." Southwind's tone was dark. "We're trying to flank the Nazis in the building. You know where they are?"

"I think so. Back that way." She pointed with her chin. "At least twenty of 'em."

"Good." The alienlike metahuman gave her a wicked grin showing small, precise teeth. "I have some frustration to work off."

Mercurye dug his heels into the air as if it were Astroturf. He did not possess the ability to fly; rather, the ability to stride through the air at incredible speeds.

He took advantage of this quirk in his ability as the Nazi troopers fired bolt after bolt at him. It had served as a distraction while his surviving comrades regrouped, but more Nazis in armor filled the Echo grounds, adding their arm cannons to the forest of energy beams. Ten became twenty became fifty. He could no longer hold their attention.

To give himself more time to anticipate the vector of the blasts, he gained altitude, driving his winged sandals against the air. Higher up, still flitting back and forth, he could see the spheroid war machines tearing at the walls of the research building with snakelike tentacles; delivery trucks disgorging more troopers; fire on the roof of the Echo museum. His heart sank.

The barrage diminished. Below, he saw two glowing forms dashing from trooper to trooper, leaving a wake of uprooted troopers. Blue beams chased the figures.

Kid Zero. He had recovered and split into his two battle forms, Kid Plus and Kid Minus. Each one could deliver an atomic-powered punch and communicate with the other through a mental link.

The two Kids moved fast enough to evade the blasts aimed at them. Eager for an earthbound target, the troopers concentrated their fire, often hitting each other.

Over the din, Mercurye heard a voice call his name.

He spotted a figure waving his arms from the shattered window of a corner office. He squinted against the glare of the hot summer sun; he recognized the face: his boss, Alex Tesla.

Mercurye was torn: answer Tesla's summons or try to draw fire away from Kid Zero's atomic forms.

In the second that he hesitated, Mercurye saw Kid Minus—the dark form—trip on a divot in the ground. The troopers wasted no time in descending on him with mailed fists. Their armored shapes enveloped the glowing form.

Out of the corner of his eye, he saw Kid Plus's energy aura turn white and expand.

Without warning, a blinding light erupted from the pileup. Mercurye threw a hand over his eyes.

A wave of heat hit him. The nanoweave fabric of his pants tensed. His exposed chest hair smoldered.

Then the shock wave, followed by the immense roaring sound of the explosion itself.

Carried by waves of sheer force, Mercurye hurtled through the air like so much shrapnel.

For a moment, a blackness as pure as the white light of the nuclear explosion swallowed him. But a shred of his consciousness remained alert—and furious. These armored barbarians had killed Kid Zero. A boy. His friend.

Mercurye, who styled himself after the messenger of the gods, had a message for the Nazi horde.

Revenge.

Weak but awake, he let his feet skid across the sky, slowing his fall. He arrived at a full stop at the main gate, where a dozen ShipEx trucks with shredded sides had been abandoned.

Mercurye looked back at the Echo campus. A miniature mushroom cloud reached toward the sky, enveloped by smoke and flames that silhouetted tall armored figures in flight. He judged that the blast had taken a large chunk out of the administration building—including the cafeteria where he had left his comrades—and left a crater in the ground where Kid Zero had fallen.

"Oi, mate." The words issued from the ruins of a guard booth. A black-clad glove protruded from the rubble. "Lend a hand?"

Still aching, Mercurye shouldered the slabs of

concrete aside with the remains of his metahuman strength. The man underneath wore a black hood and Echo uniform. His black raven wings bent at unnatural angles.

"Corbie." Mercurye hauled the wounded Englishman onto the street as gently as he could. "Where's your squad?"

"Dead. Bloody Nazis... came out of the trucks... killed Miranda and the Troll..." Corbie spit, a mixture of blood and saliva. "Played skeet with me."

"Can you move?"

"I can't bloody *fly*. I suppose crawling's an option." He stared at the column of smoke in the center of the campus. "What was that?"

"It *was* Kid Zero."

Corbie cursed. "Help me up." With a supporting arm, Corbie limped over to the guard's crushed body and took her sidearm. "Just point me in the right direction."

A sense of doom came over Mercurye. Small squad tactics he could handle, but this was all-out war, and he wanted guidance too. Even the courage of Corbie would be consumed by the inferno of violence before them. Yet, what could they do?

Then he remembered Tesla, trying to get his attention before the blast. "Better yet, I'll take you there." He gripped Corbie's uniform and took to the air, legs pumping hard in an airborne sprint.

In moments they were over the crater. The shattered forms of Nazi troopers lined the sides; Mercurye guessed that the boy's unintentional suicide bombing had taken out a few dozen troopers, leaving scores more reorganizing on the lawn. A squad pressed into the gaping hole in the building where the cafeteria had been.

He angled to the left, to Tesla's office window. They ducked the shards of broken glass that lined the window like jagged teeth. Their booted feet crunched on the debris-strewn floor.

Tesla was nowhere in sight.

"Alex!" Heart in his throat, Mercurye scanned the room for a bloody corpse.

Corbie nudged him. "In there, maybe?"

A bookcase stood at an angle to its compatriots to reveal a narrow staircase lit by dim fluorescent lights. Mercurye peered down the space between the rails. "This goes all the way down to the subbasement. Some kind of escape tunnel?"

Corbie limped over to the entrance. "If it is, there are a lot of blokes who can put it to use."

"I can find out quick enough." Mercurye vaulted over the rail, arms tight to his sides. There was just enough clearance for him in the gap to drop down past the flights of stairs. As he approached the bottom, he churned his feet to gain purchase on the air. His last step, from two feet above a concrete floor, he took as though stepping off the stairwell itself.

Beyond the stairwell, a door led to a small room glowing with multicolored lights from consoles up to the ceiling. Alex Tesla stood beside a chair with an elaborate helmet on his head. White noise growled out of a speaker mounted next to a viewscreen on which flickered a stylized symbol of a star over an eye. He twisted dials and cursed between calls of "Uncle! Uncle!" into thin air.

"We're not beaten yet," Mercurye said to his back. Tesla whirled, pointing a needle-nosed, wicked-looking gun that Mercurye had not seen in his hand.

Fear and doubt played across Tesla's features. "I thought you were killed."

"Helps to be airborne in a shock wave," Mercurye said. "I'm pretty sturdy." He looked at the unfamiliar gun more closely. It resembled a prop from a Buck Rogers serial. "Is this your secret armory?"

"No. It's . . ." The doubt returned, and Mercurye recognized the look of a man scrambling for a plausible lie. "It doesn't matter what you see if the Thules kill us all." He pounded on the screen. "Come on, answer!"

Mercurye hesitated. The room offered no exits other than the door he had come through, so his hope for an escape tunnel was dashed. Frustration overcame his deference. "What are you doing? You're needed out there. We're scattered all over the place, getting picked off like—"

Tesla cut him off with a hand. A voice came through over the static. "*Metis . . . can't . . . interference . . .*"

Metis? Mercurye knew that word, but from where?

"Come in, come in. Please! Can you hear us? Send backup . . ." Noise drowned Tesla out. He dashed the helmet to the ground with a curse and glared at Mercurye.

"Did you get through?"

"I don't know. The Thules are jamming every frequency, even our secret ones." He paused, sizing Mercurye up. "We have to assume we're on our own."

"Um, yeah . . . listen, these Thules—the Nazis—they're slaughtering us. OpTwos, Threes, all going down. We have two hundred metas in Atlanta. If we can just mount a counteroffensive—"

"And how do you propose to do that? I can't even use my goddamn cell phone." Tesla scowled. "It's worse than you think. Echo isn't the only target. They're torching the Perimeter."

Mercurye gaped at him as the words sank in. "The Perimeter? How do you know?"

"Never mind that. There are too many innocent lives at stake to worry about the Echo campus. Let them destroy it. We need our teams out on I-285." Tesla shoved the gun into his pocket and began to climb the stairs. Mercurye followed him up the narrow stairway, although he could have floated to the top in a fraction of the time.

"Okay, how do we do that without radio contact?"

"That's where you come in. Mercurye, messenger of the gods."

Comprehension dawned. "Oh."

Gunshots interspersed with incomprehensible Cockney swearing echoed down the stairwell. An explosion sounded, followed by more gunshots. "That's Corbie. He must have found some targets."

"Then we'll take a shortcut." Tesla pressed a hand against a specific spot on the wall. The featureless concrete lit up with a web of glowing blue circuitry; the shape of a door defined itself. As it opened, they heard more gunfire and energy beams.

"I think we've found the front line," Tesla said, retrieving his gun from his jacket.

Mercurye missed his sidearm and his caduceus. "Is that little toy going to make a difference?"

Tesla almost grinned. "You'd be surprised."

"Not today I won't."

The last time Ramona had seen the rotunda, it was full of gawking tourists. Now, above her, tons of rock and metal lost their support and fell towards her in what seemed to be slow motion.

"Oh God," she breathed.

As if united in thought, the Four Winds rose into the air and extended their arms to the onrushing debris. Wind howled around them; the fall of the wreckage slowed. Ramona stared, transfixed. Could the Four Winds' combined telekinetic power hold up a building?

Bare arms wrapped around her waist and yanked. Her sidearm flew out of her hand. Someone moving faster than a human hauled her to the front entrance and let go. She tumbled to a halt next to a pair of legs.

The owner of the pair of legs helped her to her feet. "We've got to get out," Alex Tesla said urgently. Ramona did not hesitate; she pushed the glass doors—miraculously intact, at least for the next ten seconds—and ran out into the daylight.

The smoke-free air tasted as sweet as bourbon to her. She turned to see Mercurye hauling his comrade Flak past them. Air whooshed out of the doorway at their heels.

Ramona threw Tesla to the ground and covered his body with her own, despite the sharp pain in her ribs. The ground floor of the Echo administration building exploded in a deafening roar.

Dust enveloped them in a daylight-defying cloud. The glass doors they had passed through moments ago showered on Ramona's back and cut her exposed skin.

For a moment, Ramona blanked out on everything but the pain from her lacerations. The screams of buried men and women reached her. She could hear a lone voice calling out the name "Kevin" over and over, more distraught with every repetition.

Lesser pieces of debris continued to hit the ground around them; beneath her, Tesla squirmed and tried to rise. She pressed her hands against the ground to push herself away from him and from the broken glass.

Mercurye stood over her. He took her hand and lifted her to her feet as if she were a feather. Bloody cuts crisscrossed his bare chest, the blood mixing with dust.

"I'm okay," she said before he could ask. The sadness in his eyes was unbearable. "Thanks." On impulse, she squeezed his hand and held it.

"Alex," Mercurye said, "do you still want me to play messenger?"

"More than ever. We need to concentrate our forces on the highway."

"The—what?" Ramona goggled at him. "What highway? The Nazis are right past that pile of rubble." She pointed at the demolished building and the rising cloud of dust.

Flak came up behind them. His black face shone with bruises. "I ain't gonna retreat," he·said wearily.

"They're attacking civilians on I-285. The ring of fire." Tesla brought out a strange-looking pistol. "Our first duty is to the citizens. The campus—we can write it off if we have to."

"And what about *our* people who're getting wiped out?" Flak said.

Tesla said nothing.

"He's right. Atlanta's depending on us. We can't dig a hole and hide in it." Mercurye released her hand. "We have to do what we can."

"I'm not sure I can do *anything*. I don't even

have a gun anymore—I'm just a detective. Where are the OpThrees? The OpFours? Aren't there a few in Atlanta? That spooky Greek lady, Amphi-something."

"I'll find them," Mercurye said quickly.

"No, you won't. Atlanta has five million people. Are you planning to go door to door?" Ramona blew air out of her cheeks. "Without radio we're screwed."

Tesla's jaw dropped. He stared at her.

"OpFours. I know where one is." He turned east. "He's not close. Fifteen miles at least."

"Who?"

"The Mountain."

Flak snorted. "The big guy in Stone Mountain? He's never left his hole where the Confederate memorial used to be—before he smashed it."

"And he won't talk to anyone," Mercurye said.

"That's true," Tesla admitted. "But he's also a hundred feet tall. He could tilt the balance in our favor."

Mercurye rubbed his chin. "Fifteen miles I can do in five minutes."

"With a passenger?"

He nodded. "Maybe. Yes."

"Then you can take me to Stone Mountain before you round up our troops. I'll order him out of hiding."

"No." Ramona stepped in front of her boss. Tesla raised an eyebrow. "You're needed here, sir. Besides, depressed men don't want to be bossed around. They need to be cajoled. That's a job for a woman."

"Like in *King Kong*," Flak said.

"Damn right," she said.

Tesla paused only for a moment. "All right. Get to it. Flak, you're with me." The two men spun on their heels and raced back into the dust cloud.

Mercurye and Ramona watched them disappear into the darkness.

"You ready?" he asked, spreading his arms.

Ramona straightened. "Take me. I'm yours."

Ramona pressed her head against Mercurye's chest, squeezed her eyes shut, and tried not to scream—though in fact she could barely breathe, and every breath she did take cracked her abused ribs. The wind roared in her ears and tore at her hair like a beast with a million claws. Mercurye ran at full speed, nearly two hundred miles an hour, a thousand feet up. She could taste blood mixed with sweat and dust on his skin. Her eyes teared up every time she glanced at his face. It was a mask of concentration and strain.

She dared not look down.

The roar increased in volume to a howl straight out of Hell. Ramona tried to breathe through her nose in the air pocket against his chest, but before she blacked out, she felt his arms squeeze her tighter. Then—

"Hey. Hey, wake up. Come on." Ramona's eyes flew open. She lay on hot granite that seared her palms. The sun glared down behind Mercurye's head, giving him a golden, winged halo.

"Christ." She rolled over to shield her eyes. "We made it."

"In record time. Congratulations." He felt her cheeks and the pulse in her neck. "That was equivalent to riding a plane bareback. You're one tough chick."

"Next time I'll skip the window seat. Help me up." Ramona sat up painfully and grabbed his hand as her head spun. "Gah...I need a cigarette."

"I hear that a lot." He winked at her and strode

to the edge of the abutment. Stone Mountain was a barren chunk of granite shoved eight hundred feet up through the flat Georgian plain by ancient volcanic pressures. In the early 1900s, the Daughters of the Confederacy and the Ku Klux Klan raised funds to carve the world's largest bas-relief into the side of Stone Mountain. Unsurprisingly, the subjects of the carving were the heroes of the losing side of the Civil War: Robert E. Lee, Jefferson Davis, and Stonewall Jackson, all mounted on horseback. Some Southerners regarded as divine justice the emergence of Mountain from the very center of the bas-relief—until he declined to take up where Lee, Davis and Jackson had left off.

Mercurye peered over the edge at the gaping hole in the mountain where the monument had been. "I don't see him."

Ramona wobbled to her feet. "He's probably sulking in there. Or asleep."

"There's no ladder. I'll fly you down." He scooped her up again and stepped onto air as if it were a staircase.

They landed on the lip of the cave. The sunlight illuminated the first forty feet; beyond was darkness.

"Wonderful," she said. "I forgot my hardhat and lantern. Silly me." She dug around in her pocket for her lighter. "This will have to do."

"Just look for the giant made of stone. You can't miss him."

"Thanks for the ride, handsome." Ramona stood on her tiptoes and planted a kiss on him.

To her surprise, he kissed back, pulling her close. For a moment, she forgot about the agony in her chest, the death and destruction in the city, the horror of the invasion, and lost herself in the sensation of his lips.

They broke. She took a deep, creaky breath. "Wow. Okay, get going."

Mercurye nodded at her, his cheeks red with a boyish blush. "Good luck." He sprang into the air. With a single stride he covered fifty feet.

"Ramona!" She shouted after him. "My name's Ramona!"

But he was already out of earshot.

The cyclopean tunnel curved to the left, out of the sunlight. Ramona paused for a minute to let her eyes adjust to the dark. Rumor had it that the Mountain had dug his way out of the heart of Stone Mountain, where he had come to life. He was no supernatural creature, though; he had been an accountant, or project manager, or something mundane. No one knew what sparked his horrendous transformation.

Ramona debated whether or not to announce herself. This was essentially his home. Would he resent her intrusion?

She resumed walking. The tunnel floor had been smooth before the bend. Here she began to see stones and boulders of increasing size; the light faded rapidly. Ramona fingered her lighter but resisted pulling it out until absolutely necessary. She put a hand out to guide her along the wall. She felt it curve away from her; had she entered a chamber?

Suddenly, boulders blocked her way. The smallest was five feet tall. She clambered onto it and flicked her lighter. A rockslide of some sort had blocked off the tunnel.

"Oh, damn. Damn, damn, damn." Tears welled up in her eyes. All that effort, and the poor bastard had been buried in his own home.

She had failed them all.

The lighter sputtered and went out. Ramona sat on the boulder and let the dam break. Sobs wracked her body. Never before had she felt so worthless.

The boulder moved.

Only a few inches, but it jarred Ramona as though an earthquake had struck. She held her breath and waited for it to happen again.

It did.

And then the boulder lifted her into the air. The tunnel reverberated with the sound of rock grating against rock. Ramona worked her lighter until the flint caught. The tiny flame cast enough light to illuminate the cavern.

What she had believed was a rockslide formed itself into a head, shoulders and arm. The head tilted, ever so slowly, to reveal a grotesquely massive face, fifteen feet from chin to brow.

Eyes that glowed like a volcano regarded her. When the Mountain blinked, it sounded like a car backing out of a gravel driveway.

He extended the finger on which she stood and studied her as if she were a butterfly.

Ramona's heart pounded. The Mountain could have killed her with a casual gesture; in fact, he might do it accidentally. She fought down the urge to run.

"Hello there," she said. Her voice sounded tiny. She took a deep breath. "Hello there!" she shouted.

The Mountain's mouth opened. A blast of super-heated air washed over her. A sound like a sonic boom shook the tunnel. She covered her ears.

Then she realized he had said "hello."

"Can you speak softer?" she said as loudly as she could.

The head tilted. "I can," the voice said, this time without the deafening volume, though she felt like she was having a conversation with a thunderstorm. "Who are you?"

"Echo Detective Ramona Ferrari. I take it you're the Mountain?"

The giant shook, rocks falling from the cave walls. He was chuckling.

"Okay, that was a stupid question. Listen, there's an emergency. Echo needs you."

The Mountain stared at her without speaking.

"We're under attack. Nazis . . . I know, it sounds crazy, but there are hundreds of them. They're big—I mean, not as big as you, but eight feet tall and heavily armored. Bullets won't hurt them."

She waited for him to respond. After an awkward silence, she said: "They're killing us out there. And they're on the Perimeter, Tesla says, so civilians are dying too. It's a war. All-out war . . ." Ramona took a breath. The Mountain said nothing. "Can you hear me?"

"Yes," he rumbled.

"I feel like I'm babbling. Does this make any sense to you?"

"I like it."

Ramona blinked. "What?"

The giant looked around the tunnel before resting his eyes on Ramona again. "First person . . . to talk to me . . . in a year."

"Really?"

"I like your voice."

"Oh." She cleared her throat. "But did you understand what I said? About the Nazis?"

"Yes."

"Oh, good. Then you'll come back to Echo with me."

"No."

Ramona gaped at him. "No? People are dying."

"Don't care."

"You . . . don't . . . care?" Her face flushed. "What kind of monster are you?"

The giant's glowing eyes stared at her. His silence spoke volumes.

"Ah. Right. A giant rock monster." She remembered what she'd told Tesla about cajoling the reclusive OpFour. "I'm sorry. You have to understand, I've just come from a war zone. It's a miracle I'm still alive. If it weren't for my friends, I wouldn't be here at all. But you have a right not to care. You're safe here."

"Alone."

She nodded. "I'm sure. You don't exactly roll out the red carpet for guests. Does Echo even look in on you?"

"By helicopter."

"Sure. That makes sense, since there's no way to get up here otherwise." She made a show of inspecting the chamber. "Nice place you have here. Cozy. How's the TV reception?"

The finger shifted, knocking her off balance. "Mocking me," the Mountain said.

"You're goddamn right I am. You're worse than a teenager, moping in your room!" She pointed towards the mouth of the cave. "I just told you people are dying as we speak, and you don't care because you're *lonely*. How the hell should I take that?"

"You don't understand."

"Honey, *no one* understands what it's like to be a walking office building but you. That's a given. Now, what are you going to do about it?"

"Nothing."

"I see that now." Ramona judged the fall from his finger to be ten feet. "Put me down."

The Mountain lowered his finger. She clambered off. "I need to get back to HQ. You're of no use to anyone, not even yourself."

Ramona turned her back on the giant and walked toward the light. She heard him shift behind her.

"Divorced."

She stopped but didn't reply.

"Wife divorced me. After this."

Ramona began to walk again. She heard more movement, like a dozen sidewalks buckling.

"Lost everything."

"You're still alive," she said over her shoulder. "That's more than a lot of people can say for themselves today."

"Wait."

"I can't talk anymore. I have to figure out a way down this mountain." Ramona walked to the lip of the hole.

The Mountain crawled behind her. The sound of so much mass in motion elicited a primal fight or flight response from her, like a deer fleeing an avalanche.

Stone Mountain looked out upon the city. Atlanta burned; smoke rose from a dozen conflagrations. One of them was Echo, she realized.

The giant groaned when he came into the opening. "Fire," he said.

"Brilliant observation," Ramona said. "Are you going to help me down, or do I have to turn into a mountain goat?"

He had not taken his eyes from the view. "Long way," he said.

"Long way down," she agreed.

"Long way to Atlanta," the giant said firmly. There was a hardness in his voice that was not present before. Ramona turned to face him.

"You know, the best cure for the blues is to work out your frustration," she said, jerking her thumb at the city. "I bet you have a lot of rage to vent."

"I do." The giant laid his palm down on the cave floor. Ramona mounted it. The Mountain brought his hand up so that she could safely climb onto his shoulder.

The Mountain lowered himself from his den. His first step towards Atlanta covered twenty yards and nearly crushed a parked SUV. Looking out over the forest and the highway beyond, Ramona realized she had a whole new problem: how to get a ten-story stone giant through an urban area without killing anyone.

"Watch your step," Ramona yelled up to his ear. "We have a lot of distance to cover."

If the city wasn't under attack by Nazis, Ramona thought, *they'd be mobilizing the National Guard against us right now.*

The Mountain took long strides—long meaning he covered nearly fifty feet a step. From her perch on his shoulder, she got the distinct impression that she had been drafted for a Godzilla movie.

Every step the giant took jeopardized something: a house, a car, trees, a swimming pool. He left five-foot-deep indentations in the ground as he passed. The damages incurred by his stroll would cost the city millions of dollars and give insurance companies epileptic fits. People screamed and ran at the sight of him.

"Watch out for the houses," she called to him. "Oh, crap! Dog at twelve o'clock! Um...damn." She sighed as she spotted a flattened German shepherd in a bus-sized footprint. "Mountain! Hey, damn it, slow down!"

"Thought it was war," he said, but he stopped. Atlantans gathered at a respectable distance and clutched each other in fear.

"Not on *them*." She pointed at the crowds. "You have to be more careful. Echo prevents civilian deaths, not causes them."

"Hard," he said. She understood what he meant. As they had left the park, Atlanta's urban sprawl took over. There was literally nowhere he could step without crushing something.

The All-Star game had jammed the highways to bursting, so those were out.

"Go back." He sounded like a despondent foghorn.

"No, no! Let me think." What she needed was a megaphone to warn people in their path.

"I got it. Mountain...wait, calling you that sounds stupid. We're co-workers. What's your real name?"

The giant tilted his head. "Bill," he said.

"Okay, Bill, remember when you nearly deafened me for life in that cave? Now's the time to make use of those lungs...or whatever it is you have in there."

"What do I say?"

"Anything. We just want to clear a path."

"Hrm."

Ramona edged away from his mouth and covered her ears. "Ready!" she said. She felt the giant's chest expand.

"COMING THROUGH!" he announced with the force of a rocket engine. Despite being behind the sound wave, Ramona's ears rang.

The Mountain looked down upon his fellow citizens as they ran in a panic. He huffed, and Ramona recognized his geologic-sized chuckle.

He took a careful first step in an abandoned front lawn. "STAY IN YOUR HOMES," he said. It made sense: a house was easier to avoid than a tiny dot of a human.

"Watch out for dogs!" Ramona said.

"I like dogs." The Mountain hunched over—carefully, so as not to dislodge his passenger—and studied the ground as he chose his steps.

Thus they made steady—and loud—progress through the Atlanta suburbs. When they reached Tucker, on the cusp of I-285, they got a glimpse of the white-hot thermite fires being sprayed by the spheroid war machines. The hellish orange glow of the war machines' antigravity propulsion systems—a technology Ramona had not believed possible—lit the highway under the vast ceiling of smoke like a vision of hell. The Mountain paused.

"Fight them?" he asked.

Ramona bit her lip. "Keep going. If we can free up the Echo campus, every goddamn meta in the city can give those bastards the fight of their lives." *Assuming there's anyone left alive at headquarters*, she thought, but didn't mention. She prayed she was right about the rationale for sending him into the city proper.

"Come back," he said and began his careful walk again, punctuated by bellowed warnings. They moved south, avoiding the Perimeter until they had to cross it. Inside the Perimeter, houses were packed too closely together for the Mountain to traverse safely.

Three war machines peeled away from the highway

and approached them. Ramona remembered what they had done to the Echo administration building. "Bill! Bogeys at five o'clock! Do you have eye beams or something?"

The Mountain plucked Ramona off his shoulder and concealed her in his palm. With his other hand, he swatted at the war machine closest. It exploded into flames and debris. The other two veered away and kept a respectable distance.

"Good enough!" She had to shout at the top of her lungs now that she was so far from his ear. "We're close! Keep going!"

The Mountain gave each of the war machines a dirty look and resumed walking towards a central column of smoke in the distance: Echo headquarters. The Mountain began to take larger steps, using city streets as a pathway. He shouted his warning repeatedly. Ramona put fingers in her ears and grinned like a tank commander homing in on enemy troops. Someone as big as the Mountain didn't need the element of surprise. Right about now, she figured, those chrome bastards should be wondering what all that noise is.

They came into visual range of the Echo campus. A dozen war machines hovered in the sky above. Blue beams launched into the sky at a handful of flying metas. Fires from the colossal explosion had spread to the security building and the hangars.

"ECHO OPFOUR, THE MOUNTAIN, REPORTING FOR DUTY!" the giant roared, making his first step onto the grounds of the Echo campus into one that crushed a dozen Nazi troopers. Ramona laughed out loud.

She stopped laughing as the Nazis turned their beams

from human-sized targets and aimed for the walking mountain that approached them. Each beam tore a chunk the size of her head out of the giant's stony hide. A few beams struck the hand she crouched in.

The giant sank to his knees. She held on to his thumb, horrified that she had overestimated his resistance to pain. He was a walking target.

"Oh, no, Bill," she said.

But the giant merely laid his hand flat on the ground furthest from the Nazis and opened it to let her disembark. Now she understood: he wanted two hands for fighting.

She waved a fist at him. "Sic 'em, buddy!"

The giant took advantage of his proximity to the ground to sweep up an armful of Nazi troopers and send them sprawling, then pound them into the dirt like a child torturing ants. More accurately, pound some of them deeper than the water mains.

With the aid of the Mountain, the battle quickly swung in Echo's favor. The Nazis could not ignore the hundred-foot stone giant stomping on them with gusto, leaving the remaining Echo personnel to take aim for vulnerable knee and arm joints.

Three of the Four Winds led the final charge against the Nazis. Southwind, in particular, blasted at them with desperate brutality, screaming as he did. The sight of the towering alienlike beings cutting invisible swaths through the troopers was terrible to behold.

Ramona did find Tesla again. He crouched behind a toppled wall and picked off troopers with his tiny raygun. The beam it emitted heated their armor to a red-hot glow until the metal melted. The men inside the armor were doomed.

He exchanged a wave with her and kept firing.

A figure approached Ramona out of the smoke. She carried two rifles.

"Midori!" Ramona hugged the woman fiercely.

Midori laughed with delight. "You did it, you did it!"

"He's the one doing it. I just guilt-tripped him into beating up some jerks."

"The perfect boyfriend," Midori said, handing her a rifle.

"Oh, the stories I could tell you." Ramona scanned the sky for a running figure. "What's this for?"

"Atlanta SWAT stopped by with a tip. Shoot for the knees. They used these rifles for 'antimateriel' work."

Mercurye darted across the sky, stopping above Tesla's head and leaning in for a quick consultation. For a brief moment, he met Ramona's gaze before zooming away.

Ramona loaded the rifle that Midori had given her and took aim at a retreating Nazi trooper. Her first bullet caught him right behind the kneecap. He staggered and fell.

A warm feeling of vindictiveness spread from her belly to her grin. The day was improving, after all.

Moscow, Russia: Callsign Red Saviour

Chug had gone berserk. His fists crushed body armor, helmets, and energy rifles in a flurry of rage. The troopers pounded on him and shot him point-blank, yet he only roared and threw them into the flames.

"Push them back to the trucks!" Red Saviour doubted her commands could be heard over the cacophony. She drove a glowing fist into the chest of a trooper as his arm cannon spewed energy at her feet. He collapsed, gasping for air, and she let the concussive force of the blast add to her own airborne propulsion. From her vantage point, she saw Supernaut, Svetoch and Firebird grimly advancing, sweat pouring down their exposed skin. Supernaut stood partly in the flames as if he were a demon in Hell.

The fiery trio paid no heed to their surroundings, so focused were they on maintaining the wall of fire's onerous crawl. Only Red Saviour saw the squad of a half-dozen troopers charge from the flames at the right flank of her flamethrowers.

She took off towards them, throwing a ball of energy to divert their attention. It burst in their path, staggering two who bore the brunt for their comrades. The other four trained their weapons on her friends and cut loose.

The beams tore into Svetoch and Firebird with lethal precision. Strangely, the troopers' beams had missed the giant Supernaut. He looked around wildly as two thirds of the flame wall dissipated.

"Vassily," she shouted, her voice hoarse with sobbing, "we need more fire!"

"You will have it, *sestra!*" Supernaut bulled forward, adjusting controls on his armor. The squad turned their weapons on him; she swooped down to collide with the frontmost trooper, unleashing her energy to knock him back into the others. She and the Nazis collapsed into a pile of armored—and unarmored—limbs. The heated armor seared her skin through her bloody uniform.

Red Saviour struggled to her feet first, avoiding grasping hands, in time to be blown over by a massive, fiery explosion erupting from Supernaut's vicinity. The Delex trucks bowled over and their trailers detonated, striking the second wave of Nazis and their war machines.

Everyone on Red Square was dashed to the ground; those in the heart of the firestorm, the remaining Nazi troopers, dropped their weapons as they became living bonfires. Natalya heard them screaming through the helmet radio of the nearest trooper.

"Oh, Vassily," she said. "You crazy bastard."

Fortunately, only the strongest of the CCCP were close enough to the blast to feel its effect; Supernaut knew how to control fire up to his dying moment. Worker's Champion and Molotok smoldered, their clothing destroyed. Chug did not appear to have noticed the explosion. He bellowed and smashed the nearest Nazi into pulp.

"Is best not to start fights you can't finish," she told her opponent in Russian. He cocked his head, and started to shake. Red Saviour took a step towards him, ready to capitalize on his fear. But his rifle arm lurched straight up in the air as if a puppeteer had tugged his strings.

She felt the hum before she heard it: the two war machines floated above the conflict, rattling teeth with their eerie gravity-defying propulsion system. Something flashed past her, flying up into the sky: the helmet of the trooper People's Blade had beheaded. The trooper before her followed, clamping his arms to his sides as though he were a rocket.

Every Nazi trooper stopped fighting as invisible strings tugged them into the air and to the hull of the war machines, which began to resemble oversized, iron dandelions. They rotated in the air to find space for the troopers, who impacted with flat metallic thuds.

Defeated troopers, dead or unconscious, floated up in the magnetic net cast by the war machines.

"Stop them!" she called desperately. "Don't let them escape!"

It was too late; the magnetic pull was too powerful. Those with the physical strength to resist it hadn't had enough warning to brace themselves and take hold of a fallen trooper. The CCCP and the protesters watched the war machines spin in the black smoke, catching their troops. Without ceremony, they gained altitude and vanished into the clouds.

Atlanta, Georgia, USA: Callsign Seraphym

She arrived the day of the invasion. She and her siblings were all Instruments on that day, but Atlanta was hers, hers alone to defend. In the tangled futures, a nexus point.

Once, in the conflict known among humans of Terra as World War I, a bit of apocrypha, legend rooted in fiction, was created, the story of the so-called "Angels of Mons" that rode across the battlefield saving Allied lives.

She and her siblings, however, were very real. And they had been given extraordinary license on this one day, as well as one simple command.

Save as many as you can.

The futures knotted and tangled too closely at this point to be sure of who was the most important to save, until the very moment came to save them. In some cases, it might never be clear. Even an angel could only do so much, being only a facet of the Infinite and not the Infinite itself.

So she wielded her powers, her spear of fire and her flaming sword, across the face of ravaged Atlanta. She saved those she could, and regretted those she could not.

She *felt* every person that fell, felt their pain, their lives, their transitions. Sometimes, without meaning to, she Looked at them, and at those she did save, and saw their lives laid bare before her, and their pain became her pain.

She raged across the sky with the curiously impartial anger that only an angel could sustain, using her powers with surgical precision. She could have flattened the city, but a Seraphym is absolute power constrained by absolute control. She used only what she had to: no less, but no more.

Not all those who saw her, saw her for what she was. That was a matter of belief. Virtually all the metahuman magicians knew her, of course; they were used to thinking in terms of transcendence. Those who believed in *more* saw her in her full glory, robed in flame, fire-crowned, embraced in Light and borne upwards on the Wings of the Phoenyx, with the Sword of Michael in her right hand and the Spear of Justice in her left.

The rest saw another metahuman, one they did not recognize, who must, by the success she was having against the Thulian constructs, be at least an OpThree. One more who wielded metahuman fires with the precision and accuracy of a needle laser.

It did not matter to her how they saw her. She had her mission.

Save as many as you can.

She did not answer prayers. She ruthlessly followed the web of the futures, bending her intellect upon the paths that told her *there, that one!* and sent her flashing across the sky like a comet. And perhaps that broke the faith of some, who saw her and her siblings making seemingly arbitrary or even senseless decisions if one weighed those decisions only in terms of faith.

But their duty was to the future, not faith.

If she had been mortal, she would have long since fallen to earth exhausted. But when darkness, lit by the fires of burning buildings as well as her own, closed over the city, when the last of the war machines had swept up as many of the fallen as they could and made their escape, she took to a perch atop the building that her omnipresent intellect told her was called the Suntrust Plaza and brooded down over the ruins.

She and her siblings had done what they could.

And now it was time to wait for the futures to settle into a new configuration, bent into new patterns by their intervention.

Then came the still, small voice in her heart.

An Instrument is still needed. Will you stay?

A Seraphym is not often startled. This made her raise her head.

She—Angel of Fire and Love as she was—loved humanity. And not with the abstract *agape* of her siblings, but the warmer, closer-to-mortal *filios*. For as long as there had been creatures that stood upright on two legs on this world, she had watched them, studied them, cared about them. Her chosen form even imitated theirs. And sometimes, in the past, she had regretted, deeply, not being permitted to intervene.

But now an instrument was needed.

I will stay.

New York, New York, USA: Callsign John Murdock

The city was in chaos. Fires were still spreading, even though the attackers had retreated more than a dozen hours ago; their "death spheres" had dragged all of their dead and wounded out of the city once they had their fill of killing. Buildings had collapsed, cars and homes destroyed, and the majority of the municipal personnel were overloaded, scattered across a dozen different crises, or dead. National Guardsmen and disaster relief workers had been called in, but there weren't nearly enough. After John had been revived and put to service helping rescue survivors, he learned that the attacks weren't isolated to New York; almost every sizable city or one with a national significance had been hit, in America and the world abroad.

But of them all, Atlanta had been the hardest hit. Echo headquarters had been under siege for hours. There were rumors that even the legended OpFours that no one ever really saw had been called in. The coordination and terror were mind-blowing; no one had even bothered to try to estimate the casualties in New York, let alone the United States as a whole or the rest of the world.

John's wounds had been hastily tended to; there were a lot of wounded, and none of his injuries were critical enough to warrant more than some slap-on first aid administered by a Girl Scout. Of all the damned things... it was the Boy and Girl Scouts, the Guides, the Campfire Girls, all those kids' groups, that were being pressed into service as first-in first aid. There were kids in uniforms all over the city right now. *Who'd a thought it.*

He'd been pressed into helping clear rubble and searching for survivors as soon as it was apparent that he was going to live himself.

A motley group of scouts of all stripes, rescue workers in blue and white vests, CERT workers—community emergency response teams—in green and white, and bloodied citizens were busy clearing a downed brick apartment building; John was among them, doing what he could by hand. A single backhoe had been brought in, which was more than most of the groups operating around the city had been able to get. This one was donated by a contractor who'd been doing sewer work in the area.

A husky woman in a man's work shirt and jeans, head bandaged and hair shaved around a scalp laceration, took the place of the guy who'd been working at John's left on the brick line. She glanced at him a couple of times, sharply. Finally she said, "You were with that kid, right? Burned up those robot guys?"

John stole a glance at her, still working at clearing rubble. After a moment, he responded. "Yeah, I was." He still didn't know the kid's name; he didn't even know who to ask to find out. He probably never would.

"You Echo guys, what were you doing here, anyway?" she asked. "I mean it's lucky for us you were, but..."

He shook his head. "I'm not Echo; I just found that kid on the street when I was tryin' to get the hell outta town, after those Nazis—or whatever they were—attacked."

"I thought all metas—" she shook her head. "Never mind. Well hell, if you aren't you should be. They lost a pile of metas out there today. Seems like they all oughta be coordinated like the Scouts or something."

John gritted his teeth. "You had it right at 'never mind.' It's not my problem." Wasn't it?

She gave him a funny look. "Mister, from here it looks like it's everybody's problem now."

John paused, looking to the woman again. He worked things around in his head for a moment, then went back to working. "Well, maybe."

John spent the next two days alternating between resting and helping with rescue efforts. He found a couple of people in the rubble that had survived, but not too many. John thought a lot as he pulled bodies out of the rubble; he thought quite a bit about the kid and what the woman he had been working beside had said. And . . . about what he had seen after the kid had died.

John took measure of himself, and figured he would have to go to where he could do the most good. Five days after the attack, John left for Atlanta, hitchhiking and walking south.

Moscow, Russia: Callsign Red Saviour

The attack had taken a dreadful toll on her team. Of her roster of the seventeen Moscow CCCP members that had been with her at her hearing, only seven had survived: herself, People's Blade, Soviette, Chug, and Soviet Bear—assuming the doctors could restore him to consciousness—plus Worker's Champion and Molotok.

The *militsya* and army had arrived to clean up the aftermath. Ambulances jostled for position, hospital helicopters hovered overhead, and paramedics shouted orders. Red Saviour stood apart from her comrades, knowing that if she spoke, despair would pour out like a thunderstorm and wash over her.

Reporters led camera crews around the periphery of the square. They strained against the police cordon to capture glimpses of the carnage.

People's Blade stepped over the plastic body bags with an almost surreal air of calm.

"Natalya," she said in her patronizing instructor

voice, "you haven't the luxury of shock right now. Please center yourself."

"I am fine. I'm alive."

Setting down her coffee, she tapped at her lapel comm unit. The white noise of an open line greeted her—the radio was no longer jammed.

"Meet me by Saviour's Gate," she murmured into it.

The gate had taken several direct hits, demolishing the iron grill and parts of the stone façade. The ceremonial guard's halberd lay on the ground. She wondered if he survived the attack.

Her people gathered, pale-faced and silent. Only People's Blade retained her serene countenance.

"Any word on casualties?" She let the question hang.

"Three hundred and counting," Worker's Champion said. He wore a borrowed *militsya* jacket over his demolished suit. "Indications are that this was an isolated incident."

"I doubt that, *tongzhi*," People's Blade said. "The Nazis utilized advanced military armaments and discipline in their deployment. That implies they were part of a larger force, which in turn implies that their masters have a purpose served by a larger force." She answered Worker's Champion's scowl with a small smile. "I recommend we issue warnings to the United Nations."

"One moment," Red Saviour said. The comm units had come online minutes after the Nazis vanished; she adjusted her comm unit to tune in to Interpol's bulletin system. A reedy voice spoke over the tiny speaker: ". . . strikes in Prague, Atlanta, New York, Washington, DC, Los Angeles, San Francisco, Las Vegas, Hong Kong, Jerusalem, Tehran, Sydney . . ."

She shut it off, her mouth a grim line.

"Invasion," she said.

"Then they've been biding their time ever since we beat them back in the Great Patriotic War," Worker's Champion said. "Sixty years of plotting to take over the world."

"Perhaps not," People's Blade said. "What we fought today was nothing more than a small expeditionary force. Regardless of their individual power, the troop allotment was too small to occupy any territory."

"They killed most of CCCP." Rage colored his voice. "Here, Novosibirsk, St. Petersburg, Ykaterinaburg, Samara, Omsk..."

"That may have been the goal." The Chinese woman turned to Red Saviour. "The Gentle Wind Through the Grasslands."

"Spare us your poetry," Worker's Champion said.

"It's a military maneuver from her time," Red Saviour said, moving her hands as though they were a gust of wind. "Attack fast, without entrenching. Retreat quickly when you've done your damage."

Molotok's eyebrows rose. "Blitzkrieg."

"Bah." Worker's Champion scowled more. "She has a point."

"She often does." Molotok pursed his lips. "But Blitzkrieg was often followed by an occupying force."

"Unless Germany has been hiding an army of giants in basements, that seems unlikely." Red Saviour fished out her cigarettes.

"So now what, Commissar?" Soviette's smooth contralto broke the silence.

"Don't ask me. The council was about to fire me."

Worker's Champion grunted. "We'll see about that." Without ceremony, he turned and walked off.

An ambulance backed into sight. As the reporters shouted, mourners wailed, the *militsya* counted the dead and paramedics dressed wounds, she explored the exhausted faces of her comrades, thinking: *war has found Russia again.*

Las Vegas, Nevada, USA: Callsign Belladonna Blue

Bella Dawn Parker wanted to sit in a corner, wrap her arms around herself, rock back and forth and cry.

She didn't have that luxury. She was still one of the few medics on the ground here, and there were casualties everywhere. Crying was for later.

At least her parents were safe. That Cold War–era bunker her dad had herded everyone into had somehow escaped the attentions of the Nazi metas. Maybe it had looked too old, too abandoned, too archaic to matter. What had been state of the art in 1950 wouldn't have held up too long against those energy cannons; the only reason that the bunker was expected to survive a direct nuclear hit on Groom Lake was because the eight floors of underground labs and offices above it would have served as ablative armor.

Bella let her thoughts ramble while she served as a kind of automatic healing dispenser. Someone had found a supply of pure glucose solution; while people who qualified as "walking wounded" were being patched up by non-meta medics, she was hitting all the black-tags, the victims triaged as "not expected to survive," too badly hurt for conventional emergency medicine. The guy serving as her coolie had a lab cart loaded down with the bottles of glucose and was following her around while she went from triage point to triage point. She'd gulp down a bottle of glucose, lay her hands on the victim, and—do her thing. It had never been so clear or strong before... it was as if she could look inside them, see what was broken, and then, just like some movie-special-effects sequence, make it knit itself back together again just enough that they would live. It was... scary, was what it was. She'd have been freaked if she'd had any time to be freaked. But she had lost too many today, and she didn't intend to lose any more.

Finally she reached the main triage center, a big open courtlike area in front of the vaults. She'd only heard rumors about the vaults. Her folks didn't talk about what they did here. Rumor had it that this was where all the weird-ass inventions that the US government could get to before Echo did were kept. And this was where all the weird-ass weaponry went that government scientists, rather than Echo scientists, created. And, rumor had it, this was where all the alienware from all those supposed flying saucer crashes confiscated by the government went.

Well, she didn't know anything about saucer aliens, but here were the vaults, all right. They ringed a giant open space lit from above by a single solid panel of... something... She'd never quite seen lighting like that before. The floor was something else she didn't recognize—not concrete, because it was warm to the touch and deadened sound rather than reflecting it. Its uniform gray surface was untouched by battle. There was one tunnel entrance coming into this place, and one going out. Forklifts, carts, front-end loaders, other machines, presumably meant to get things too big to carry into and out of the vaults, had been parked in orderly rows here. Someone had used a skid loader like a bulldozer though, to shove a lot of it out of the way to make room for the injured and dying, being too impatient to start up and move each piece of equipment individually. Around the periphery were the vault doors, some of which were two stories tall, all of them shiny and silver-colored and with no visible way of getting them open. The Nazis had been coming here, that much was clear by the path that Bella and her team had followed. But they hadn't actually gotten here, because the makeshift meta team had stopped them.

There was only one vault door open now, one of the smaller ones, and a white fog coming from it suggested it was refrigerated. As Bella settled down by the side of the first man in the black-tag section and her body slave handed her a bottle of glucose, she saw a lab-coated scientist with a pair of uniformed bruisers drive up to it in a little golf cart pulling a wheeled platform loaded with Nazi bodies. They began carrying the bodies into the vault as she laid her blue hands on a man's pale, chilly forehead. Whatever disgust she might have felt at the vultures carrying on business as usual was swallowed up in the overwhelming sensations and half sights coming to her from the man's broken body.

She was jolted out of her trance some time later— fortunately she was mostly done at the time—by the sound of shouts and screaming. Her eyes flew open, her heart racing, as she reached for the sidearm she'd been given. "What?" she snapped at her assistant, who had his radio out.

"Something—" A smattering of voice in a surge of static came from it. "Something's come back. One of those flying things. It's—" Another babble of voices, more static. "—they say it's not firing, but the meta-troopers that they cornered upstairs and all the bodies are, like, flying towards it—"

"Shut the vault!" The imperious order rang out over some hidden PA system, and the door of the refrigerated vault swung ponderously closed. With a dull, booming sound, it came to rest, and the clank of what must have been huge bolts shooting home signaled that it was locked.

And that was when the bodies still on the cart began to glow.

"Take cover!" screamed one of the soldiers who had been moving the bodies into the vault a moment before. Instinctively, Bella and her helper ducked behind a forklift, as the bodies glowed red-hot, then yellow, then white, then too bright to look at, and the metal cart they had been lying on slagged and sagged to the floor, the rubber tires going up in flames, triggering the overhead fire-suppression system. Not sprinklers, no. A dozen nozzles protruded from the ceiling and doused just that spot with foam and a cooling mist which never even reached the injured.

Within minutes, the fire was out, and the metal cooling down through red... but there was nothing left of the Nazi metatroopers but slagged metal indistinguishable from what was left of the flatbed and the little electric cart that had pulled it. The air was full of the smell of hot metal and burned plastic, although the ventilation system was quickly pulling all of the smoke and stench up towards the ceiling.

"What the hell—" she gaped at the remains.

"I guess they didn't want us looking at their suits," her helper said, and handed her a bottle of glucose.

With that reminder, she gulped it down, and moved on to the next victim.

It got to the point where not even pure glucose was making up for all the energy she was putting out. She felt feverish, light-headed, and oddly thinned out. Next to her, the vault door had been opened again, and from the activity inside apparently whatever had caused the Nazi armor to melt down out here had not gotten through the vault shielding. At least three people were in there now, and they sounded busy. Her helper had been looking concerned about her for the last three victims, and now he put his hand on her shoulder.

"You need to stop now, ma'am," he said quietly. "You're about to fall clean over."

But the last of the black-tags had been pulled back from the brink, and she was halfway through the red-tags—

"Ma'am, the doctors from Nellis are here now. You can stop. And you better." The hand on her shoulder got heavier. "I got my orders, ma'am. Nothin' is supposed to happen to you. Echo says."

Only now did she look at the logos on his fatigues, and realized that this was no GI, this was an Echo OpOne. She felt herself flush. "Can't let the prize cow drop, huh?" she drawled, thinking angrily of how she had been pulled away from her station, her crew, when they needed her the most. Of course, she had been needed here too, but—those were her guys... and some of them had been missing....

"Ma'am, I have my orders," he repeated. "You do what you can here, and I keep you in good shape while you're doing it, I make sure you're fit when you're done, then we go to Atlanta—"

"Atlanta!" she shouted. "Like hell I'm going to Atlanta! When this is over, I am going back to my crew, back to my station, and—"

The sound of someone shouting louder than she was interrupted them both, as three men came stumbling out of the vault, two of the three looking green and the third looking white.

"Get the general!" shouted the white-faced one to one of the nearest soldiers. "Get the Echo re—there you are!" He pointed at Bella's helper. "Get in here! You have to see this!"

"I'm keeping tabs on our newest OpTwo," the man began, his demeanor changing in an instant from subservient to commanding. "There can't be anything in a pile of powered armor more important than that."

The white-faced man began to laugh hysterically. "Oh god," he gasped. "Oh god, if only you knew! That's just it. It's what's in the armor!"

The white-faced man sat abruptly down on the floor and began to cry. Bella got up, took one of the glucose bottles and handed it to him, and began to soothe him. It felt like she was sending out waves of quietude somehow . . . like the mental blasts, like the vastly increased healing powers, this was just . . . coming out of nowhere for her. At this point, she wasn't going to question it. She just used it.

Her helper stood there uncertainly for a moment, then his expression turned decisive. "Don't let her get herself into trouble. I need to make a call."

"The President?" asked one of the green-faced men, with a gulp.

"No," the answer came back as the man sprinted up the tunnel, heading for the surface. "Tesla."

CHAPTER FIVE

The Seventh Circle

MERCEDES LACKEY, STEVE LIBBEY,
CODY MARTIN, DENNIS LEE

So, there we were. Civilization as we knew it had just had its ass handed to it. Turned out that most of the communications satellites were out for civilian media—cell phones, and so on. Military still worked, and so did landline. And nearly every city had what came to be called "destruction corridors"—paths of complete devastation leading to wherever in that city the Echo HQ had been. It was clear, very early, that the Nazis had meant to take out Echo entirely, and any other enclave of metas, but when they couldn't, they pulled out, falling back to some contingency plan. And initially, that made people angry, as if some serial killer was going around sniping firemen. That worked in Echo's favor, and Echo was going to need all the favors it could get.

Little did we know there was a favor out there that was as big as anything that had happened to us already.

Atlanta, Georgia, USA: Callsign Seraphym

As the smoke rose and the flames died, Seraphym remained, an unmoving, ever-watchful icon atop the Suntrust Plaza Building, taking only sporadic part in what lay below her. She knew everything that was going on, of course. Her connection to the Infinite allowed her, if not omniscience, then certainly broad and deep knowledge within a limited sphere. The futures were still settling; out there, metahumans whose powers had been awakened during the worldwide battle, or those who had finally acknowledged those powers and the need to use them for good, were deciding to come to Atlanta—or not. And as for Seraphym herself. . .

The multiple futures would drive a mortal mad. All those possibilities—most of them ending in blood, terror and death, with the Thulians ruling as despots over a world enslaved—and beyond that, the terrible swath of destruction across the entire Universe that had been the reason *why* she and her Siblings had been sent here. It was hard, so hard, to thread the way through the futures. Most of the ones that ended in a free world had a maddening blank spot in the middle: futures that she could not see her way to, even with her connection to the Infinite. She could only steer her way by avoiding the worst, finding the abyss by avoiding the edges of it as best she could.

She could not be everywhere, but she did not act nearly as often as mortals thought she should. There were those who saw her for what she was and did not understand why their faith was not rewarded by her presence in their moment of peril. But she had to choose, and she had to make her choices by the paths of the future. Some people were crucial to it; those she had to save. She heard, in her heart, the wail of "Why? Why him and not me?" and she could have answered it, but the answer would have shattered them.

In some hearts and minds, she watched as long-buried fires broke through the insulating cover of the ashes of the past and began to reawaken. She watched as new possible futures spun off from their decisions and began to sort and categorize those futures: this, desirable; that, not. It was not yet time to act, however. Though the Thulians had placed their counters on the board, the resistance had been greater than they had anticipated, and they were still sorting through *their* possible options. And behind them...the others...

And then...she felt it. A mind, a mortal mind, in unimaginable torment. A mind that, like hers, saw the futures. It was far away in mortal terms, but not far for her. And this could not, should not be. Mortals were not meant to know the futures. Not as she did. Not as this mind did.

And this mind...did not want to. It cried out in pain and fear.

She opened her heart to the Infinite. *Is this permitted?* she asked.

Instantly came the response. *It is.*

They called Matthew March "autistic" as a child. What no one had known was that he was not closed into a world of his own, he was far, far too open to the real one. From the time he was eight, he had seen things, seen what would happen to people around him, but more than that, seen what *might* happen to the people around him. The older he got, the more *maybes* he saw, until he was surrounded by them, choked by them. And he became paralyzed, not by confusion, but by his inability to choose. This one, and not that one—help a friend, who would later kill a child in a hit-and-run accident while drunk. Keep a girl from heartbreak only to have her grow into a lawyer who successfully defended known criminals.

He could not choose. He could not. His inability to act confined him to a bed, his muscles atrophied, and only a few psychics could fish out his most powerful visions from his mind.

And that had been bad enough. Until today. Until now. When the attack began, and all he saw was the beginning, and people dying everywhere, and the end, in the future, far but not far enough. Slaughter. Terror. Horror. Everywhere he "looked" the end was the same. He felt himself screaming inside, helpless, hopeless—

And then she came.

She was in his mind, but so much clearer than the psychics he was used to working with. And then, she *embraced* him somehow, sheltered him from his terrible visions, and held him while he cried. Was she only in his mind? He so seldom opened his eyes anymore . . . but this time, he did.

She was real. And she was beautiful. And she was . . . must be . . . an angel. Nothing else could look like that, so powerful, so strange, so otherworldly. She was wrapped in flame, and her wings were of fire, furled closely against her back. Her eyes . . . her eyes were red-gold, and had no pupils. They looked on him, and he sensed she was seeing in too many ways for him to comprehend.

How did you——?

She only smiled, sadly. *None will disturb us while I am here. I hold us out of time.*

He began to tremble. *What I see—is that what is going to happen?*

She hesitated. *It is the most probable.*

He began to cry. He couldn't stand this. This time, it wasn't inability to act that paralyzed him, it was that there was no way for him to make a difference. It was the end of everything good, everything worth living for.

I don't want to see it!

Then you need not.

He went very still, taken aback. *I—how?*

I can take you with me, to the Heart of All Time, where you may rest. It is permitted.

She stretched out her arms to him.

Wait! he said, seeing a tiny, tiny glimmer of hope in the mad tangle of death and destruction. *I need to warn them!*

She nodded gravely. He scrabbled for the pen and pad of paper kept at his bedside for the psychics that ventured into his brain. Hastily, he scrawled everything he could, then pitched the pad as far away from his bed as his weak and uncoordinated arms could manage. *Now. Now I'm ready.*

Come to me, child, she whispered, her power shielding him from the pain, as the Light opened up before him. *I will take you Home.*

Echo Headquarters, Atlanta, Georgia, USA

Ramona sipped her coffee noisily, letting the warmth dull the pain in her ribs. She had refused a trip to the hospital; there was too much to do. She scanned the sky for her scout.

Ten feet up, Mercurye sped across the ravaged lawn and slowed to a halt before her. He stepped down onto the ground. His expression was easy to read.

"No luck?" she guessed.

"Nothing. No sign of the Commandant or his lady, or your shape-changing friend—assuming I would even recognize him. I retraced your path through detention." He took a deep breath. "It's a charnel house. I doubt there's a prisoner left alive."

Ramona perked up. "Hey . . . there's one! I forgot about him in all the noise." She scratched a name down on a pad. "Get this to Sheryl. She can look up his file."

Mercurye's shoulders sagged. He shook his head slowly. "I'm sorry. They found her body an hour ago."

"Oh." Cold gripped her stomach. "Well, then, I guess I have to do my own legwork, huh?" Her eyes drifted to the ground. Suddenly Sheryl's face became indistinct in her mind. "Yeah. Part of my job, you know?" Her throat closed. Words stopped coming.

Mercurye enclosed Ramona in his arms. Grief hit her like a freight train.

"Go ahead, it's fine," he said.

"Jesus Christ," she said, between sobs. "And I was holding it together all this time. I was doing so well." Ramona's tears smeared on his bare, dust-encrusted chest. Mercurye stroked her hair for minutes while she bawled like a baby.

Her breath returned in gasps. "Okay, I just have to tell you, I don't normally cry like this. Crime scenes, mangled corpses, beheaded cheerleaders . . . I'm a pro."

"You wouldn't be the first person to lose it today."

"Oh yeah? I thought metas don't cry."

"We do," he said. "But we can also find a cloud bank to hide in."

A chuckle escaped through the sobs. She gave him a squeeze. "Thanks, handsome. Back to work, I suppose. We need Slycke's dossier from the database."

Mercurye shook his head. "Totaled. Alex took a team of programmers to rescue what data he could."

"Damn." The Echo metahuman database had been fed by virtually every law enforcement agency in the world; algorithms so elaborate as to approach artificial intelligence sifted that data into categories of relevance. It was the greatest tool a detective could have for tracking a powered fugitive. There was only one copy, though, the idea being that a lack of copies meant fewer security risks. Didn't anyone see the *Star Wars* movies and learn about the dangers of single-point-of-failure systems?

"Eisenfaust was our key, Merc. That Bermuda Triangle story sounded like a weak TV plot until his former comrades-in-arms came knocking on the door to shut him up. What he told Slycke was important enough that he didn't even try to fight for his life. I have to find that perp." The details of the incident were becoming hazy in her mind, just like every witness she interviewed. *Certain details outshine the others; soon all that's left is a snapshot.* She needed to write it all down.

"At least he's ugly," Mercurye said. "Hard to conceal that."

"That makes it worse," she said. "He'll avoid contact entirely. Fewer witnesses. If he has any sense, he'll head for the swamp. God! If only Eisenfaust would have given a proper statement, we'd have been ready for this attack."

Mercurye snapped his fingers in realization, a gesture so corny that Ramona found it immediately endearing. "That reminds me. Alex wants me to transport Eisenfaust's body to a secure location."

Her brow furrowed. "Really? That's odd. Plenty of ambulances here."

"Orders are orders." He grimaced at the makeshift morgue across the lawn, where hundreds of body bags had been lined up for identification and tagging. "Let me know if you need help with Slycke. Things will be chaotic here for a while."

"I'll call you when I find out something worth sharing."

"Call anyway. Keep me in the loop." He flashed her a smile. "Okay?"

Her cheeks warmed. "Okay. Now scoot."

Mercurye tipped his helmet to her. "Off to the underworld," he said before leaving. Ramona watched him approach the grim black line of corpses, a man given the duties of a god.

The Omega Airlines official scribbled the food order on a pad of paper. "Got it. I'll head out now. Is there anything else you need?"

A time machine, Alex thought. *A way to go back and save every employee of mine who died today.* "Nothing else. Thanks. We appreciate it."

"Our pleasure, sir." The official pushed his glasses up his nose and hurried off to Alex's favorite Waffle House to bring back food for the crew.

A guard stopped them as they approached a checkpoint in the underground tunnel leading to Omega Airlines' Secure Computer Center. The man was apologetic but firm as he indicated an aging retinal scanner. "Just a formality, folks."

"Of course." Alex wondered how his eyes must look to the machine: bloodshot, exhausted. The machine dazzled him with a bright flash. A somber and respectful guard handed him a visitor badge.

The others took their place at the scanner: Shahkti, each one of her four hands holding a bag of equipment; Ihsan Muhammed, Echo's lead programmer, whose broken leg had bound him to a wheelchair, though he had refused painkillers; and Jules and Lauren Kaivers, fresh from the Belgian office and sightseeing at the time of the attack.

The Thule Society's Blitzkrieg attack on the Echo campus—ending abruptly with an improbable magnetic evacuation by the war machines—had taken a dreadful toll: early estimates ranged from half to two-thirds of the Echo meta population, and possibly more of nonpowered personnel.

This loss demolished him. He was a shell of a man, yet his intellect issued him orders to carry on: a heartless to-do list for a man who had lost his heart.

Echo owned its own communication satellite for the comm system, yet from the moment of the attack, the comm system had gone dead. Techs worked to reroute it to local cell towers. The computer network, physically damaged from the collapse of the administration building, had suffered an attack of its own: a malignant virus ripped through the system and destroyed all data by changing binary code to strings of zeros, moving on to Echo servers around the world. Jules Kaivers had dubbed it *Lebensraum*; it had become the second, ruthless digital wave of the invasion.

His wife, Lauren, had suggested a call to Omega. She had written code for the airline decades before, and watched them construct a hardened, underground, computer reservations and operations facility using government funding. The entire system operated on copper landlines, which hadn't been updated to fiber optic cable or satellite feeds. The advantages of such a primitive system were obvious: the facility was still online while the rest of the country struggled to reconnect the internet trunks that the Nazis had destroyed while tearing through outlying regions on their way to attack urban areas. One further advantage of old tech: people simply forgot it was there and went after what was more shiny.

Scanned and cleared, the tech led them through a pair of blast doors and down a corridor where the giant springs that supported the installation and protected it from shock waves of earthquake magnitude were visible through painted metal grills. The Cold War paranoia invoked by the precautions did not seem so outlandish today.

The control room had been modernized and decorated with faded Omega destination posters: Greece, Rio de Janeiro, Rome. They made Alex want to talk to every single one of the fifty Echo facilities in the world. He settled into a desk and opened his laptop as his companions powered theirs up. The Omega tech handed out Ethernet cables like they were Halloween treats.

"Let's see what we have," Alex said.

Ihsan typed code into his command line interface at machine-gun speed. "Connecting now. Two mainframes left in Atlanta."

"Infected mainframes," snapped Jules.

"I'll be careful."

The Omega tech eyed the programmers with trepidation. "I, ah, gave you all direct lines to the trunk. You won't be able to access the Omega reservation database."

"We could if we wanted to," Lauren said, not taking her eyes from her screen.

"Behave, *chérie*," Jules said. "Make nice."

"*Désolé*," she muttered.

Jules offered the tech a wink and began to hook the portable RAID to a hub for all the laptops to access. They hoped to scrape the data out of the network before *Lebensraum* wiped it clean.

A silence descended on the room, punctuated by keyboard taps and whirring hard drives. Ihsan sucked air through his teeth. After the third time, Alex shot him an inquiring glance.

"Whoever coded *Lebensraum* is an evil genius. It's clawing at my firewall right now." He shook his head. "The port should be closed...damn it..." With a fast movement, Ihsan popped the battery out of his laptop, shutting it off instantly. His dusky face had gone pale.

"That fast?" Lauren said. Ihsan nodded.

Alex did not like the fear and confusion in his crew's faces. "Try Chicago. Try L.A. Hell, try Paris. The virus can't be that aggressive." The statement felt foolish as he completed it. "I mean...okay, I know geography isn't the same to us as it is to code. Just...just try."

Shahkti set a phone on his desk with a sheet of paper covered in numbers. "We're ready. Dial nine to reach an outside line."

Where to start? "You call Europe. I'll call the US. When you're done, start at the end of the list."

The Indian meta took her seat and two phones in her hands. Her free hands danced across a laptop keyboard, stopping only to dial a new number.

The news was grim from every facility. Albuquerque: twenty metas dead, two missing. Amarillo: no survivors. Baltimore, major damage, and virtually all metas killed in an ambush. Boston: demolished, fifty metas dead. Anchorage, with its station of two OpTwos, was the sole bright spot, though what Alex was told made no sense—that two angels and three hitherto unknown OpThree metas had virtually cleared the area of invaders, even bringing down their Death Sphere fundamentally intact. *Well, I suppose if I were being defended by a pair of OpTwos, and three OpThrees showed up out of nowhere, I'd be seeing angels too.* He made a note to collect that sphere as soon as there was time.

The voices on the line were dull with anguish, as if they were just waiting for the day to end. Alex kept the discussions short, issuing crisp orders for able-bodied personnel to assist local law enforcement and patrol for lingering Nazi units. Yet the reports were the same: massive loss of life, no sign of the troopers.

And from a remote medical facility: "We lost Matthew March."

"The autistic clairvoyant, right?" Alex said. "He was bedridden. Did his heart give out?"

"No. Suicide. He set himself on fire."

Alex tried to remember March's dossier. "He could move?"

"Evidently he could move and write. He left a note, barely legible. It will take time to decipher."

"Save it. I need to deal with the threat at hand first. Then I'll be ready for further predictions of doom."

Alex concluded the call and sat back in his chair. A sigh escaped him. Anchorage had provided the first piece of good news today, but it came with a mystery attached—one that would have to wait for an answer.

Shahkti slid over a list of casualties from Europe. Across the board, hundreds of metas had been lost, hundreds more nonpowered personnel, and the civilian casualty estimates mounted every hour as more bodies were found. The Thule Society had wielded their shock troops like a scalpel, slicing deep into the infrastructure of every target country, in addition to all kinds of inexplicable targets like restaurants and warehouses. The news wire reported attacks in remote locations like the Congo and Tibet; yet the bulk of enemy forces had assailed major cities in the richest nations of the world—with the exception of Germany. The birthplace of National Socialism was untouched. The German government had scrambled to issue a statement condemning the attacks before the smoke had cleared; their parliament was meeting at this very moment to send aid to the affected developing countries. Yet their offers of peacekeeping forces went unheeded. The world watched their every action with suspicion.

"Call the rest of the American bases," he told Shahkti. "I need to think."

Shahkti laid a spare hand on his shoulder. "You need to rest, sir. An exhausted leader makes hasty decisions." The Indian woman spoke without recrimination, but her serious tone overcame matters of rank.

"I know, I know. But it's important that they hear—"

She cut him off. "They *will* hear from you, in time. Echo facilities were designed to act autonomously in times of crisis. This is such a time. Our comfort is of minor importance. What matters is the actions Echo takes next."

"Finding the Nazis," he said.

"Yes, sir, but that is a job for Echo metahumans." Shahkti's voice hardened. "We're eager for a rematch, believe it. But you, yourself, are the face of Echo to the world. Right now that face is too haggard to win the public's trust."

"I don't follow you," he said. "We protect the public."

"All they see are two metahuman forces waging war against each other. Most take our side, but some will question why they have been caught in the crossfire." She raised a finger to still his tongue. "*Regardless* of who instigated it."

"Blame the victim," he said with bitterness.

"Do not fall into such thinking. Warriors can never be victims. We have accepted the risks." She sounded to Alex as though she had had this argument before. "You have a new war on your hands. Keep us in the people's hearts."

Alex took a deep breath. Shahkti was right, and he should have recognized this problem twelve hours ago. In the modern world of instant communication, you cannot wait to explain your position, lest you find your enemies have explained it for you. The most casual observer of presidential elections knew this maxim.

He could see the ramifications now. The President would probably invoke the War Powers act—but against what? An enemy that vanished, with no country to make war on? Congress would flail about trying to enact antiterrorist legislation, but these weren't terrorists . . . in fact, as news wires came online, there were reports, and plenty of them, of terrorist training camps reduced to smoking holes in the ground. The Thulians didn't want any guerilla opposition—and didn't want anyone else taking credit for their blitzkrieg, he reckoned.

But they had to get this under some kind of control before Echo got hobbled. He scribbled a number on the list. "Call this number and ask for the Spin Doctor. Tell him Alex is calling in that favor."

"Right away." The woman flashed him a rare smile that was momentarily dazzling. "Now you will get some sleep, yes?"

"Not quite yet." Hope, as dangerous as it was intoxicating, bubbled through Alex. He *would* control this situation; he would not be beaten. "Ihsan, report. Have you gotten through yet?"

The Turkish programmer groaned. "*Lebensraum* has brutalized the network unhindered, thanks to the outside attack." His voice betrayed the pain his leg was causing him. "Anyone who could have thrown up a defense was killed or running for their lives."

"No matter. Zero out the trash it left behind. Wipe it clean for reuse. I have a solution." The programmers perked up. He fished out an unlabeled CD-ROM from his laptop case. "This software may do the trick."

Lauren stood and took the CD. "What is it? Black ice? Something illegal?"

Alex thought fast. The CD contained a simple, unbranded gateway protocol—into the Metis computers, deep under the Andes, where Uncle Tesla and Enrico Fermi's electrical intelligence matrices lorded over the system like kings. Every byte of Echo data had been secretly duplicated in their vast banks of the secret science city's holographic storage devices, under cover of a simple periodic heuristic virus-check routine that sent copies—literally mirrored, thanks to a light-beam linkage—of any changed files through one of Alex's hidden rooms. If anything could resist *Lebensraum*'s destructive rampage, it would be living computer programs derived from the brain patterns of the greatest scientific minds in the history of the world. They didn't have ice and defense programs, they had immune systems.

Revealing that secret to the uninitiated, however, was another matter.

"Something from Homeland Security," he said.

Jules blew a raspberry. "*Those* amateurs?"

"Hey, give 'em some credit. Trust me, this is powerful stuff."

"I'm sure it'll do a heckuva job," he muttered as his wife ran the install on her machine. "Threat Level Ochre Paisley, America, run in circles and panic."

Alex frowned a moment and rubbed his hands together. He'd solved two problems, for now at least. What next?

Shahkti's arched eyebrow answered that question: sleep.

"Two hours," he promised. "Wake me up then. It's going to be a long, long night."

Moscow, Russia: Callsign Red Saviour

The woman known to Russia as Red Saviour jerked awake from a fitful half nap haunted by dreams of daggers and swastikas. Sitting up so abruptly caused her bruised and fractured ribs to howl in protest. When she had finally permitted the paramedics to examine her after the Saviour's Gate Massacre—so

the world media had already labeled it—they wanted
to send her to the hospital at once. Her strenuous
objections intimidated them enough that they settled
for binding her torso in stiff bandages and rubbing
salve into her burns. The ribs had already knitted
themselves together.

Natalya sat stiffly at the edge of her cot—she
couldn't bend over without aggravating her wounds—
and massaged her temples. The clock on her laptop
read 4:15 P.M., an hour after she dropped down to
close her eyes for a moment. Something had registered subconsciously to rouse her from what could
have been a deep sleep.

"Commissar Saviour." The soldier's voice was timid.
"You have a visitor."

"He can wait, comrade," she said. She knew she
shouldn't sleep while the Nazi invaders were still on
the loose somewhere in the countryside, but she could
enjoy a moment of solitude for a few more minutes.

The tent flap opened. A short, balding man with
an air of entitlement stepped inside, his features lost
in the glare of the harsh northwestern *Okrug* summer
sun. His silhouetted form wore a windbreaker over a
suit and tie, as if he'd come from a board meeting.
Two hulking forms stood behind him.

"Out," she snarled, "whoever you are—unless you
have news of the *fashistas*."

"That's just what I was going to ask you, Natalya
Nikolaevna." The man stepped forward so that the lamp
illuminated the face associated with the familiar voice.

She struggled to her feet. "President Batov," she
blurted. "*Izvinit* . . . I didn't mean . . ."

Batov held up his hands. "No, please, don't get up."

He moved forward to clasp her hand and guide her back down to the cot. "They warned me you were badly injured. Give yourself a rest." Smiling warmly, he sat down on the cot next to her to force her to sit. She blushed and found a comfortable posture that put the least amount of strain on her ribs.

"*Spasibo*, sir," she said.

"I have looked forward to meeting you for a long time. I regret that it could not be under more relaxed circumstances." The bags under his eyes told her that he hadn't slept much since the attack either. "The major general provided me with a detailed briefing, but I want to hear your perspective of the events."

"They are the same, I am sure," she said, uncomfortable at his unblinking gaze. "The terrorists traveled packed in delivery trucks to the Square. They attacked the protesting crowd"—bearing signs against her—"and killed most of my comrades before we fought them off."

Batov pressed his lips together. The silence stretched until she thought she'd burst. At last he said: "Have you been following the news?"

"*Da*, sir. Attacks worldwide with the same blitzkrieg tactics—"

He shook his head slowly as though she were a child. "That is not the news I mean. Russian news. *Pravda*." He released her hand. "They have a name for the incident."

"The Saviour's Gate Massacre."

"No." Batov's gaze was steady. "Another name. Red Saviour's Massacre."

Her chest constricted. "Who . . . ? Why? I don't understand."

"Critics have seized upon the attack as an opportunity to criticize the government. You led the civilians into battle. You are a convenient target."

Her fists clenched. "That is unacceptable! Now is a time for Russians to pull together, not bicker . . . you must silence them!"

Batov laughed coldly. "Oh? By sending them to the *gulag*? It is the twenty-first century, not 1950. You think like a dinosaur."

"I think Nazis in powered armor is the problem! Excuse me for saying, comrade President"—her words stumbled out before she could correct her form of address—"but we're camped in the shadow of *Polyarnyye Zori,* a nuclear reactor! We have eye-witnesses that saw the Nazi warships pass directly overhead—over our nuclear facility, over Murmansk and the nuclear subs! Unhindered!" Natalya's face burned. "I think that is a more serious security threat than what some nattering *kulaks* in the press say about me!"

Batov backed away from the cot. She hadn't realized how much anger she was projecting. His bodyguards dropped their hands to their belts.

"Forgive me, sir," she said. "I'm very tired and frustrated. Our satellites have been destroyed. NATO's are gone, even weather satellites are down or offline. The Nazis disappeared off ground-based radar minutes after the attack, and we haven't picked up their trail yet. This is at the forefront of my mind."

"And so it should be," Batov said cautiously. "Just as the perception of the government is my priority." He let the sentence hang.

"We'll find them, sir. We'll find them and hang

them for what they did." *To my team,* she added to herself. *To the innocents in the Square.*

"Thirty-six hours and you've turned up nothing." The President spoke with care. "The trail is cold, but I think our friends in America have a lead for you." Without prompting, one of his guards produced a folder for her. "How is your English?"

"*Is beink flawless with no accents,*" she replied in English. The folder contained a printout of a communiqué and a pair of photographs—and a dossier reproduced from Great Patriotic War records. "Eisenfaust," she read from the photo's caption.

"Your father's old enemy."

She glanced at the dossier. "His deceased enemy. This is sixty years old. What do I care about dead Nazis? I'm hunting live ones."

Batov smiled thinly. "Eisenfaust turned himself in to Echo the day before the invasion—alive and well. Until—" he pointed at the second photograph.

Natalya fished it out and winced. The graininess tipped her off that it was a capture from a spy satellite feed—probably the last picture the satellite ever took. The same face—young, proud, square-jawed—had been smashed to a pulp and was now framed in a body bag's shroud. The time stamp on the photo dated it the day of the invasion.

"*Nasrat,*" she breathed. A caption in Russian read: *Killed by intruders during siege of Echo campus.*

"It is puzzling—and thus a clue to our puzzle. Read the first message from Mr. Tesla."

The stationery bore the alchemical symbol for air: Echo's logo, jagged from the low-quality fax. It was dated the day before the attack.

*We have a guest at our facility who
claims to be none other than Eisenfaust,
the war criminal lost at sea at the end of
World War II. Death appears to have treated
him well. He hasn't aged a day. This man
says that he has important information to
impart. His story is dubious, but he insists
that we confirm his identity with someone
who knows him—and most of the names
he gave us are of WWII metas long dead
from old age. However, there are two still
alive: Worker's Champion and Red Saviour.
May we fly them to Atlanta to meet with
this man? All expenses paid, of course. If
it turns out to be a hoax, I'd be honored
to treat them to a night on the town and
pay their consultation fee.*

*Thank you for your time and consider-
ation, Mr. President.*

Alex Tesla
CEO, Echo

"It is a coincidence," she said. "Why did he ask
for me?"

"For your father, actually. But I'd like you to go
and meet Mr. Tesla. In the past, we have resisted
Echo's efforts to establish Russian branches of their
organization, but in light of current events..." His
voice trailed off, awkward.

"You mean the obliteration of CCCP."

"I'm sorry. Yes. And the controversy surrounding the
way the attack was handled"—he held up his hands
again—"which I do not personally question, of course!

But it puts me in a very difficult position. Half the public wants to give you a medal, but the other half wants you jailed for gross incompetence."

She gritted her teeth. "You know we did the best we could."

"I know. Now you must let me do the best I can." He pointed to the dossier. "Accompany Worker's Champion and your father to America. Interface with Mr. Tesla about Echo's intelligence efforts on the Nazis—they suffered more than we did. Let the furor cool down, let the dead be buried in peace."

"I can't rest while they're still out there to strike again."

"We'll be ready for them." He paused and bit his lip. "It is best that I tell you this in person. The FSO has been ordered to decommission CCCP for the time being. We've activated the Supernaut program to fill the gap."

Natalya leapt to her feet, ignoring the pain in her ribs. "*Shto?*"

Batov's guards interposed themselves between her and the President. "We cannot leave Russia undefended, I'm sure you'll agree?" He didn't wait for her reply. "CCCP has been gutted—I'm sorry, that's a poor choice of words—hindered by a personnel reduction. While you head the investigation into the whereabouts of the terrorists, the Supernaut squadrons will be activated to guard key targets. I thought you'd appreciate the homage to your comrade's sacrifice."

So they have renamed the military personnel armor program after Supernaut: that pompous, overbearing, ambitious boor. What about the others that died? "Da, it is a fitting tribute," she grumbled.

Especially since Vassily Georgiyevich was little more than a puppet for the Kremlin anyway. She left the thought unvoiced.

"Good. Then it is settled." He brushed his hands together. "I will repair your reputation in Russia, and you will find these killers for me. And when you do, Natalya Nikolaevna..." The curtains of diplomacy seemed to open to reveal a furnace of anger to her, a heat to be shared between grieving siblings. "Do not be gentle with them."

"This is a promise I can keep, comrade President." She gave him a crisp salute, which he acknowledged with a confidential smile.

"Make me proud, Natalya." Batov turned and pushed past his guards. They followed him out of the tent, leaving Red Saviour alone with her thoughts and the story of Eisenfaust's life—and death—rendered in black and white in her hands.

Atlanta, Georgia, USA: Callsign John Murdock

The sound of wheels on tracks had lulled entire generations of the rootless and restless to sleep, and John Murdock was no exception to that lullaby. He lay stretched out on top of stacked cases of bottled water—not yuppie water, this was stuff in plain plastic jugs, pulled straight from municipal water supplies and labeled "Not for Sale: Emergency Supplies."

This was the last stretch of track before Atlanta, and this train was not going to stop until it got there. He had time now, time to think, to watch the landscape roll by, to think about what the hell he was getting himself in for.

It was a bizarre landscape, too. On the long stretches of Georgia hill country, red clay and tiny farms just barely scraping by, it looked as if nothing had changed since the 1950s. There wasn't a sign of trouble from the train, and if the people out there were shaken and scared and scarred by what had happened in the cities, the train sped by too quickly for it to be noticeable.

And then the train would slow, sometimes to a crawl, to get through an industrialized area. The rust-belt towns weren't nearly as bad as the bigger cities, but... still. And it would all hit him, with the stench of burning still hanging in the air, the National Guard troops patrolling, the cleanup going on. Near as he could tell, a lot of these spots must not have had more than a single truckload of troopers hit them: one patrol of armor, and none of the fancy flying machines. But one patrol had been more than enough to turn factories and warehouses to rubble. Small-town cops and private security armed only with handguns hadn't even been a blip on the radar to those troopers.

John just hoped they'd cut and run, putting their priority on getting the civvies out rather than making a stand.

What am I doing? Well, that was the question, wasn't it? Along with *What am I going to do?* He hadn't really considered much past *Get down there, sign up, put what I can do to good use.* Someone had given him one of those combination pen-and-radio novelties, and he'd been trying to pick up FM stations along the way. The reach wasn't much, but it was enough to get scattered fragments of news. Most shocking, Echo had lost half, closer to three quarters, of its OpTwos and Threes and there was no real tally on how many OpOnes or SupportOps they'd lost. He wished to hell he had something useful, something he could use to help rebuild and clear...as far as search and rescue went, a good rescue dog was of more use than he was, augmented senses and all. But...*three quarters*...good God.

No one knew where the Nazis had gone. And they sure hadn't been *beaten*. True, they had been losing the fight in Atlanta, but in plenty of places elsewhere they'd had it all their own way. But for a reason only known to them or their commanders, they had suddenly broken off combat, all over the world at the same moment. The flying death machines had gathered up surviving troopers and bodies, and just...vanished.

If anything, that made people more scared than the attack. They'd come out of nowhere, gone into nowhere, and who knew when they'd be back? The only defense was Echo, and Echo was gutted.

All right. He could help with that.

John could see smoke still rising from Atlanta, even from thirteen miles out. It'd been over a week since the attack had happened, and the city was still burning.

Ambivalent did not even come close to describing how he felt about this. It was a complete one-eighty from the way he'd lived his life for the past five years. Until now. He was driven to do this, and he wasn't sure by what. Or when it had started. Back at the bar, and all of the glass and fire and blood? Or the redheaded kid, and more fire?

It wasn't that he hadn't had plenty of time to talk himself out of this on the way here, either. With all of the destruction and death, he hadn't had to worry about getting booted from a train by a railroad bull, low-paid legalized thugs sent to make sure vagrants and bums weren't stealing things or catching a ride. Oh, there were guards on some of the trains—the armaments trains—but there were a lot of trains running. The Nazis hadn't taken out the rail system but they had done a number on the Interstates.

Without having to worry about getting hassled by some low-rent security detail, his only concerns were catching the right trains and not getting run over by one. He'd even been able to crack the doors on some cars and ride inside, up on the tops of cartons of beans and bottled water. He'd learned a couple of years ago to try to avoid the livestock cars, even if they were empty, though nothing was empty right now. Even the livestock cars were put to use hauling emergency supplies. Generators, mostly. Livestock cars were ventilated, so gas and diesel fumes wouldn't build up, but they were metal-sided and could be locked, making them harder to loot. Generators were at a premium right now. There were rumors that this would accelerate Tesla's old dream of broadcast power for everyone. There were rumors that the head of Echo was behind the Nazi invasion so that he could profit from that. Conspiracy theories.

And there he was, hiking in towards the city. He hadn't realized, until he looked at a roadmap, that it was going to be like getting into a fortress in a way. Atlanta was surrounded by a ring-shaped superhighway, and from the buzz at the gas station, that ring had been devastated, which meant a lot of rescue people, a lot of clearing, and if he wanted to get in quietly, a lot to keep out of the way of. John had decided that the main arteries into Atlanta would be too clogged with fleeing inhabitants, disaster personnel, and much needed supply trucks. Entering the city through one of the industrial areas would be easier, and leave him less likely to be noticed. Plus, it was more expedient, with the train tracks stopping off closer to the factories and manufacturing plants than to any of the municipal roads or thoroughfares.

It still didn't make any sense, but he was here. John Murdock had arrived in Atlanta.

John shrugged his small backpack further onto his shoulder. It wasn't exactly heavy for his enhanced muscles, but the crude straps still cut into his flesh after a while. That was a new acquisition; he'd lost about everything he had in the fight, but there were plenty of folks handing things out right and left to anyone volunteering with search and rescue. He'd practically had all of this thrust into his hands. The backpack itself, green with the letters CERT emblazoned on the side (along with a green plastic hardhat and lowest-bidder goggles) now held a couple of changes of clothing. He picked those clothes up from a sidewalk dump, an impromptu supply depot made up of folding tables and tarps. He sorely needed some new clothes, since his shirt and jacket were bloodied rags and his pants not much better. The rucksack with his few belongings, left in a bus station locker, was long gone. Water bottles, toiletries, and a hand towel with a duck on it were in the backpack too. Hotels had been handing out their amenity kits as if they were candy at Halloween. John had a couple of them emblazoned with the names of places that would have had their security people giving him the hairy eyeball if he'd even looked at the front door a month ago. Funny what rich people thought were "necessary items." Soap, shampoo, comb, toothpaste and a brush, yeah. Sleep mask, earplugs, and *socks?* Who would forget their own socks? Who needed hotel socks? Well, actually, he did.

John was just getting into the outskirts of the city's heavily industrialized area when it happened. His mind was elsewhere, and his senses were at a disadvantage; the smoke stung his nose and eyes, the sounds of sirens and distant gas explosions from still-raging fires all worked against him to cut off any early warning he might have had. It wasn't until he was already around the corner of a brick factory and in the middle of the street that he saw the scene that was playing out.

He only needed a glance, and knew the entire story of what had happened. A group of rough-looking men were busy rifling through an overturned truck, tossing out boxes and crates to be picked over by more thugs, dirtier and seedier than the ones in the truck. An unconscious civvie wearing a corporate jumpsuit and bleeding from the head lay in a nearby gutter, avoiding the goons' collective attention for now. These bastards had taken advantage of the chaos in and around Atlanta to do some jacking and looting. An improvised roadblock made of debris and wrecked cars turned on their sides finished the picture.

But wait—why? This wasn't a truckload of DVD players and high-def TVs . . . and it wasn't a truckload of food and water either. What could have been so important as to make this truck a target?

John didn't have much time to contemplate that. This bunch wasn't terribly bright or observant, but they spotted him quickly enough. Someone let out a whistle, and everyone snapped to very quickly. Initial confusion and even a little panic on their part rapidly turned to anticipation and greed. John was traveling alone, with an emergency worker's backpack, and lone people were easy prey. He might be a paramedic.

He might have drugs.

An unshaven greaseball with a beer gut stepped forward, and stabbed a sausage finger in the air at John. "Where do you think you're going, pal?" *No getting out of this, apparently.* "You deaf? I'm talking at you, pal." The rest of the greaseball's troupe put aside their distractions, instead focusing on new prey. John unslung his backpack, tossing it back towards the corner of the brick factory. The group of ruffians began shuffling towards John, forming a rough semicircle as they approached. This wasn't their first time ganging up on someone. Still, they weren't particularly smart. If they had been, they'd have just shot John and then looted his body.

The greaseball, relishing the chance to taunt his next victim, laid it on thick. "Just talk to us, pal. We won't hurt you." John kept his trap shut. He quickly surveyed their armament; pipes, rebar, some chains, and a pistol. Normally, he'd have kept walking, let them have their fun. No point in doing something as stupid as getting into a fight on behalf of someone else. But—

But they were pissing him off. John felt the hate rising in his belly, felt the disgust and the sickness. It took him about a second to figure out how to deal with them, how long to wait to move. His timing was ruined, however, by the poor chump in the gutter.

The driver for the truck started to move around, trying to pick himself up. He whimpered and tried to call out for someone to help him.

Crap. The greaseball's head was already turning, his gang following suit. John had to do it now. "Hey. You just gonna stand there, or ya gonna get on with it?" Bullies don't like being talked back to; the leader of this rabble was no exception.

Some smirking skinhead wielding a bent piece of rebar piped up. "You going to let him talk to you like that, Al?" The greaseball shot a venomous look to the skinhead, then switched the stare to John. A heartbeat later, and he was charging, his pistol held high and ready to beat John with it. Quite a tell: apparently he didn't have ammunition to spare, so pistol-whipping was the move. John waited for the man to close within a foot of him before reacting. He sidestepped the thug, using his rooted left leg to trip the man. Off-balance, he took his assailant's gun hand into both of his own fists, latching on and spinning Al around. Al shrieked in pain and the sudden realization that he was in more trouble than he bargained for. After locking Al's arm under his right armpit, John loosened his grip enough to wrench the gun from the screaming thug's hand, breaking two of his fingers. For spite, John broke the man's arm.

Al went down, his ruined appendage wobbling uselessly at his side as he writhed on the ground. The rest of the looters were stunned into inaction for a moment, but John never stopped moving, gliding quickly towards the loudmouth skinhead. The loudmouth was able to raise the rebar over his head in an overhanded blow before John was right next to him. John plunged Al's revolver into the skinhead's belly, quickly emptying the cylinder. Two shots: yep, they'd been low on ammo. The thug collapsed, a bloody hole through his abdomen. John didn't skip a beat, dropping the pistol and moving to the next one. *Four more to go.*

The next two thugs took the initiative, running at John to attack him at the same time. John ducked under the swung chain of the first one, pushing him in the back with a well-placed elbow. The man's momentum carried him forward, out of the fight for the moment. The second looter tried to skewer John with a jagged-ended pipe; John twisted in place, avoiding the thrust and escaping with only a gouge to his right side. He jabbed at the thug's throat, stunning the man as his throat closed up. Throat shots tend to break anyone's rhythm. A front kick to the thug's groin, a leg sweep to trip him, and another boot to his temple knocked him into unconsciousness. The first thug had regained his composure, and was marching towards John while whipping the length of chain around over his head, as much buying time as he was showboating.

Chain-thug was varying his speed, using the chain to keep his distance from John. When the strike finally came, it was well executed. John barely had time to throw up both of his arms and save his eyes. The chain struck, and then the guy was on top of John, trying to force him to the ground. John fell backwards with the thug, locking him in a bear hug. The cracked asphalt bit into John's back and head as he impacted it, the added weight of the man on top of him worsening the situation. Before the stars in front of his eyes could clear, John reflexively tucked his chin to his collarbone, and then rammed the top of his skull into the punk's nose twice. Blood gushed, and the thug was now trying to roll off of John. Wasting no time, John kneed the man in the groin, and rolled out from under him. Standing up as quickly as possible, John slammed a boot into the back of the man's head.

John was up and in a boxer's stance, hands up and ready. He heard the footfalls of one of the thugs running away; the last one was shaking in place, ready to bolt. Normally, John would have let him get away, end the fight as soon as he could and move on. But he didn't run, and now John was ramped up and the energy, the fury, had to go somewhere. *Too bad, so sad.* John walked forward, grabbing the man by the throat as he moved past him. Holding the frightened punk against the wall with one hand, John started to relentlessly punch the man in the face with his free fist. A good while later, John wasn't sure how much later, he stopped, letting the pulp of the man slump to the ground.

It took a few seconds for John to get his breathing under control, to let the blood throbbing in his ears quiet itself. Once he'd had a moment to ramp everything down, he began to look about at the destruction he'd caused. Most of them dead, dying, or wishing they were dying. One that got away, but that wasn't too much of a loss. He added up the number of thugs again mentally, and came up short—

"Over here, you asshole!" Greaseball. He was standing over the prone and sobbing form of the driver, who had crawled from his relative safety in the gutter. Maybe to get at a radio in the cab of the truck, or a weapon. It didn't matter. The greaseball had used the commotion of the fight to get away and get into the crates from the truck. He had some sort of . . . glove, or something, on his whole arm; the broken one was still limp at his side, some of the compound fractures bleeding noticeably. How the man was even standing, John couldn't fathom. Drugs, maybe. The glove was humming, with Al the Greaseball pointing it at the head of the driver.

"You're dead meat, pal! You hear me?" Spittle flew from his mouth, punctuating the curses and questions.

John had had enough. He didn't know what the glove did, but he didn't like the ominous hum it was emitting. With all of the techno-gizmo-whatever junk floating around nowadays, it could be part of some new bit of power armor, or some meta's arsenal. *Or it could be a toaster for all you know, idiot.* He looked at the driver, then the glove, then the last remaining looter. The driver would probably get killed as soon as John did anything. The greaseball knew it, too.

Except for one small fact . . .

"Screw it." The first lance of flame from John bit into the thug's uninjured arm at the elbow, severing it cleanly. Al fell backwards, his mouth wide in an O of silent agony. He waved the stump around in the air, unable to clutch at it with his other arm.

John walked forward, watching the thug push himself away from the driver and John with his legs. John seethed and raged on the inside. More fire answered that rage, sweeping up the thug's body in slow, measured waves. John took his time, hating everything about the man, about the world, this city, the invasion, and more than anything, himself.

John finally stopped when there was hardly anything

left of Al to burn. There was a scorched silhouette of a person against the asphalt. John felt sick looking at it, thinking of the "shadows" against a brick wall in Hiroshima. He turned away in disgust, facing the driver. John kicked Al's gloved hand into the gutter— the armor on the glove had kept the hand intact—as he walked up to the driver. "Are you all right?"

The driver was clearly in a bad way. He was dying. John knew the look in those eyes, that gray face. But dying or not, he was afraid. Scared to death of John. He tried to drag himself away from John, dying eyes fixed on John's face, horror transfixing his own.

That look drained everything from John in an instant. The rage, the high from the fresh kills, the power—all of it gone, except for the disgust. It came back and redoubled, stronger than ever. John started for the man, to try to help him, get him to a hospital. But then he thought better of it. This guy was going to do himself more damage trying to get away from John. *Leave him alone. Maybe he can get to a radio and call for help before he passes out.* He walked back to the corner of the brick factory, stepping over the bodies in the intersection.

Shouldering his backpack, he started down the street again. He made sure to fix his eyes intently on his own feet.

He couldn't, *wouldn't*, look at the driver again.

And then—

It was a flash of light, a wash of fire in the sky. Instinctively, he ducked; instinctively, he looked up.

Instinctively, he felt himself ramping up inside again. Fight or flight. But with him . . . it was always fight. Right down to the end of the road, it was always fight.

But what alighted beside the driver was . . . not what he expected.

His mind flashed back to that moment in New York when that poor, poor kid had exploded all over the sky. The wash of flames, and bursting through them, that . . . *being*, that fabulous winged creature cradling the kid's still form in its arms.

She . . . it was a she this time, oh yes. She stood beside the wreck of the truck, a flawless body clothed in flame. She had scooped up the driver in her arms as effortlessly as if he weighed nothing. Her flames licked harmlessly at the driver; his eyes were closed, but his chest was still moving. And the expression on his face had gone from pain and terror to—impossibly—peace. He even smiled a little.

Huge wings of flame stretched out behind them, poised as she was to launch into the air again. And only after taking all that in, did John raise his eyes to hers, to look into *her* face.

Beautiful. Terribly beautiful. Inhumanly beautiful. He looked into her eyes, and felt her gaze lock with his, and the impact of that drove him to his knees as his insides went to water. He felt all that he was being laid out in front of her, felt her examining it in that nanosecond of time. All of his self-loathing was a flood of thin, filthy water gushing from him to evaporate at her feet.

A pair of tears, like crystal pearls, slowly moved down her cheeks. She was *sorry* for him.

And then, the great wings cupped air, thundered, flashed, and she was an arrow of fire across the sky, the driver still held in her arms.

John got slowly to his feet, then stood stock-still

for a couple of beats before he finally came back to life. He shook his head, then cupped a palm over his eyebrows to look at the sky. *Insane. You have to be.* He shook his head again to clear it, before setting on back down the street, but it didn't work at all.

Atlanta, Georgia, USA: Callsign Seraphym

Seraphym returned to her perch only minutes after she had left it. Metas with the power of flight came up to her perch, some to try and speak with her, to convince her to help them. But she had her own path to follow this day, and it was not theirs. As always, some could see what she was, and some could not. She ignored them. Not one who came to her was one who had any great part in the web of futures as she saw them.

The same futures Matthew had seen.

Then came one she could not ignore, purely because of his persistence. The face and body of a god, and the name of one too, if not the power. Tesla's Messenger trod up the air to her, and stared. Why had he come to her? He had seen her flames. He had heard about her and he did not know her. And he was passionate in his loyalty to Echo and Tesla, and he would, if there was any chance, lure her to them.

"Who are you?" he asked, finally.

I am what you see.

He started, his head jerking a little, to hear her voice in his mind. "I mean, are you a meta? Is this all some sort of illusion?"

The only illusions here are those that come from within you, and prevent you from seeing me truly.

"Echo needs you—"

*Echo must go on needing. I am not Tesla's property.
I serve another Power.*

"But—" She sensed his anger, his frustration. She
couldn't blame him. Echo did need, with so many
dead, so much in ruins. Echo needed.

Tesla would have to find his answers elsewhere.

"You can't—" he began, his voice rising a little.

She raised her eyes at last, and Looked at him. Saw
all of him laid out bare before her. Every memory. Every
thought. Everything he was ashamed of, everything
he dreamed of. She felt him understand what she was
doing; sensed him recoiling from the things he would
never, ever have revealed to another living soul—

—of course, she was not, precisely, living. In a way,
she was more. Superliving.

She saw his immediate future, the ship come to
take him to a place he had not even dreamed of, to
a new course for his life. That she did not allow him
to be aware of. Only a few, a very few, mortals would
be permitted to know their possible futures, and this
time, he was not among that select few.

He was aware of all else though. Aware that she was
nothing like he had thought. Aware of what she truly
was. It was he that cried out, turned away, and fled,
running along the paths of air with terror chasing him.

Fear not, she sent after him. But of course it was
a little too late. Her kind almost always said something like *"Be not afraid"* to mortals, but honestly,
they never had been very good at making that work.

The immediate future became present, then past, and
she gazed. Days and nights, seen as blended frames,
and she acted as best she could to steer a course to

that place that was more a hope than a destination. And then, one afternoon, she sensed a clear calling. One mortal was dying who would be needed. She could scoop him up and take him to those who would heal his broken body before it was too late. She *should* do that. If he lived, his power would bloom. He would be indispensable, not because he would be powerful, but because of who he would save with *his* power. One tiny keystone to the arch...

She launched from her perch and dove for the spot. The man, now a simple transport driver—though that would change the moment she touched him and became the catalyst to bring out his power—lay in a broken, bleeding heap on the asphalt. There had been a fight, and a bloody, terrible one. The driver had been ambushed, but someone had taken on his ambushers and left nothing of them. But...

But there was a blank here. She could not See who had come to the man's rescue.

Startled by the sound of someone nearby, she looked up, and into the gray eyes of a single man who, until that moment, had not existed for her. He had been a blank spot in the canvas of the present. She was seldom surprised by—anything, really, but this surprised, shocked her.

And she Looked at him. And his pain, pain even he did not really understand properly, struck her like a blow to the face. Here was loss, betrayal, the death of all hope. Here were tragic flaws, great courage, and a yawning chasm of desperation. Here was one who could have been, and could be, noble—as noble as the angels...or a terrible, soulless creature. Or he might simply lie down in despair and die.

She Saw what he was, much of his past, and what he might become—

With a shock, she realized that much about all the futures around him was...undefined. And not because the futures themselves had not settled. Because there was information being withheld from her, things about this man that the Infinite did not *want* her to know.

Curiosity sparked in her. She opened herself to what knowledge the Infinite would give her.

His name was John Murdock. She noted him in her mind, but curiosity became more than a spark, it became a flame.

But also, there was fear. For the first time, Seraphym knew fear. Why would the Infinite keep knowledge from her?

A soft moan woke her to the present again. The man she held needed help. And the world would need him.

She broke off eye contact with Murdock, realizing only at that moment that his pain had made its way into her heart, calling two slow tears from her eyes. Shaking her head with an inaudible sob, she spread her great wings and took to the sky, trailing fire behind her.

Atlanta, Georgia, USA: Callsign Mercurye

Mercurye slapped two twenties on the counter of the roadside bar. "Whiskey. Line 'em up."

The bartender, a gaunt man with frown lines entrenched in a drawn face, took a step back. His gaze moved from Mercurye's face to the body bag flung over the meta's shoulder.

Mercurye hunched over the bar. "I swear to God, my friend, if a man ever needed a drink, it's right now."

This was language the barkeep understood. His hand moved across the bottles on the wall and settled on Bushmills Irish. He set five tumblers on the bar with the wooden clatter that ordinarily soothed anxious customers. The only other sound in the bar emanated from the jukebox—an old Aerosmith song. Old men and tattered women stared at the muscular, bare-chested metahuman and his morbid cargo.

The meta slammed back two drinks in as many seconds.

"Tough times," the bartender said with a raised eyebrow. "Hell of a thing."

"Hell's the right word for it," Mercurye said. The whiskey distracted him from the whirl of emotions tearing his head apart. He downed two more as if he'd come from the desert. "Keep 'em coming."

"No problem."

An ancient man limped up to the bar with his wallet in his hand. "You're not paying while I'm in this room, son." Mercurye turned his head wearily. He forced himself to smile in thanks, but the man sought no reassurance. He pushed Mercurye's money back to him and replaced it with his own.

A second man, younger but still gray of hair, reached over with another bill. "'Nam, sixty-eight," he said, and jerked a thumb at the old man. "Korea."

The blowsy woman at the bar added to the pile. "My son was in Kuwait," she said.

Five belts later, Mercurye felt his back relax. He looked to each of his patrons. "Thank you," he said. "Stay away from the city if you can. It's a mess."

The Vietnam vet shook his head. "Driving in tomorrow with water and food. I ain't afraid of a war zone."

The meta nodded.

"That a friend?" With his chin, the vet indicated the body bag, now propped against the bar.

"Never met him." Mercurye remembered Eisenfaust's face, blackened by bruises. Ramona had filled him in on the man's role in the invasion, which led him to believe that Alex had a special plan for the body. "Sorry I brought him in, but..."

"Don't suppose you could have left him in the car," the bartender said.

"I'm on foot," Mercurye said with a weary grin. "I won't be long."

The Korean war vet unexpectedly laid a hand on Mercurye's shoulder. "It ain't my place to speak for what any man thinks or feels after coming out of war, but if this is your first time, listen. I remember the faces of the men I killed every day, just as good as I remember my friends that died." His rheumy eyes bore into Mercurye's. "You just got to make it through each day. No one will understand, even when they say they do. It's a part of your heart now."

The hand moved from his shoulder and waited, outstretched. Mercurye took it, wondering what this man had to muster up to survive his war, half a century ago, without metahuman powers or stamina. Just courage.

Braver than we are.

"We'll do our best," he said, feeling ineloquent.

"Well, now, you got to, don't you?" The old-timer showed his rotting teeth in a smile. "We're too old and tired to kick your asses."

Mercurye finished his whiskey and asked for directions to Ten Falls Road, where Tesla's remote lab lay hidden from the world. The locals all knew it as a cinder-block building distinguished only by the electric fence at its perimeter. He hoisted the body bag to his shoulder and left the bar with a wave.

Striding through the air, high above the sporadically lit rural highway, the farms, the swamps reflecting moonlight, and the carpet of firs, he tried to resist the thoughts that burrowed up from his subconscious. That woman—that entity—had frightened him more than the Nazis had when they slaughtered his friends. Violence, hatred, death—these were human experiences, grounded in the natural world. Mercurye had encountered telepaths as well, who could rifle through his mind like a customer in a record store, yet he had been taught techniques to resist their intrusions: the mental version of hiding around the corners of your own house from an intruder.

Yet the woman—what could he call her anyway?— the *angel* had ripped open reality itself to spread his entire consciousness out before him. As a child he had believed angels would show up on one's doorstep with bland good tidings; so were they depicted in his mother's surfeit of Christmas imagery. He had expected to see them at the mall, placid and mild, handing out presents or inviting hobos to soup kitchens.

The fiery woman atop the Suntrust building had been neither bland nor mild. As though a star had come to life, she had regarded him as if he was an ant. He could appear on worldwide television, address a stadium full of screaming fans, face down superhuman monsters, but after contact with *her*, had there been a nearby cave, he would have huddled in it like a Neanderthal terrified of lightning. His face ached from forcing a stoic expression ever since.

Mercurye concentrated on the resilience of the air beneath his feet. Ramona's wry grin welled up in his consciousness like a remembered candy in his pocket. The plump detective had become a beacon of sanity for him during this miserable time. Glamorous women pursued him relentlessly. Once he dropped off this corpse, he could be in one of their beds within the hour. Yet Ramona blotted out their faces; her voice drowned out the professional coos of groupies as famous as he was.

She was a comrade. He could call her. He knew she would welcome it.

On a night like this, he wanted to share the darkness and the misery with comrades who understood pain and loss, not sympathizers whose caresses were intended to make his grief disappear as if no one had died.

He shouldn't have kissed her. A stupid mistake—and not the first time he'd acted without thought around women. A call from him at so late an hour had connotations he didn't want to tangle with, not today.

All at once, he spotted sodium lamps illuminating gray brick with pale orange light. The Echo lab building. From his vantage point, it resembled an abandoned gas station.

Mercurye landed in the overgrown yard, crunching gravel and dried weeds under his boots.

"Last stop," he said, lowering the body bag containing the dead German metahuman. Crickets chirped in the grasses; bats flew overhead. Nothing indicated that the lab had been used in the last five years. The blue paint on the metal front door had succumbed to rust. A deadbolt held the door against his tugs. He could have knocked it down with a good rush, but what was the point? There was no one here.

I must have made a mistake, he thought, until he glanced at the side of the building and saw the correct address in tarnished brass numbers bolted to the wall. A small plaque with the alchemical symbol for air, Echo's adopted logo, declared it for authorized personnel only.

He fished out the pay-per-call cell phone they had handed out at the campus. Alex had programmed into it the number for his emergency crisis center in the Omega Airlines complex. Mercurye felt too foolish to interrupt Alex in his efforts to rescue the database from the Thule virus.

I could call Ramona, he mused. *She might have an idea...or at least commiserate with me.*

A subsonic hum roiled his guts. Could the disrepair of the building be a sham? He might be standing on top of a massive hidden complex. Jumpsuited Echo Ops with clipboards could be waiting for him to find the concealed switch to activate a giant elevator...or something equally absurd.

I'm too tired and drunk for subtlety, he decided. He pounded on the metal door, which rung with a satisfying clangor. "Hey! It's Mercurye! Open up, will ya?"

The hum increased in volume, accompanied by a rush of air. He scanned the yard for some indication of elevators, platforms, anything. In the nighttime dark, he could only barely make out the grasses waving.

Above him, a black circular shape blotted out the

stars; it was at least fifty feet across, larger than the war machines that had attacked Echo earlier. No details were visible, just a deeper black than the night sky. The descending object lacked the wicked orange glow of the Thule crafts' propulsion system.

Nevertheless, Mercurye unslung his pistol, though he knew he ought to flee.

Blue lines coalesced on the belly of the silent craft. They joined to form a symbol: a star floating over an eye, the same Mercurye had seen in Tesla's buried room.

The craft halted twenty feet above the ground. White light poured out of an aperture, from which a ramp snaked down and gripped the ground before stiffening. Three figures stood silhouetted by the glare.

"Alex *kanyat*?" A woman's voice called.

"Not quite," Mercurye answered, shielding his eyes. "Why don't you come down where I can see you?"

The figures trotted down the ramp, resolving into the recognizable forms of human beings. All three wore matching two-piece outfits that reminded Mercurye of psychedelic-era Nehru jackets, with their raised collars, plastic sheen and straight seams. Two had golden skin and Latin features; the third, a middle-aged woman with a wide, soft face, possessed preternaturally pale skin. She looked him over with a quizzical expression.

"Oh my," she said in a melodious voice, with an accent he couldn't place. "You aren't kidding about not being Alex. I don't think he ever looked so good shirtless." She gave him a once-over as if he were on display at a butcher shop. "To what do we owe this pleasure?"

"To this poor bastard." Mercurye nudged the body bag containing Eisenfaust. "Heinrich Eisenhauer, late of the Third Reich, or so he claimed." He craned his neck to peek inside the craft. "If you folks are from the funeral home, you've really upgraded your hearses."

The woman's brow furrowed for a moment before opening up in a toothy grin of understanding. "Ah! We are here for the body, it is true. Your witticism makes sense in this context. Would you care to lower your weapon?"

"Ah, right. Sorry." He tucked the gun back in its holster, feeling embarrassed. The woman emanated nothing but serenity and calm. He recalled Alex bellowing at a screen in his secret room. "Ms. Metis, I assume."

The woman tittered. "Oh, no, silly boy. My name is Mable." She extended a hand. "Pleased to meet you."

"Mercurye." Her hand was soft, as though it had never done a day of work. "I just assumed..."

"It's quite all right. I see now why Alex sent you, Mercurye. You live up to your name." Mable gestured at the body. "Escorting the dead?"

"Hopefully it's a temporary assignment. Hauling around corpses isn't what I signed up with Echo for."

"Oh?" She raised an eyebrow. "Then what? Adventure? Mystery? Excitement?"

"Something like that."

Mable nodded as if she had made a decision. "Then you're about to get all three." She turned and spoke a few unintelligible words to her two companions. One produced a slender, silver rod from his belt and pointed it at the body bag.

The bag floated into the air.

Mercurye gaped. The silent craft, and now these wands—these people, dressed like refugees from a sixties science fiction movie, possessed antigravity technology. Aside from the powers of a few metas and an army of Thule troopers, Mercurye had not believed antigravity was possible until today.

"Who *are* you people?"

Mable gave him that sweet smile again and wrapped her arm around his. She led him up the ramp into the dazzling light of the flying saucer. "Alex hasn't told you? We're from Metis, my handsome young messenger. You'll be there soon enough, and you can decide for yourself who we are."

Atlanta, Georgia, USA: Callsign Red Djinni

Every morning the lights come on and that dull electric hum that seems to permeate this place builds to something I can't ignore. A perpetual hum, a constant buzzing, and my skin feels like it's being fried. It's in the floor, the walls and ceiling, it courses through the air itself. I suppose I could have asked for something to shield me from it. I doubt they would have complied, but I could have asked.

But no, I won't have it. I welcome the sensation, knowing just days ago this would have been torture. And I don't just mean the invasive humming, but the cell they've put me in. To be caged up like this, to be denied simple freedoms, would have been too much to take. But things are different now. I'm different. The pain that courses through my skin forces my eyes to open and the dreams to stop. My dreams are now haunted grounds with faces that I don't wish to see. It's only when I wake that I can block them out. Only awake can I find some peace.

So each day I stay awake for as long as I can. Each day is now a ritual of distraction. I know this can't last, and that sooner or later I'll have to face some hefty consequences. But at least in here, locked away, I can remove myself from the world. Maybe someday I'll be ready to pick myself up, to heal and to fly back into the fray. Maybe. Someday.

But the world isn't ready to give up on me just yet. *Someday* comes a lot sooner than it should.

I warm up with stretches, push-ups and crunches. There really isn't room to do any more. As I finish my last set, like clockwork, I feel the telltale footsteps of the guard bringing my breakfast. This is all part of the ritual. Between meals there is nothing, so I have to amuse myself. I try different faces, all from memory. I don't have a mirror, so god knows what I look like. It passes the time, it keeps my face from reverting to its natural state, and it keeps the mind busy. When I pause, when I *falter*, that's when my eyes close. I don't like it when my eyes close anymore. I don't like what I see.

As each boot slams rhythmically down on the concrete, I gauge the guard's weight and distinguishing gait, and I mark his progress. This is now the extent of human contact for me. I'm the only prisoner in this wing. From what I understand, the Nazi Blitzkrieg pretty much cleaned out the prisoner population here at Echo headquarters. The guards have learned not to talk to me. I'm hungry for any kind of diversion, and I've said some pretty appalling things just to get them to stay. None of them are very quick. All of them have vulnerable points to provoke. So who is it today? Reeves, the family man? Hollister, the holy optimist? Or is it Falladay and his crusade to bed his way across all of Atlanta?

It's none of them. Lying flat, I feel the vibrations coming up off the floor and get a better sense of the man. His footsteps are too heavy and too measured to be one of the guards. A big man, and the steady march screams of military. Sitting up, I'm almost surprised when the cell door opens instead of a tray being shoved through the grate at the bottom.

Towering above me is the largest Echo meta I've ever seen. He's got to be seven feet tall, and built like a tank. Stepping in, he places a tray on the ground. I assume it's my breakfast. My eyes don't leave his, not until he turns and closes the door. Wait. He *turned away*. I've got a clear shot at driving my claws into his neck, and he doesn't care. There's no fear there.

"Red Djinni. I'm Bulwark, Echo OpTwo. I'm here to discuss the terms of your stay."

You ever hear your name spoken by someone who believes he is authority personified? It's pretty annoying. As I get to my feet his eyes fall to his clipboard, and they stay there. No, he's not worried about me at all.

His voice isn't forced. He doesn't talk, he *rumbles*, but it's quiet and reserved, like speaking any louder would pulverize the walls. His understated movements belie his size. He doesn't need to project any weight or authority, *he just does*. I smell officer training here. This is obviously a man who is used to people following his orders.

I don't like him.

"The terms of my stay? Well, a TV wouldn't hurt. Can you guys get me a Tivo in here?"

He lets that slide. He doesn't even look at me. He

just stares down at that damned clipboard. At last, he puts the board behind his back and sizes me up. I read nothing from him, not a thing. The cold bastard just stares me down.

"I see you've been practicing your faces," he says finally. "Alex Tesla?"

"Did I get the mole right?"

"Should be a bit more to the left."

"I'll have to remember that."

Still nothing, not so much as a smirk. This guy is stone cold.

"Red Djinni, as a metahuman with no public record save your alleged crimes and misdemeanors, you are a ghost in the system. You are not subject to trial or hearing, nor are you under the jurisdiction of any formal tribunal except those bound by international law. As such, you are the responsibility of any internationally recognized law-enforcement agency that has the misfortune of apprehending you. In this case, that would be Echo. Since your incarceration here, you have remained silent, with the exception of inflammatory statements that have made your guards cry, soil their pants, or scream for your blood. Hardly productive. Do you wish to make a statement now?"

"Gosh, Occifer, you really think I should?"

Bulwark just looks back at his clipboard. "I'll take that as a no. You've been active for a few years now, by our records. Alone or with a troupe of other mercenaries, you're suspected of committing any number of high-profile thefts, acts of terrorism and assassinations. You have never been apprehended, until now."

"Alleged crimes? Suspected acts? Anyone ever tell you that you suck at interrogation?"

"This isn't an interrogation, Djinni. There's enough on you to suggest you've been careful to cover your tracks, but nothing we can hold you on, not for long, and you know it. So let's stop wasting our time and get to the point."

He pauses only to look up.

"I'm here to offer you a job."

He's not looking away. He's watching to see how I take this. I don't bother to hide the surprise. Why bother? He'll take it as shock that Echo would be willing to take on a known metahuman felon, or distrust, or skepticism. Truth is, I should have seen this coming. The world got hit hard that day. It's all the guards can talk about. Across the globe, the invasion decimated the metahuman population, from both sides, from all factions. There's a shortage of meta-powered people now, and armies like Echo must be scrambling to fill the void. With me, they think they're taking a calculated risk. If they've done their homework, they know of my brief stint as a vigilante years back. Since then, they have stories of a disreputable thief who's been hired to off a few crooks here and there. They obviously don't know the full story. They don't know about the Vault, or about the blood on my hands from that day. After Jack took off, the only person that could damn me was the last member of Vic's crew, a trainee meta named Howitzer, and he's dead. My eyes close, and I see him again, another unwanted face. He's got a wry grin, appalling since he's missing both legs now. We were clearing civilians off the highway while OpThrees went to work on a group of Nazi troopers. He almost made it, until one trooper threw that car at him. His legs got crushed. Stupid kid died from the shock while we were waiting for paramedics to show. That last look he gave me, that look...

I had done it again; I had tempted fate and gotten away with it. No one would know what went down at the Vault that day. I read that in Howitzer's bemused eyes as the light faded from them.

It's classic Djinni. Everything has to be ironic. The day I finally succumb to that nagging voice of morality and try to do the right thing, I get nicked. What's more, I wanted to be caught, to be put away and escape. But even a cell in the heart of Echo's fortress isn't safe. The prisoners were massacred here just days ago, and my one wish to sit and wallow in my own emotional filth is now shot to hell by a *job offer* from Billy Bob Jarhead! .

"The hell do you want *me* for?"

"Information, to start," he says. "Like what happened to you that day. You were seen with Howitzer, the only member of Agent Amethist's squad accounted for."

I fight down an involuntary shiver.

"Thanks, but no thanks. I'd rather gargle battery acid."

"This is important to us, Djinni. To..."

He pauses, and finally lets something slip through his cool military demeanor. He needs something from me. There's something I have, or something I know, that this man desperately needs. It's his eyes. It always comes back to the eyes. His look haunted, and I'm struck with the thought of looking into a mirror.

"You're a demanding jackass, aren't you, Bulwark? We're not going to get along, are we?"

"Probably not, but that hardly matters. You're needed. So what are you going to do about it?"

My eyes close again. I see them all. I see Duff's headless body fall. I see Jon ripped apart by energy blasts. I see my claws tear into that rookie guard.

And Vic. I see Vic. Not how she died, but that tranquil look of hers whenever she needed to calm me down. That look of trust. Damn her and that look...

Reaching over, I pick up my tray and start to munch on some bacon.

"What's the job?"

"I want you to find a few people for us."

Atlanta, Georgia, USA: Callsign Victoria Victrix

A week after what had seemed like the Apocalypse, the city was just starting to pull itself back together. Vickie's neighborhood had actually come through in pretty good shape. They had never lost services except for a brief period during the invasion itself. Well, all but the Internet, that is. That was down. Vickie wasn't surprised. And thanks to her folks, she had a backdoor into what remained of Darpanet, which operated on old-fashioned copper phone lines and DoD trunks, so she could still talk to people who had access to the old system. Slowly. But the web, web shopping, deliveries—she depended upon those, and they were gone for now. She would have to go *out*.

She had managed to crawl...almost literally... out to the supermarket after three days, retrieve her car, and stock up on staples for Grey thanks to the police stationed at the store. They'd looked at her cart oddly to see it wasn't full of bread and milk. A deputy even loaded the cat food and litter for her. She, damaged goods that she was, actually *had* human staples stockpiled for herself. She could live quite well for a month on the MREs stored in an otherwise unused closet. They were there against the possibility that she would one day be too frightened to leave her apartment for that long.

Right now, that wasn't a possibility, it was a probability. She had been threatened twice on the way to get her car by roving hoodlums, and even though she had left both of them under heaps of dirt and asphalt, she had been nearly mindless with panic by the time she'd gotten to the grocery. She had nearly run people down in her haste to get back home, and once there, she had locked the doors and windows and vowed not to leave again.

Then, a week after the invasion, there came a knock on the door. She sat in her chair for a moment, frozen. The knock came again.

Slowly, stiffly, she got up. She forced herself to go to the door. Trembling from head to foot, she peered through the peephole.

On the other side of the door was a nondescript man in a dusty Echo uniform, very much the worse for wear.

Echo? What could they want with her?

"Charles Burns, ma'am, Echo SupportOp. Is this Victoria Victrix Nagy?"

"Yes," she replied cautiously, and did not even put her hand on the lock.

He waited, and when nothing more was forthcoming, sighed. "Will you let me in please, ma'am?" Without waiting for her to answer, he held up his ID to the peephole.

It seemed genuine all right. Reluctantly, she took

down the chain, undid the bar locks, flipped the deadbolts. Finally she opened the door just enough for him to squeeze through.

Then she beat a hasty retreat to the farthest chair in the room, but remained standing. Burns—oh the irony of the name!—stood there looking at her, and sighed.

"Ma'am, you registered with Echo a while back."

"I was rejected," she rasped.

"I know, ma'am." He looked at his PDA. "Says here, you can't leave your house?" He glanced around the room. "Ma'am, Echo needs all the able-bodied metas we can get. We lost a lot of people a week ago. We could sure use you."

She shook her head, violently. "I can't—" she choked out. "I can't—"

He stared at her. She knew what he saw. Someone young, apparently healthy, nothing outwardly wrong with her. And out there—out there were metahuman and unpowered Ops and SupportOps of Echo, some wounded, some worse than wounded, all shell-shocked, and all of them doing the work of three people or more, because there were so few of them left.

His face grew impatient. "Ma'am—"

"I *can't!*" she said, through gritted teeth, bile rising in her throat. "If I could, I would. I . . . can't."

She was drenched with sweat now, and probably white as a sheet. He stared at her, and finally sighed. He put a small card down on the end table nearest him. "If you change your mind . . ." he said, shook his head again, and let himself out. The moment the door closed behind him, she ran to it, slamming home bolts, chaining it up, locking herself in again.

With her barrier against the world sealed again, she put her back to the door and slid down it, landing with a thump on the carpet. She began to cry silently, eyes squeezed tightly shut, tears etching their way down her cheeks.

She felt the pressure of Grey rubbing against her legs. Pressure would be all she would ever feel there. Would he have understood, if she had managed to strip off a glove and show him her hand? Tell him that her entire body was like that, scarred from neck to feet? Would he have understood that the psychological scarring was worse, far worse, than the physical scarring?

And even if he had, were there any resources at Echo left to deal with someone like her? If there were, they surely had their hands full right now.

<Easy, kiddo.> The voice in her mind was soothing. Pulling her slowly back from the abyss in her own mind, from the contemplation of guns, drugs, knives, ropes ... of her failure. There it was, they needed her at last, and she couldn't even leave the house. He had been right. They had been right. She was worthless, useless—

<Hey. You're plenty useful. I can't use the can opener myself, you know.>

Grey's wry comment cracked through and startled a laugh out of her. She opened her eyes to see his green ones gazing unabashedly into hers.

<Check out that card he left. There's a Darpanet-accessible address on it.>

She scrubbed at her eyes with the back of her hand. "So?"

<So maybe you can do computer work for them from here. You know. Contact lists. You have the

inside track when it comes to the magical community. Find out who survived, and if they aren't in Echo, persuade them to join up.>

She bit her lip. Yes. She could do that. In fact, most of the mages she knew were *not* in Echo. Mages were very good at hiding what they were.

<So go write him an email. Tell him what you can do for him, what you can't, and why.>

She pushed herself off the door, and stood up. She picked up the card and went to her computer.

By its nature, Darpanet was hard to shut down. While shiny new stuff was brought online all the time, the old stuff was still out there somewhere, whirring away, forgotten in corners of servers and switchers. In these days of easy drag-and-drop interfaces, nobody remembered command-line stuff even existed, except for the very old-school and the very clever. While millions might panic over "the Internet" being gone because they couldn't reach their favorite websites, Vickie brought up Darpanet and the slow, robust, primitive email program it supported.

Mr. Burns, she wrote. *I'm sorry our meeting went so badly. . . .*

PART TWO

The Hunt

INTERLUDE

So, dear audience, whoever you are out there—if there is anyone left other than cockroaches at this point—that is how, from my perspective, it all ended. The day, the week, when the world didn't just change, it shattered. Everything was different after that day, literally everything. The old rules didn't apply any more. Life was no longer a kind of game of cat and mouse for the metahumans of Echo, a game where everyone more or less played by the rules.

We had met the enemy, and he was so unlike us that we were left floundering.

We were going to have to play by some new rules. We were also going to have to make it up as we went along.

Governments flailed. War declarations were in order, but against whom? You could call up troops, but where to send them? You could try and enact draconian antiterrorist laws, but despite the terror, these hadn't been terrorists per se. They had come openly, and gone—where? There wasn't a single known terrorist organization that wanted to claim them, only a few radical neo-Nazi groups...and the minute they had, vigilantes had descended on them and stomped them *into paste. And everywhere, the questions were: Why had they stopped? Why weren't they attacking again? When would they? Their actions made no sense. Even their targets were confusing. On one hand, these shock troops and war machines hit critical strategic targets. But they also hit things like paint factories, DYI stores, even car dealerships. One Cadillac dealership and one Hyundai dealership were leveled to the last hubcap, but the Honda place between them was untouched. One shock troop attacked a mountainside in Montana full force, but the missile silos twenty miles away were untouched. A war machine torched every Taco Bell in two cities, then went after a National Guard base, in that order. Why?*

The world being what it was, there had always been the haves and the have-nots, but never before in America had the divide been so deep as in the aftermath of those attacks. On the side of the haves, once the initial rubble had been cleared up and their services restored, it was pretty much business as usual. On the side of the have-nots, it was living in the ruins of Kosovo, of Darfur, of Sarajevo—living in a war zone where every day was a battle for the basics.

To many of us, it felt like the end of everything. And oh, how wrong we were. It was all just beginning. The assembly point was Atlanta, where Echo had begun, and where it had almost ended. We had no idea where we were going, but we knew that it was move, or die.

I hope you are out there, dear audience. I hope you are me, actually, laughing over this and getting ready to edit it down. I hope you aren't them—laughing over this and getting ready to . . .

I'd rather not think about that.

If you're not me, and you're not them, you might be wondering why most of this was in writerly third person and some was in Red Djinni's own words. Both are easy to answer. When I write about myself or almost anyone else, it's easier to put myself at a kind of mental distance, third person, to write down the horrors. But his story is from files I found on my computer, and it felt wrong to change them. If you've read this far, you know how he studied people, and he probably knew I was going to make this record before I did. I want—I need you to hear his voice.

I'm rambling and I don't have leisure to ramble. Better get on with it.

Oh, how I hope you're me. I feel so out of my depth.

CHAPTER SIX

Red, White, and Blues

STEVE LIBBEY & MERCEDES LACKEY

Stranded travelers and airport personnel alike stared at the only three figures marching out of Gate 29 of Atlanta's Hartsfield-Jackson Airport. The shortest of the trio, a statuesque woman with raven hair and tight red clothes bearing Russian iconography and the Cyrillic letters CCCP, nevertheless stood at over six feet tall. She surveyed the chaos of the closed airport with a haughty air. Russian military transport went anywhere it wanted to.

The two older men behind her wore crisp black business suits that failed to conceal their remarkable physiques. One man's sharp, foxlike features resembled the woman. The other loomed over both of them with shoulders that would be the envy of professional wrestlers everywhere. All three stared at the conglomeration of knickknack shops, franchise coffee stands, and overpriced fast-food counters with faint looks of disgust.

An airport official flanked by security guards bustled up to them, waving papers. The woman shouldered her overnight bag and spat out her words: "We are here on state business. You will direct us to Echo representative for transporting."

The official, already exhausted from dealing with thousands of furious air travelers who no longer regarded the danger of being shot out of the sky by Nazi war machines or the demolished tarmacs as a reasonable excuse for flight cancellations, sighed with resignation. He repeated the phrase that had been etched into his brain: "I'm sorry, ma'am. We have no information at this time."

"*Shto?* What nonsense is being this?" Red Saviour glared at him. "Do we look like tourists to you? Fetch the Echo liaison at once."

"Liaison? Ah . . . um . . . There're no Echo folks here. The campus isn't far, but it's not open to the public right now."

Red Saviour turned to her father, who stood by with a condescending smile, as if he were watching her learn to ride a bike. "Papa," she said in Russian, "this cretin knows nothing and says less. Shouldn't we have an escort?"

"Our hosts may be distracted. Remember they too have lost comrades, Wolfling."

She scowled at him; whether or not the Americans could understand their Russian, the childhood nickname wasn't appropriate in public. She was hardly a little girl.

"Then we will have him call and remind them they have guests," she said, but her father touched her elbow to interrupt her.

"Excuse us, my friend," he said with a surprisingly gentle smile to the official. "We have been confined in an airplane for too long. I am sure a taxi would suffice."

The man's entire body telegraphed relief. "Right this way, sir."

Nikolai Shostakovich winked at his daughter, who puffed out her cheeks at him.

The American taxi was of astounding size: an entire minivan, typical of American excess. Natalya offered Worker's Champion the front seat, which made the cabbie smile nervously. The big hero folded himself into the seat with a grunt.

Luggage stowed, the driver pulled away from the curb onto a strangely empty street. "Where to, folks?"

"Echo headquarters," Red Saviour said.

Nikolai leaned forward. "By way of I-285, please."

The cabbie shook his head. "No can do. The entire highway is closed except to rescue teams." He shuddered. "You wouldn't want to go there anyways. It's one long grave right now. I don't know if I can stand to use it again when they reopen it. Besides," he added with relief, "it's not on the way."

"I have seen enough of bodies," Red Saviour said with a pointed look at her father.

The car trip took twice as long as it would have in ordinary circumstances. Police stopped the taxi twice, and held it up several more times to allow tanks or bulldozers to pass. "City's gone crazy. National Guard has the city under lockdown but Atlanta's a big place. The murder rate's gone through the roof, and you still see looters." The cabbie nodded at the glove compartment. "You can bet I'm packing."

"You are moving away?" she said.

"No, no. Packing. Packing heat." He paused. "A gun."

"Ah!" Red Saviour reached past his arm, opened

the compartment and pulled out the pistol, eliciting
a yelp from the cabbie. She looked it over with a
practiced eye. "Nine-millimeter Glock. You must be
good shot to use toy gun."

"*Natya*," her father said.

"I am just being helpful." She returned it to the
glove compartment. "Needs cleaning and oiling," she
told the driver. The driver nodded numbly, then jerked
his attention back to driving and took several long,
deep breaths. If not for the fear of repercussions from
what were obviously foreign metas, he'd likely have
thrown them out right there and left them looking
at taillights through tire smoke.

The cab reached a police line, marked off with
yellow tape. Beyond the tape, a dozen gutted ShipEx
trucks lined the entrance to the Echo campus. Red
Saviour knew at once what had burst their sides.

"End of the line," the cabbie said. "Can't go further."
He unloaded their bags for them, accepted his tip and
waved to them in farewell. "Welcome to Atlanta," he
shouted out the window as he rolled away.

Nikolai waved back. "Southern hospitality," he
told his dour companions. But Red Saviour paid no
attention to the departing cabbie. Her attention was
riveted on the devastation before her.

The Echo campus looked as though a bombing
squadron had made several passes overhead. Two
buildings remained standing; three more had been
sheared in half or leveled entirely. The smell of smoke
and dust hung in the air. Black gashes violated the
lush green lawn, which was dotted with temporary
trailers such as those she would see on construction
sites—which, she presumed, this mess would soon

become. Makeshift memorials of flowers, photos and white crosses lined the driveway.

A police officer in full combat regalia approached them, assault rifle at the ready. "Move along, please."

"We are expected," Red Saviour said. "We are delegation from *Super-Sobratiye Sovetskikh Revolutzionerov.*" The man gave her a blank look. "CCCP. From Russia."

He shook his head slowly. "First time I've heard of it. You'll have to come back later. No visitors allowed."

Indignation welled up in her, but her father stepped between her and the officer. "Alex Tesla asked us to consult on a case. Would you notify him that we are here, at least? He can reschedule our meeting if he wishes."

The officer muttered into his radio, glancing from Red Saviour to Nikolai and back again. His frown deepened.

"This is ridiculous," Red Saviour said to her father in Russian. "Southern hospitality indeed. They treat us like *we* invaded *them.*"

"Be patient for once."

"Bah." She fished out her sole pack of *Proletarskie* cigarettes and lit one. "No wonder that the Nazis took so many lives here. These Americans can't even be bothered to get off the couch."

"Hmm. I think I will do the talking," her father said.

"Papa!"

"Hush, child. Try to smile for our hosts."

Red Saviour looked to Worker's Champion for support, but he only nodded in agreement with Nikolai.

"Fine. *Horosho*. I am on display like a mannequin." When the officer's gaze fell on her again, she showed all her teeth in a smile. The man visibly winced and turned his back on her.

"Lenin's Beard," Worker's Champion said. "We should have left her in Moscow."

Nikolai chuckled. "Believe it or not, she has improved immensely. That's enough, Natya."

Red Saviour glared at them both and puffed on her cigarette with newfound vigor.

The officer flicked off his comm unit and approached them. "That's a negative on the appointment. If there was a record of it"—he waved at the massive pile of rubble—"it's buried under that. Your best bet is to call the public line tomorrow and request—"

With an exasperated snort, Red Saviour threw her cigarette on the ground and pushed the officer aside. She stomped down the driveway towards the trailers, head held high. The man regained his bearings and raised his weapon to her head, advancing and barking orders. Without looking back, Red Saviour grasped the gun barrel and shattered it with a flash of blue energy.

"*Where . . . is . . . Alex . . . Tesla?*" she bellowed into the air.

Worker's Champion restrained Nikolai by the arm. "*Nyet.* Let her learn. You coddle her too much."

Nikolai resisted the iron grip for a moment before shrugging in defeat. "You have obviously never raised a child, Boryets."

The disarmed officer shouted into his radio. Police, Echo SupportOps, and metahumans converged on Red Saviour, who imperiously strode across the grass with folded arms, calling Tesla's name. The police and SWAT commandos leveled their rifles at her amidst cries of "Stand down!"

Within moments, forty armed or meta-powered personnel swarmed her. Red Saviour pretended to ignore them, forcing the circle to move along with her towards the trailers.

"Alex Tesla! Is that you in the riot helmet? *Nyet?* Then why haven't you fetched him, dolt?"

Two burly Samoan men in OpTwo uniforms blocked her way. "Easy there, sister. No one wants to get hurt here," said the smaller of the two.

"Oh! You are being Alex Tesla?"

The Samoan shook his head. "Matai, Echo OpTwo. You can't—"

"Then get out of my way, Mr. OpTwo. I have an appointment." She resumed walking.

Matai put a hand out. "Stop right there."

Red Saviour locked eyes with him. "Do not touch me, *tovarisch*, unless you wish to lose hand."

With a grin, Matai reached for her shoulder. To an expert practitioner of *Systema,* this was an open invitation for a takedown. In an instant she had seized his hand and redirected him into the ground, yanking his arm back and placing her bootheel at his neck.

Dozens of rifles aimed at her throat. Grass and turf surged up onto the second Samoan's form, doubling his size. He loomed over her with fists the size of air conditioners.

"Easy! Easy everyone!" Matai said. His eyes watered from the pain.

Red Saviour surveyed the assembly disdainfully. "Very impressive, you Echo boys. Now which of you is man enough to inform Tesla that one single little *devushka* has come for tea?"

The crowd muttered amongst themselves. Motu opened and closed his fists, making a sound much like a landslide.

At last, one of the security guards made a call. A lone figure appeared at the door of the centermost trailer and approached the mob. Guns ready, the operatives parted for him.

Alex Tesla, with the solemn dignity of an exhausted leader, looked Red Saviour over curiously. At last he asked: "Can I help you?"

"That is why we are here, to help you."

She released Matai, who flopped onto the grass. He picked himself up at once, trying to appear casual.

Red Saviour offered a hand. "Red Saviour, Commissar of CCCP, Russian Federation. You sent for us."

Tesla hesitated a moment before shaking her hand. "Alex Tesla, Commissar of Echo, USA. I'm sure I have no idea what you're talking about." He gestured for his people to lower their weapons.

"I spent twenty hours cramped in military transport plane with no smoking allowed. Please get idea quickly."

"Excuse me, Mr. Tesla. My daughter lacks manners." Nikolai stepped into the circle with a telegram. "Nikolai Shostakovich. This man is Worker's Champion. What she *means* to say is that we received this message from you, and we came at once."

With a flourish, Nikolai presented the telegram. Tesla scanned it. "I didn't write this."

"Then perhaps your secretary, *nyet?* We've all had a trying time these last few days. Such a small detail could easily be lost."

Worker's Champion spoke, his voice a commanding rumble. "This is not a matter to discuss in front of underlings. Dismiss your people."

Tesla bit back a reply. "Very well. Back to work, folks. The situation is under control."

The crowd dispersed. Massaging his arm, Matai shot Red Saviour a sour look as he left. Tesla led the Russians into his trailer, where papers, maps, photographs, telephones, radios and rifles covered the surfaces. He offered them metal folding chairs, which creaked under their weight.

"Sorry for the reception. We're a little jumpy right now."

"We did not mean to cause a commotion," Nikolai said, silencing his daughter with a touch on her arm. "We are still reeling from our own tragedy."

"I heard. You have my condolences."

"And you have ours. Let us not, how do you say, get off on the wrong foot."

Red Saviour rolled her eyes. "*Da, da.* I apologize for pushiness, Mr. Tesla. Nazis are still being on loose and I have sense of urgency to get back to Russia and find them, instead of sit in plane for entire day."

Nikolai and Worker's Champion exchanged looks.

"So now you can tell us about dead *fashista*. Where is being his body?"

Tesla met her gaze with his own shadowed eyes. The silence stretched out until the strain hinted of secrets concealed. "Ma'am," he said at last, "I'm afraid I can't produce it for you."

"Then why are we here?" she snapped.

"I told you, I don't know." Tesla picked up the telegram again. "I'm getting an idea, though. The writer of this telegram is an associate of mine."

"*Horosho!* Send for him."

Tesla frowned, dragging the tips of his mustache down. "He's indisposed."

"'Indisposed'? I do not know this word."

"He ran into a squad of Thule troopers during the attack. Luckily he'll pull through. He's a tough—"

"Thule!" Red Saviour nearly jumped out of her seat. She turned to her father, a light in her eyes., and spoke in rapid-fire Russian. "Papa! That's where I recognized the commander's insignia. Your scrapbooks from the Great Patriotic War—there was a man with the Thule emblem on his uniform. A dagger wreathed in ivy against a swastika."

Nikolai paused, thinking. "I do recall that picture. It was Boryets that ran into the Thule Society, however. A pack of mystics—"

"Madmen," Worker's Champion said. "They believed that the Germans originated on another planet, orbiting the star Aldebaran, I think." He noticed Tesla's look of confusion and repeated the discussion in English. "In the Great Patriotic War, I broke up a ring of Nazi magicians who believed they could summon angels to strike the Russian people down and turn the tide at Stalingrad. It was our good fortune that there are no such things as angels, particularly ones who would aid fascists."

He inclined his head in respect. "I am impressed, Mr. Tesla, that you are familiar with the Thule Society. Hitler officially dissolved them before the Nazi party took power."

"Echo's memory of World War II runs deep," Tesla said. "You recall that my father founded Echo in Atlanta at the urging of Yankee Doodle and Dixie Belle."

"Da, da. I remember Yankee Doodle," Worker's Champion said.

"And I remember Dixie Belle. *Quite* well." Nikolai winked at his daughter. "However, I regret to say that Yankee Doodle and I did not get along."

"Do not remind me," Worker's Champion said. "Let me assure you that impetuousness runs in the Shostakovich blood."

"Bah," Red Saviour and her father said in unison.

"It was of no consequence. Your founding heroes fought bravely at our side, Mr. Tesla. It saddens me that they passed away before I came to their country to visit, although this tragedy would have broken their hearts."

"They would have been right in the thick of it."

"Indeed, if they had to choke the *fashistas* with their crutches." Worker's Champion smiled. "Our countries have had a tempestuous relationship during my overlong life. Yet in these modern times of unity, I would think that your organization and mine could work together against this threat. Cooperation makes us stronger, does it not, Natalya?"

She frowned. "*Da.* Of course. Just what I was going to say."

"She speaks for all of us," Worker's Champion said with a straight face. "Commissar Red Saviour is the official representative of the CCCP. I am but a functionary, and Nikolai merely consults now and again, when his ladies will let him out of the house. Red Saviour should be the point of contact between Echo and CCCP."

"A splendid idea," Nikolai said.

"Well, we can use all the help we can get." Tesla spread his hands. "You can see what we've been reduced to. It's pretty clear the Thule Society targeted Echo facilities throughout the country and Europe, aside from the Red Square incident and a handful of others. They knew our radio frequencies and jammed them exclusively. No attempt was made to hold ground or steal our assets. The attack was a surgical strike."

"A blitzkrieg," Red Saviour said.

"Exactly, which raises the question: what next? Why preemptively attack metahuman law enforcement if not in order to open the way for a larger force?"

"What next, or where next?" Nikolai said. "Metahuman reinforcements can move quickly in a crisis. The goal may have been to weaken all outposts equally— every link in the chain becomes a weak link."

"Thus the Moscow attack," Tesla said.

"Unless that was merely revenge for handing them their heads in the Great Patriotic War." Worker's Champion stroked his chin. "It is an obvious motive."

Tesla raised a finger. "Only if they're German."

"They wear swastikas, they speak German . . . how can they not be German?" Anger passed over Red Saviour's face. "And Germany itself suffered no attack. Is obvious connection."

"Lots of Nazis weren't German. But look, Germany's tripping over themselves to offer aid to affected regions. The government issued a strong denial *and* an apology for even being associated with the Thules sixty years ago." Tesla shook his head. "Whether the Thules are a renegade military force or World War II holdouts supplied by a serious blacksmith, I don't think they have any genuine connection to the German government. No government could hide that kind of a force for so long. In fact, the very fact that they left the Berlin Echo facility alone suggests that they're trying to make Germany a red herring."

"Or it could be a ploy by the Germans to confuse us while they prepare another strike," rumbled Worker's Champion.

"The war ended sixty years ago, Boryets. The world

has moved on. Someday you will, too." Nikolai returned the elderly hero's icy glare. "Alliances have shifted. Would you have been welcomed in America in 1967? Hardly. They would have treated you like a stray fighter jet—and rightly so. Now we are sitting in Atlanta, in America's own Georgia, with our new friend, discussing our shared campaign against a common enemy. If you keep seeking hidden motives where they do not exist, you will miss the true motives."

Worker's Champion's expression froze. His jaw muscles worked under his skin. Red Saviour tensed for an explosion of rage. Her father had a way of getting under people's skin, for good or ill.

Yet the brawny old man merely crossed his arms and looked away with a pout.

Natalya relaxed. Worker's Champion had the capacity for ruthlessness if he did not get his way. In the context of an FSO council room, it carried all the shadowy power of the Russian government, with its various shades of authoritarianism. In Alex Tesla's trailer, however, it came across as petulance. She flushed with shame that she had been acting the same way out of frustration and exhaustion. Her father and Boryets had been trying to maneuver her back towards behaving like a leader instead of a spoiled princess.

I must regain lost ground with Tesla, she decided. "You are, of course, correct. The world is complex place today. Bald-faced aggression by first world government is unlikely. However, we must deal with immediate problem at hand. Comrade Tesla, please to tell us what CCCP can do to help you."

Tesla suppressed a grin. "Thank you, Commissar. I'm sure you saw how much our city has suffered at the hands of the Thules. Their attack was designed to reap as much chaos as possible in a short amount of time."

"Let me propose something," her father said quickly. "We traveled directly from the airport to your facility. My daughter has a keen eye for civil emergencies, thanks to her years with our *militsya*. May we impose upon you to provide her a tour of the affected areas so that she might formulate a better sense of the damage you've sustained?"

Red Saviour nodded in agreement until she realized what her father had asked. "Papa, should we not—"

"Of course, an excellent idea. One hour in Atlanta will tell you more than I could in a week. I'll make the call at once." Tesla brought out a cell phone and spoke quietly.

Natalya gave her father a quizzical look. He smiled in response, a smile she remembered from when he and her mother were still married and wanted to discuss their daughter's future without her presence.

"We still have much to discuss," Worker's Champion rumbled.

"And so we shall," Nikolai said. "When Natalya returns, she can brief us on her findings. And then..." he paused long enough for her heart to sink, "we can brief *her*."

"Old men," Red Saviour grumbled, puffing smoke like a factory and then flicking away ashes. "Every decision on planet is made by old men. Why not just demote me and end farce?"

After being sent away like a child, the sound of her own anger gave her some relief. "Take her on a tour of the damage" meant "find her a playmate while we solve the problem." Granted, her reputation for a quick temper preceded her, but this was her father and Uncle Boryets, not the cringing bureaucrats of the FSO. If anyone understood her position, it should be those two.

Had she crossed the line one too many times? Was she nothing more than a liability?

Echo personnel bustled past her as she leaned against Tesla's trailer. Aside from furtive glances—news traveled fast—no one paid attention to her, which was just as she wished it.

With a slow, deliberate twisting of her bootheel, she ground her first cigarette into the dirt—and lit another.

"Those things will kill you," a woman's voice chirped at her side. Red Saviour glanced up to see a slender, blue-skinned young woman in Echo Damage Control Officer attire. Curiosity gave the girl's delicate features a warm cast that belied the icy color of her skin.

"Not fast enough for my enemies," Red Saviour said, inhaling the nicotine-laden smoke. "Echo Damage Control, *da*? Let me guess: you are Ice Pack Girl."

"Belladonna Blue."

"That was being my second guess." Red Saviour returned to surveying the dark Echo campus.

The girl shifted her weight from foot to foot. "Tesla told me to accompany you on a tour. I'm also new to town."

"I am not 'new to town.' I am merely visitor. As soon as they—*we*—are finished with consultation, we return to Russia where we belong."

"Ah." Belladonna Blue scratched her head. "I heard about the ruckus you caused today."

"What is 'ruckus'?"

"Commotion. Incident."

"*Da.* 'Incident' is my middle name."

"It is?"

Red Saviour snorted out a cloud of acrid smoke but still did not face the girl. "*Nyet.* It is Nikolaevna."

"Ah." Belladonna cleared her throat. "Well, *zdrastvuitye, Commissar Krasnaya Spasskaya.* Welcome to America."

"*Shto?*" Red Saviour turned to look at the girl again.

"Sorry, my pronunciation is off."

"Was actually being quite good. Where did you learn Russian?"

The blue girl spread her hands. "My folks are scientists. Politics can't get in the way of a good debate about particle accelerators, so I met a few Soviets as a girl."

"Is that so?" After a pause, Red Saviour offered a hand. "Natalya Nikolaevna Shostakovich, Commissar of CCCP."

"Bella Dawn Parker, but everyone calls me Belladonna."

"Everyone calls me Commissar, and salutes," Red Saviour said with a hint of a smile. "Tell me, Belladonna, what have you done to deserve tour guide duty?"

"Nothing. Like I said, I'm fresh off the boat from Las Vegas. I think *she's* our guide." Belladonna pointed with her chin at a blond woman in a standard issue Echo OpOne outfit, stepping gingerly around piles of rubble.

Red Saviour forced a smile.

The petite woman who stopped before them stooped slightly, as if hiding from enemies in the shadows. Cropped blond hair dangled over her forehead. The collar of her Echo uniform was drawn tight around her neck, and long black gloves covered her hands. Her bright blue eyes never rested on one spot for long, and especially not on someone's eyes. She had an Echo-issue messenger bag on one shoulder, and a bottle of water clenched tightly in one hand.

"You have business with us?" Red Saviour asked with an arched eyebrow.

"Oh, yes. I'm sorry. Victoria Victrix Nagy. Vickie." She extended a hand. "Echo OpOne."

The two women introduced themselves to her. Red Saviour remembered to smile. "Nagy. Russian?"

"Hungarian." The young woman paused. "With many ties to the old country."

"The American South is not being what I expected."

"Oh, this is Atlanta, not the South. An hour out and you'd see the difference." Vickie took a deep breath but found no words to follow it. An awkward silence settled over the women.

Belladonna broke it with a thoughtful nod. She gestured at the still uncleared debris. "I know, it's bad. Were you on the campus when it happened?"

"No. It's not that." She shook her head. "Never mind. You ladies ready for a whirlwind tour of our fair city? They gave me orders to drive you for two hours."

"I have no choice. Please to lead on." Red Saviour tugged at her tunic impatiently.

Vickie led the trio to a purpose-built Echo sedan. The gull-wing doors lifted out of the chassis as they approached.

"Fancy," Red Saviour said. "Such decadence is unbecoming in law enforcement." Nevertheless, she folded her tall frame into the front seat without difficulty.

Belladonna patted the extended doors as she climbed into the back seat. "Better for car chases. Easier to fire out of with a sub-machine gun."

Vickie practically shrank into position to drive the vehicle. She thumb-swiped the tops of two Echo prescription bottles, which clicked and allowed two pills each to fall in her gloved palm. She very deliberately placed them on her tongue and then squirted water in after them, swallowing with just a hint of frown. Bella knew capsule color and stripe codes by heart, like any long-term pro in emergency medicine, and she could tell these were heavy-duty antianxiety drugs. Someone new to her powers, maybe? Or did their driver have deeper problems than that?

Vickie pulled her seatbelt tight and pressed the ignition button. The car emitted a quiet hum. The sound of gravel crunching drowned out the electric motor as they rolled into the street. Vickie's knuckles were probably white under the gloves, by the way she held the wheel.

"First time in a broadcast power car?" Belladonna said to Red Saviour.

"*Da.* Feels like amusement park ride."

"They're a lot like hybrids, except the batteries are continually topped off by Tesla-design broadcast power as long as they're in range of the towers. A lot are still standing. There's also a tiny gasoline generator, for long distances. These babies can do zero to sixty in five seconds. They top out at one hundred eighty miles per hour."

Red Saviour mentally converted the figure to kilometers and whistled. "Quite acceptable for police work." She tapped the glass of the windshield. "Bulletproof?"

"And armored. Ramming plates front and back.

We're riding in the smallest, quietest tank on the planet. Better than an armored personnel carrier, actually. You may have seen some of these used by heads of state."

"I am being impressed."

Vickie managed a shy grin. "Unfortunately, the rest of our trip won't be so impressive. Atlanta's a mess right now," she commented. Her voice had a tremor in it. As if to illustrate her point, she maneuvered the car around a crater in the road, roped off with yellow police tape and orange cones.

"I haven't seen much yet," Belladonna said. "They settled me into a bunk in a trailer first thing. Folks are spooked around here."

"Who can blame them? The Nazis made a beeline for Echo HQ."

Red Saviour found the control pad for the window and lowered it before lighting another cigarette. "Is true that Echo has giant statue who fended off Nazi force?"

"It is," Vickie said. "But I didn't see him. They drove him back to Stone Mountain before I . . . before I was activated."

"Drove him back?"

"They sat him on a massive flatbed truck used for moving cranes. Actually two trucks. The first one's suspension gave out halfway through Tucker." She glanced at the Russian heroine. "It's not easy being a hundred feet tall."

"We could have used a giant in Moscow."

An awkward silence settled over the car. At last Belladonna spoke. "Casualties?"

"Most of my team." Red Saviour puffed on her cigarette. "Hundreds of civilians."

"That's . . . appalling."

"What is appalling is being forced to stay in America while bureaucrats replace my CCCP with army of blundering idiots in metal monkey suits. And *I* should be in field commanding search teams. Oh, but look, here is being Waffle House. Again. *Horosho*. Is important I see these things."

The car passed a brightly lit Waffle House, ubiquitous in Atlanta. A vinyl sign hung under the iconic yellow tiled sign: STILL OPEN FOR BUSINESS. FOOD BANK DROP BOX.

Belladonna's blue face darkened. "I know what you mean. I should be in Las Vegas. LVFD took as hard a hit as Echo."

"Why Tesla thinks now is time for niceties is beyond my understanding. Our united purpose is clear: search and destroy. What is need for secretive discussions?"

Red Saviour and Belladonna watched the city pass by in silence, mulling over their resentments. Vickie drove north on side streets into downtown Atlanta, where sodium lights flickered on in anticipation of dusk. Storefronts stood dark; some had been boarded up. The usual tourist foot traffic had disappeared, leaving only the homeless and the sinister.

"It's weird to see it so quiet," Vickie said with an odd hint of relief. "Hard Rock Cafe, Planet Hollywood. Tourist traps, and all empty."

"I know of Hard Rock. Is giant one in Moscow on Old Arbat Road."

"You've been there?"

"Was thrown through window by giant robot. I think I crushed guitar of Dean Reed. I did not stay long enough to find out." Red Saviour sniffed. "I do not welcome such capitalist decadence in my country.

Old Arbat was once beautiful historical district. Now is magnet for credit cards and spoiled youth. Fortunately, Range Rovers smash robots well."

"But your people have embraced capitalism," Belladonna said. "Democracy, free markets, freedom of the press. Don't you think these are improvements over the Communist authoritarian state?"

Red Saviour gave her a cold look. "I *am* an authoritarian, *sestra*. My father fought to uphold power of the State and I carry on his legacy."

"Ah. I see."

"You are surprised?" She indicated the hammer-and-sickle badge on her uniform. "I do not wear this because capitalist outfit is being at cleaners. Law and order requires strong State. Without strict controls, there is no incentive for capitalists to curb their greed."

"In America we vote."

"You can vote for puppet president, not for plutocrats who are tugging on his strings. Power in this country hides in dark back room filled with cigar smoke and deal-making."

"And in Soviet Russia, decisions were made by democratically elected officials? Spare me, please. I may be a lefty but I'm not naïve. How does a Russian make their voice heard in the government?"

"By getting job with government, like me. I serve the proletariat."

"And are you serving them right now, or just being trundled around Atlanta by flunkies while Tesla and your people decide your fate?"

Red Saviour opened and shut her mouth. Belladonna moved in for the kill.

"Our leaders may make a lot of noise about patriotic

nonsense, but they know the American people won't let them cross the line. If any politician infringes on our rights and gets caught, there's hell to pay. We've fired presidents for that crap. When's the last time Russia impeached a corrupt politician without using tanks? 1905?"

After a pregnant pause, Red Saviour grated out: "You are having lot of nerve to speak to me so."

"Nerve is one thing I never run short on."

"Ladies, please," Vickie said. "Can we find a less divisive topic? Or should I drop you off at the gym for a few rounds in the ring?"

The woman in red and the woman in blue locked eyes over the seat back, jaws clenched, brows furrowed. At last Belladonna looked away with a frown. "She's the guest here, I suppose. Do whatever she wants."

"*Da*, I am guest. Get me out of this consumer playground and take me to where proletariat lives. We will see how well American Dream is playing out in big city."

"That would be south Atlanta," Vickie said. "It was rough before the Nazis plowed through it on the way to Echo HQ. Now it's a total mess. Echo sent several teams over to quell riots and looting."

"Is perfect. Step on gas . . . or whatever car uses."

Within minutes they had left the gathered skyscrapers behind. By a series of overpasses braided around each other, Vickie entered the sporadic traffic on I-20, the east-west corridor leading to the poorest sections of Atlanta. Military vehicles and ambulances mixed with utility trucks, big rigs and police cruisers. No high-glitz vehicles were anywhere to be seen.

"I don't know that part of town so well," she told Red Saviour, who only shrugged and watched the industrial warehouses pass beneath them. "Are you sure you want to go there?"

"Of course. Is where action is, as is said in movies."

Vickie blew air out her cheeks and hunched forward over the wheel. Red Saviour gave her a sidelong look.

"You're frightened. I see it in your shoulders."

"Just concerned. Mr. Tesla is counting on me."

"To what? Control overbearing Russian metahuman? Ha!" Red Saviour snorted a laugh. "Is good joke I make. No one, man or woman, has ever controlled me."

"Not even Worker's Champion?" Belladonna said with a smirk.

"Keep testing me, little blue girl, can put ice pack on yourself." A look of consternation crossed her face as Vickie exited the highway. "Why are we stopping?"

"I, ah, I need to check something..." Vickie's voice was small even in the silent car. "Just...just relax, okay?"

The exit ramp deposited the sedan directly on a street, just north of an intersection. Vickie pulled up to the curb and stopped. She lowered her head to the steering wheel.

"Are you carsick?" Belladonna asked, placing a hand on her shoulder. "I can cure that in a jiffy. I am a healer, you know."

"I'm fine. Can I have a minute?" Her voice almost cracked. "Alone?"

Red Saviour and Belladonna exchanged a look. "Sure, Vickie. Take your time. The Commissar needs a smoke anyway." The two women stepped out of the vehicle.

Red Saviour lit up a cigarette. "Agoraphobia," she said quietly. "Or maybe panic attacks. Or both."

Belladonna raised an eyebrow. "Very good. I saw it too. You have medical training?"

"Five years in *militsya*. We received EMT training, victim evaluation, such things. I learned to tell difference between serious threat, drunk and mental patient." She pointed with her cigarette. "She is no soldier. Was probably seamstress or grocer. Poor comrade is barely holding head on straight."

"Our bickering probably didn't help."

The Russian grunted. "She should stay out of Russia, then. Arguing is our favorite pastime." She craned her neck to survey the street. "Hmm. Very downtrodden, like Moscow ghetto. Economic class disparity in your country astounds me."

Belladonna sighed sadly. "It astounds us too, those who care."

"I suppose this is what we have to look forward to in my country, unless Communist Party can regain trust of people. Allure of televisions and fashion accessories have wiped memory of Marx from the proletariat's mind."

"Then you're catching up with the rest of the world. Consumer culture seems to be the norm." The blue meta snorted; she didn't seem particularly happy about that.

Red Saviour peered into the gloom. "It takes many forms. Look."

On the next block, a dozen young men, black and white, stood on the corner. Their exaggerated gestures conveyed their bluff machismo even at a distance. One leaned on a stopped car, passing a plastic bag into the open window and accepting a wad of cash in return. The car sped off and the man rejoined his friends.

"Drug dealers. You have heroin here?"

"Crack's predominant in the south. Out west it was meth." Belladonna screwed up her face in distaste.

"This is tolerated? Where are being *militsya*?"

"Cops? Probably on riot duty. These jerks are small fry."

Red Saviour cast her cigarette aside and started forward with long strides. Her hands glowed with azure fire.

"Hey! What are you doing?" Belladonna ran to her side.

"Frying small fries. Drug trafficking is crime."

"Easy, lady. Echo tries not to step on the local police department's toes." She interposed herself between the Russian and the drug dealers down the street. "Plus there's the Extreme Force law."

"*Horosho*! Now you are talking my language." Red Saviour grinned widely, appearing genuinely happy. "I approve of extreme force."

"No, no. The law *prohibits* the use of metahuman Extreme Force against non-metas except in life or death circumstances." She jerked a thumb at the dealers. "It sounds crazy but we should radio this in and let the boys in blue handle it. They get touchy if we steal their fire."

"Ridiculous."

"Every country has laws governing extralegal metahuman organizations like Echo to prevent abuses of power. I'm sure Russia has such laws for Echo."

"I *am* Russia's Echo, and I am bound by no such foolish law. Are you going to stop me from arresting these perps?"

"Did you say perps?" Vickie asked.

"'Perps' is term learned from military advisor who liked American cop shows," Red Saviour answered.

Belladonna chewed her lip. "How will you arrest them? You're not licensed. You can't even make a citizen's arrest."

Red Saviour took her hand. "Then I will need you. Come with me, citizen." She tugged Belladonna down the shoulder of the road. Atlanta was notorious for lacking sidewalks.

"Listen, Saviour—"

"Commissar."

Belladonna lowered her voice as they came within speaking distance of their prey. "Okay, Commissar, I grant you that these scum are breaking all sorts of laws, but they're more symptoms of a greater problem. The Narcotics Division works every angle to find these guys' suppliers, higher up the food chain. Brute-force tactics only interfere with their investigations."

But Red Saviour had reached the outer fringe of the group. In the orange light, Belladonna's blue skin appeared to be a dusky—and normal—brown. The men hooted at the two women and made lewd suggestions.

"Hey, baby," said the man who had sold drugs to the occupants of the car. He smoothed his overgrown mullet. "Damn, you look fine. What can I do for you?"

Red Saviour jerked a thumb at Belladonna. "My friend here is wanting to know name of your supplier."

"My—huh? Why?"

"So she can move up food chain. Please to give name and location."

The other dealers gathered behind him, muttering suspiciously. The mullet-haired man shook his head and chuckled. "I can't do that, darlin'. You want sweets, you buy from Timmy T."

With lightning speed, Red Saviour decked him. His jaw broke with a loud, sickly crack. "Is wrong answer, Mr. T. I will ask your friends." She stepped over his writhing form to face a massive black man with cornrows. "You, *bolshoi* big man. Give me name and location of your supplier."

"Hell I will," he said, balling up his meaty fist and swinging at her. With *Systema*'s deceptive casualness, she caught his arm and slammed him into the ground. Bracing her foot, she twisted his arm until the bone snapped, and let the arm flop to the ground. The bone jutted out from the skin. The man shrieked and bled, and stayed down, clutching at the break.

"Christ," Belladonna said, sounding both appalled and in awe.

"I will ask again," Red Saviour announced. Her next target flinched away from her. She grabbed his collar. "Your supplier, *svinya!* Be smart and spill beans."

"Lemme go!"

"My friend is being authorized to arrest you." She pulled the man to her. "All I can do is hurt you."

The dealer's eyes were wild. "You a cop?"

"*Nyet*. I am a Communist." At her grin, the man strained to escape.

Belladonna stepped forward. "Echo OpTwo Belladonna Blue. You boys are all under arrest for selling illicit substances."

Two of the men laughed. Two looked worried. Several pulled aside their oversized jackets to reveal handguns.

"There ain't but three of you," one man said. "How 'bout we whip your asses like them Nazis did?"

"Three?" Red Saviour glanced back to see Vickie, as pale as a sheet, standing behind them. "You should stay in car, *sestra*," she said softly.

"Belladonna's right. This is a police matter," Vickie said, her voice thin. "I've made the call."

"Cops don't care. They ain't comin'," the dealer said with a sneer. "This town's *ours* now."

"Not while I'm here," Belladonna said, her voice hard. "Or while I visit."

"Right." Vickie took a deep breath. "I can subdue them until the police arrive."

"*Nyet.* Extreme Force law, yes? No powers." Red Saviour twisted her captive's arm behind him. "Will have to restraint them old-fashioned way." She kicked out his legs and threw him to the sidewalk. His squeal of pain was cut off by a quick kick to the head.

The swift act of brutality ended the standoff. As one of the dealers surged forward, Red Saviour grabbed the fist of her first attacker, broke it, and kneed the man in the stomach as he sailed past her. She spun around him and punched another dealer in the face.

"*Davay, davay!* Come on, my friends!" There was no mistaking the savage joy in her cry.

Belladonna hesitated. "I'm a DCO now. I'm not supposed to fight!" Nevertheless, she performed an aikido throw on the man who dove at her. "I'm a healer!"

"Someone has to be hurt before you can heal them," Red Saviour called back. "Must I do all work myself?" A fist caught her in the jaw. She grinned and wiped blood from her lip, then seized the man's arm and cast him at a nearby attacker with a club.

"Look! A weapon. This qualifies for life or death, *nyet*?"

"*Nyet*," Belladonna said. "Has to be lethal."

"Club can be lethal," the Russian said, pouting. "Vickie! I am needing backup from you. Please to injure someone."

Vickie backed away from two advancing thugs, hands

up to ward off their attacks. Tears spilled down her cheeks. "I . . . can't. I can't! Stay back!"

"I'll give you a reason to cry," her attacker said. "You better bring your game, you gonna mess with us."

She stumbled out of the way as the other man lunged at her. His laughter was the harsh laughter of a sadist with a victim in his sights.

Red Saviour pushed through the mob gathering around her to reach Vickie. "Fight them!" she shouted. A drug dealer grabbed her hair and pulled her back into the arms of his cohorts. A dozen hands clawed at her. She had lost her advantage of mobility.

"Damn it," Belladonna said, clenching her fists. The blue girl's orders crippled her, Red Saviour realized. As a Damage Control Officer—a role that Soviette filled in CCCP—she was to let her teammates do the fighting, and instead concentrate on healing and protecting bystanders. Yet Vickie was as helpless as a bystander, and the rest of Bella's "team" consisted only of Natalya. If this was law enforcement in America, Red Saviour wanted no part of it. The FSO council of old men were permissive in comparison.

"She mine," a cruel voice nearby said, and with a glint of steel gave Red Saviour the opening she needed. A knife glittered in his hand, and his smile promised that he knew how to use it.

"Knife!" Red Saviour strained to be heard over the chaos. "Is life or death?"

"Yes!" Belladonna said.

"*Horosho.*" Energy had been surging inside her, excited by the danger of the fight. Now she could release it. Her fists glowed once again. Those restraining her jumped back in alarm. So did the knife wielder.

"Oh man. Take it easy, lady," he said.

Red Saviour laughed and unleashed a blast of blue-edged energy. It enveloped the man and hurled him out into the street, a limp lump of flesh.

"Medic! Please to fix him." She cast about for the thugs menacing Vickie. Neither they nor the metahuman were anywhere to be found.

"We have lost Nagy," she said. "Let us finish quickly." With a glowing hand, she swatted a man away with a disturbing crunch of breaking bones. "Fix him next."

A cluster of dealers had backed away and drawn their guns. Red Saviour launched into the air on a column of energy and hurtled down into their midst. Her fists struck the ground; the resulting explosion of energy sent the remaining criminals sprawling.

"Oops. More damage to control." Red Saviour grinned. "Medic on team is being very useful. I do not need to restrain myself."

Belladonna cradled the knife fighter's body. "If you don't mind leaving these men as cripples."

"I will lose no sleep over it." She sent a blast into the back of a fleeing drug dealer. "These *svinyas* have made their choice. I am the consequence."

A wounded drug dealer raised his gun and took aim at Red Saviour's back. Belladonna spotted him from her vantage point on the ground and hurled a bolt of psychic energy at the man's mind. His eyes bulged and he collapsed in a quivering heap with a strangled squeak. Red Saviour spun on her heels, fists ready.

"Got your back," Belladonna said with a hint of satisfaction.

"*Spasibo*. I think we have run out of citizen arrests to make."

"Where's Vickie?"

"*Borzemoi*! I had forgotten her."

Belladonna flicked on her comm unit. "Come in, Vickie. Where are you?"

A plaintive voice with a metallic twang came over the tiny speaker. "I'm sorry. I couldn't help it." Vickie said. "I'm so sorry..."

The blue girl frowned. "We need your location."

They heard only the sound of sobbing.

"She's losing it," Belladonna said. "She couldn't have gone far."

"She is in that alley." Red Saviour pointed down the street.

"How do you know?"

"I could hear voice resonating on ventilation grill. Enclosed space." She began to build up energy. "Tend to wounded. I will bring her back." Blue light illuminated them as she released a burst of energy from her feet and shot into the sky. She arced over the street, towards the alleyway.

A pair of large mounds of concrete and asphalt guarded the entrance to the alley, making it inaccessible to cars. Victoria Victrix huddled against a dumpster. She had closed off from the world, arms covering her head. Blond hair fell in a curtain over her face. She shook with sobs.

The two drug dealers who had pursued her were nowhere to be seen.

Red Saviour cut off her propulsion and let her momentum carry her into the alley. She hit the ground and rolled into a crouch. The American showed all the signs of a full-fledged panic attack; using a blast of energy to land like a rocket would only upset her further. She noted with mild satisfaction the metallic grate over the woman's head.

"*Sestra*." Red Saviour laid a gentle hand on her shoulder. Victoria pulled away with a gasp. "Victoria, please listen to me. You are being safe. I am here now."

Belladonna's voice chirped in the woman's earpiece. Red Saviour removed it with careful, nonthreatening movements. "Commissar here. Can you hear me?"

"Yes. Is she injured?"

"No injuries here, just one frightened *devushka*." She surveyed the alley. "And no sign of attackers."

"Roger that. I'll stay here with your...perps. They'll live. I think."

"*Horosho.*" Red Saviour pocketed the device and turned her attention to the sobbing woman. "Victoria, please to be talking to me. Are you all right?"

Her nod was almost imperceptible in the dim light, but the woman tried to squeeze herself into a tighter ball. Natalya searched her memory for her *militsya* commander Yvegeny Petrovich's advice on agoraphobics. Perceived threats frighten them as much as real ones, he had said. They want to hide from the world.

Thus Vickie had squeezed into the smallest space she could find. Deliberately, Red Saviour interposed her body between Vickie and the rest of the world. Their hair intermingled, and when their foreheads touched, and Vickie did not flinch, Natalya knew she had crossed a threshold. She slowed her breathing to match Vickie's.

"Is all right," she said, wishing her English vocabulary contained more words of comfort. "Will be fine. You are safe." She repeated the words: *all right, safe, fine, okay.*

Her ungloved hand pulled Vickie's gloved hand from her face and squeezed it. Victoria's breath came in big gulping heaves, but her eyelids flickered open. For minutes, they held hands and breathed, while Red Saviour whispered the soothing phrases over and over.

A rock fell off the nearest pile with a clatter that echoed in the quiet alley. Red Saviour leapt to her feet, fists aglow. Yet there was no one in the alley besides her and her charge.

Another rock tipped off the mound as she watched.

"I was scared..." Vickie whispered, and the shame in her voice became evident.

Realization hit Natalya all at once: two attackers. *Two piles of rocks.*

She dashed forward and struck at the pile. Concrete shards and asphalt chunks spattered against the alley walls. A human hand quivered in the dirt.

"Oh, *nasrat!*" Using her power to blast away the stone, she dug the criminal out of the pile of rocks. Dirt clung to his skin and clothes. She felt for a pulse: weak, but present. With care she laid him on the ground and switched to the other pile.

Dust and gravel fell from the man's mouth and nostrils. Red Saviour could feel no pulse in his neck. Roughly, she cleared his passages. He hung limp in her arms. She spread him out and began CPR.

After thirty seconds of compressing the man's chest and blowing air through his filthy mouth, his body convulsed in a cough. She turned him over and let him vomit out the remaining material in his system.

Belladonna's voice came over the comm unit. Red Saviour answered it: "Commissar."

"How's our girl?"

Red Saviour glanced over at Victoria Victrix, who had unraveled herself to a normal sitting position on the ground, yet still had not raised her head to acknowledge her surroundings. Blue strobe lights reflected through the alley now. "She will be fine. Is perps you should worry about."

"What did you do to them?"

"Saved their lives. You did not tell me our meek friend had aspirations to follow in Premier Khrushchev's footsteps."

"Ah . . . what? Never mind. Atlanta PD are on the scene. I'm heading over."

Belladonna drove them back to Victoria's apartment in Peachtree Park. Red Saviour kept an arm around the woman's shoulders as they walked her to the rickety elevator and escorted her to her door. A gray tabby hissed at them as Victoria pushed the door open with a shaky hand. He interposed himself between her and Red Saviour as though he were a protective parent. She shoved him aside with her foot and got a swipe as a reward.

"Nice kitty," she snarled. "Where is pest control?"

"Sit her on the couch," Belladonna said.

Victoria Victrix tilted her head back and exhaled. Home at last, she relaxed for the first time since they had met her. The cat leapt into her lap and smothered her with purrs. She removed one of her gloves to stroke his fur—and despite the dim, incandescent light, Red Saviour noticed ugly mottling and knotty ridges on the back of her hand. And the fingers were almost skeletal.

She tried not to stare, though her eyes could not resist swooping in for more visual clues. Instead, she scanned the woman's bookshelves, crammed with the spines of both popular paperback romances and leather-bound tomes in unrecognizable languages, DVDs and CDs, all carefully arranged and orderly. They formed not a collection but a reference library.

Belladonna brought her a warmed cup of coffee, which she accepted with her gloved hand.

"Thank you," she said. "I'm sure you didn't expect to have to babysit a meta tonight."

Red Saviour pursed her lips, biting back a reply. Belladonna smiled sweetly at the woman. "Part of our job. Just relax and decompress here. We'll return the cruiser and file a report. About the arrests, that is." The unspoken question hung in the air.

"*Da*. You have earned your rest." Red Saviour proffered a hand. "Was good to meet you, Victoria."

"And you." Again, Victoria used her gloved hand. "I appreciate your backup. I—I have a lot of ramping up to do."

"Bring shovel next time." Red Saviour winked at her. They left wordlessly, as if both were unwilling to let anything be said where others could eavesdrop.

Back in the car, Red Saviour lit up a cigarette and savored the harsh bite of the Russian tobacco. "She is dangerous. Too much power, no control. Tesla must be desperate to activate so unreliable an asset."

"We need all the metahuman help we can find."

"*Nyet*, you do not understand me. Comrade Victoria is not metahuman, or if she is, is not where her power is from. Was magic that nearly killed those *svinyas*. Are you familiar with magic?"

"I grew up in Las Vegas. Of course I am."

"Not trickery. *Sorcery*." She uttered the word carefully, as though it were the very thing it described. "My country is ancient land. There are those unwise enough to explore the dark old ways banished by Orthodox Church. Do you know story of Rasputin?"

Belladonna nodded, keeping her eyes on the road.

"*Nyet*. You only know official story, which church issued to quell frightened population and to discourage curious workers from exploring same paths. Rasputin truly possessed magical powers gleaned from his research into ancient traditions. He was killed—with difficulty, as you know—to prevent him from spreading knowledge, but ideas carry on wind like seedlings."

She paused to draw smoke into her lungs as if to scourge a memory. "I have dealt with his kind, his inheritors. Magic is poison. We saw things—from our own minds—that cannot be forgotten."

"Hallucinations."

"Nothing so simple. I cannot explain it well—this is nature of magic. Cannot be explained, cannot be controlled. Echo would be well served to eliminate any practitioner of magic as precaution."

"Eliminate? You can't seriously mean we should kill Vickie?"

"*Da*. And cat, for safety's sake. Is preemptive strike. She may be on your side now, but that is being almost as dangerous. Did she bury perpetrators out of fear or out of spite?"

"Fear, obviously." Belladonna cast her a sidelong look. "Besides, if magic is so unpredictable, that could be good for our side. I think you're overreacting. If she's Echo, it means she can be trusted."

"I only trust what I can control. Good intentions can change to bad with simple twist."

"And then there are people like me, who give trust to get trust."

"I am here to protect innocents like you."

"We 'innocents' are here to help you, or at least save you from yourself." Belladonna started the car and pulled away from the curb.

"Or so you want us to believe."

"Jesus, Natalya, that's some classic Soviet paranoia, there. The Cold War ended long ago."

Red Saviour raised an eyebrow at her.

"Oh, how rude of me. I mean, *Commissar.*"

The honorific hung heavy in the air. Passing street-lights animated the seat between them with sharp-edged shadows.

At last Red Saviour smiled. "Natalya is fine, Comrade Bella."

They found Nikolai, Worker's Champion, and Alex Tesla standing at the lip of a crater partly obscured by rubble from the collapsed administration building. Crews had roped off the site into a grid. A metahuman with robotic arms dug patiently through the concrete and steel as construction workers directed halogen lamps to shine into the holes he created.

Red Saviour introduced Belladonna to her father and Worker's Champion. Both looked pleased when the blue girl greeted them in Russian.

"Back so soon, my dear?" Nikolai kissed his daughter on both cheeks. The formal greeting made her suspicious.

"I have seen enough. Mr. Tesla has much work to do to restore order in Atlanta. I am reminded of the work that awaits us back home."

Nikolai cleared his throat. "*Da, da.* Well, you see... about that, my Wolfling—"

"You are staying," Worker's Champion interrupted. "Piotr Dzhavakhishvili will make the arrangements."

She stared at them, stunned. Her father gave her an apologetic smile and shrugged.

"You—you are teasing," she said in Russian. The ground seemed to cling to her, the Southern humidity a dewy net. "You cannot be serious."

Alex Tesla stepped forward to shake her hand. "I can't tell you how much we appreciate your generous offer. They said you had suggested it on the plane ride over. Really, we're touched."

She barely gripped his hand; her eyes never left her fellow Russians' faces.

"Since you two have had some time to get to know each other, perhaps Ms. Parker will be willing to serve as your liaison while your team establishes itself in the city."

Belladonna raised an eyebrow at Red Saviour. "I can do that."

Tesla offered his own weary smile. "As the man said, 'this could be the start of a beautiful friendship.'"

Red Saviour shook her head from side to side, slowly, as if denial could erase the terrible orders she was receiving from Worker's Champion, her father, and by extension, the government itself.

This was not reassignment—this was exile.

CHAPTER SEVEN

Headhunters

DENNIS LEE & MERCEDES LACKEY

In a lone cell deep within the shattered Echo headquarters in Atlanta, Red Djinni was coping with his latest crisis. He sat, motionless, and stared at a list of names clutched tightly in his hand. Across from him a hulking figure leaned against the cell wall, watching, his arms crossed.

If only he would twitch a little, would reveal *anything*. In the short time he had known him, Red had conceded that this man, this Bulwark, was inscrutable. This worried Red, who had made a career out of reading people.

Red went through the list of names again. It wasn't a very long list. Even now, desperate for bodies to fill the void left by the invasion, Echo was only willing to go so far in lowering their standards for meta-powered personnel. Each name had a criminal record of some sort, but mostly misdemeanors and nonviolent felonies. During Red's short career in the metahuman underground, he had encountered many such individuals. While he was surprised by how many he had burned his bridges with, he was amazed to be presented with a near complete listing of their names. Bulwark couldn't have concocted this list from Red's records. If he had, Echo would have had enough to put Red away for the duration. If they knew all the details of Red's life as a mercenary and thief, they wouldn't have done this. They wouldn't have been able to trust him.

The list, as far as Red could see, was a compilation of people that he had completely screwed over. Criminals, all of them, and he was now charged with finding them, approaching them, and convincing them to be law-abiding supercops. He was convinced. There was a God—a God who watched, pulled his little strings, and laughed at his puppets with a keen sense of humor.

At long last, Red looked up. His face, though cloaked by his signature scarf, couldn't hide his resignation. He squinted up at Bulwark in disbelief.

"You don't approve?" Bulwark rumbled.

"You have got to be kidding," Red snorted. "How did you come up with *this* lot?"

"From what was left of our data banks. These were the names flagged with potential for rehabilitation."

Red pointed at one name. "This guy's an arsonist!"

"He picked his targets carefully," Bulwark countered. "He's never actually harmed anyone. His psych profile suggests therapy may help."

"All right then—" Red tapped three more names. "Kleptomaniac; extreme, bipolar, wacky fun time; and this one has spastic panic attacks at the sight of her own super slobber."

"We don't discriminate on account of mental disorders. We can help these people just as much as they can help us."

"You say that now. I wonder if you would feel the same after being on the receiving end of anxiety-induced hundred-mile-an-hour projectile vomit."

"I imagine I would," Bulwark replied. "I'll just stand behind you."

Red paused, and then chuckled. "Funny. When did you develop a sense of humor?"

Bulwark shrugged. "I noticed you quell your opponent's arguments with levity. I surmised the same tactics might work on you."

"Typical," Red muttered, shaking his head. "Leave it to you to find the cold, calculating side of comedy."

"You will find them?" Bulwark asked. It wasn't really a question.

"I said I would!" Red snapped, his eyes falling back to the list. "I just don't know where to start."

"Go by the numbers," Bulwark suggested. "By location, who might we attempt to approach in one trip? Who might be the most amenable to joining an organization like Echo? Which are the most likely to earn our trust?"

"Earn your trust?" Red said. "I hope that's not your opening line."

"Unfortunately, it is. We can't afford to get careless here. Oh, and speaking of—" Bulwark stepped forward and shackled Red's wrist with a stout metallic bracelet.

"The *hell*—?"

With a soft click, the metal began to hum as tiny red-and-green LEDs flashed into existence across the inflexible band. After a moment, the humming and lights subsided. The bracelet, however, was locked tight around Red's forearm.

"Nothing to worry about," Bulwark said, gauging

the anger that flashed from Red's eyes. "It's just a tracer. Standard issue when we're transporting felons. It'll give us a lock on your position, in the unfortunate case that we get...separated."

Red took a few calming breaths. "I suppose this means you're coming with me."

Bulwark nodded. "I am, and a few of my trainees. I figure this sort of field exercise would be of use to them."

"And you don't think having a small army of Echo Ops descending on your quarry just might make them a wee bit skittish?"

"Oh, we're hardly an army; just a training master, a few rookies and one of their own—you. I think we'll be just fine."

Red held up his arm. "And this? What if I don't care for this arrangement?"

Bulwark spread his hands in a mock gesture of helplessness. "Then we're at an impasse. The tracer is not negotiable. It's been hardwired with fairly stiff countermeasures. The casing is self-enclosed so you can't pick the lock. If tampered with, the tracer will inject you with enough GHB to drop you instantly and send out an immediate location beacon. Now, if you want to renege on our agreement, you can stay in this cell until we get around to bringing you up on whatever charges we find."

Bulwark held up a hand, halting Red's retort. "Yes, yes, I know, we can only hold you so long on charges. But I just had the most informative chat with some of our detectives. As you know, we don't have much at the moment, but I'm sure we can pin *something* on you, given enough time. And wouldn't you know it? We've got a state of emergency on our hands. This has given us license for a certain laxity in holding procedure. Who knows? This might drag on for years. What do you think are the odds of finding some damning piece of evidence on you, or stumbling across some willing witness if we applied enough pressure?"

Bulwark didn't wait for an answer. He turned and opened the door to Red's cell.

"We're taking no chances, and you're no exception. So where do you think we should start? I can have a transport prepped and waiting within the hour."

Red glared at him, and gave the list one last look. Bulwark watched him sag and knew he had won.

"Detroit," Red growled. "We're going to Detroit."

Descending from an altitude of 18,000 feet, Echo Transport 72 entered Michigan airspace after enjoying a turbulence-free flight with sunny skies. The carrier, resembling more a pregnant whale than the sleek, swift jets used by Echo's rescue crews, was one of dozens brought out of retirement to fly daily allotment sorties spanning the continent. The invasion had crippled Echo in some cities more than others, and the quartermasters had been working feverishly to reallocate their remaining resources. Transport 72 was filled to capacity, a testament to the heavy losses experienced by the Motor City. Loaded with supplies, weapons and a handful of armored vehicles, the flight manifest would not have normally allowed for passengers. Bulwark had pulled a few strings. The Detroit branch office would have to do with one less APC, at least for a day.

Huddled together between crates of burst rifles

and ammunition, three Echo trainees lounged on makeshift seats. Scope, the oldest and most seasoned of Bulwark's apprentices, had remained silent for the bulk of the trip. She seemed absorbed in repetitive cycles of dismantling and assembling her new side-arms, checking and rechecking that the parts were well oiled and calibrated.

To her left was the picture of tranquility. Harmony, a statuesque girl with long flowing blond hair, sat in lotus position with a thin smile tugging at her lips.

To Scope's right, the young boy known as Acrobat continued to rock back and forth, his arms wrapped around his knees. For the entire flight he had not stopped talking, and only about one thing.

"Can't believe it," he whispered *again*. "Wow. Can't believe it. Red Djinni. It's Red Djinni. We're working with Red Djinni."

On the other side of the cargo hold, Bulwark sat sifting through a stack of reports. Behind him, Red sat with his legs crossed, his back to them all, staring intently into a mirror.

"Check him out," Acrobat continued. "Guy's a rock. He hasn't moved in an hour."

With a grunt, Scope put down her assembled pistol, reached over and smacked Acrobat across the head. He yelped in surprise.

"Not going to tell you again, Bruno," she growled. "Knock it off."

Acrobat rubbed his head and shot her a hurt look. She didn't notice.

"I'm sick of hearing your fanboy crap," she muttered, and appraised Red with a glance. "Besides, he don't look like much to me. He can change his face.

So what? Don't know what Bull expects us to learn from this guy, stupid power like that."

"He's gotta have something else," Acrobat insisted. "I heard he's the guy that infiltrated the Goldman Catacombs. They say he, like, teleported in or something. How else could he have gotten past the motion sensors? And remember those hits on Horatio and Crackdown? Word is the Djinni did them solo. They were found together, both decapitated. Clean cuts too, right through their reinforced neck harnesses. Dude must be hiding some major muscle!"

Scope answered with another smack to Acrobat's head.

"Scope!" Bulwark barked across the cargo hold. "He better have deserved that!"

"Yes, sir!" Scope answered, coming to attention. "He did, sir!"

"Very good," Bulwark replied, looking back to his reports. "As you were."

Scope sat down and turned to Acrobat. "First, the Goldman Catacombs were never infiltrated. That was a hoax. Second, Horatio and Crackdown were taken out by the Blood Brothers, everyone knows that. Third, you're an idiot. I liked you better when you were too shy to take a dump without permission, much less shooting your mouth off every ten seconds with the latest from the Geek Report and IPwnHotGirls.com."

Acrobat turned red and pouted in petulant anger.

"I'm *not* a geek," he mumbled.

"Sure you are."

"Am not. I'm a *superhero*."

"I rest my case," Scope replied and resumed inspecting her pistols.

At last, Harmony chimed in, her voice gentle and

soothing. "Scope, will you please put those guns away? They're making ripples in my peace pool."

"Never," Scope replied, touching the cold metal and fiber grips with reverence. "State of emergency, girls! I finally get to carry a real piece. Thank God for the Invasion!"

She paused, and then muttered a low curse. In her excitement, her voice had carried a little too far. She caught Bulwark's gaze over his papers. Red Djinni, who had finished altering his face, had turned around. They both shared the same, pained look.

Scope stood up, her mouth open, trapped in the awkward tension. She didn't have the words. She was saved by static as the transport's speakers blared to life.

"We're about to set down in Detroit, folks. Best get up here and strap yourselves in."

Bulwark gathered his files and marched away. Scope ran to catch up with him, tripping over herself in apology.

"Sir? Sir? Hey, Bull, wait—"

Harmony, her expression now marked with sadness, gathered up her yoga mat and followed at a respectful distance. Bringing up the rear, Red walked alongside Acrobat, who seemed simultaneously apprehensive and giddy by Red's proximity.

"Hey, kid," Red whispered. Acrobat felt a star-struck jolt of terror. "Remind me later to tell you how I cut through those neck guards."

As Red steered the old rusted Ford into the alley, he dimmed the lights and eased the old boat to a halt. The car was an obvious choice; it blended in with the surroundings. He had chosen an appropriately worn face and threadbare work clothes to complete the illusion that he was just another blue-collar worker. He was pleased to note that Bulwark had followed his lead, looking very much like a foreman in need of a stiff belt after a hard day on the job site. His trainees, on the other hand, entertained transparently romantic notions of undercover attire.

"So what's our story here, Bull?" Red asked as they piled out of the car. "You and I are out for a drink or two, perhaps to discuss our in-depth knowledge of struts and conduits, and we brought our three contract killers along to coordinate our part-time gig as enforcers?"

"Nice trenchie, Acrobat." Bulwark said, ignoring Djinni.

"Cool, huh?" Acrobat grinned. "It's all long and black and stuff."

"You all look like rejects from *The Matrix*," Red muttered. "Screw it. Not much we can do about it. There's no way to make this lot look like it'll fit in here anyway."

"Why raise such a fuss about it then?" Bulwark asked.

"It's the principle of it," Red snapped. "When you do a job half-assed with more people than you need, things *will* get messy."

Bulwark responded with a level gaze. That had sounded like a promise.

Red led them along the alley, whispering instructions. "All right, we get in, sit down and wait for Vivian to come talk to us. Bull should do the talking. Neo, Trinity and Switch here will shut up and watch. You're here to learn, not mess up the negotiations."

Acrobat sighed, looking bashful and guilty. Scope's

eyes widened and she started to retort in anger but was interrupted by Harmony.

"Who is Vivian, and how do you know she'll approach us?"

"She's our first mark and she can lead us to the others. She also owns this place. You're looking at one of the last true speakeasies, with a long bloody history that trails back to Prohibition. This place has bullets embedded in the walls from the Purple Gang, the Chambers Brothers and was almost totaled during the Twelfth Street riot. These days, it's a hideaway for vagrant metas. I suppose it's safe to say that cops aren't really welcome here."

Harmony looked confused. "So . . . why will she come over to us?"

"Because everything about this group screams *cops*."

"Even you?" Bull asked.

"We'll see," Red answered evasively. "It might help if they didn't see me shackled like this." He held up his arm and gave Bulwark a pointed look. Bull merely shrugged, and motioned Red onwards.

Djinni led them through a dark entrance and up a long, narrow flight of stairs. They emerged in a smoke-filled tavern dimly lit by hanging oil lanterns. As they took seats around an old wooden table they noticed a few of the patrons fishing bills out of their pockets, dropping them by their unfinished beer steins and quietly exiting through the back. The bartender, an attractive black woman with short-cropped hair, sighed and strolled over to their table.

"What can I get you?" she asked, her eyes cold and uncaring.

"A round of whatever you have on tap," Bull replied.

"Coming up. That'll be three hundred dollars."

"Beg pardon?" Bull asked, pausing as he reached into his wallet.

"For this month's protection," she replied. "You can tell Alistair I'm getting tired of him crapping all over the agreement. He should know better. Donovan might be pricier, but he didn't make captain for nothing. He knows the rules and he'd stick to the terms. He wouldn't be sending his flunkies into my bar to chase off my customers like this."

"I think there's been a misunderstanding," Bull said. "You're Vivian Wilde, correct?"

"How do you know that name?" Vivian demanded.

Bull reached into his wallet and slapped some bills down on the table.

"Five hundred," he said, "provided you have a seat and talk to us. We're not who you think."

Vivian's eyes narrowed. "Guess not. You might not be Alistair's, but you *are* cops, and I really don't like cops who know my full name." Her eyes fell on Red. "And *you* must have balls of steel to get anywhere near me again."

Red chuckled. "Y'know, Viv, someday I'm going to figure out how you always know it's me."

"Good luck with that, you backstabbing piece of crap," Vivian replied. "You're all about bad habits, Red. I know you too well. Even you can't hide them all."

"Please, Miss Vivian," Bulwark said, pulling a badge out of his jacket and laying it face up on the table. "We only wish some of your time. How much time is entirely up to you."

Vivian stared at the Echo insignia and pulled Red towards her by the neck.

"Ow," Red winced as she dug her nails into his flesh.

"Echo?" she whispered. "You told Echo where I was and brought their dogs into my bar? This is low, even for you."

"I sense you're angry," Red noted blandly.

"This isn't angry," she said in a dead tone. "You've seen me angry." Her nails dug in harder. "*This* is irritated." She spun and caught Red with a solid right hook, which got him to his feet and staggering. "*That* was annoyed." She finished with a strong kick to his groin, and Red landed in a groaning heap on the floor. "And *that*, well, that was just fun."

Scope nodded in appreciation. "I don't know about the rest of you, but I kinda want to see her angry now."

"No," Red gasped, clutching his genitals. "No, you really don't."

"Please, Miss Vivian," Bull repeated, motioning to Red's vacant chair. "Please sit with us, we just—"

"I'm retired," Vivian said. "I don't pull jobs anymore, there's no peace in it." She turned to Bulwark, and her features softened and sagged in weariness. "I'm not a danger to anyone, not anymore. I'm just trying to have a life here, man. Can't you people respect that? Can't you just leave me be?"

"In a sane world, we could. We did." Bulwark said. "But we don't live in that world anymore."

Vivian stood her ground for a moment and eyed the crisp bills Bull had placed on the table. She reached out slowly, like putting her fingers into a fire, and took them. She tucked them gently into her shirt, and took a seat.

"You've got five minutes," she warned him.

Bulwark nodded, and began his pitch. He told her

of Echo's need for personnel, of the terrible deficit left by the invasion day and the lengths they were willing to go to. Full pardons for a select few; their past wiped clean upon successful completion of a five-year service contract. He watched her carefully, gauging the effect his words had on her. There was guilt there, and remorse. Her records were rife with the sort of intrigue and violence common to those who chose the dodgy vocation of a cat burglar. On paper, Vivian was just another calculated risk, perhaps even more of a risk then Red Djinni. But Bulwark wasn't the sort to give up on people based on cold, hard facts. He had researched his potential recruits extensively and had flagged those he needed to meet. You could only read so much from a dossier. Vivian Wilde had been a victim for most of her life, and Bulwark needed to size up what strength she had left. He glanced over to Red, who had crawled over to the nearest wall and was trying with difficulty to get up. She was still a fighter, it seemed, with a heavy kick.

There came a long and uncomfortable silence as Vivian considered Bulwark's words. Finally, she shook her head.

"You don't want me," she said. "No matter how desperate you say you are. You need people who are ready to go, and right now. I still . . ." She paused.

"You still have control issues," Bulwark offered.

"Yes," she said. She held up her hand. Small bolts of electricity flashed between the digits. Acrobat gave a surprised yelp and teetered on his chair. Scope's hands went to her guns but then relaxed. Harmony leaned forward and stared at Vivian's hand in fascination. Bulwark didn't react at all.

"That's about as much as I dare to do," Vivian admitted, closing her hand. "Great for popping doors, overriding circuits, messing up pretty much anything with a current. Anything more and I risk overload."

"We can help you with that," Bulwark said. "We have the best trainers—"

"I don't care," Vivian sighed. "I never wanted this, y'know. I've learned to live with it, and I'm in a place now where I never have to use it. Don't you realize this is for the best?"

Scope snorted her disgust. "That's it? This is who we came for? Some pathetic mouse who's got some punch and won't use it?"

"You don't know what you're talking about," Vivian said quietly.

"Like hell I don't," Scope snapped. "Your grand scheme is to curl up in a ball and hide until you die."

Vivian nodded. "That was the plan."

"We're offering you a place to help those you care about," Bulwark said. "In time, we can arrange a placement here in your own city, to help protect your own. Perhaps even alongside those you've come to trust." He reached into his jacket, produced a small card, and laid it in front of her.

Vivian hesitated, but her curiosity got the better of her. She glanced over the list of names. "You want the Spitter?"

"We want help," Bulwark said. "We want *your* help."

"You're not just talking about me," Vivian said, her eyes now very bright. She flung the card away and stood up. "You want me to lead you to the others. Well, you can forget it!"

She turned on Red.

"How could you do this?" she cried, her voice breaking. "*Again?* Wasn't last time enough? You took her away! She was the one thing...the *only* thing that mattered, and you...you—"

Red felt her hands on him, her fists and incoherent sobs beating into his chest. He didn't fight her off. He came to his feet, all pretense of his pain gone and his hands held deliberately high. The locals sat in shock as Vivian, whose icy stare and detached demeanor had become local legend, screamed her rage and lashed out in wild blows. Red stood and merely watched her pound into him. He was watching her.

No, Bulwark thought in alarm. *He's* gauging *her!*

"Djinni!" Bulwark shouted, rising from his seat. But he was too late.

Red had let Vivian's tantrum rise to a fevered pitch. He caught her arm tightly, and squeezed. Vivian's cries stopped with a startled yelp of pain. Red delivered a smart slap across her face and leaned in with a smirk.

"She thought you wanted her to go," he said. "She thought her mommy didn't love her anymore."

Vivian came to a stop and Red watched as her emotions played themselves out. Shock, then anguish, and then there was just hate. She broke free of Red's grip, her fingers darting for his eyes.

"You worthless, piece of...!"

She faltered and her hand stopped in mid swing. Vivian staggered back, her mouth agape in a quiet scream of horror. She began to glow, and her light coalesced into crackling threads of electricity. She grasped at empty air, struggling for control, but her aura only intensified. Brighter and brighter, the lights arced and danced about her, swarming away and back to her shaking hands. She doubled over, trying to contain the pulsing waves of energy, but she had reached critical mass. With a scream, her limbs flew outward and the waves fled from her with a deafening crack. The EMP tore through the room, and out.

Breaking news on the local channels would report a freak electrical disturbance on Detroit's south side, stunning locals and knocking out all electrical equipment for nine city blocks.

It took a few minutes for Bulwark to wake up, clawing back to consciousness and shuddering to clear his mind. He picked himself up and surveyed the room. Most the bar's patrons were still knocked out, though a groggy few, including his team, were beginning to stir.

"I feel terrible," Harmony groaned.

"Breathe, Harmony," Bull said, propping her up to a sitting position. "Let your mind clear a bit."

"Uh, Bull?" Acrobat whispered. He jerked a thumb towards the bar. "What about . . . ?"

Bulwark glanced over at the patrons. Most of them were groggy, but a few had murder in their eyes.

"Miss Wilde," Bull said. "I believe your friends will need some assurance that we mean you no harm."

No one answered.

"Miss Wilde?"

Bull's eyes darted everywhere but to no avail.

Oh great . . .

Vivian and Red Djinni were gone. All that remained was a ruined tracer bracelet, abandoned and lifeless on the hardwood floor.

❖   ❖   ❖

Vivian was in love.

A few weeks back, she wouldn't have thought it possible. It was tough for a single mom to find someone, someone who was willing to look past the five-year-old child stubbornly glued to her leg every waking moment. Adele was a sweet, shy kid and so unlike her parents. This was a good thing. Her father, Victor, was a monster. As for her mother . . . well . . . how many mothers were armed with twin Glocks, habitually crawled through ventilation shafts and could bypass the security of state-of-the-art strong rooms? No, it was best for Adele to be as different from her parents as possible. It was her only hope for a normal life.

And that's what this job promised. Enough capital to run, hide, and start up a life in exile. Of course, running from Victor was easier said than done. He had eyes everywhere. It was miraculous that Vivian and Adele had made it this far. From the moment Adele had been born, Vivian had taken her into hiding. Twice now, Victor had found them, and both times Vivian had managed to thwart Victor's goons, to free Adele from their clutches and spirit her away. Barely.

Well, no one said a single mom's life would be easy.

And this time, she was close. She was so close she had to fight to keep from shivering with excitement, to keep the fantasy from clouding her judgment, but the man she had found seemed perfect. The timing was miraculous. He had sprung into her life, out of nowhere, and with the perfect job lined up. She was a little rusty, having been on the run for several years, but the schematics seemed tailored to her. His crew was a skilled lot, but for this particular gig they needed someone who could bypass a vault in absolute silence, without the usual explosive clamor involved in blowing safe doors. They wanted an experienced cat burglar, with a little something special on the side.

In the weeks spent planning this job, Vivian had become close to this man. It was almost eerie how much they were drawn to one another. He opened up to her, told her things he probably shouldn't have, and when she saw him for all he was, from the hardened mercenary to the vulnerable child he kept hidden away, she was lost. She was lost in a love she had not thought possible. She responded to him with everything in her. She embraced what he was, had revealed her own naked self to him, and after the job was done, he would follow her. Her and Adele. He had said so, and she believed him.

He was the answer to all her problems, to all her desires. And damn if you couldn't bounce a dime off that ass of his.

She felt another shiver and fought it down. This wasn't a good time to laugh. The slightest twitter would be disastrous. She spared a brief moment to look at the alarm. The red light blinked back, daring her to make a sound, just one clear sound to trigger the security siren and alert the forty-odd men with big-ass guns that intruders were in the building.

And again, as he placed a soft hand on her back, she clenched her teeth to fight from shaking. Just his touch, damn him. He knew what he did to her, insane man. Just enough pressure to let her know he was there. Just intimate enough to keep things interesting.

She bit her lip, enduring a frantic moment of ecstasy as his mouth closed in on her ear. It was hardly a whisper, he barely exhaled, but in the still, she heard it.

"Set the stage."

Vivian nodded, and with practiced precision her fingers delicately turned the dial. The small portable speakers crept to life and soon a low humming filled the room. Vivian watched the alarm, gauging the flickering light against the crescendo of white noise. She kept her breathing deep and silent. The flicker of red stuttered and briefly accelerated as the alarm adjusted to a new baseline of sound, then fell back to a plodding blink.

She felt his breath on her ear again.

"Flash test," he whispered.

Vivian held up her hand, and let a current ride across her fingers. The soft crackle went unnoticed, masked by the hum of the sound machine.

"Showtime."

Vivian pressed her hand to the vault console, and fried it. The digital display went black, and the small door swung open with a barely audible hiss.

He pushed her gently aside and reached in. Retrieving the files with one hand, Red Djinni pulled down his scarf with the other and brought her close for a kiss.

"Was it good for you too?" he whispered, and she smothered a mad desire to laugh.

"Aren't you going to miss this?" she whispered back. "I know what it means to you, I can feel it."

"You're worth it," he said. "You're all I want now." He held up the packet. "And this is our ticket out."

Later, at the safe house, the need for silence was long gone. There was much cheer and celebration. Jon was taken with the music, her body an extension to the beat. Duff was taken by the booze, but his exuberant praise for Vivian was genuine. Vivian took his compliments with good-natured laughter, but she was starting to look restless. She had been away from Adele for days now. Soon, Red had promised her. They would make the drop, receive payment, and would be on their merry way to a long, blissful retirement. Vivian and Adele would never need to run again. He sealed it with a kiss. It seemed to reassure her, and she sank deeper into the plush cushions of the loveseat, sipping her scotch from a tall glass.

Red stepped out into the cool bite of night air. Jack was muttering into his cell. Looking up, he grunted and closed the handset.

"We're set," Jack said. "Package One is secure. Package Two?"

"It's complete," Red nodded. "The raw data is intact and ready for delivery."

"How do you want to do the ditch?"

"I don't," Red answered. "Job's done, and there's no way she can catch up to the boss now. I'm going to tell her."

Jack swore. "Great. You fall for this one too?"

Red nodded. "I owe her the truth, from my own lips. She's no idiot. She'll figure it out anyway."

"This I've got to see. The last time you pulled this too-little, too-late crap, the girl in question almost tore you apart with her screaming. This one can fry your brain with a touch. You're a sick man, Red. Ah well, should be entertaining, if nothing else."

Red didn't answer and reached for the door. He stopped, his hand resting on the doorknob.

"I don't know what to say," he admitted. "For once, I don't have the words."

"Sure you do," Jack said. "You give it to her straight.

Hey, Viv? Surprise, darlin'! Your ex hired us to keep you busy while his boys took your little girl away. She's with her scumbag crime lord of a dad now, and you're never going to find them. Since the day we met I've done nothing but lie to you, just to keep you stupid and romantic and oblivious."

"That's not the truth," Red muttered.

"Yeah, it is," Jack said. "You played this one, like all the others, and we got the job done. This one got under your skin though. Enough that you feel you have to stick around to satisfy your warped sense of morality. It's all a game until Red gets that twitchy feeling. You're lucky we find it funny, would have plugged you with bullets long ago if we didn't."

"You think you could?" Red asked. "You think you could go that cold on me?"

"You think a few honest words to Viv will tip the karmic scales in the least?" Jack countered.

"No," Red said. "But I'll say them anyway. I just didn't think this one would get to me. I've seen the best of her, Jack. I told her I'd be there forever, and it almost felt like the truth."

Jack shrugged. "Yeah, well, get ready. You're about to see the worst in her." He motioned to the door. "Let's go see what she's like when she's mad."

The Tunnels.

The cops knew of them mostly by rumor. Rumor painted them as a complex maze of underground burrows and corridors that might date all the way back to the days of the slave trade, and at least dated back to Prohibition. What the skeptics said was that a few tunnels ran from a couple of basements down to the river, where illegal hooch was brought up from Lake Michigan via rowboat and offloaded for the speakeasies. And as usual, the truth was somewhere in between.

What certainly was true was that the cops didn't know most of what lay beneath the streets. And Red knew the Tunnels like he knew every line and crease of every face he'd ever had to wear.

He hadn't used Viv's exit; no sense letting her know he knew the location. Instead, he'd used an old riverfront entrance, currently hidden in the old storage areas of what was now a very high-end restaurant. A white kitchen jacket and a harried expression got him into the basement; the hidden catch in the back wall opened the door into a dank, cold, brick-walled corridor lit not at all at this point. Which was why he had also filched a flashlight.

His only company until he got to the rendezvous point were the rats the size of cats. Their eyes glittered at him in the flashlight beam, but they seemed inclined to leave him alone.

Two more sets of eyes glittered dangerously at him out of the darkness; there was a low-wattage bulb here and he shut off his flashlight as he faced those pairs of eyes. One set blazed with anger, one set regarded him as coldly as the rats had, measuring him up for something.

"Jack," he acknowledged that second set. "Viv. You've been a busy guy, Jack. So how's Blacksnake as an employer?"

Jack had picked a "neutral" spot for the meet; above them was a Cafeebucks. Then again, what wasn't under a Cafeebucks these days?

Jack grunted. "They got dental."

When Jack's escape plans had been slipped under

the door of Red's cell at Echo HQ, his first thought had been, *I'm going to kill that son of a bitch!* Maybe he would, someday—but not now. Not until he knew what the score was. Not while Jack could be useful. Just as Jack wouldn't kill him—not while Red was, or held, something he wanted.

Red's second thought had been, *I wonder which shiny, mild-mannered Echo agent is really a Blacksnake plant?* There had been no scent, no distinguishing stomp of Echo standard issue bootheels on the cold cement. Just a single sheet of paper with Jack's signature snarky handwriting. Somehow, Jack knew Bulwark's intentions, and he had an idea how to turn it around. But they needed a third party.

Red gave Viv a quick, appraising glance. Jack might have wanted Red alive, but Viv, on the other hand, might kill him any second now. Sure, she'd been recruited to get him free of the bracelet, but that could have been for her own reasons. And after what he'd just done to her back in her bar . . .

Red crossed his arms and leaned against the damp brick, keeping Jack between himself and Viv. "So. What's the pitch? You're working for Blacksnake. And Blacksnake, God knows why, wants me. Right? Okay, I'm valuable, but not that valuable, not with Tonda breathing down my neck."

Vivian was looking now between him and Jack, enlightenment and outrage showing on her all-too-expressive face. She was, for once, speechless.

Not for long, however.

"You . . . you . . . you rat *bastard!*" she spluttered, her eyes finally staying on Jack. "You . . . this was all so you could *recruit* him? For *Blacksnake?*"

"Not just him, darlin'," Jack drawled. Before Viv could react to that, he'd turned back to Red. "Tonda's been taken care of. With extreme prejudice. That was part of my deal. Viv here was happy to help spring you after I offered her that. No more Victor Tonda, no more problems for either of you."

Red sketched a nod. No doubt she was—since Jack undoubtedly included getting his hands on Adele as part of that deal, and Viv would have nominated Red Djinni for Pope if doing so would get her little girl back to her. He didn't show his relief at hearing that Tonda was dead, but that fact changed the entire landscape of the future. With Tonda out of the picture, there would be no one left who knew anything about that little contract to rob Echo . . . and even if there was, Tonda's lieutenants would be so busy fighting each other for the empty seat at the head of the table and restructuring the organization in the wake of the invasion that no one would care about administering the penalty for Red's failure.

With two hot spots of red burning her cheeks, Viv turned on Red. "You didn't tell me you were going to do that to me!" she accused.

"Couldn't," Red replied curtly. "You have to be angry to go *boom* like that, Viv. And without the boom, I'd still be wearing that Tiffany knockoff." He raised an eyebrow. "And nobody told me I wasn't the only one he'd asked to the prom."

"And *you*—" she continued, rounding on Jack. "I thought all you wanted was to cut Red free of that bracelet! You didn't tell me you wanted to recruit out of my address book! I thought all you wanted was him!"

"You were both told only what you needed to know," Jack said curtly. "Viv, you've got what you wanted. Djinni,

Tonda's dogs aren't sniffing after you any more. Either of you going to argue with my results?" He waited while they both fell back a mental step or two. "Thought so."

Viv's eyes burned and tiny crackles of electricity arced across the knuckles of her clenched fists. "I am *not* going to help you track down my friends so you can shanghai them into—"

"Hold up." Jack spread his hands wide. "Relax. There will be no shanging of anyone's hai, and that's a promise. I'm just here to give them my pitch. No coercion. Not for anyone. But, darlin', the world's not the same anymore. They're gonna start running out of places to hide before long. Sooner or later they're gonna have to sign up with someone. It might as well be us. No?"

"Well," Djinni drawled, pushing off from the wall and bracing himself. "In my case...that *would* be a no. No thanks, Jack. I'll pass. I'm not joining Blacksnake, and I'm not going to help you recruit for them either." He smirked. "Echo has a better dental plan. And chiropractic."

For a moment Jack stared at him, and Red felt a grim satisfaction rising in him. Jack had actually not expected this. It was sweet. It didn't make up for Jack trying to kill him—

It didn't make up for Amethist—

But these days, the Djinni was grabbing every molecule of pleasure he could salvage out of the train wreck his life had become. And the look on Jack's face was one to be savored.

As Jack's teeth ground, he growled out, "When I get done with you, you're gonna need chiropractic, you—"

"Now, now, no coercion, you said. For anyone." Djinni's smirk turned into a mirthless grin. "I'm just going to make my offer, like you are. Let 'em choose between us, or go back to their holes, all fair and square."

"Why the *hell* did you go along with my plan, if you intended to do what they wanted all along?" Jack burst out.

And for a moment, Red was unable to answer.

Finally... "When I do a job, I do it on my own terms," he muttered. "I don't like leashes."

It was more than that, of course. When that shackle had been snapped around his wrist, he'd had the same visceral reaction of any wild animal in a trap. He'd have appointed Jack as World Dictator if it would have gotten that damned thing off his wrist.

"Anyway, same deal. I say my piece, no coercion. Just like you." He matched Jack glare for glare as Viv's eyes narrowed. She looked him in the eyes and licked her lips.

"What?" he asked.

"You've changed, but not too much." She paused as an expression of bitterness and anger spread over her features. "You're still using people."

She turned back to Jack, pointedly ignoring Red. "All right. Follow me and you can make your pitch. Both of you. And after that..." She paused again. "After that, it won't matter. You'll never find us again."

She turned to look at Red. "Jack tells me you're bulletproof now," she said levelly, looking him right in the eyes. That look...

"Well, not really—" he began.

Before he could react, she reached around to the small of her back, pulled out a .38, and fired it point-blank into his gut.

He had *just* enough time to harden his skin, so the bullet didn't penetrate far—not to the vital organs—but it *felt* as if it had. The impact drove him back into the wall and he folded up around the wound, dropping to the cold cement floor.

"I'm not ready to kill you," she said, looking down at him, her eyes hot and cold at the same time. "But I wish you a *world* of hurt."

She turned and stalked off into the darkness, leading Jack away.

Behind them, Red caught the bullet as it pushed out of his stomach; with one hand clutched to the healing wound, he lurched to his feet and followed them, stumbling against the walls, half-blinded by pain.

I am really *getting tired of getting shot. . . .*

Bulwark stood at stiff, and very military, attention as Yankee Pride hauled him over the carpet. "You think that just because we're in a crisis you can pull some maverick stunt and no one is going to notice? You think because of all this"—Pride waved a hand at the window, showing the construction and demolition outside—"that the rules don't mean anything? You were on thin ice before, Bulwark, and you just broke through it. Maybe you thought your record went away when we lost the computers. Maybe you thought we would just ignore thirty-one citations for insubordination. Did you?"

An answer seemed called for. Bull answered stiffly, "No, sir."

"What is your malfunction, Bulwark?" Pride continued, scowling. "Do you get some kind of kick out of being the champion of the underdog? Or do you just enjoy being the best of a lot of misfits that no one in their right mind would take on or even give half a chance to? How many times do you think you can pull this kind of crap before—"

He was interrupted by a delicate cough. "Sir, Bulwark's record is not that bad. He does get things done. And the recent unfortunate—"

"I am well aware of his circumstances, Operative Jenson. That's why we loosened his leash. And this is what we get. First the Incendiary Incident—"

"Sir, you said you wouldn't bring that up again." Jenson looked pained.

"Now this. Not only did he drop the baby, he brought home his team half dead from a bar fight—a *bar fight*—and he lost the Djinni." Pride turned to face Bulwark again. His index finger was extended. Bulwark knew he was about to pronounce a permanent demotion—

That was when the intercom buzzed urgently.

Pride whirled. "What?" he barked.

"Uh, sir, this is the front gate, sir. There's—you need to take care of this, sir." The gate guard was almost stuttering. Bulwark felt his hackles going up. More Nazis? Another invasion?

"Excuse me?" Pride's tone nearly froze the intercom.

"Sir, please turn on the video. You'll see."

With a growl, Yankee Pride stabbed at the buttons on the intercom, activating the tiny screen. And his jaw dropped.

It didn't show much but what it did show...

"Come on, get the boss on the horn," said Red Djinni, hanging half out of the driver's side window of a rusted Winnebago. "I got a dozen metas in here, the can is backed up and the shower doesn't work. Get me clearance and get us in there before something bad happens in here."

The Djinni had not exaggerated. He did have a dozen new meta recruits, and the smell inside that Winnebago was probably banned under the Geneva convention. There was a hurried conference among Yankee Pride and several of Tesla's aides. Finally, one of them turned and addressed Bulwark.

"As you were, Operative Bulwark," the aide said, before leading the rest away.

Pride paused and fixed Bulwark with an icy glare.

"Thin ice, Bull," Pride said before marching off.

"I apologize for the transportation," Bulwark said politely, turning to greet the new metas. "If things had gone according to plan, you'd have been flown back several days ago." He punctuated this with a withering look at the Djinni, a look which glanced right off him, from all appearances. "Operative Taylor here will show you to your new quarters, and we can begin your orientation after you get a chance to clean up and—whatever else you need."

They all looked tired, but they perked up at the mention of cleaning up. They certainly followed their escort willingly enough, leaving Bulwark and Jenson alone with the Djinni.

"So?" Bulwark said, looking him up and down.

"Job's done," Red replied.

"And that's supposed to be acceptable?" Bulwark said, struggling to keep his voice calm.

"Job's done, and that's all I promised. You want more, then we'll need to renegotiate our arrangement.

Throw whatever job you want at me, Bull, but chaining me up will never end pretty." The stance, the eyes, all told Bulwark one thing: this was not a challenge, this was a *need*.

"So it would seem," Bull said, finally.

"Should I take him back to his cell, sir?" another guard asked.

"No," Bull said. "Take him after the other recruits and have him pick out a room."

"Good start," the Djinni said as he sauntered away after the guard. "And I'll be wanting a raise," he called back over his shoulder.

When they were at last alone, Jenson gave Bull an exasperated look. "You're doing it again!"

"Doing what?" Bulwark replied, his mind already racing out elsewhere.

"Giving Pride more reasons to bust you down." He grimaced as he looked at the wreck of an RV being driven off somewhere by a guard. Hopefully somewhere to be incinerated. "Djinni belongs in a cell, and you know it. Maybe we don't have enough on him to put him away, but we both know—"

Bulwark shook his head. "I'm not treating him like a prisoner anymore. I need him. He obviously won't work under duress. We need to bring him into the team; it's the only way we can get him to cooperate. Look what he did! He could have run. We all thought he had. Instead, he finishes the job."

"We can recruit more without him," Jensen insisted. "You don't need any more of this kind of heat right now; you don't need..."

Bulwark fought down a welter of emotions, allowing only insistence to show in his voice. "I need him.

He's my only lead. He's the only one who might know what..."

Jenson held up a hand, his expression one of sympathy tinged with reluctance. "I'm sorry, Bull, I'm sorry. We all miss her, but we need *you* now. You can't let this interfere with your work. You need to do your job, and let me do mine. I'll find her for you. Just give me a little time."

Bulwark closed his eyes a moment. Yes, Jensen had been assigned to find Echo Ops missing in the invasion. And yes, he was good at what he did. But...

"I hope you will, but you know as well as I do that if you haven't found her by now, the trail's cold."

Cold as the grave. Cold as death. If she were alive...we'd know by now. The Psy-Ops would have found a trace. Someone would have recognized her. But still, he had to *know*. And Red Djinni was the only key he had.

The last time anyone had heard from her was when her partially scrambled comm link had reported her to be "somewhere" in the downtown area of Atlanta as the invasion started. The last time anyone had seen or heard from any of her team had been when Howitzer had been spotted fighting the invaders alongside... the Red Djinni.

Since Howitzer had gone down about a half hour after that...

"Djinni might be all we have left."

Djinni had been very close-mouthed about what he'd done or been doing just before the invasion started. And short of violating every law about psions in the books, not to mention psionic ethical codes, and sending a psi-talent in to hose out his memory, the only way to find anything was to wait until Djinni himself was ready to open up.

But Jenson's jaw was clenched, and Bulwark knew that he'd already made up his mind about what he would and would not do, and none of those plans included the Red Djinni in any way, shape, or form.

"I'll find Amethist, Bulwark," was all he said, before stalking off. "Whatever happened to Vic, I *will* find your wife."

CHAPTER EIGHT

Moving Day

STEVE LIBBEY

The salt-and-pepper-maned Piotr Dzhavakhishvili animatedly described the purchase of the building whose lobby he and Red Saviour currently occupied. The American holding company had painted a rosy picture of the building's condition, and when Dzhavakhishvili threw his hands in the air and stormed at every gross exaggeration, they backpedaled and denied ever making the claim. By the end of the negotiation, the hyperactive, well-coiffed, and overdramatic Russian liaison had bullied the owners into fully halving·the price.

Red Saviour chuckled as he related the story. "It serves them right," she said.

"These slumlords are scum," Piotr agreed. "We're their karma coming back to haunt them."

"It is specter of Communism that will haunt them," said Natalya. The famous phrase felt awkward in her mouth as English words—a sensation which defined her daily existence in Atlanta. She pointed out the window. "Look at this neighborhood. So much money in this land, but there are perfectly good workers sleeping in cardboard boxes. I am thinking there is big difference to be made here."

Piotr frowned. "America likes its TV and malls, Commissar. You may find it hard to sell that line of reasoning in this country. Their complacency is overwhelming."

She shook the curtains, causing a dust cloud to settle to the floor. *This headquarters is little more than a decrepit office building with an obsolete, hurriedly installed Russian computer network*, she realized. Three floors and a basement, with a garage for the modest fleet of vehicles allotted them. The basement was blessed with high ceilings, so Petrograd immediately staked out the former laundry room as his lab. Storefronts divided the first floor, worthless to a metahuman peacekeeping force. She had ordered an overhead projector and screen to convert one of the storefronts into a classroom. Another of the storefronts had served as a restaurant in happier times. The kitchen could feed the CCCP and its staff ten times over. Walking through the space sent ideas swirling through her head.

The second-floor offices still contained shabby desks and filing cabinets too heavy and cheap to be worth selling off. She chose an office with a view of the street and a large window that could be used as an exit, at least for those not bound by gravity. A windowless interior room served for the computer network's core. An air conditioner down the hall blew freezing cold air over the servers through an insulated tube. The setup looked as primitive as an old science-fiction movie.

People's Blade divvied up the hastily converted quarters on the third floor, leaving space for showers and an adjoining infirmary, weight room, and social area. For herself and Red Saviour, however, she suggested that they take the smallest rooms. "As the new team grows, we will be first to have apartments of our own, as befits our rank. Until then, we will give the benefit to our comrades," she'd said.

"Correct thinking," Red Saviour replied, though she'd winced at the tiny bed, whose thin mattress grazed two walls. "I will keep my clothes and boxes in my office."

Fei Li carried her suitcases into her room. Red Saviour watched her go, back straight. *Fei Li loves this*, she thought. *The Spartan arrangements, the military overtones. I, too, but now I find that I miss Papa—and Molotok. He and I are expected to live up to our parents' legacy, but they had the Great Patriotic War to inspire their rise to glory. All we have is a recalcitrant bureaucracy, a decadent capitalist city and a ramshackle building.*

Still, she assured herself as she unpacked her suitcase on the bed, *Marx wrote his Manifesto one word at a time, with but pen and ink. Modest tools that moved a world! So shall we.*

"I need a signature here," Piotr Dzhavakhishvili said, standing at the door with a clipboard. "For the reinforcement of the roof."

Natalya grinned. Even as an airborne meta, she relished what that reinforcement made possible. "The helipad," she said. "CCCP's own personal air force." The work order seemed straightforward, typed on a carbon form like she still found in Moscow. "I am not used to *Amerikanski* dollars. Is this good price?"

"Beats out the competitors," he said. "This kind of work is never cheap."

The work order had been signed by the salesman, initialed by Piotr...yet something was missing. She tapped the pen on the clipboard.

"What's wrong? Did I forget something? The tool shed, landing pad, lights...they're all there."

"*Nyet, nyet,* is something else. Is...hmm..." She drew a circle on the form absently, then it hit her. "Is not union shop!"

"Huh?"

She held out the form for his inspection. "'Look for the union label,' says old song. In America, strict rules for use of union logo, for union members only. But no logo on this quote."

He took the clipboard back and scratched his coiffure. "I never thought of that. I just put the bids out."

"Unions are last vestige of collectivist thought in labor movement. *My* CCCP is union shop. I reject this bid!" She turned her back on the bewildered liaison. "Find me union quote. *That* I will sign."

Annoyance crept into his voice. "The FSO gave me a budget more modest than modern, Commissar. Unions will charge you twice as much for the same work."

"Is savings at expense of unionized workers! What kind of Communist do you think I am?" She spun on her heel. "CCCP holds to higher standard than cheap *Amerikanski* Pay-Mart culture. We will begin to set good example—by using union labor." Fury built up inside her, as her zeal for rehabbing the building dissolved in a sea of bids and shady contractors. "Now, get out of my room, *svinya!*" She threw a thick copy of *Das Kapital* at the wall over his head. "Out!"

"Madwoman!" he shouted, stomping out. The floorboards groaned under his weight.

Fei Li peeked out of his own room, holding a crisply folded shirt. "Natalya? What is the commotion?"

"Nothing, nothing," she said with a sigh as she picked up the book. "Just misunderstanding over contracts. First of many, I am thinking."

"Don't alienate our American allies just yet with your temper." Her voice took a familiar, gently scolding tone. "We have lost much of our leverage. This is not Moscow."

Natalya scowled at her as she bowed and ducked back into her room. Down the hall, Soviette directed an equipment-hauling Chug into the infirmary. Thanks to the squat powerhouse, they had no need of forklifts to haul heavy loads.

"Wait, Chug," Soviette said. "Try this wall."

"Okiez," Chug rumbled, setting the EKG down. Even though his voice resembled a collapsing cliff face, much like his skin, his joy was evident. Chug was as eager to please as a puppy—one that was five hundred pounds and covered with an impenetrable rocky exterior. Had Soviette asked him to move the entire building, the CCCP would be homeless as the place fell down around a faithfully-trying Chug.

"Jadwiga," Natalya said in Russian, "how is infirmary coming together?"

The elegant Soviette sighed like a nun in a jungle mission. "It is little more than a playpen for doctors. If anyone gets more than a scraped knee, they'll die of gangrene. This room is unsanitary, underpowered, poorly ventilated..."

Natalya held up a hand. "Enough. I get the point. We are underfunded, it is true, and Moscow's purse opens for us no more. We must make do, *sestra*."

The doctor pursed her lips. "There is no making do while we lack even the most basic medical equipment. You wanted this infirmary to save us exorbitant American hospital bills." She shook her head. "It won't do that."

"Hmm. But what about that?" She pointed at the unplugged EKG, whose dials and switches fascinated Chug. He hummed tunelessly as he flipped them on and off. "It is very impressive looking."

"Right now, all it does is tell me when you've died in my primitive emergency room."

"But you can heal with a touch. What need have we for surgical equipment?"

"I am not Jesus Christ," Jadwiga said with barely restrained anger. "My powers convince the body to knit itself back together, but they are not magic. With serious injuries, there is no substitute for genuine medical knowledge. Besides," she slapped Chug's hand away from the EKG, making him cringe, "healing and diagnosis are two different things. Unless you want to pay Echo's medical center every time Chug gets a stomachache from eating chairs, find me proper diagnostic equipment."

Natalya bit back a retort. Soviette had been Medic One for years. Her combination of medical knowledge and empathic healing powers had saved many comrades' lives in the past. Natalya respected her opinion above any other doctor she had met—and there had been many—and Jadwiga did not exaggerate to make a point.

"It's that bad?" Natalya said softly.

Jadwiga flushed, embarrassed by her outburst. She petted Chug's head to soothe him. "*Da*, it's bad. Do you think it's a deliberate slight from the old men in the Kremlin?"

Natalya shrugged. "Who is to say? But when in doubt, I just assume it's politics." She smiled sadly. "Make me a list. I'll pass it on to Molotok and we'll do what we can."

"*Horosho*. I trust—well, I am sure you and Moji will find a solution."

"Well . . ." Her voice trailed off. "Are you done with Chug?"

"*Da*. There is nothing left to carry." Jadwiga winced at the abruptness of the comment. "For now," she amended.

"Work on the list. It is important to me." She squeezed the woman's shoulder. "I promise."

Jadwiga's smile broke through her ordinarily aloof expression to show the great beauty she possessed. Her smiles were rare and to be treasured.

"*Davay, davay*, Chug! We have furniture to move." Natalya took him by the hand and led him downstairs as if he were a child.

"Chug hungry," he said.

Natalya groaned. Chug's strange metabolism ran at lightning speed and allowed him to digest anything. Anything, including plants, machines, concrete—and furniture. She had little time. They passed the comm room, which would contain the advanced radio equipment and video monitors. Bubble wrap and cardboard boxes were stacked haphazardly in the corner.

"In here, Chuggy," she said. "You can eat the bubble wrap, and the boxes, but nothing made of metal or plastic. Understand?"

"Chug unnerstanz," he said. Within moments bubble wrap filled his mouth, popping like a miniature strand of fireworks. It would tide him over for an hour, she guessed. If he made up his mind to follow the packing material with a dessert of high-frequency radio transmitters, there was nothing she could do to stop him, aside from scolding him like a child. Chug possessed enormous strength, exceeding that of Worker's Champion. She had never seen him wounded or injured, only stunned for a moment, when hit by a tank—the entire tank, thrown like an American fastball.

Fortunately, Chug adored the members of the CCCP, particularly the women, who doted on him. Natalya had to admit a fondness for him, and a bit of guilt that she regarded him as a pet.

The bubble wrap was nothing more than a memory and a burp, yet Chug was not satisfied. He eyed the cardboard boxes.

"Go on, but just the boxes."

"Dank youz," he said, seizing a pile of folded-up boxes like a hamburger. Chug was not a quiet or dainty eater, but did it matter when all he left were cardboard shavings? She would have to sweep up in here later.

With Chug temporarily sated, they began to move desks out of the rooms designated for meetings, resources, and—although she neglected to advertise it—interrogations. These were no snap-together particleboard pieces of junk, but rather hulking brutes from a time when a desk was expected to outlive its users. Constructed of solid oak and thick rolled steel painted an ugly olive, the desks weighed at least three hundred pounds apiece, enough to put the fear in ordinary movers.

Chug carried the desks in turn, maneuvering them as if they were oversized bags of groceries. A desk for the Commissar's office on the second floor, three shared desks for the comrades, three in the resources library, leaving one for the reception area. Chug talked to himself as he trundled them up and down the stairs.

Fei Li would surely lecture her about some obscure aspect of feng shui, but the Chinese woman had taken one look at the weed-infested side yard and squatted down to clear it out.

Facing the door would be best for the reception desk, she concluded, recalling some tenuous strand of a feng shui conversation when Fei Li trained her in martial arts. Something about not having one's back to the door, and that made sense to the soldier in her. Chug, however, had deposited the desk at the foot of the staircase, down the hall. He thumped around upstairs, probably busy trying to remember her instructions.

Natalya rubbed her hands on her jeans, crouched, found a handhold on the desk and heaved. Her meta-human physique afforded her triple a normal man's strength, and the heavy desk put it to good use. She braced it on her belt and marched it down the hall. Craning her neck to see around it, she guided the desk into position and eased it to the floor. *I should move furniture more often,* she thought. *It's a better workout than a gym. Good practice for throwing dumpsters and trabants at perps, too.*

She pushed a dusty office chair behind the desk and sat, looking out the door to the street beyond. Feng shui appealed to her sense of paranoia. She peeked in the drawers for abandoned office supplies. When she looked up, a man opened the door and strolled in as if he owned the building. Balding, large but not obese, he had the sturdy confidence of a man used to changing his environment with his hands. He wore a tie poorly and a workman's jacket with ease. His metal briefcase showed signs of wear.

"Hello there, gorgeous," he said. "I'm here for your boss, Red Saviour." The man drew a card and held it out to be viewed. "Ross Hensel, Hensel and Hewitt Builders."

Natalya snatched the card from the man before he could pull back. "Why do you think Commissar Red Saviour should talk to you?"

Hensel narrowed his eyes. "That's between me and the Commissioner, little lady. As much as I'd enjoy talking to ya, your boss needs work done and my company is the one to do it."

"I think I am beginning to understand. You want to bid on renovation work on CCCP headquarters, *da*?"

"You got it. Russian, are ya? They sure grow 'em pretty there, I can see. I can tell why old Red keeps you around. You ain't hard on the eyes." He grinned, genuinely thinking he was being complimentary, and cast his eyes around the room. "Got any coffee? I take mine black, two lumps."

Natalya stood. Hensel came up to her chin. "This logo here, is union logo?" She flipped the card at him.

"AFL-CIO, Building and Construction Trades," he said. "Member since 1974."

"*Horosho*. Since you are fellow worker, and member of labor union, I give you another chance." The man frowned at her words. "You are perhaps accustomed to sexist hiring practices in capitalist country. Is understandable." She stepped out from the desk. "I am Natalya Nikolaevna Shostokovich, known in Russia as *Krasnaya Spasskaya*."

"Kras—" He lost the rest of the syllables.

"Red Saviour. Commissar Red Saviour, Comrade Hensel."

"Well, hell," he said, turning red. "My apologies. Sitting at that desk you looked like...never mind. It's a pleasure, Ms...."

She shook his hand. "Commissar will do."

"Commissar. Your man Dzha...Dzhavak..." He fumbled again.

"Dzhavakhishvili," she said.

"Thanks. He indicated that the bidding process had been reopened, and that you expressed interest in our bid."

"I said no such thing. He oversteps his bounds, but now that you are here, let us talk about your bid." She gestured him to follow. "We will speak in cafeteria, where there are more chairs. Today is being moving day."

"I can see that. Who're you using?"

She pointed. "Him." Chug rounded the corner with the last desk propped up on his shoulder.

"I'll be damned," Hensel said under his breath. Chug favored them both with a stony smile.

"I'm doing gud, Commissar Savyur," Chug said. "I only got lost twice. I learn fast!"

"*Horosho*," she said. "Carry on."

The stony creature giggled his way past them.

"His English is improving. I would not have thought anything would get through that boulder of a head."

She brushed off a space for them to sit, using a discarded rag. "Phew," Natalya said. "Filthy. I don't need this much space for comrades' dinner. We will rarely be off duty all at once."

Hensel settled onto the bench with the care of a heavyset man. "You folks plan to keep busy, eh?"

"Television and McDonald's has made your *Amerikanski* metahumans lazy...and fat," she said with a pointed look. "They seek fame like moths attracted to flame, but they take no care to avoid being burned. In Russia, metahumans are champions of proletariat."

Hensel frowned. "Don't think we have proletariats here."

Natalya pointed at him, and then at his clipboard with the union logo. "Proletariat is *you*, Comrade Hensel. Is workers your union represents, and workers you unite with to battle against capitalist owners."

"Yeah, well," he began, searching for words. "I gotta tell ya, Miss Saviour, the unions got over that talk early last century. We're about as capitalist as you get. We work hard for a day's wage. And, no offense, but the final product is a damn sight higher quality than your forced labor."

Natalya blew air out her lips. The Cold War ended years ago with *perestroika*, but Marxist thought still found a chilly reception in the country that believed it had "won" by outspending the Soviets. Not until the American proletariat truly suffered under the yoke of oppression would the tenets of Marx and Engels gain any ground with them. *I am just planting seeds,* she reminded herself.

Reigning in her temper, she forced herself to smile at the man. "Well, is pleasant bantering about politics with so sturdy a worker as yourself, but let us move on to matter at hand." She indicated the clipboard. He spun it around for her to view.

"Most of those figures concern reinforcement of

your roof there," he said. "You're gonna want I-beams at six-point-five-foot intervals—er, about two meters. Doubling the load-bearing capacity, you know. Roofs ain't made for supporting the weight of anything besides a bit of snow." Hensel's discomfort at his earlier blunder had disappeared in a sea of shoptalk. He was in his element now.

"You are charging for extra load-bearing columns on all floors. We only need underneath helipad."

He leaned forward. She smelled cigarettes on his breath and craved one for herself. "That's where you'd be wrong, Commissioner. Where's the pressure going after you shunt it through the third-floor supports? To the second floor, where you got nothing. Takes longer to cause damage, but once you're sagging, you're look-ing at replacing the whole damn roof." He grinned, satisfied with his explanation. "I bet your low-ballers didn't tell you that."

"*Nyet. Horosho* point you make."

"Say again?"

"*Horosho*...is good, is good point you are mak-ing." She put her palm on the tabletop and pushed. "Weight doesn't disappear altogether. Is distributed to weak spots in structure."

"You got it." His eyes strayed to her chest, lingered, and snapped back up. "I can see why they put you in charge."

She looked down her nose at the man. "*Svinya.* Now, tell me..."

"Come again?"

"*Svinya.* Means...it means 'fellow worker,'" she lied. "You have charges here for refurbishing this room."

Hensel swept a hand in a semicircle. "It's a good

space. I just figured since you got a virtual army living here, and you got a mess hall, you'd be using it. No sense in letting it go to waste."

"I was going to store equipment in here. We do not need all this space for dining."

He produced a red pen and scratched a line through the columns relating to the cafeteria. "Too bad. You could open a little Russian restaurant or something. Feed the workers."

Natalya's eyes went wide. "Feed the..." She imagined the tables full of proletarians, eating and talking...or listening. "Not restaurant," she said. "What is place for poor people called?"

"The poor house?"

She shook her head. "*Nyet, nyet.* Where exploited workers and disenfranchised come to eat."

"McDonald's?"

"*Nyet!*"

His eyes roved the room. "A soup kitchen?"

Natalya slapped the table, sending up puffs of dust. "*Da!* Soup kitchen, where we feed comrades for free."

"There's one down the street," he said, inclining his head west. "Saint Francis, I think."

"Then there is room for another. But will be for Saint Karl!" She stood and spread her arms out. "We serve good sturdy food: borscht, potatoes, stew. Workers can eat for free, as long as they listen to lecture." She made a fist. "Thus we endear ourselves to proletariat and plant seeds for worker's revolution in America."

Hensel grimaced as if she had broken wind. "Um, I think they call that sedition, lady. You can't preach the overthrow of the government here. It's a free country."

"*Da!* Is free country, with free speech laws. You

might not like to hear it but is perfectly legal. If they want to eat, they have to listen to us explain to them why they are hungry in first place."

"I don't know," he said. "I mean, Russia's our ally now, but this is like the bad old days of..." He stopped as she initialed his estimate on renovating the cafeteria. "Of... well, I guess we can accommodate you."

"*Horosho.*" She grinned in triumph, still awash in the vision of delivering a rousing lecture on ideology to the American poor, who stared in slack-jawed realization of their plight. She would budget for inexpensive, student editions of the *Communist Manifesto*, to be handed out for further reading. A whiteboard...

"I want whiteboard, too."

"Sure thing," he said, jotting it down. "Commissioner, while we're on the topic, I took the liberty of preparing an estimate for the living quarters for your people." Hensel pulled a sheaf of papers from his briefcase. "I think you'll find this fits right into your budget."

"Excuse me," a soft feminine voice said. They turned towards the source of the interruption: Fei Li, the People's Blade, in a muddy T-shirt and jeans. She held a trowel in one tiny hand. "Please forgive me, but I believed you would want to be notified. A gang of street hoodlums is attacking a local grocery, according to the local police band, and aid is called for. They are understaffed in this neighborhood, it appears."

"Our first operation!" Red Saviour exclaimed. "Excellent! How many *svinyas*?"

Hensel's brow beetled at the word he thought he knew in a different context.

"Twenty," the Chinese woman said. "Apparently there is a metahuman presence, which causes the local constabulary some concern. This particular gang is known as the Rebs."

"Oh, damn, the Rebs," Hensel said. "Bad news. If you're going after them, you ladies better bring that rocky guy."

Red Saviour turned on him. Such disrespect was intolerable! She opened her mouth to excoriate the man, at last.

"Natalya." Fei Li had read her mind.

Fei Li's voice had not risen, but it deflated Natalya's anger. Her former teacher could command a legion with a single upraised eyebrow.

"Fine. Then, Comrade Hensel, you will be my guest. Bring your papers; we will discuss your plan for our barracks."

"Your g-guest?" Hensel said. "I thought you were going to tackle a street gang."

Natalya gave him a wolfish grin. "You're coming with us." She held up a hand to stifle his protest. "If you want contract, that is."

Natalya and Fei Li went for their uniforms and dressed while Hensel waited in the lobby. Feeling a little guilty at the look of fear on the man's face, Natalya had Soviette fetch the man a bulletproof vest they kept as a reserve. It could not stretch to fit his bulk, leaving three inches unprotected. His protest went unheeded.

"Pistols tend to stray to the left. You will be fine," she said. The lie didn't reassure him.

Natalya tugged at her white-banded gloves. She

had chosen her favorite uniform, a tribute to her father. The outfit had the added benefit of being a fine nanoweave that could stop a medium caliber bullet. It might break a bone, but she would survive the wound.

Her red headguard protected the sides of her head from impact trauma and held her wild raven hair in check. Some metahumans preferred to go masked, but she had to issue orders, and she could not do that hidden behind fabric.

"I ain't so sure about this," Hensel said.

"Why?" she said. "Because is just People's Blade and I?"

"Yeah, that, among other things."

"We will give you good show," she said. "Now, tell me about barracks."

"Right." He unfolded his proposal from his pocket. "You got eight rooms for a predicted fourteen people. That's getting cramped, unless you're a freshman in college."

"I have my own room, as does comrade Soviette and Fei Li."

"Knocks you down to five rooms to sleep eleven people."

Fei Li jogged into the room. "Forgive me for being so slow. Let us not tarry any further." She adjusted her cloth belt around a loose-fitting tunic, into which she had tucked the metal sheath of the fabled blade, Jade Emperor's Whisper. Red Kevlar-paneled tights, at Natalya's insistence, gave her legs some bullet protection.

"Keep talking, Comrade Hensel."

They oriented themselves on the street. "Four

blocks," Fei Li said, pointing west, past a row of ragged tenements.

"We'll race," Natalya said. She thrust her arms under Hensel's from behind. "Comrade, don't drop anything."

With a confident smile, Fei Li pushed off the sidewalk as if she were a swimmer at the bottom of a pool. At once she had leaped twenty feet into the air, tapping a telephone pole for additional footing.

"Holy crap," Hensel said in a stage whisper.

"Bah," Red Saviour said. "Is nothing. Hold tight."

Directing the energies under her feet, she and Hensel floated into the air. After a brief lull, the energies exploded under her in a white flash, propelling them forward at the speed of a motorcycle.

Hensel howled in fear.

"Close your eyes. You will get bugs in them." She adjusted her grip on the big man. He weighed less than the desk.

Bystanders craned their necks as Red Saviour and Hensel blasted by them. She let the energies burst out, making light and noise. Ahead of them, somehow, People's Blade sprang off a window ledge.

The blocks flashed by. Red Saviour stayed behind People's Blade, knowing that she would draw fire from their civilian observer.

"Tell me about five rooms, comrade." She dodged a power line.

"Five rooms," he said. "Not-not to mention limited bathroom facilities. The room with the drain can be converted—"

"Is for interrogations. Not negotiable."

"Interrogations? You can do that?"

A column of smoke rose from a storefront ahead.

Men in white outfits waved Molotov cocktails, baseball bats, and pistols. She estimated over a dozen targets.

"Put me down here," he said. "Keep me away from those nutcases."

"Too far. I will not be able to hear you. Aha!" Shifting their weight, she skimmed the sidewalk, then twisted abruptly to halt behind a parked SUV with shot-out windows. Hensel let out a lungful of air.

"Stopping's worse than starting," he said, hunkering down behind the car.

The Rebs stuck to their theme: white jeans and shirts, with Confederate flag armbands, resembling a streamlined, modern-day Ku Klux Klan. Hooting and hollering, they reveled in the fear of their Korean victims and onlookers. Molotovs had ignited the produce cart in front of the small market. More smoke billowed out from the broken plate-glass window.

"Jesus," Hensel said, peeking around the bumper. "That's a lot of guys. You sure you don't want backup?"

"Comrade, give us credit, *da*? I did not become Russia's bestest hero by calling for help." She looked up through the broken windows of the SUV. "Besides, Blade Shuai has decided to make her move. Just watch."

"That slip of a girl? Unless that sword of hers—"

"You are shutting up and watching." Natalya grinned, getting excited. "By the way, I like large mirrors in bathroom. We will need sauna, also."

Fei Li dropped from the sky, sun at her back. She hit the ground and rolled through the open doors of the store, right between the legs of a Reb gangster. Silent and swift, she was inside before the gang members had a clue what the tiny blur was.

A cry arose from the grocery, then a yell of pain.

A single, bare-chested Reb flew out the front window, spinning like a toy, and landed on the street. Blood seeped out of the figure 8 carved into his chest.

"Eight inside," Red Saviour said with satisfaction. She shrugged at Hensel's look of horror. "Will be easier when we install radio network." Her fists began to glow. "Now, stay put. This will take moments."

"Metas!" cried the Rebs. Weapons were brandished, and all heads turned towards the store.

"*Svinyas*," Red Saviour said, stepping out into the street. The Rebs spun at the sound of her challenge. "Is time to give up your decadent, exploitative lifestyle and get good factory jobs. You now face real proletarian warriors."

"What Bond movie is she from?" one of the Rebs said. Another snickered.

In response, she blasted the joker with a streak of blue energy. He skidded across the concrete.

"Well damn! That ain't right! Get 'er! Get 'er *done!*" The Rebs swarmed on her with their chains and bats. Red Saviour waited for them to come within arm's reach, then she stepped under the downswing of the nearest bat-wielding gangster. She wrenched his arms, seized the bat, and jabbed him in the stomach. She swung it up to clip his chin and followed through to parry a bike chain with the bat.

Her foot lashed out and shattered the Reb's rib cage. Another tried to strangle her with a noose and received an elbow in the throat for his efforts.

"Bathrooms!" she shouted.

Hensel realized he was being addressed. "What?"

"Bathrooms are in tatters. Can you work on plumbings?"

He ducked as a two-foot splinter of broken bat flew past his head. "I got a guy for that."

"*Horosho*. Add"—she backhanded a Reb—"to"—then flipped over the head of a fat one and kicked him in the spine—"list!"

"Got it," he called back.

People's Blade stepped out of the storefront, wiping her blade on a Stars and Bars bandanna. Groans resounded from the storefront, but no one moved.

A heavyset, bearded Reb in a denim vest approached her. She leveled her swordpoint at him.

"I suggest you stand down," she said in a quiet tone that brooked no dissent.

"I can't hear you," the man boomed. "Why don't you . . . *SPEAK UP?*" In an instant, his voice rose to the roar of a hurricane. The force he generated blasted the car in front of the store—and People's Blade—through the façade with a terrific crash. There was no dodging the sonic assault.

Red Saviour had instinctively covered her ears. A Reb scored a hit with his baseball bat; her cheek reddened and blood spurted from her broken nose. She shook her head to clear the fuzz while the Rebs hooted around her. A boot caught her in the stomach and her muscles tensed to absorb the blow.

The metahuman loomed over her. "Let's send these commie bitches home to daddy!" Before she could react, he seized her hair and pounded her face into his thick knee. Nose cartilage crunched even more. Bats and fists fell on her back and legs.

The pain and disorientation began to draw her down into unconsciousness. How did she drop her guard? She would never have let this happen in

Russia—it was her homeland, her turf, where she and CCCP had kept the peace with an iron fist. Yet most of CCCP had died protecting her countrymen from the Thulians. Why had she survived? To experience further humiliations, like being beaten by a pack of ignorant Americans and their smelly leader? Was this the fate of those who fought for international socialist brotherhood?

Nyet.

She blocked out the pain and gathered her energies for an explosive burst. Such a sudden release could injure her, she knew, but her head swam too much to zero in on the dancing targets around her.

"Now hold on there!"

The beating halted.

It was Hensel. He had waded into the fray and interposed himself between the Rebs and her prone form. He swatted at a gangster with his clipboard.

"I am not going to stand here and watch you goddamn hicks whip on a woman. No way, Jack."

The metahuman screwed up his face in outrage. "You ain't from around here, boy."

"Brooklyn born and raised and damn proud of it."

"A Yankee." He raised his arms to his gang. "We know what to do with carpetbaggers, don't we, boys?"

The gang surged around him, those who Red Saviour had blasted still wobbly but fired up by their leader. They hollered back at him incoherently.

Hensel narrowed his eyes. "You jerks just keep on yammering. You want a piece of the Commissioner here, you gotta go through a union man." He stood straight and tall in the midst of the predators.

The filthy metahuman burst out laughing. "If

that don't beat all! All right, union boy, you'll get your wish. I'm a-gonna show you why they call me Rebel Yell."

He drew a deep breath. Hensel raised his clipboard as a shield. The Rebs behind him scrambled to get out of the way.

Rebel Yell opened his mouth. The merest exhalation before his vocal cords took hold of the air had the basso, thundering quality of an onrushing tornado.

But no sound emerged except for a surprised squawk. His eyes flew wide and a red droplet leaked from his lips—then he vomited a mouthful of blood.

A slender, inhumanly sharp blade jutted out of his chest: Jade Emperor's Whisper.

Fei Li withdrew it swiftly. Rebel Yell clutched at his chest and turned to look at her in shock. His breath wheezed out from a gaping jaw.

"You—you stabbed me—" he gasped.

Her smile had no sweetness. Fei Li's delicate features had subtly changed to project a cold, superior and impersonal harshness. For a moment, Red Saviour could not even recognize her friend and teacher.

This—this was Shuai: the General Shen Xue himself.

Rebel Yell fell to his knees, blood seeping out from his fingers.

And then the People's Blade—Natalya could not think of her as Fei Li just then—put a tiny hand to her ear and tilted her head.

"I can't hear you," she said.

The southern metahuman plopped facefirst onto the street.

Hensel offered a hand to Red Saviour. Standing, she saw that the Rebs milled about, angry to see their leader incapacitated—possibly killed—by a mere woman. Their numbers still gave them confidence.

Horosho, she thought.

"Comrade Hensel, you have convinced me that you are the man for the job. You're hired."

The union man chuckled. "Thanks, lady. But these rednecks don't look too happy about their boss."

"He will survive," People's Blade said, soft and sweet again. "Metahumans heal quickly."

Hensel picked up an aluminum bat. "I think we still got work to do."

"Oh no." Red Saviour cracked her neck. "We are off the clock now. This is *play*."

Back to back, they raised their weapons—fist, bat and sword—and faced their enemies.

INTERLUDE

Remember when I said that the divide between the haves and the have-nots had never been deeper? The actual destruction was relatively "minimal." For those of us actually in it, it didn't seem that way; it felt like we were living in the Apocalypse. But for most of the rest of the US, within weeks, it was business as usual. The destruction corridors had mostly marched around or through low-income and slum neighborhoods; for the rest of the population, after the supply situation sorted itself out and there were goods in the stores again, the only difference between then and now was the perception of Echo, and the news stories. After all, no one like them, no one they knew, no one they could connect with, had really suffered.

It could have caused an internal war of the sort that Marx and Lenin predicted and hoped for. Instead, it was the destruction corridors that saved the haves. The have-nots couldn't reach them, and were, in any case, too busily focused on basic needs and defending those basics from each other. Were the Thulians planning on a class war to follow their initial blitz? I'm betting on it. But they undid themselves with their own plan.

CHAPTER NINE

Hoods

CODY MARTIN & MERCEDES LACKEY

John Murdock had been in Atlanta just about two weeks, and this was rapidly becoming the most surreal experience of a life stuffed full of unreality—at least by the standards of Joe Six-Pack and Jane Soccer-Mom.

He'd found a squat: a couple of rooms in an abandoned industrial building. He had the feeling it had been some sort of lab, or maybe it had once been for a live-in caretaker. It had two rooms. The first room was a bare concrete box with a single, heavily barred window, but plenty of electrical outlets and marks on the floor that looked like the outlines of cabinets or benches. The second was a smaller concrete box, but this one had a shower, sink, and toilet in it. For some reason, the electricity and water were still on; maybe this had been overlooked. Maybe it was on for whoever was trying to sell the place. He was surprised that no one else had claimed it, except that it was on the top floor and the door was almost hidden behind some piled-up sections of movable partitions. He had only found it because he'd been looking for someplace he could secure against the looters. There had already been a hasp on the door. He only had to get a padlock, and install more locks on the inside, in order to secure it.

It was grim, grimy, but it was private and, for now, it was his. Slowly he had accumulated some possessions besides the ones he'd carried in his backpack when he'd arrived. All of them were things that had been discarded, but were still useable. A two-burner electric hot plate of which only one burner had worked until he'd fixed it. He had an old mattress to sleep on now—he'd poked over quite a few of those before he found one that hadn't smelled of urine or cat spray. Instead, it smelled like Eau de Old Lady, a kind of mingling of musty lavender, cheap soap, and dime-store perfume; it looked like it was probably fifty years old, battered and lumpy, with some blued-cotton batting spilling out of a popped seam. A couple of plastic cartons served as tables supporting scavenged lamps with bulbs just bright enough to read by, a cheap windup radio-flashlight he'd been given as part of the CERT pack that gave him thirty minutes of music for a minute of cranking, and a TV that had an apparently unfixable orange tint across the top with an antenna made from a coat hanger. A couple of boards and some bricks made a bookshelf he was slowly filling with whatever he could find. Best of all, he had a tiny refrigerator that he had pulled out of the same abandoned RV he got the TV from—a rusted-out Winnebago with a stopped-up toilet that had smelled like a dozen winos had been living in it. He had carefully cut a thick piece of cardboard to fit over the room's window at night, to prevent any light from showing. All in all, it was a dump, but it was more home than he'd had in a while. And it was free, a big plus.

He still was not sure why he was here. He'd initially thought he would go straight to Echo HQ and sign up, but one look at that half-wrecked place had raised the hackles on the back of his neck. Partly it had been the way he'd been treated by the uniformed SupportOps guarding the entrance to the site—like he was a nuisance, but potentially a dangerous one, one that they eyeballed warily, with hands hovering too near their weapons for comfort. Partly it was the feel of the place; it reminded him of a bivouac that had just been shelled, full of grass-green troopers who had never seen a fire fight in their lives and were trying to sort out their nerves while still under the gun. Echo had been whipped, whipped good, and the metas were still in shock, disbelief, and fear. That was simply not something he wanted to get tangled up in the middle of. If they found out where he was *really* from, as opposed to the cover story he'd concocted, they'd probably turn him in, what with the mood that they were in.

He should have moved on from Atlanta. Yet he had stayed. Part of it was because it was easy; there was money to be picked up in odd ask-no-questions day-labor jobs, enough to buy food and coffee. He had a squat. And it felt like he should be here, although he couldn't have said why; besides, where else was there *to* go? Every major city had been hit, just about. Small towns were no good; he'd stand out. And he wasn't sure his bolt-hole in Minnesota was reachable right now.

His building was on the edge of one of the neighborhoods, old and run-down, red brick and wood frame, two- and three-story buildings. It was mostly intact, and bounded by two of what the government reps called "destruction corridors," swaths of war-zone wreckage where the Nazi war machines had just plowed through, blasting everything in their path. Minimal power and water had been restored very, very quickly here—nobody wanted blackout rioting—but after that, it was as if the city promptly forgot about them.

Maybe they had.

There was plenty to be done in the neighborhood, and with a blanket here, a T-shirt there, a book; it added up to more comfort. Some of the locals knew about his powers after a while; he kept it very low-key and so did they. Still, the people of this area were fairly tight-knit, and word spread. Having a unique ability put him in high demand; after all, he could weld without needing a rig, and he could lift and haul more than three men his size. It might have been taking slight advantage of these folks when they were in need, but they couldn't complain too loudly; they were getting help that they couldn't get anywhere else. Sure, truckloads of donated clothing and household goods had been dumped here, but nothing else. Forget about getting any handymen in here to fix things; they were all on high-paid jobs in the richer parts of the city. Echo hadn't been seen in this area since the attacks; it seemed to the residents that they were too busy looking after their own hides to spare any time for people that didn't have flush bank accounts.

Today, the job was helping a local bodega owner to get into his store. It was located on the east side of the neighborhood, right on the edge of one of the destruction corridors that had turned this area into an island. The owner's name was Jonas; he was an elderly black man who had a kind way about him. John liked him immediately upon meeting him.

Jonas sighed, looking to his right, at what John could only compare to the bombed out ruins of the cities of Bosnia. "Y'know, it seems to me that when things like this happen, the only people really hurt bad are the ones that just happened to be in the way. Maybe this wasn't the best part of town, but... a lot of good folks lived out there. A lot of them are dead now, and they never hurt nobody. Only the Lord knows where the rest of them are."

John shook his head, walking past a large pile of rubble. "There's never any rhyme or reason to things like this. At least no good reason."

"I'm old enough to remember the peace marches in the sixties, because, hell, I was marching with 'em." A wry expression passed over Jonas's face. "Funny how it seemed like there was an awful lot of black and brown faces in Vietnam all out of proportion to the population, you know? We had that chant—'War! Huh! What is it good for? Absolutely NOTHIN'!' And I don't see anything here to make me change my mind."

"Well, now we just need t'get ya elected, Jonas." John grinned. They had arrived at their destination. The bodega was located right on the corner of the street—what used to be a street, anyhow. Part of the building above the entrance had been collapsed, somehow; stray weapons fire, more than likely. Tons and tons of twisted rebar, bricks, and building refuse prevented anyone from even seeing the door. Corrugated steel "riot shutters" were pulled down and locked over the windows. That was what John was to remove.

"The smell in there is probably enough to choke a mule," Jonas observed ruefully. "But the canned goods should still be good, and Lord knows that there is an acute shortage of diapers around here. If I can just get the store running, I might be able to get someone to bring in stock for me."

John nodded, pulling back the sleeves of his shirt. "Just show me where t'cut, and we'll get ya back to runnin' this joint."

"The locks first, then the hinges, there and there—" Jonas pointed. "The shutters should just fall off."

John relaxed, focusing on his breathing and untensing his muscles. Once he was sure that he was concentrating on what he had to do, he spoke. "You'll wanna look away for this; it's gonna be pretty bright." He waited a heartbeat before he started the flames. Small at first, no bigger than what a Zippo would produce. That was always the hardest part—keeping from releasing all of the energy at once. The flames started a few inches in front of his fingertips; they coalesced, and then intensified. A few seconds later, the fire was white-hot and steady. John willed the flames to where they were needed in a rigid stream, sending sparks into the air each time he contacted metal.

Behind him, he heard people congregating. Not many, and they were quiet. One kid piped up with "Mister Jonas? You guys gonna open the store? Ma says if I don't come back with laundry soap she's gonna make *me* wash them diapers!"

A couple folks chuckled at this. "We'll help you clear out the garbage, Jonas, if that'll get you goin' faster."

John was just about finished with the last hinge on the shutters when company showed up in a nearly silent sedan that probably cost more than any ten houses here, put together. The doors scissored up, and four men stepped out. Their distinctive Echo uniforms were unmistakable. Tight black pants and form-fitting jackets with little Nehru collars, looking as if they had come straight from a 60s sci-fi show about the future—one in which these guys were the storm troopers. Over the right breast was the Echo logo in red. Knee boots of shiny stuff that was not exactly leather completed the image of the sci-fi flashback; all they lacked to make the image complete was a perky little cap. Now, supposedly the reason for the color, or lack of it, was the special fabric—"nanoweave" it was called—and it didn't take dye. This was its natural color. That knowledge didn't help.

Goon squad. John extinguished his flames in an instant; even though the molten metal from the locks and hinges was still cooling on the sidewalk, he didn't want to be too obvious if he could help it. The Echo squad made its way through the crowd, which parted readily. Folks around here had grown to mistrust anything in a uniform after years of being targeted for "routine policing," and with the neglect of this 'hood, Echo wasn't really a home-crowd favorite.

Jonas stepped in front of John, fists on his hips, looking the Echo patrol up and down before he spoke. "Anything we can do for you boys?" he asked, with perfect diction and pronunciation, making sure that his gray hair and age spoke for him as well. "Or do you think you can give us a hand getting into my store so I can start serving my neighbors here again?" He cast a sidelong glance at one of the little kids. "Seems Jamel here is going to have to wash diapers unless I can sell him some soap for his mama."

One of the Echo operatives stepped to the front of the group, a distinctly displeased look on his face. He was a thin man, in good physical shape like almost all of the Echo personnel, but with a look of irritation so ingrained in his features that it probably never left his face. *He could use a perky little 60s cap to cover his bald spot*, John thought. Normally, he would have laughed right in front of the man, but this wasn't a particularly good time to show his disdain for uniforms and the folks that wore them.

"I don't suppose you have any proof you own this business?" the leader, an OpOne by the insignia, said through gritted teeth.

"Sure I do. In the store." Jonas jerked a single thumb back towards the inaccessible bodega. This caused more than a few people in the crowd to chuckle; they were definitely not on the Echo leader's side, and he knew it.

"Hey," said one lanky bystander. "Use that head. That store's been a wreck fer two weeks. Stuff's been rottin' in there. Who'd break in there when even my dog knows old Jonas ain't never kept no cash past closin' time an' there ain't nothin' in there now but stink an' soap an' canned beans?"

The Echo leader frowned even more, which John hadn't thought was possible without the man's face splitting in half. "Right. I can only guess that I'll find plenty of folks in this crowd that'll vouch for 'Jonas' here, so I'll save my time. I've got more important things to do than contend with this."

"Like get the bastards that torched my car?" called someone.

"Or the jerks that're sellin' crank in the next block?" asked another.

"No. With the primary attack from the invaders being centered on Echo Headquarters, we're understaffed.

We lost a lot of *good* people, and need to refill the ranks to meet the demand for security around the city. We've received reports of a metahuman in this area, an unregistered one. We're willing to offer a reward for anyone that wishes to cooperate."

Dead silence followed his words. Jonas scowled.

The metahuman looked over the crowd, looking down his nose at them in a way that reminded John of a middle-management type that had shown up to "inspect" a worksite he'd once done day labor at. The man exuded an "I'm better than this" attitude, and it was apparent to the gathered crowd.

"You are under martial law," the leader said, his voice sounding a little shrill. "I'll have you know I have the authority to arrest anyone I suspect of harboring an unregistered metahuman and incarcerate them for as long as I care to."

Mistake. The only thing that could have been worse would be if he had started firing into the crowd with a sidearm. The residents started protesting loudly, some of them a little bit more aggressively than was comfortable for the officer. He realized his mistake too late; what had been a gawking crowd standing around waiting peaceably was turning very ugly. The man's own squad exchanged incredulous glances.

"You can't do that!" someone protested, but the man next to him elbowed him viciously.

"He's a cop," someone else said, with a resigned sneer. "He can do whatever he wants to."

John stepped forward, holding up a hand to quiet everyone. He settled his gaze on the Echo leader. "Cut the crap, fella. Whaddya want?"

"Are you the unreg—"

John interrupted him. "Yeah, yeah, save it. I'll repeat myself: whaddya want?" John crossed his arms in front of his chest, waiting for a response.

The man started to sweat. "I'm authorized to order you to come in for registration and recruitment into Echo. Failure to do so—"

"Bull, pal. You've got no such authority. You never did before, an' nothin's changed since. The Constitution is still around, I'm assumin', so unless y'got me doin' somethin' wrong, you've got no right to drag me in. If y'wanna ignore that, I doubt that you an' yer Boy Scouts here could do the job." John casually pointed a finger at the group of three Echo SupportOps behind the leader; they were huddled together, almost defensively. The shocked looks on their faces told him that their putative leader had stepped far, far over the line. "They're green, and you're so full of it I'm surprised that yer eyes aren't brown." John took a step forward, igniting his flames so that they sheathed around his right arm as he moved. "So, y'wanna make an issue of it, or can I go back to helpin' out another law-abidin' citizen?"

It was a no-win situation and the leader knew it. Whatever his powers were, they could not possibly equal John's; even with his flames out of the picture, John had several "modifications" that would still put him over par with these chumps. What was more, the crowd was still looking ugly; they were firmly in John and Jonas's camp to begin with, and more so now that the Echo leader had opened his mouth.

The man turned red with fury, but at least he finally had the sense to realize when he was whipped. "I'm going to report this!" he sputtered, pointing an accusing finger at John, and then Jonas. "And when I do—"

"It'll go in a big old file drawer that nobody ever opens, along with everything else about this neighborhood," Jonas said. "Y'all can talk, and when y'all are down here actually doing something for *us,* maybe we'll listen." The Echo leader looked as if he wanted to retort with another snooty comment, but thought better of it. Still red in the face, he turned on his heel and marched back through the crowd, his squad in tow. The crowd jeered and hollered as the uniformed meta left, but their attention turned back to John and Jonas after the Echo personnel were out of sight.

"Jonas, y'ready t'get back into business? Looks to me like y'got plenty of customers here waitin' on ya." John shut off his flames again, setting his fists on his hips.

"There is nothing I would like better, my brother," replied Jonas with a smile. John threw him a lopsided grin in return, and set about prying off the shutters. He didn't like the fact that Echo had heard that he was in the area, and knew he was a metahuman. Any time something like that had happened in the last few years, John had gotten the hell out of Dodge as fast as he could. He'd been careful not to let his name slip during the conversation with the Echo stooge just now, but that wasn't much comfort. Despite the home-team support from the neighborhood, he didn't doubt that there'd be someone who'd be willing to talk, whether through being bribed or under duress. So far, the neighborhood only knew him as John the Welder.

Ah, shove it. He'd stay put for now, and see what more he could do. If things went south, he could fade away into the background chaos of the city. He pushed those thoughts to the back of his mind. Right now, all he wanted to worry about was whether Jonas had any beer left in his shop.

John stumbled through the open door of his squat in the old industrial loft, a day's worth of sweat and grime covering him from head to toe. He shut the door behind him, latching it shut, securing deadbolts he had installed there himself; there were more security devices on that door than there were on most people's cars.

Feeling a modicum of safety, John stripped out of his "work clothes." When he was done, a Kevlar assault vest, a pair of tactical boots, and two armored shoulder pads lay in a messy pile at the foot of his mattress. All of them were well worn, with various disfigurements marring their once new exteriors. An acid burn here, a tear from a knife there, a rip caused by sheer bludgeoning; these wounded garments were a reflection of the past experiences of their previous owners. John still didn't have a great deal of money, but when a person knew where to look, there'd always be bits and pieces of equipment lying around just waiting for someone to snatch them up right now. He'd once thought himself to be above scavenging, much less looting the dead, but necessity and time had worn away at some of his scruples.

Still soaked through with sweat, John stood panting with his back to the door, surveying his apartment. This inspection was to make sure that everything was how it had been left. Not that there was much that could have been tampered with.

Having decided that his sanctum, if you could call

it that, was still inviolate, John went straight to the bathroom and stood in the cold shower until he felt marginally clean. Pulling on tattered pants and a shirt, he walked over to the mattress. He flopped down on it hard, sighing heavily as he did. He figured he still had some time to steel himself for the shakes that always came after a night of "work." He sat up straight, then pulled his knees to his chest. His teeth clenched, he tried to regulate his breathing a little. Then the shakes started.

Every day, John Murdock would wake up, put on his work clothes, and be one more set of hands putting the neighborhood to rights. Every night, he would put on the other set of work clothes and go out to put things to rights in other ways. And then, when he got "home," he'd fight himself. It was an uphill battle, getting steeper each day. And at the end of every night, every bout of shakes, he'd clean up, and swear he'd never do it again. Never run down an alley, only to meet a chorus of shotgun blasts. Never plod through a dank, abandoned building, wondering which shadow wouldn't really be just a shadow. Never have to listen to the cries of some innocent schmoe, waiting to die or worse, someone at the wrong place, at the wrong time, screaming for help. *Save me. Please. Help.*

But then he'd think about what he'd done. Before the Nazis. Before the invasion. What he'd done, and what had been done to him. And her.

Then he'd slowly stop shaking, and turn on the television. Pick up a book as he absorbed the yammering of some bright smile with haunted eyes, gibbering about the latest news as if the invasion had never happened, or as if it didn't matter as long as people absorbed their babble, and bought what they advertised. There was something especially sickening in how a news announcer's voice would be full of strain and fatigue, and then it would be followed by a recording made months before in an ad agency's perfect little recording booth, when nothing could be so awesome and right in life as having their product. And then, back to the newsreader's soul-weariness in eerie contrast. John's life was like that too, and maybe that was why it bugged him so much. He'd get his fill of giving people a little bit of hope, and then fight some of what took their hope away, and never quite do enough. He'd maybe eat, and then he would sleep. And repeat it all the next day.

After running into the Echo patrol—Echo press-gang would have been a more fitting term—it hadn't taken long for the locals of this isolated neighborhood to accept that John was more than just another refugee or drifter. Things started to quickly ramp up, after the confrontation, and now his metahuman nature was well-known in the area; a local grocer needed protection from the gangs, a building full of concerned tenants that were tired of the drug dealers using the abandoned apartments of their home for deals, and so on. John was all they had. And he was finding it hard to say no.

It was against his best interests to do anything high-profile; just running around at night and taking care of the worst of the criminal element was already plenty stupid, by his estimation. But . . . there was still something that wouldn't let him ignore these people. It went against his instincts, honed after the last few years of surviving all alone, but the small-timers that were preying on the remains of the destruction, like carrion feeders—they irked him on a personal level.

He'd started working on a better plan, though. There were two gangs in this neighborhood that had banded together after the attacks, for mutual protection. In truth, they were closer to militias, which gave John something to work with. He had talked with the leaders of both groups; they were criminals, all right, but he wasn't exactly a saint either. His plan was to organize both groups around the neighborhood they shared, with the purpose of taking care of the area's basic needs. This would afford the groups a measure of responsibility, which was close enough to power to water the mouths of the gang leaders. Initially, they resisted John's plan; that quickly faded after he had properly demonstrated his powers on a ruined car during one of the first joint meetings he'd held with the gang leaders and a council of some of the more prominent neighborhood residents. There was one thing that always made sense to criminals, and that was violence, or at least the threat of it. John hated doing it, but it was a necessary evil in order to get them to listen.

Now things were happening; space was being cleared for a guarded community garden, classes were being organized for children and adults alike, a minor clinic had been set up one day a week by some hippies called Hog Farmers, and they had even managed a rudimentary sanitation service. Between the two destruction corridors, the neighborhood looked like it might get close to normalcy. It was akin to how the Black Panthers had made neighborhoods self-sufficient back in the 70s; the key difference being that this neighborhood had banded together in the face of shared hardship and recent horror, instead of against racial discrimination.

That night, John was reading Kierkegaard's *Purity of Heart*, when he actually bothered to pay attention to the television. A group of metas, wearing red uniforms, were displayed in a video clip, fighting the Nazis against a background of what looked like the Russian version of the Invasion. The newscaster offered his sardonic commentary about a group of radically leftist heroes, calling themselves the something unintelligible and Russian, which seemed to have the initials "CCCP." Then, another shot, of some of the same people arriving on the concourse of Atlanta Hartsfield, escorted by Echo personnel, warily avoided by the civilians, over whom most of them towered, Especially one striking woman, dark-haired and stunning, with cold eyes that measured everything and found it substandard.

Apparently they had come to help.

"While the name would imply a closed membership of Ruskie hard-liners," the frozen-bright smile and empty eyes blathered, "the group declares that it welcomes anyone willing to fight for the greater good of the working class. And I'd thought all that was so last century." The bleached-and-teased newscaster smiled and laughed with his bleached-and-teased co-anchoress. Disgusted, John shut the television off. His interest had been piqued, though. Maybe if he had time tomorrow...

There were several places in the city where Seraphym took up perches; she didn't eat, didn't sleep, and one place was as good as another to her. The

Suntrust Plaza Building was the most obvious. But there were others. When she tired of being stared at, there were places she could go to be unnoticed, to sort through the futures, sifting through the threads of what-might-be. It was difficult to do this when you were being gawked at or shot at. The gawking wasn't so bad, but the bullets were annoying. The tug on the lines of the present would disturb her and she would have to deal with the would-be killers, sometimes losing her train of thought for an entire minute.

Even if she had not been very close to omniscient, it would not at all have surprised her that there had been people trying to kill her. It was not just the two metacriminals that had made the first attempts on her life; those she had left in fetal curls after exposing their innermost thoughts and revealing to them every darkest secret they attempted to deny. After seeing on the news what she could do, she still could not imagine why they had thought they could take her. Humans were unfathomable sometimes.

There had been one televangelist whose empire had come crashing down in the wake of the Thulian attacks. He blamed her for not saving his elaborate church complex from the Thulian troopers. His motive she could at least understand, and his anger had been fueled by self-righteousness to the point where he was, as she understood the term, insane.

She had melted the barrel of his shotgun, and exposed him to all of the pain he had caused others by taking the money they could have used to support themselves in exchange for his false promises of salvation. He had not been left in a fetal curl; he had collapsed and crawled away on hands and knees, passing out of her sphere of interest. However he chose to redeem himself, or if he simply died, did not matter to the futures.

There had been contract killers—a mercenary group called Blacksnake for two, a freelance for one—who had been hired by other "religious" men, because she did not act as they felt an Angel of the Lord should: to wit, to act for *them*, as "God's personal enforcer" of what their narrow view of morality encompassed. Therefore she must be Fallen. As if they had any notion just what the Fallen were like. The contract killers she had dealt with simply; she allowed their victims access to them, or rather, the spirits of those victims, those who had not forgiven and gone Home, that is—which was quite a few. Chased by the haunts they themselves had created, again she dismissed them. They had no impact on the futures and thus no further impact on her.

Still, the interruptions were annoying. So she had a perch or two that no one knew about, where she had never let anyone catch sight of her. This was one, this rooftop on an abandoned industrial building. It was the one that she most often chose, not only because she could sit here unobserved, but because this was a place that ate at her. It was a blank spot in the futures, a hole in the intricate threads she was trying to sort. She could not yet understand its importance, so she would come here to try and make some sense of it, prowling mentally around it and sniffing suspiciously, like a cat around something that might be a coiled snake, or might only be a coil of rubber hose.

She had come here tonight just after midnight, wearying of the everlasting gawkers trying to take pictures of her. She could go about her rescues just as easily, and less visibly, from here. Things slowed just after midnight, leaving her to settle, wings close-furled, in the chill, damp air of predawn, to blank her mind and wait for direction.

But it was not a clear direction that came.

It was a man.

He strolled casually from the roof access door, bringing a bottle of beer to his lips as he walked. Seraphym could see his physical body clearly, even in the gloom; he was dressed simply, with a sweat-soaked A-shirt and a pair of ratty jeans. In another instant, she scanned him, trying to determine the futures and threads connected to his existence—and was surprised to find that she couldn't. Recognition replaced the novel sensation of astonishment almost as quickly as it had come over her. This was the man she had seen a few weeks ago, when she had saved one particular soul that had the misfortune of being ambushed by looters.

And another surprise: the Infinite was still not going to reveal his futures to her. He existed for her only in the present, and an unfamiliar sensation sizzled quietly through her. After a moment she recognized it.

Fear.

She tasted the sensation; it was very new to her. Never in all of her long, long existence had she personally felt fear until she had been made incarnate here. She'd fought some of the darkest entities in existence, and braved horrors that would have shattered a mortal mind. But never had there been this sense of dread. She knew why she felt it now, of course; she was made in Man's image and when humans encountered something they did not recognize, that was alien to them, they felt fear.

Why could she not See him?

He stopped, bottle forgotten in his hand, and stared at her.

Who are you? she asked, fixing him with her gaze. The novelty of this sensation, this *fear* as well as the uncertainty itself, had her slightly unbalanced. Now that she had him in her physical sight, she knew his name. It was there, in his mind, in her memory. John Murdock. And this was not the first time he had made her feel fear, and for the same reason. She knew him only through emotions. Doubts, fears, horrors—but no hopes, no dreams; he had given those up long ago. To read anything more, the things that were not in the front of his mind . . . that was hard, harder than it should have been. She could not actually see his past unless he chose to think about it, which was the last thing he wanted to do. And he was the nexus of a surprising number of paths leading to him. Yet none that she could perceive led *away* from him.

She did not know what he would do, what he could do, what he would be, not in the futures, not in *a* future, not in the next minute. The hole in the futures was not this place. It was him. And she had been brought to him; even now she felt in herself a connection to him that, in the context of what she herself knew, made no sense.

An inquiry confirmed what she had surmised. The Infinite was still withholding things about this man from her.

And she did not know why.

"Who . . . are you?" she said aloud, as humans spoke, her voice sounding strange and hollow in her own ears.

He regarded her for a moment, and then scoffed

before taking a swig from his bottle. "I thought that'd be apparent," came the laconic reply. "I'm your Creator. You're a figment of my imagination, after all, ain'tcha?"

That shocked a startled laugh out of her. "My Creator, John Murdock, is nothing you believe in. Why can I not See you?" Her wings stirred restlessly, made of tongues of flame for feathers that gave off their own light for those who could see them. She herself glowed, soft and golden, in the darkness.

John leaned forward, counterbalancing himself with his bottle in hand and squinting at her. "You've got me, Harvey Rabbit. I guess you can't really see me, period, since you don't exist, but that's waxin' a bit too philosophical for my tastes." He stood back up straight, ambling over to lean against a wall.

There came the faintest stirrings of . . . now what was this? Irritation. She was piqued that he did not believe she was real! Up until this moment she had been utterly indifferent as to whether mortals believed in her or not. Why should she care about this one?

Yet she did. She was determined to prove to him that she was as real as he was. As he raised the bottle to his lips, with a thought, she changed the beer to spring water. John sputtered his next gulp in surprise, then looked at the bottle in annoyance.

"Well, that was a waste." He chucked the bottle away, letting it clatter against the roof and off into the darkness. "Y'know, I've known that I'm crazy for a while. I just wish I could still enjoy a simple beer."

"One should not litter, John Murdock," she chided, and held out her hand. The bottle flew to it. She handed the bottle back to him, full once again, and felt a strange tingle as her fingers brushed his. Potential.

Potential of the futures. He was awash with them. He was a nexus of many, many important things that might happen—and yet she groped after them blindly, unable to sort them, able at the moment only to understand that they were there. "Perhaps this German beer will be more to your liking—although I can make it be Guinness or Foster's, or...the beer from the recipe of Pharaoh Ramses if you prefer."

He accepted the beer, took a long pull from it and sighed before speaking. "Y'just might be of some use here, Harvey. Erm—whaddya call yourself, or do you want to call yourself anything? Harvey probably fits well enough, considering, but it feels a bit odd saying it to a really *pretty* hallucination, y'know?"

She blinked, both at the question and at his flippancy, so at odds with what lay beneath his surface. She had never had a name before. She was an individual, yes, but...what she had to identify her was a fragment of the Song, not a name as such.

"In the mortal media...I am known as the Seraphym." She frowned. "And I am the creation of the Infinite, not of you."

John shook his head dismissively. "That's too much of a mouthful; how 'bout Sera, for starters?"

"It is no better and no worse than any other name." *Sera. Que sera, sera—what will be, will be. Am I what will be?* Her mind flitted around him and his potentials, trying to guess what she could not see by the shape of the void of which he was the center.

"Sera it is. Now, what's this 'Infinite' schtick? Some sorta band?"

She blinked, and took a nanosecond to sort through all the possible meanings of his words before the most logical presented itself. Surely he could not think—she answered his question as if it had been posed in all seriousness. "The Infinite is All. It is and was and always will be. It contains everything and is everything, and we Siblings sing the Song of Its Creation."

He stared at her for a few long moments, clearly not happy with her answer. "So it is a band. Whatever you say, Obi-Weird. What are ya doin' here, if I might ask?"

She hesitated. This would be the first time she had told a mortal of her purpose. It was the first time she had felt a need to do so. Oh, there were those who had recognized her for what she was, at least in part, but she had never let anyone know her purpose here in so many blatant words. Again, she felt unsettled and off-balance. Why was it that she felt moved to tell him her purpose? What was it about this mortal? Why should she answer him? Was it even permitted?

The answer came before she even posed the question. *It is permitted.*

That unsettled her more. Now, it was one thing for those who *could* do so, to see her for what she was and recognize it. It was quite another for her to tell someone, someone who apparently had no faith in any power beyond that which he could discern with his own five senses.

"What do you see?" she asked, not wanting to look into his mind just yet. Something...was making her hold back.

He quickly looked away from her, standing up straight to walk over to the side of the roof. Resting his elbows on the short wall there, he looked up at the cloudy night sky. He picked a cloud, gesturing to it with his beer bottle. "I can see a cricket in a top hat. How 'bout you?" He was . . . hiding something, refusing to say what he wanted to. And she could take that thought from him—but she would not.

She tilted her head to the side. "You do not answer the question that I asked, John Murdock. Why is that? Why do you fear the answer?"

"I'm fickle like that," came the unenthusiastic response. "To be fair, ya haven't answered my question, either. What are ya doin' here?"

That was fair. Information for information. "I am a servant, an instrument, of the Infinite. The Infinite cannot intervene directly in mortal affairs but . . . there is a shadow on the futures of this world, and a darkness to come to it and worlds beyond this one, unless . . ." She paused. She knew what she did, but how to phrase it? She searched through things that wise humans had said. "'God does not play at dice with the universe,' one of your prophets said. What most mortals call God does not *play* with the universe at all. The creatures of life are given a gift, that of Free Will, and the means to steer their own course. But sometimes—this time—some of those creatures have gone too far. What they may do will undo the fabric of Creation, eventually, or at the least cause significant damage. So . . . I am here to . . . show options. It is for mortals to choose, once they know what the options are." And that was when it hit her. Options. This man had none. Or rather, he had no future at all, or else . . . hidden inside the man was something entirely new, something that could not be tracked, nor anticipated.

He was just one man—except . . . he might be one of those she was expected to try to save. If this mortal in the equation ceased to be able to affect the mortal world, it might be hard to find another to replace him.

But telling him would serve no purpose, not just now. She had to learn about him, learn about him the hard way, as mortals did, before she could decide what to do about him.

Seraphym, you have Free Will too.

She felt breathless, shocked to her core at the thought. The Siblings did not have Free Will; they were infinite reflections of the Infinite. Except...she had been given Free Will. What did that make her?

"And I am here, on this roof, because it is quiet. I suppose you could call me an angel," she said, speaking before she thought.

"Well, that answers your question for ya, too."

"Which question?"

He turned his gaze back to her, soberly. "What I saw when I looked at ya: an angel, in every sense." John didn't look at her for long, breaking eye contact and returning to stare at the night sky. "It's bull, but that's what I saw."

So, he had seen her in her full Aspect! Yet he was not a believer, nor was he gifted with the clear sight of the magicians. That was unexpected. Everything about him was unexpected. She sensed that the time to end this conversation was now. She needed to think. But...

"'Oh Lord, I believe,'" she quoted wryly. "'Help thou my unbelief.' I shall give you a new thing, John Murdock. Something that you may feel with your fingers, smell with your nostrils, taste with your tongue. And it will be there when I am gone, to help with your unbelief. Here."

She took one of his hands, feeling again that strange tingle, and put something in it. A pottery jar, corked with a lump of unbaked clay. "This is the beer of the Pharaoh. You will not like it. It is made by fermenting barley bread."

And then she spread her wings and launched herself skyward. Out there, she sensed already there was someone she should save. It never ended.

Could she save John Murdock?

John turned back to stare out at the city. Most of the fires were out, but there was still so much smoke and dust in the air. It ruined what would otherwise be pretty decent nights, like tonight. It wasn't just the haze that messed it up, it was the stink of smoldering tires, burnt plastic and other less-identifiable things that put instincts on edge.

He wasn't terribly sure of what to make of Sera. He'd seen at least one of the news broadcasts detailing the "Seraphym phenomenon" that had been documented in cities all over the globe. Some of the pundits speculated that it was a group of mind-linked or body-duplicating metahumans, while others contested that it could be a single, sufficiently "talented" meta sending out projections. He had dismissed what he had seen in New York as a trick of his anguished mind and the terrible explosion that had been the red-haired kid going nova. Ever since he got to Atlanta, he hadn't given the "being" he'd seen at the truck ambush much thought, but now he was certain that it was the same as his newest acquaintance.

He didn't like any of it. Her knowing his name, showing up on top of the roof of *his* building, not any of it. He'd done a good job of hiding it, but every instinct in his body had railed against his will to strike out and attack her out of surprise when she'd first shown herself on the roof. Attack her reflexively, or run as fast and as hard as he could in the other direction.

Under it all was sheer, mind-blanking terror. It was one of the constants of his life in the past few years, but never had it been as strong as it was now. Everything he was doing nowadays—none of it made any sense. He wouldn't make it through if he kept up like this. He ought to pack up and leave tonight—to hell with that, just leave. He didn't have anything he couldn't replace. One of the advantages of being a vagrant: picking up and running was a simple affair.

But . . . still. He couldn't, despite the fact that leaving would be the first smart thing he'd done since the Nazis showed up.

When he'd looked at her . . . something had quaked inside of him. Something primal and horrible, and he knew that he couldn't ignore her. And with that realization came the other constant emotion of the past five years—hate, mostly of himself.

John ran his fingers through his hair, finishing his beer. He left the clay jar that Sera had given him on the ledge, and went back inside. He had a lot of thinking to do.

CHAPTER TEN

Bad For Good

MERCEDES LACKEY

"Miss Parker, you must be getting at least as tired of this as I am, but unfortunately, you seem to have violated the Damage Control Officer's Directive again." Yankee Pride glared at Bella. She shrugged.

"I was with an OpOne and two SupportOps and they lost control of the situation," she replied. "I restored it. I'm supposed to maintain a safe zone, right?"

"Yes, but—"

"And you would agree that a goon in cyber armor—cobbled together from the stuff in his garage and the bits he snagged from looting research firms—running rampant through Five Points is not safe, right?"

"Yes, but—"

"And he managed to knock Corbie out in the first ten seconds, ran Silas up a tree and had Grainger peeing his pants. And there was no backup. Dispatch said so. The SWAT sniper squad was stuck on the other side of the destruction corridor, and that assumes they would have found a chink in that armor when they finally did get there. If they got there. Which was looking dubious." She kept a deadpan expression on her face. "I saw he was wide open telepathically, and I dealt with him. End of story."

"You hit him!"

"With a psionic blast that put him into an epileptic fit, yeah."

"You walked up to him—"

"From behind. Whatever he was using for a heads-up display and scanners sucked. Anyone could tell that. He had about thirty percent straight-ahead vision, no rear and no peripheral. That's how Corbie got on top of him in the first place."

She glanced over at Corbie, who was in rather better shape after her psychic-healing treatments now than he had been when the goon had thrown him into a building. "I'd have had him, if the taser hadn't malfunctioned," Corbie grumbled. "Piece of shite—Yank, if you're gonna expect me t' be getting physical, you gotta give me better equipment."

"I'll discuss that with you later—" Yankee Pride turned back to Bella. "You walked up to him, put your hand on him, and you hit him!"

"I'm a touch-telepath, if you want reliable," Bella sighed. "I've told you that before. After five feet, things get weaker, after ten, dicey and after that—"

"I don't *care* about that! *You hit him!* You're the DCO!"

"Yada, yada, healers aren't hitters." She returned his outraged glare. "You're too used to Einhorn, who'd rather cry and hope the *big bad mans* folds. Who else was going to? You had an out-of-control situation, I controlled it. Like I was supposed to. Protect the civilians. Right?"

"She's got a point, mate," Corbie said laconically.

"You stay out of this!"

Yankee Pride, Bella thought, was starting to unravel. Just like Tesla. Echo was in a siege mentality, and for Pride, that meant "stick to the rules no matter what, because that's all we have left."

And Bella was violating the rules with practically every breath she took. *Echo healers do not operate offensively. New Echo personnel do not live off the campus. Echo healers do not practice medicine on citizens without a license. Yeah. That'll work.*

She already had her eye on an apartment near that little magician. She was operating a roving Free Clinic out of a van. The van in question was operated by a hippie commune that was going into the 'hoods and helping people set up gardens, and distributing anything in the way of food and help they could get their hands on.

"The rules ain't workin', mate," Corbie persisted.

Yank very nearly exploded at that point. "That's not *your* call. That's not *my* call. We follow the rules!"

"Ja, ja," Bella muttered, "I vas only followink orders." Fortunately Yank didn't hear that, though Corbie did, and smirked.

"The rules are there for a reason, Parker!" Yank was saying, losing the "miss" now. "You DCOs get involved in combat, you make yourselves targets, you make your patients targets, and if you go down, who's going to protect the civilians and keep the team on its feet?"

"And when *none* of the team is on its feet?" She wasn't giving an inch on this one. Lost Wages FD didn't tie the hands of its paramedics when they went into a dangerous part of town. If you wanted to carry, and you got the permit, you were allowed to carry on the job. Bella's hammerless Taurus .45 was in her luggage, and when she got her own apartment, it would be in her headboard. "When the rest of the team is outgunned and outmanned, you *still* want me to sit on my hands? Dammit, Yank, the Fire Department let me carry a gun as a paramedic! You don't want me using powers, *fine,* then let me pack heat!"

"Damage Control Officers do *not* act offensively!" He was on his feet and yelling.

"Then make me something besides a DCO!" she shouted back. They glared at each other for a good minute, before Yankee Pride threw up his hands melodramatically and marched out.

She stared after him, sourly. She hadn't won, and she knew it.

The apartment was good-sized, and the price was a great deal. The building was old, and it was in the blue-collar part of town, but it came with appliances and some furniture, there was cable and...

Bella stared at the metal box by the socket in the wall. "Is that a T1 line?"

The super made a face as if to say *hell if I know.* "That's what I'm told. Little gal next door to you, the writer, had it put in a good while back. Asked for permission, owner said if she put it in her own place she had to put it in everyone else's. She didn't bat an eye. Guess those romances pay good bucks."

"Either that or she's got connections." There was definitely way, way more to Vickie Nagy than met the eye. "I'll take it." She signed the lease, and wrote out a check for the first month plus deposit then and there. "In fact, can I take it now?" On the off chance that she'd be able to get a place today, she'd loaded everything she had brought with her in the Echo van she had borrowed.

The super shrugged. "The utilities are on, the companies are sayin' that they want people to do stuff over the 'net instead of tryin' to come in. If you got a credit card an' can make deposits?"

"Within fifteen minutes of plugging into that T1 line." Bella eyed it with greed.

"I'll help ya unload."

Shortly the living room was full of boxes and bundles, the super had a twenty-dollar "thank you," and Bella had a new home. She took off from unpacking just long enough to get the van back, and she got a break on that. One of the SupportOps she worked with was just coming on shift and needed it and was willing to come there to pick it up. He brought pizza, she paid for it for both of them and passed him a six-pack of beer. Easy peasy.

Good thing about being a meta; they all seemed to have some slight component of superstrength and endurance. By sunset, Bella had everything unpacked, the boxes broken down, and her own bed with the NASA foam mattress made up and ready to sleep in. Now all she needed to do was find the laundry room....

Down in the basement, laden with basket and soap, she pushed at doors until one gave—

Victoria jumped back against the wall with a screech that was not quite covered by the sound of the washing machines.

"Whoa!" Bella dropped the basket and put out both hands placatingly, and concentrated on putting out a soothing vibe. "It's just me. I'm your new neighbor. Thanks for the fat 'net pipe, by the way."

Vickie's pupils were as big as coat buttons and she was shaking. And for once there weren't any gloves on her hands. Bella deliberately did not look at them directly, but she had excellent peripheral vision and what she saw definitely gave her food for thought. The skin was horribly scar-seamed and tight-shiny, the fingers skeletal. She knew that look. Burns, bad ones. Things began to fall into place. She wondered how much Echo knew....

"Steady. Deep breaths. You know the drill, right?"

The tiny blonde nodded, and without taking her eyes off Bella's, began taking deep, shuddering breaths. Slowly her pupils contracted. Slowly she stopped shaking. Finally she peeled herself off the wall. "You're— my neighbor?"

"Right next door. I'm pretty sure our bedrooms share a wall. I don't snore."

Vickie managed a ghost of a grin. "Yes. Yes, well. Good. As long as you don't get into knockdown drag-out fights with your boyfriend. Or at least, if you do, I get the right to record everything you say, and use it in a book later."

Bella rolled her eyes. "Now I know why that apartment was going cheap. Okay, since I don't have any boyfriends, done deal. It's worth it for the T1 line." She kept her tone light. Vickie had endured a very rough time of it from the look of things. Panic attacks that fierce, coupled with obvious burn scars and severe body-shyness—well, it was safe to assume whatever did that to her wasn't the common, garden variety of domestic violence that Bella was so familiar with from the ambulance runs.

Maybe someone decided to burn the witch, she thought, with a shudder she took care not to show. At a very young and impressionable age, she had watched Bergman's *The Seventh Seal*, and the image of the young woman being burned for heresy still came back to haunt her nightmares. And certainly Red Saviour seemed only too willing to take that route with Vickie.

"Anyway, I am all moved in, so don't freak when you hear someone next door tonight. And I sing, so if I get too loud, don't hesitate to bang on the wall." She grinned. "Sorry about barging in like that. I figured, it was Friday night, who'd be doing laundry?"

"The person who has panic attacks leaving her apartment," Vickie responded, with a bitter-sounding laugh. "Who else?"

Time for a peace offering. "Look, if you've decided to try and beat this thing, you go, girl. But it doesn't have to be all at once. I can do your shopping for you. And I can do your laundry when I do mine. How much stuff can two women filthy-up in a week anyway?" Bella grinned. "Save your strength for the battles that count, don't wear yourself out in the skirmishes."

Vickie looked at her, dumbfounded. "I—I'm not sure what to say—"

"Say 'Thank you, Bella,' then go upstairs. I'll babysit your underwear. I owe you that much for scaring the whey out of you."

The blonde let out her breath in a long sigh that seemed to let a lot of tension out of her as well. "Thank you, Bella."

"*De nada*," Bella replied, with a casual wave of a blue hand. As Vickie scuttled out, she loaded up the other two machines and made herself comfortable, propping up her feet, opening her book, and sticking her MP3 player earbuds in her ears. And wondered what the cits would think to see an OpTwo meta parked in a laundry room.

The Hog Farm Commune had been established back in the sixties. Forty years later it was, somehow, still going strong. Perhaps it was the ethic, or perhaps the fact that the founders managed to embrace every alternative lifestyle there was without making anyone feel excluded or picked on. Although its head and home were in Mendocino County in California, it had branches all over the country, and one of those branches was outside of Atlanta.

Red Earth Hog Farm had been—no surprise there— completely untouched by the Nazis. And in the tradition of Hog Farmers everywhere, even before the last of the big fires had been extinguished, Hog Farmers had loaded up their psychedelically painted vans and headed for the inner city, laden with food and help.

Hard as it was to imagine when you looked at the destruction corridors, life for the wealthy had gone pretty much back on track by this time. In the gated communities, and in the whiter suburbs, the grocery stores were being supplied again with most of what people had come to expect and plenty of luxury goods. In the 'hood, grocery trucks were coming a lot less frequently even to the big chain stores. Plenty of people were cut off from those by destruction corridors, and as for the mom-and-pops and corner bodegas that people depended on . . . as might be expected, the chains got first priority, since they had their own supply fleets, and the indie distributors supplied them first because they were more of a guaranteed paycheck. That didn't leave a lot of deliveries for the small stores. As for folks that had once had jobs, sad to say, a lot of them either didn't anymore, or couldn't get to them. That meant no money for supplies anyway.

Hog Farmers to the rescue, with food and anything else they could scrounge up that might need passing out. They showed up by the tie-dyed score, with tools and expertise and seeds to help people turn even tiny lots into gardens. Bella knew all about the Hog Farmers from her parents, who'd been activists in the sixties. As soon as she knew they were in the 'hoods, she signed up as a medic. Or actually, not "signed up" as such. The Farmers weren't big on paperwork and paper trails. Technically she was practicing medicine without a license, but AMA doctors were in short supply, and not inclined to set up free clinics. No, officially she was along to "guard the food." And if people happened to get better when she was around, well, wasn't that a miracle, praise Chee-zus!

She was very careful not to keep anything desirable in her little jump bag on these jaunts. Nothing expensive—in fact, nothing a school nurse wouldn't have, and no drugs of any kind. She and the Farmers were very clear about that to everyone that came looking for medical help—just as she was very clear that there were some things she could not help with. Recent injury, most disease, yes. Cancer . . . maybe. Genetic defects, old injuries healed wrong, heart disease, diabetes—maybe sometimes, but it was chancy. There were a lot of things she just couldn't do anything about, though it made her want to cry or throw things when she had to turn people away. Echo would have

had a fit if they had known about this. She was already
doing long shifts—they all were—but she had never
needed much sleep, and this . . . this was important.

But it seemed that not everyone had gotten the
memo about what she didn't carry.

Bella was just packing up her bag, and Zeke, Moonfairy and Brown Derby were folding up the cardboard
cartons, now empty, that had held the diapers the
commune made from discarded T-shirts, and the cans
of formula and condensed milk. This one had been a
special "baby run" scheduled ahead of time. A lot of
moms here had been caught short by the Invasion;
they were used to running to the bodega for dispos-
able diapers, and most of them had never seen a cloth
diaper until now. Bella had her hands full with unhappy
babies of all shades over the past hour. She'd had to
keep a firm rein on her temper a time or two when
it was obvious that some of these women were keeping fretful kids quiet by feeding them booze. But she
had a canned answer for that, one she'd gotten from
another of the paramedics in Vegas. "You know how
you feel with a hangover? Well, that's what your kid
has. A spoonful is a lot of liquor for a baby, and giving
it to him to quiet him down is only going to give him
a hangover when he wakes up. Then you get to listen
to him cry for a whole day instead of only an hour."

She was thinking about the kids as she packed up,
satisfied that she had done just about the best that
she could, when suddenly that silence descended that
made all the hair on the back of her neck stand up.

She finished packing her bag, and only then did
she turn around, slowly.

Six of them. Gang-bangers without colors, the kind

of gang that forms from bangers kicked out of *other* gangs. All buff, all packing. And oh, how she regretted that her .45 was still in the headboard...

"Whatcha got in the bag, bitch?" The leader—oh, she got bad, bad vibes from him. There was something very cold about his eyes. Whatever was looking out of them was only remotely human now. Before she could reply, he jerked his head at one of his boys, who snatched the bag out of her hands. Out of the corner of her eye she could see Moonfairy, who had his cell phone out, dialing 911. But help was not going to come very soon, if at all.

"Please don't do that," Zeke said carefully. "All we're carrying is diapers and baby form—"

The thug had already emptied her bag on the ground, and was pawing through it, looking for drugs. What he found was her speculum, blood pressure cuff, stethoscope, packets of bandages, tongue depressors, swabs, sample tubes of ointment, alcohol wipes, plastic gloves and not much else.

"Where's the stuff, bitch?" The leader smashed at her instruments with his boot. She seethed. Ointment squirted out of the mashed tubes.

"Please don't do that," Zeke said again. "We don't have drugs. Miss Parker is a meta, she—"

"I wasn't talkin' t'you!" The leader nodded at another of his boys, who backhanded Zeke into the side of the van. "I asked you, Blue. Where's the stuff? You craphead hippies always have stuff. You meta freaks, we *know* what you could get aholt of."

She shrugged. "Couldn't tell you. Don't have any."

"Wrong answer." He grabbed for her.

The instant he touched her—she knew. Knew that

his boys were edgy from doing without. Knew that the Hog Farmers' usual please-and-thank-you routine was not going to work.

Knew that the hand clamping down on her bicep belonged to someone who had murdered over thirty people, all of them up close and personal. He *liked* to kill. He had his own addiction to feed—he never had any intention of going away quietly, even if he had gotten drugs from them. She saw in his mind what he was going to do to her, and then, what he was going to do to the others. While they lay bleeding, he was going to take the last survivor, force him to drive the van full of his boys back to the Farm, and he had a plan for what they were going to do there....

There was never any question in Bella's mind of what *she* was going to do.

She let him haul her into his grasp, let him get his arm around her throat, let him get his gun to her temple. She let her anger and outrage and fear build to a lethal level.

Then she reached inside his brain; she found the control centers she wanted. She seized them and twisted. Fatally, with a dual jolt of psionic power to exactly the right places, paralyzing him, then short-circuiting the breathing center.

He stiffened, unable to move, choking, dying as he stood there. She reached up and snatched the gun from a hand that couldn't stop her, ducked and writhed out of his hold even as he began a slow toppling to the ground, and whirled, training the gun onto the one nearest Zeke.

"You want a piece of me?" she snarled, as they stared, first at her, then at their leader, on the ground,

his eyes desperate but the light already starting to fade from them as he died by inches, suffocating, suffering only a fraction of what his own victims had suffered. "Didn't you cretins pay any attention? *I'm a meta.* And I don't need this to kill you!" She flicked the gun into the van, where it landed with a muffled thud among the diapers. "I can kill you by touching you! I can kill you *without* touching you!" She took one step forward, hand outstretched, mouth twisted into a savage parody of a smile. *"You want a piece of me now?"*

The leader shuddered, and died at her feet. That was enough for the thugs. They scattered, pelting away from the crazy metahuman, as fast as their legs could carry them.

She turned to the Farmers. They all stared at her, wild-eyed. Zeke recovered first.

"Bella, wha-what did you—"

"*Never* piss off a healer," she said hoarsely, feeling her gorge rise, as her entire self revolted against what she had just done. "We know how to fix you—and that means we know how to take you apart. Now, excuse me—"

She made a dash for the alley, to heave up her guts again, and again, and again, and still she could not vomit up her horror, and the sick loathing she felt for herself. The cops that finally arrived found her there, sagged against the brick wall, with her victim not ten feet from her.

For being the subject of this hearing, Bella had been given remarkably little opportunity to say anything. Spin Doctor was handling most of it; all he required of her was that she stay calm and stick to the facts—the facts being what she had seen in the gang leader's mind.

It was taking place on the Echo campus, and not in a courtroom or a judge's office, because no one really wanted this to get out. Or even rumors of it to get out. So, for the audience of a judge and the DA, first Zeke had testified to what the Farmers had witnessed. Bella stated exactly what Spin Doctor had told her to, then sat down.

The judge looked at her skeptically. "So. The claim is, she read his mind?" he demanded of Spin Doctor.

"That's what she does, Your Honor," the Echo meta replied, evenly. "The validity of what a psion reads is already established in the courts."

The judge looked sour, but Spin Doctor was already handing him a fat file folder. "Furthermore, preliminary investigation by the police, together with DNA and fingerprint matches, places the deceased at the scene of at least seven unsolved and very brutal murders, three of them involving sexual assault. They expect more to come in as they search further back. So what Belladonna Blue saw in his mind is accurate." He raised an eloquent eyebrow. "It appears she not only apprehended a serial killer, she prevented a massacre."

"Well, that's just it, isn't it?" the judge growled. "She didn't *apprehend* him, she executed him!"

"Echo metas are authorized to use lethal force under the appropriate conditions." Spin Doctor could not have looked more bland.

"And what made this appropriate?" The judge looked ready to explode. But he would not look at Bella.

"Perhaps the gun to her head?" Spin Doctor put

both his hands on the table, leaned over, and looked hard at both the DA and the judge. "Bob, give this one up, you can't win it," he said softly. "The minute word gets out of the kind of animal she put down, and trust me, I will make sure that it does, you'll have people wanting to pin a medal on her, not lock her up. Look at her! She was out helping distribute baby formula and diapers! No one is going to believe she's dangerous to the public!"

For the first time, the judge did look at her. Bella met his eyes steadily. He was the first to look away.

"All right," he growled. "We'll put it through quietly. But keep a damned leash on her." He stood up, shoving away from the table, and stomped out, the DA right behind him.

When they were gone, Spin Doctor turned to Bella, and his expression was not encouraging.

"Now, regardless of what I just did, *you* know, and *I* know, that you could have used less-than-lethal force. That thug would have been collected by the cops, he'd have been linked back to those previous crimes, and he'd have gone to jail for seven life sentences at least—"

"Maybe I could have used sublethal force," Bella interrupted, feeling her face flush. "And maybe I couldn't have. I didn't think I had a choice then, and I don't think I did now. And maybe he would have been convicted, and maybe he wouldn't have been." She stood up, and faced the meta across the table. "All I know for sure is that he had a gun to my head, and what I saw in his mind, and I don't know enough about my own powers yet to be sure of *just stopping* someone in a case like that."

Spin Doctor frowned. It was obvious that he couldn't contradict her. It was also obvious that he didn't believe her.

"I appreciate what you did for me," she said, holding back what she wanted to say. Even though *what* she had done still made her sick to think about, she would not have changed it. Where she came from, you didn't try to rehabilitate mad dogs, you shot them, before they could bite someone.

And it was true—her powers were growing and changing so fast she wasn't sure what she could and could not do anymore.

But dear God, how she sympathized with that Russian nutjob, Red Saviour, at this moment.

Spin Doctor nodded curtly, and left her alone in the room. He didn't have to say "We'll be watching you."

They both knew it. It didn't have to be said aloud.

They'd given Bella two days off as "medical leave." She was very tempted to spend it drunk. Instead, it occurred to her that it wouldn't be a bad idea to go have a look-in at CCCP HQ. She'd heard they were running a soup kitchen; maybe they could use a street healer too for a couple days.

INTERLUDE

Here's a dirty little secret. Do you know what Hollywood was doing in the days immediately after the invasion? Once they crawled out from under their desks . . . the big studio execs sent crews into the destruction corridors in and around L.A., armed with catering trucks and wardrobe trucks . . . and they filmed. They filmed thousands of non-SAG, non-BAG extras—gathered up from the isolated neighborhoods, paid in food and cash—to crawl through the debris, fight each other, migrate from one place to another, gather in torch-carrying mobs, in every sort of costume that could be pulled out of the trucks. While rescue crews were still pulling out bodies, while the fires still raged, they were filming, getting footage virtually free, for every conceivable movie that they might want to make someday that would involve mobs in wreckage.

And that sort of thinking was typical. So if these stories seem kind of schizophrenic, well, that's why. Schizophrenic thinking was endemic. There were thousands of conspiracy theories. There were people saying that the Thulians had crawled away somewhere to die. Then a single patrol of armored suits would pop up somewhere and wreak some havoc and all *the paranoia would start again. We think now, that was the Thulian backup plan—appear, terrorize, and vanish, until we were eating each other in the frenzy caused by fear and paranoia.*

Of course, dear audience, you might already know this.

I hope you care.

CHAPTER ELEVEN

Working For A Living

STEVE LIBBEY & MERCEDES LACKEY

The women's locker room rang with excited chatter. Ramona ignored the women and went to her locker, at the far end of the row.

Under normal circumstances, she might have felt intimidated by the lithe bottle-blond trophy wives that made up the usual clientele of a Workout Plus gym. Buff, beautiful, and self-assured, each one must have been detestable in high school. At least metahumans had an excuse for their perfect physiques. Ramona felt dumpier than usual.

Ramona stripped out of her jacket and skirt, and pulled on sweat pants. Topless, she could still find the nearly healed bruises where Valkyria's bullet had fractured her ribs. Today would be her first workout in a month. One of the blondes looked away as she pulled a T-shirt over her head.

It's wartime, honey, she thought. *Deal with it.*

The women hushed themselves with warnings: "Here she comes!" An expectant silence fell over the room, leaving only dripping shower heads to echo off the tiles.

Sleek with sweat, Shahkti strode into Ramona's aisle, two towels divided between her pairs of hands. The clusters of women stared as she passed them.

"Slumming, aren't you?" Ramona said, allowing the smirk to bloom on her face.

Shahkti's own dark face lit up with a comradely smile. "Hello, Detective. Have you just arrived?"

"Oh yeah. I want to get pumped up for my rematch with the Nazi dominatrix."

Shahkti opened her locker to reveal a nanoweave Echo uniform, crisply folded, and toiletries neatly arranged beside it. "Understandable. You cannot always be assured of a handy printer within reach." Without a hint of self-consciousness, Shahkti peeled off her damp shirt, maneuvering all four arms free of the sleeves effortlessly. Nude, her body was that of a goddess, reminding Ramona of the rumor that the inhabitants of her village had worshiped her as one.

Shahkti draped a towel over her shoulder. "I have finished my routine for today, but if you wish any coaching on hand-to-hand techniques, I would be happy to offer my services."

"Really? Wow. I mean, heck yeah, girl." Ramona held out both arms. "I'm a little bit unarmed for your style."

That made Shahkti laugh out loud. Ramona hadn't seen this much warmth in her, ever. "Four-armed teachers were not exactly listed in the Yellow Pages. I know many conventional styles."

"Then I'll take you up on it." She could see the metahuman was ready for her shower, but Ramona wanted to bask in her glory a little more.

Shahkti smiled. "Notify me when you are ready

for some sparring." She patted Ramona's shoulder and trotted off to the showers, leaving an audience of Atlantans behind her.

Ramona gave the room an offhand shrug. "Office talk," she told them.

Another familiar face greeted her in the weight room: Matai, easily the biggest man in the room, grunting under the leg press machine. He nodded in acknowledgment of her presence but kept up his routine. Ramona noted that he had the machine set at eight hundred pounds. She waited in awed silence until he finished.

He greeted her as he wiped sweat from his forehead. The Samoan dwarfed virtually every non-metahuman she had ever met. He would have looked at home as a defensive lineman. No, as a defensive line. Most of his size came naturally; he lacked the definition of a conventional body-builder. Matai simply gave the impression that he didn't have to make any effort to remain huge.

"So is this the new Echo gym, Matai? I just saw Shahkti." She handed him his water bottle.

"Thanks," he said after a healthy swig. "Mostly SupportOps and a few OpOnes. These machines don't carry enough weight for most of the metas."

She began a stretching routine. "Ah, that's right. Only your brother is a meta. I keep forgetting. You Samoans look metahuman already."

Matai chuckled, his round features suddenly boyish with amusement. "It's the company I keep."

"How's your brother doing?"

"Not good." The smile disappeared. "He lost a lot

of friends from R & D in the attack. I think it broke his heart."

"I know the feeling."

Matai shook his head woefully. "A broken heart's bad for people like us. Samoans, I mean. It's worse for him, I think. He's always been sensitive. At home Mama would send me out to bring him to dinner. He would be out in the trees, watching a spider building a web. Sitting for hours, just watching."

"The soul of a poet."

"Fighting isn't natural to him." Matai paused as a pair of racketballers passed them. "Sometimes I pray to God for Him to switch our places. Give me the powers. Not because I want to be a metahuman, but because he hates it. And I wish he could have some peace."

Ramona at once thought of Bill, the Mountain, back in his dark hole. "Yeah, I understand."

"Out in the field, I'm like a child among adults. Isn't that curious?"

"But you do have a power. You're a leader. It takes a certain temperament and mind-set. Quick thinking, decisiveness, alertness. They don't call you 'Chief' for nothing, right?"

"Not if I can help it, they don't." Matai exhaled as he began another set of reps. Several nearby weightlifters stopped to watch. Ramona wanted to announce to them, to everyone, that Matai was no metahuman, that his strength came from good-old-fashioned genes and willpower. Instead she punched in an ambitious program on the Stairmaster and started pumping.

She pedaled in silence; the whirring of the Stairmaster's gears and the rhythmic clank of Matai's leg presses provided a soundtrack to her questing thoughts about Slycke. She had digested his meager dossier over the last week. News searches added little to supplement the data already in Echo's recovered database. Born in Macon, Georgia, Walter Slycke had acquired his powers one night near a toxic waste dump. He had been recruited by a gang of metahuman bank robbers, the Easy Men, lorded over by a man who called himself Easy Listener, and took it upon himself to dub each of the crooks with a corny fifties-style moniker. Slycke hadn't suffered the indignity of his handle, Smooth Operator, for long. A string of increasingly violent solo crimes followed until an OpOne team apprehended him in 1999. Georgia law enforcement had refused to mount a search effort for him; they were already overwhelmed, and their unspoken attitude was that Slycke was Echo's problem.

And that's all she had to track down the only man who had heard Eisenfaust's final words.

"Matai." She tapped the Stairmaster's power button. "If you had broken out of prison, where would you go?"

"Somewhere I could blend in." Matai relaxed his legs and exhaled. Ramona laughed, but left it at that. Some jokes just wrote themselves.

"But what if your personal appearance was offputting? Inhuman."

"Ah. A metahuman. Well . . . I suppose I would try to cross the border into Mexico."

"That's a bit far from Atlanta."

Matai shrugged. "Maybe I'd go to ground until my pursuers gave up."

"I'm not giving up on this guy."

"Law enforcement has a lot on their plates now. It would be easy to disappear. Unless your perp is as big as the Mountain, he can pretty much move around at will."

Ramona wiped her forehead. The Atlanta heat managed to penetrate even this soulless, air-conditioned box. She imagined her sweat was the strange oily substance that Slycke's skin exuded. Like the Mountain, he must live in perpetual horror at his own body, cut off from society at large. Except that Bill the Mountain retained a sense of ethics, as lonely as he was, essentially dead to his wife and family.

A germ of an idea took root. Ramona had a sudden urge to dump a liter of 10W-40 motor oil over her head.

"You sleuths have the tough job," Matai continued. "I have no idea how you gather information and dig needles out of haystacks. I prefer field work: five minutes and either the problem's solved or I'm a red smear across the pavement. No suspense there. Still too much paperwork, though."

A slender blonde approached Ramona. "Are you done?" she asked while never taking her eyes off Matai.

"You can have him. Some of us girls have to work for a living." She gave Matai a wink and bustled off to the locker room, head swirling with possibility. For the first time in days, she didn't wonder what Mercurye was doing.

The first thing Jack Point did when Ramona entered his office was give her a white rose.

"Why, thanks, Jack," she said.

"Identify yourself, please," Jack Point said. His garish

harlequin three-piece suit, pink gloves and polka-dotted top hat belied his solemn, intent scrutiny of her face.

Ramona tilted her head. "Jack, Jack, Jack. How many times have we worked together? I can't believe you don't recognize me."

"You're lying," Jack said with a sad smile, "whoever you are. If we've worked together, you must be an EchoOps detective. And female... Jeanine Carlson?"

"No."

"Adrianne Penn."

"Wrong again, buddy."

Jack leaned back into his chair. "The only detective cruel enough to torment the guy with prosopagnosia is Ramona Ferrari."

Ramona clapped her hands together twice. "Brilliant deduction. Nice to see you again." She tucked the rose into her lapel. "Does that help?"

"Yes, thank you. And thank you for not lying when you say it's nice to see me again." Jack Point had relaxed from the awkwardness.

"It is nice, you freak. You always keep me entertained."

"My blindness to faces amuses you?"

"No. The workarounds you find for it impress me." She adjusted the rose. "The flower's a nice touch."

"Looks classier than the 'Hello My Name Is' badges. What do you have for me today?"

Ramona leaned forward over his desk with a photograph. "Here's my quarry."

Jack Point squinted at Walter Slycke's scowling mugshot, complete with an oily black film over his skin. "Now that's a face even I could remember. Metahuman?"

"Until the attack, he was a prisoner in the security

wing. He was too slippery, literally, for the Nazis to execute him." She passed him Walter Slycke's dossier and pointed to an italicized section. "That gunk he exudes can all but eliminate friction. With fancy footwork, he can deflect bullets."

"He'll be tough to recapture."

"I have to find him first. He's gone to ground."

Jack Point shrugged. His attention wandered to an etching on his wall: a scene from Gilbert & Sullivan's *The Yeomen of the Guard*, featuring the jester who was his namesake.

Ramona waved her hand in his face. "Stay with me here, buddy. I'm in a bit of a hurry and the courts are tied up with aftermath nonsense. Warrants and court orders are hassles I don't need. Your built-in polygraph will make interviews much more to the point."

"Jack Point, that's me."

"You bet. What kind of paperwork do I need to fill out to get you on the case?"

"Not much." Jack Point wrote "out of the office" on a Post-it and adhered it to his computer screen. "Funny how informal things have become since... hmm." He cleared his throat. "Where to?"

"The sticks. We're paying a visit to Ma and Pa Slycke."

Three hours later, Ramona wished she had requisitioned a helicopter instead of one of Echo's unmarked sedans. The Atlanta traffic had gone from bad to impossible thanks to the destruction wrought on the highways. It took an extra hour to crawl through rush hour traffic. She bit her lip and resisted the urge to activate the siren that would clear a path—and announce their presence to the world. Jack Point's top hat was bad enough; fortunately he had to doff it to fit into the car. He watched the cars creep by and glanced at his hands at regular intervals.

"Those gloves aren't going to change themselves," Ramona said.

"Hmm?"

"You keep staring at them. Did you mean to wear the white ones?"

He held up his gloved hands. "Ah. No, it's a mental trick. I'm usually the only person in the room with pink gloves, thus I know these hands are mine and not someone else's."

"Of course they're yours. You operate them, you receive tactile information from them, right?"

"Sometimes it's not enough," Jack Point said in a quiet voice.

Ramona blew air out her lips. "Sorry. I guess I forget how acute your condition is. You can't even recognize yourself?"

He shook his head.

"So you've never really seen your own face?"

"I was normal until I was twelve. That's the last time I saw myself." He smiled. "But among neuroscientists, I'm a rock star, so it's not so bad. The most acute case of prosopagnosia in history. I go right off the charts." He chuckled. "Some of them are convinced vivisecting my brain will reveal the nature of consciousness itself. I've lost count of the MRIs I've been subjected to."

"You could say no."

"They mean well and they're very grateful. Who knows? They might learn something genuinely useful. Meanwhile, Echo has use for me as a walking polygraph."

"The good with the bad," Ramona said.

"Everything's a trade-off," he agreed, giving the hat on his lap a flip.

Unsummoned, an image of Mercurye entered her mind. Handsome, metahumanly strong, able to fly... what trade-off did he make for his powers?

Suddenly she missed him terribly.

Well south of Atlanta, the afternoon sun illuminated the edges of kudzu-engulfed trees that formed a parade of grotesque shapes on the side of I-75. Traffic had died down as Ramona and Jack Point left behind the extended suburbs that established Atlanta's reputation as a major center for urban sprawl. A few intrepid commuters still drove their air-conditioned SUVs to their suburban palaces, their faces tight with exhaustion as Ramona zipped past them.

"Look at those bogs," she said. "It's no wonder there haven't been any sightings of him."

"You think he's hiding out in the swamps? How very pulpy of him. Could it be that he's trying to scare meddling teenagers away from a hidden treasure?"

She chuckled. "Not if he's smart. But right now he's scared and lost. Nothing in his history indicates he's much of a survivalist, so I'm betting he's lurking around Beechwood."

"Beechwood. Hmm." Jack Point shuffled through the papers. "Born 1974, Beechwood, Georgia. Isn't that a little obvious?"

"Slycke's trying to have it both ways." She took the State Route 401 exit off the highway, bypassing a cluster of gas stations and truckstops. "And that's how I'll catch him."

They cruised through Fort Valley and Nakomis, sleepy southern towns settling down for an evening's dinner.

Ramona stopped for a quick refuel and some gritty gas-station hot dogs. Jack Point settled for a honey bun and coffee. Twenty minutes later, as the sun set in a swath of crimson, they entered the swamps of Beechwood.

The tiny village had all the rustic emptiness that Ramona expected from the deep south: a handful of elegant plantation homes with peeling columns, surrounded by mobile homes and decaying shacks. The air lacked the pollution of Atlanta but retained the thick humidity, made worse by the earthy smell of the swamp.

Despite their map, it took three passes down Carter Lane to find the turnoff to the Slycke home. Five hundred yards through bramble and willow trees led them to a yard littered with car parts, broken appliances and overgrown foliage. A shape peered out from a stained curtain when they pulled into the driveway and parked.

"So much for stealth," Jack Point said. "What if he's bolting out the back door?"

"I doubt it, but keep your eyes open."

Wood groaned under their weight as they mounted the steps.

"Take your hat off," she told Jack. "Manners."

He sighed and cradled it in his arm.

Ramona knocked on the frame of the screen door. She heard furtive voices within, and the patter of feet. Jack Point arched an eyebrow but she shook her head.

Finally, the door opened to reveal a stout black woman in a fading pink floral house dress. Her scowl dented the folds of her face.

"What you want?" The woman's voice was deep and husky and tired. She stared bug-eyed at Ramona's companion. "You circus folk?"

Ramona smiled and flipped her Echo badge open.

"Echo Detective Ramona Ferrari, ma'am. I'm hoping you'll answer some questions for me."

The woman nodded her head at Jack. "Who's he?"

"That's Jack Point. May we come in?"

The sigh that escaped the woman had in it decades of bitterness and resentment. "Might as well," she said at last.

Inside the house, the flickering light of a television bathed the room in a dismal blue luminescence, spitting out audio from a battered speaker. A man in his sixties slouched on a dusty sofa with a can of Coca-Cola. His face bore a look of passive acceptance, as if he had given up even moving.

When Ramona and Jack Point came into view, he tilted his head with sudden distrust. "Who're you?"

Ramona repeated her introduction as the woman leaned against the wall and glared. The man grunted. "Pull up some chairs, Ma," he said.

"They ain't staying long."

"Don't back-talk me. They're guests." He made no effort to move or even emphasize his anger.

The woman dragged creaky wooden chairs into the living room. Ramona feared hers would give out, but it held firm.

"Say your piece." The man shifted his eyes from the television to Ramona.

She cleared her throat. "I appreciate you taking the time to speak with us. I promise I'll make it painless." Her smile was lost in the darkness. "We need to ask you a few questions about your son, Walter."

"We ain't got a son," the woman snapped. Jack turned his head towards her.

"Ellie's barren. We're alone," the man said.

"The female in the dress is lying," Jack Point said without umbrage. "The male on the couch is also lying. Additionally, they are frightened of reprisal."

Mr. Slycke grunted and stared at Jack Point as if seeing him for the first time. Jack Point's eyes roved the room, never meeting anyone's gaze.

"Why, I never!" The woman stomped her foot. "Calling me a liar in my own house..."

Ramona held up her hands, palms out. "Ma'am, please. We know that Walter's your son. Has he been here? Did he threaten you?"

The couple fell into angry silence broken only by the distorted bleating of the television. Neither would speak first.

"The female is too ashamed to reveal the information. The male feels familial competition with the suspect and thus may betray him out of resentment."

Like a walrus, Mr. Slycke levered himself to his feet. "You goddamn cracker freak," he said, brandishing his can of cola at Jack Point. "No man talks to me like that. No man!"

"Sit down, sir. I am carrying a firearm, and I am likely to shoot one or more people in this room if you threaten me again."

Ramona interposed herself between Jack Point and Mr. Slycke. "Jack! For Christ's sake, don't antagonize them. We're trying to get them to cooperate."

"Why? I can read them like open books. Walter Slycke was here at least two days ago." Jack Point stood and walked past the angry old man as if he wasn't there. He plucked a picture of a young boy off the mantle, holding it in his pink-gloved fingers by the frame's corners. "See?"

Ramona marveled at Jack's perceptiveness. In the dim room, he had spotted a thumb-shaped smudge in the dust on the old picture frame. To him, she realized, objects were just as communicative as people.

"Cute kid. Who'da thunk?" Ramona showed the picture to the couple. "Feeling nostalgic recently?"

Without warning, Ellie Slycke spun on her heel and left the room. Her footsteps reverberated in the kitchen.

"That was a long time ago," Mr. Slycke said into the air of the room.

"Twenty-five years, I'm guessing. Walter has been a metahuman since he was seventeen, correct?"

The man closed his eyes. "What I done to bring down the wrath of God on my boy, I don't know. Never fought, never drank. I looked after my wife and my boy like a man should."

Ramona nodded her head when he opened his eyes again. "I'm sure you did, sir."

"Walter wasn't a smart boy, but he worked hard at anything he put his mind to. Could have hired him at the body shop. It's a good job," Mr. Slycke insisted. "Honest work. Walter wasn't no criminal."

Jack Point opened his mouth to speak, but Ramona silenced him with a finger. "That changed, didn't it?"

"He and his friends were out at the dump. I don't know why—boys like to act up at that age. He didn't come back till dawn, and that—stuff—covered him like he'd changed a truck's oil without a pan. Only it wouldn't come off with rags or water or detergent. Walter cried like a baby, he was so scared. Every time Ellie tried to comfort him, even put a hand on his shoulder, it slid right off. He could barely stand, he just lay down on the floor." He pointed at the wall. "Fetched up against that wall because the foundation is shifting towards the backyard."

"That must have been horrible."

"I pray you don't have to see your children like that."

"Why didn't you contact Echo? We have specialists to help metahumans deal with their condition."

Mr. Slycke shrugged. "We just thought he got into some kind of industrial waste. The hospital's an hour away. Ellie kept trying to wipe it off him . . . I suppose we should have called someone. But after a day of worry, Walter found he could clean himself just by willing it. He put on overalls and kept the oil under his clothes. Once he did that, he stayed in his room for a week, not talking, hardly eating, just thinking. And then he left."

"To join the Easy Men."

"I don't know. I reckon he just wanted to hide from respectable folks until this 'condition' worked itself out of his system. It never did." He hung his head.

Ramona and Jack Point waited respectfully for the man to gather himself. When he raised his head again, tears glistened in his eyes. "I suppose you've come to arrest him."

"That's our job, sir. Is he here?"

"No." Mr. Slycke looked at Jack Point. "That's the truth."

Jack Point nodded.

"Was he here?" Ramona asked, leaning forward. Her heart raced with excitement.

"Three days ago."

She ran a hand through her hair, both relieved and disappointed. "What did he say?"

Ellie Slycke's voice rang out in the quiet room. "That's between Walter and his kin. Ain't none of your business."

"Ma'am, with respect, it's everyone's business. Walter may have information pertaining to the Nazi attacks. The sooner we find him, the sooner we can act on it."

The woman shook her head slowly from side to side. "He didn't say nothing about no Nazis. He felt bad about what he done, and wanted to make up for it."

"This would be a good start."

"You keep away from him!" With sudden fury, Ellie Slycke advanced towards Ramona with fists balled. "Leave him be. He's been cursed enough already."

"Ramona, these people don't know the fugitive's whereabouts, but they do know his intentions," Jack Point said coolly. "They are using hostility to deflect your questions."

"I noticed," Ramona muttered. She stood up and confronted Ellie Slycke. "I don't care a whit about your family drama, lady. Those Nazi bastards killed my friends right in front of me." Her voice rose in pitch. "If one life—*one life*—can be saved with what he knows, then I'll track him down like an animal through every stinking swamp in the state. I won't eat, I won't sleep, and I sure as hell won't be intimidated by a bitter old woman!"

Ellie Slycke blinked and backed up. Ramona pursued her.

"Your boy is a convicted criminal. Blame his 'curse' if you want, but I have co-workers in far worse shape who risk their lives every day to serve and protect. *We're at war*, lady. If Walter is withholding information, that makes him a traitor." She paused for effect. "And I don't think you raised a traitor."

"Damn right," Mr. Slycke said.

Hands over her mouth, Ellie Slycke regarded Ramona with horror and sadness. "Walter left to meet up with those thieves," she whispered.

"The Easy Men?"

Ellie Slycke closed her eyes and wept.

"The Easy Men were disbanded a decade ago," Jack Point said. "However, the female is telling the truth, as best she knows it."

"Thanks, Jack."

But Jack Point had already started for the front door of the ramshackle home.

"Hey," Ramona called to his retreating back.

"What remains to be learned belongs to them alone." The bang of the screen door punctuated his statement.

The bland whiteness of the laptop screen mocked her with its lack of information. Each of the five dossiers in the list ended with the same bad news. Current whereabouts: UNKNOWN.

In an act of desperation as much as faith, Ramona ran the names—and aliases—through the FBI database, the Interpol database, the CIA, the IRS, and even the phone book. For the second time. Just in case there was a server hiccup, she told herself, though she knew it was pointless.

With the exception of Walter Slycke, there was no official record on the Easy Men from the last decade. Before Slycke's capture, the Easy Men had a bad run and disappeared off the radar. Ramona had spent hours cross-referencing unsolved robberies in hopes of recognizing the modus operandi of the remaining Easy Men, such as a hyperspeed snatch by

Twinkletoes, or an uncrackable safe cracked by Easy Listener. Nothing.

Slycke could be anywhere within four states by now. The Easy Men could be across the world. As helpless as she felt in front of the computer, it beat pounding the pavement in Atlanta.

"You stink," she told the laptop. "Do my thinking for me!" She closed it with more force than was healthy. With a pang of guilt, she reopened it; cheery light and a logo greeted her. "Okay, okay, sorry. Take a nap for a while."

Ramona stood, stretched, dug out a cigarette. She opened the window in spite of the air conditioning. The smoke gave her a momentary boost which faded fast, leaving only the comfort of the habitual movements. Smoking did her no good aside from putting her in a reflective state.

"He's in Georgia," she said aloud. Her voice functioned as an aural whiteboard. "He's got to be. Why, I don't know, but I feel it, and if I'm wrong, I'm screwed anyway."

She wished Mercurye was listening to her. A silly urge, because he hardly struck her as a deep thinker, yet in explaining Slycke's movements to him, she might talk herself into some grand insight.

She remembered the German's posture as he spoke rapidly to the metahuman criminal: urgent, desperate, tensed and waiting for a killing blow. Whatever the man had done during World War II, her mental image of him in his last moments was that of a self-sacrificing hero. It was too much to reconcile.

The humid Atlanta air crowded into her apartment, making the cluttered mess feel even more vile.

Ramona knew a detective who thought best while cleaning, and prayed every day to become that person. Alas, she thought best when mournfully studying her mounting trash piles.

"This is why you'll never hook up with that man. You're a slob." She caught herself—why were her thoughts drifting to Mercurye like an infatuated school-girl? In this time of crisis, it was selfish and childish. But thinking about him *did* make her feel better somehow.

She put the godlike metahuman out of her mind. Too many lives depended on her ability to suss out Slycke's whereabouts and get him in an Echo inter-rogation room. If they could hold him still. A memory came back: Southwind, the gangling, hairless, pale metahuman, dashing Valkyria into the ceiling and saving Ramona's bacon. All of the Four Winds—the survivors, anyway—had varying degrees of telekinesis. A psychic hand could hold a greased pig far better than a physical hand.

When I find Slycke, I'll make sure Southwind is there for backup. After losing his partner, he'd prob-ably appreciate a chance to be a part of the solution.

She ground out the cigarette. Purposefulness filled her: she remembered one very strange resource that she had not considered until now.

Her desk was far more chaotic than the room around it, as though it were the wellspring of all dis-order. The piece of paper with the important phone number had been torn from a *Vogue* magazine. The unceremoniously beheaded underwear model on the other side was clear in her mind. For an hour, she rooted through the drawers, working from the small-est to the file folders filled with scraps of paper and inaccurate dates. Her stomach began to claw at her in hunger and anxiety.

"Oh, come *on*." She wished with all her heart that she had undertaken to organize her desk...five years ago.

At last a tanned hip flashed at her from a pile of Post-its. Ramona pounced on it and then laughed in triumph. She hadn't thrown it away after all.

She dialed the number labeled "BFH" on her cell. The number rang for two solid minutes as she chewed on her fingernails.

"It is good to hear your voice again, Ramona." The voice was delicate, breathy, low and carefully neutral.

"You knew it was me. I should have figured."

"It's my job. I know why you're calling, too. My prices have increased since you last used my services." A pause. "I want fifty thousand dollars for the information you are going to ask me."

She whistled. "That's a lot of benjamins, Benjamin. Can't Echo just write you a check?"

"No checks. No companies. No reimbursements. I only accept real money from real human beings. If you want my information, you have to bleed for it."

Fifty thousand dollars? "For Christ's sake. I don't carry that kind of cash around. Even if I had it."

"That's the price for what you need to know. I recommend that you hurry. Your bank closes in forty-five minutes."

"Wait. How do I know—"

"I'll call you when you have the money in hand. One-hundred-dollar bills, unmarked. Paper bag." The line went dead.

❖   ❖   ❖

Ramona's cell rang in time with the swish of the bank's revolving doors spitting her out. She stuffed the paper bag into her purse, feeling conspicuous about holding her life savings in a vulnerable physical form.

"Hello?"

"Walk two blocks north. Cross the street. Half a block and take a right into the alley next to the package store, before the sidewalk ends."

"Classy as always, Benjamin." The line went dead. *So much for witty banter,* she thought.

With one hand on her purse and one hand on her holster, Ramona walked briskly down the Atlanta street. Aside from sporadic commercial zones like this one, it was rare for there to be enough sidewalk for a pedestrian to get around. People standing on the streets seemed to be waiting for the next riot. Tension was in the air, and more than one bystander gave her a predatory once-over.

The city really has changed, she thought. *Where are these lowlifes coming from?*

A pair of armed guards bearing shotguns smoked cigarettes outside the package store. Ramona spied the coiled snake insignia of Blacksnake, the security contractor. The men ignored her scowl as she passed them.

I can't begrudge the store owners for providing for their own safety, even if it's through those scumbags. Hell, guarding package stores is all they're qualified for. Should just pay them in liquor.

Trash stank up the entryway to the alley. Ramona breathed through her mouth and stepped gingerly over broken bottles.

"Calling Benjamin Franklin Hotline," she announced to the empty alley. "Inquiring minds want to know about their futures."

The alley's walls caught her words in a wash of sharp echoes. She peeked in doorways as she passed them.

"Hello? Anyone home?"

Without ceremony, a slouching figure appeared in the mouth of the alley. Two large plastic buckets, one set into the other, dangled from a hand hidden by the overlong sleeves of a gray-cloth greatcoat too warm for the Atlanta summer. A floppy brimmed hat hid a pale, wrinkled face in shadow.

Benjamin Franklin Hotline separated the buckets, overturned the empty one and sat on it. "Money first."

"Nice to see you, too." Ramona opened the paper bag to reveal the sheaf of bills. "There you have it. I'll be working in McDonald's when I'm sixty thanks to you."

"Echo pays you plenty. Drop it in the bucket."

She removed it from the bag and started forward. Benjamin Franklin Hotline held up a palm. "Bag too."

Ramona shrugged and did as he requested. She loomed over him. "Didn't bring a seat for a lady?"

"Ask your question."

"I have a few."

"I'll answer one."

Ramona gaped. "I just paid you fifty grand! You should be writing me a goddamn novel! What the hell's happened to you?"

Benjamin Franklin Hotline didn't look up, but his head swayed in acknowledgment. "Fair enough. I'll stop you from asking the wrong question."

"Christ. Fine, Mr. Genie from a Bottle." She lit a cigarette. "Let me think."

"He's alive and safe, but that's not the man you're after."

"What, Slycke? He's—"

"Echo OpOne, code-named Mercurye."

Her cheeks burned. "You read my mind."

"I read *everyone's* mind. That's my job. Walter Slycke is the question here."

"Yes, yes, yes! Where is he?"

The psychic paused. Street noise filled the air around them.

"Well? Is that the right question?"

"It is. I can give you an address."

"The Easy Men, right?"

"What remains of the Easy Men. He will not be there long, I wager." Benjamin Franklin Hotline leaned over his open bucket and reached inside. The sound of sifting papers reached her ears. He never looked at the papers, but eventually the hand came up with a scrap.

How appropriate, she thought.

"Here," he said. "I strongly recommend you arrive there before six P.M. tonight."

The address was unfamiliar: Osierfield, GA, in Irwin County. That made it two hours away by car.

"What happens at six?"

"I can't answer that question without another payment." He stood and dropped the open bucket into the one he used for a seat. "You're better served making haste."

"Right, right. Thanks."

"I don't require thanks. You paid for it."

"Then don't spend it all in one place." She opened her cell as he hobbled away. She needed a team, and fast.

Fifteen minutes later, Ramona stood in the parking lot of the last team member's current location, and it was not a place she had ever expected to be. Her call to Echo had produced a helicopter and a pickup squad: Flak (Mercurye's squad leader, but Ramona put that out of her mind), Silent Knight, and the mind reader she requested, Pensive. One team member that worried her was the new Damage Control Officer, Belladonna Blue, who was on probation for flouting procedure. And Southwind, on whom the operation hinged, had gone AWOL.

Well, AWOL here.

"I have to have a telekinetic. I'll settle for Carrie, or get me Mintohk from Williams Street, or some teenager's poltergeist. Anyone."

"Southwind's the only one," the dispatcher had assured her. *"He's your man, if you can call him that."*

Ramona didn't know if it was a crack about Southwind's sexual orientation or his alien appearance. *"I have an hour and a half to nab this perp and he's the only one who can do it."*

"Like I said, his comm has been off for days." The dispatcher lowered his voice. *"There are rumors, though . . ."*

And thus Ramona strode up to the burly, shirtless bouncer at Menergy, the all-hours club. "Looking for Southwind. You can't miss him: eight feet tall, bald, looks like he double-parked his flying saucer."

"Not here." The bouncer had to raise his voice to be heard over the pumping Euro-disco music. He wore leather pants and suspenders that didn't conceal his nipple rings. "I can't let you in."

"What?"

"We're at capacity. You'll have to wait."

She blinked. The dimly-lit dance floor could have

fit a bulldozer in between dancing couples. Ramona drew herself up. "Do you know who I am?"

"Don't care, sister."

"Oh, you will. Because either I pull out my Echo ID and pull rank, or I pull out my Echo sidearm, drop you like a frickin' roach, and write a report about how you interfered with a peace officer in the course of performing her duty." She gave him a steely glare. "The first choice hurts less and involves no paperwork, but I guaran-damn-tee you I like the second one better."

His jaw twitched.

"Well?"

"I promised Rey he would be left alone." The man's face softened. "He's in *mourning*. We all are."

"Then he'll want to hear what I have for him—a little chance for revenge."

The bouncer's eyes narrowed, then he stood aside. "Second red door on the right. Knock first."

Ramona passed through the barroom quickly. She was the only female in the room. Menergy appeared to cater to the macho gay crowd: black leather and facial hair abounded, though there was a selection of young men decidedly more effeminate than the bouncer and his ilk. Nevertheless, the bright desperation here was the same you'd find at happy hour at any bar.

She pounded on the second red door.

"Occupied!" The voice was familiar.

"Rey! It's Ramona Ferrari. We have a situation and you're needed."

The voice was slurred in a comic parody of intoxication. "Who—oh, Christ. Get lost."

Ramona tried the handle. Someone—or something— held it firm. "Either come out or let me in, Rey."

The metahuman barked harsh laughter. "I came out a long time ago, before I turned into a freak. Leave me alone."

She glanced at her watch. Ten minutes had already been lost with this unsavory detour. The amusement in the copter pilot's voice when she told him to rendezvous with her at Menergy was bad enough. Now she had yet another self-pitying metahuman to deal with.

"I am going to count to three... Oh, the hell with it." She drew her pistol and fired five swift shots around the doorknob, angled towards the jamb. The wood holding the bolt shredded. Ramona gave the door a kick before Southwind could force it shut.

A leather modular couch took up most of the room, which stank of sweat, smoke, and booze. Southwind reclined across the entire length of the couch, wearing nothing more than a thong. Two pale and similarly underdressed young men had cast themselves under his arms in fear.

Southwind rolled his giant, bulbous eyes at her. "Rah rah, very exciting. You scared my friends, mean lady." He patted their heads. "You're not going to use that big bad gun on little old me, are you?"

"Cut the crap. I need a TK for a mission right now."

"So what? I quit. Or I will when Echo finds me." He considered. "Which, I guess, it has now, right?"

"No. We're at war, soldier, and you have marching orders."

"Forget it. Echo let Kevin die in their stupid war. They don't deserve me."

Ramona locked eyes with him—a feat considering that his were the size of her hands. His transformed features did not express emotions as a normal human's face might, instead seeming to switch between serene and evil. What he truly felt was unreadable, but she could guess: grief, rage, loneliness, resentment.

"Listen, mister. Echo didn't 'let' Kevin die. And we're doing a snatch-and-grab on a meta that has intel on the Nazis—the people who actually killed your boyfriend. You want revenge, this is the place to start." She holstered the gun. "You in or not?"

"You're serious?"

"Helicopter will be here in minutes. Only a TK can catch this guy. Without you I'll just send the chopper home and call it a night. So?" Ramona put out a hand to him.

Southwind took her proffered hand and stood, nearly smacking his head on the ceiling. His boytoys fell to the floor with yelps.

"Yes, ma'am!" he said with a crispness that betrayed his military past. A pile of clothes floated past her head and unfolded. Ramona had never seen clothes put themselves on before. In seconds he was dressed in a spindly Echo uniform and giving her a snappy salute. "Ready for deployment."

Interstate 75 cut through the verdant Georgian landscape that blurred underneath them as the Echo copter carried them to their destination on spinning blades and roaring jets.

"This is where we get off," Ramona shouted over the headset.

"We're ten clicks from the target, ma'am!" The pilot jabbed a finger at the heads-up display. "I can put you right on their roof."

"That's a negative. One perp has metahuman hearing. Southwind will take us in." She tilted her head at the giant meta hunching over in the cabin. He nodded. "Head over the highway and circle it until you hear from us. With luck, Easy Listener will mistake you for a traffic helicopter."

"I'll lay off the jets, too."

"Good boy." She turned to the team. "All right, folks. With the exception of Flak, none of you have worked with me before. Flak is the squad leader but he'll be executing my orders. This is a snatch and grab against meta Ones. These guys are not known for excessive force but are known for skilled escapes. They will be frightened, so be prepared. Our target, Slycke, is carrying critical intel. He must be taken alive at all costs. Pensive will make the read on the scene, which makes *him* mission critical as well."

"Another point," Pensive said. His wild eyebrows and graying hair gave him the air of an art-film director. "Should we not have more combat operatives for this mission?"

"That's what Silent's for." And, she added to herself, the best she could do given the dubious response she'd gotten from Tesla when she described her hunch about Slycke. She had to call in favors to get Flak and Silent Knight.

Southwind crouched at the helicopter door. With a flick of a finger he opened the latch and slid the door open. The roar of the blades swelled.

"Form up, close as you can, and I'll grab you. Close your eyes if you feel dizzy." He removed his headset and rolled out of the hatch, looking for a scary moment as though he were committing suicide—and then he floated alongside the helicopter, utterly relaxed. One spidery hand urged them forward.

"I hate this part," Flak muttered before he pulled his headset off. The five clustered together, Silent Knight hulking behind them like a pet truck.

Southwind raised both hands. A million miniature hurricane winds wrapped their bodies and dragged them out of the helicopter. Ramona shut her eyes to the vertigo overwhelming her. Over the sound of the blades she could hear Flak swearing loudly, using curses that would make a sailor envious.

In seconds the helicopter peeled away from them. Southwind kept them hovering in the air until the helicopter had become a speck in the distance. Aside from the susurrus of the prevailing winds, silence enveloped them.

Southwind chuckled. "That's better, isn't it? You should see yourselves with your faces all screwed up."

Ramona opened her eyes. The unincorporated landscape of Irwin County stretched out beneath her like a verdant woven blanket. Floating in the sky, she was reminded of the time as a child when she had taken a hot air balloon ride at a state fair, and the world had seemed vast beyond comprehension.

Silent Knight, who, true to his moniker, had been virtually silent for the entire trip, surprised her by speaking first, though the words seemed out of place in his computerized voice: "A lovely sight."

Flak pointed towards the destination. "They may have spotters. Can you take us in low?"

"You got it. The view won't be as pretty. Ah, close your eyes again. Trust me on this one." He dropped from view. Ramona squeezed her eyes shut as they began a free-fall. Her stomach lurched and panic rose inside her.

As quickly as it started, the descent ended in a gentle slope. The ground was a mere five feet below.

"Sorry," Southwind said. "But we're under the radar now." Force built up behind them.

Once they began a horizontal vector, genuine meta-human flight was actually rather relaxing. Southwind deliberately steered them towards the tree line to take advantage of cover. Ramona forced herself to gather her thoughts about the mission. She checked her watch: 5:45 P.M.. Slycke would be on site for another fifteen minutes. She asked Southwind for an ETA.

"Five minutes, ma'am." His exaggerated features were screwed up in concentration. Given that he was working hard to keep from slamming them into obstructions, she decided not to pester him.

She addressed the others. "We're going to deploy without any chatter, so listen up. Slycke is going to bolt when he gets wind of us. Southwind's job will be to lock him down—he's the only one who can hold onto him. Flak and Knight will run interference. Pensive will remain outside until the area is secure. I'll do the talking."

"What about me?" Belladonna asked.

"You're the DCO." Ramona frowned. "Listen, Blue, no trouble from you, please. Just watch our backs."

"She'll keep it tight," Flak said. "We've been over this already, believe me."

They emerged from the grove of trees. A tattered Texaco sign stood sentry over a concrete box labeled COUNTRY STORE. A flickering fluorescent light proved the power was on, in spite of the store's ramshackle appearance. Ramona held up a hand for Southwind to reduce their velocity.

Good old reliable Georgia mud, Ramona thought. Parallel tracks led away from the door. She pointed them out, and Southwind followed them at a slower pace along the overgrown gravel road. The country store was still in sporadic use, it appeared. Ramona had a guess who was the primary customer.

Abruptly, Southwind halted them. A wing of a dilapidated antebellum mansion peeked out from behind looming stands of hydrangea. Time had weathered the walls and columns, leaving only a few dirty shreds of white paint to mottle the gray, water-stained wood. A rusting tractor stood watch by the driveway.

Ramona waved them on. Silent but for the air they displaced, they entered the yard.

At once, a raucous sound of shrieking and scrabbling startled them. Guns swung around to find a target in . . . a chicken, loose in the yard and surprised by the floating visitors.

Pensive pointed to the house and held up four fingers. He folded all but one and nodded meaningfully. Southwind let him down in the yard.

Her watch read 5:55 P.M. Ramona put a finger to her lips and gave a single nod.

Southwind guided them towards the double doors of the front porch. They glided like ghosts over the stairs and a makeshift ramp. Inside, angry voices volleyed back and forth. Invisible hands swung the doors open before them with a woody groan.

The interior of the house, while not restored, had been cleaned of dirt and grime. The voices echoed out from the dining room. Southwind floated them over the buckling hardwood floorboards to a clear view of the occupants seated at a table.

Ramona's heart raced. Walter Slycke stood with his back to them, hands gesticulating wildly. An elderly, gaunt man in a jacket and tie sat across the table in a wheelchair and winced at the volume of Slycke's voice. A slender, blond man in a dirty hooded sweatshirt ignored them both and picked at his food, but the thick-armed, bare-chested man in overalls glared in anger at Slycke.

Twinkletoes and Musclehead, she realized. And Easy Listener was in worse shape than she had expected.

Ramona cleared her throat. "Excuse me, folks. Need a word with your slippery friend here."

Slycke whirled around. His skin oil had been flowing freely over his face and neck, as if he were a mechanic bungling an oil change.

"Oh, hell no," he said.

Her feet touched the floor, making it easier to aim her sidearm. "Oh, yes. Thanks for distracting your host for us, Mr. Slycke. I trust you can guess who we are."

Body tensing, Slycke scanned the room for a bolt-hole. Southwind raised a hand and the shutters of the windows clattered shut.

"Area secure, ma'am." His smirk twisted his thin features disturbingly.

The old man scooted back his wheelchair. "Miss, please. Lower your gun. No one wants any violence here. Walter was just leaving."

"Damn right," Slycke said. "And you ain't gonna stop me."

Ramona grinned at him. "Not me, Walter. Meet my friend Southwind here."

With a howl, Musclehead launched the entire table at them—at *her*. She reflexively threw up her arms.

Silent Knight stepped in front of her, palms outstretched. Musclehead's howl—and every voice heard in the last two minutes—played back as a tight-beam, amplified and focused sonic burst. She had never been so close to Silent Knight in action; it was tantamount to unleashing a hundred thunderstorms in a small room, and she blanked out momentarily. The table exploded into splinters.

Easy Listener fell out of his wheelchair, covering his ears and wailing. Twinkletoes appeared over Ramona in a blur, her sidearm now in his hand. As rapid as a machine gun, he emptied the clip into Silent Knight. Most of the caseless rounds ricocheted off the metal and nanoweave—she had not loaded armor-piercing bullets. Still, the impact staggered Silent Knight and blood sprayed out from his stomach.

Twinkletoes stared at the crumbling giant in shock; it was obvious that he hadn't been in a fight for years. Ramona, on the other hand, had been so keyed up in anticipation of this confrontation that she was ready to act. She wrapped her arms around the metahuman's legs and put all her weight against his knees. He tumbled to the floor with a yelp.

"Stop, please!" Easy Listener's anguished plea went unheeded. Flak had pinned Musclehead's arms behind him and held tight as the strongman bucked like a bronco.

Twinkletoes raised the empty gun to pistol-whip Ramona. In his hands, even an unloaded gun became a deadly weapon. Ramona blanched. Yet the gun leapt out of his hands and bounced off the ceiling.

Southwind had nearly dropped Slycke from midair so that he could turn his attention to protecting Ramona.

She pulled handcuffs from her jacket and slapped one on Twinkletoes' ankle. "Hey!" he protested, but before he could squirm out from his weight, she cuffed his other ankle. She rolled off his legs and caught her breath, half crawling to retrieve her pistol.

Her cell phone vibrated.

What lousy timing, Ramona thought. She struggled to her feet, ears ringing, and scanned the room. Slycke floated in the middle of the room under Southwind's control; Flak had Musclehead in a half nelson and grunted under the strain of keeping him still; Easy Listener had curled up into a ball, blood seeping from his ears and crying. Twinkletoes clawed at the handcuffs preventing him from using his speed to escape.

Belladonna crouched by Silent Knight's prone form. Her hands moved over the ragged, bloody holes in his nanoweave shirt. Ramona leaned in. "How is he?"

"I can handle it," the blue girl snapped without taking her eyes from Knight.

Ramona exhaled in relief. The moment of terror and violence had ended in relative success. Her desperate curiosity about Eisenfaust's final words came back in delicious anticipation of gratification. She even smiled.

"Hot damn. Now we can get started."

Slycke flailed his arms as Southwind held him fast, three feet above the floor. He glared at Ramona with undisguised hatred. A faint scent of oil wafted off him, spread by the displaced air from Southwind's telekinesis.

"Walter, Walter, Walter." Ramona tapped her cheek with her gun. "Whatever are we going to do with you?"

"I ain't going back to lockup," he said.

"That's up to Southwind, honey, and his magic fingers. But if you cooperate with us, I can ask for your sentence to be reduced."

"Bull."

"Hey. I'm not the criminal here. You make me an offer. Why shouldn't we throw you back in a hole?"

Oily liquid formed patterns over Slycke's blunt features. His eyes narrowed. "What do you want from me?"

"Information, Walter. You're a witness to the murder of Heinrich Eisenhauer—Eisenfaust. His last words were addressed to you."

"Yeah. So? Lots of killin' that day. Hell, I thought they killed *you*."

"Which explains why you're so happy to see me again. Walter, what did Eisenfaust say?"

"Let me down first. I ain't no animal."

Ramona snorted. "Not according to your dossier. Spill the beans. Now. Or I get the psion to scrape out your skull, and believe me, *that* is unpleasant."

Walter Slycke glanced around nervously. A long moment passed . . . then her phone rang. Again. She hit the Ignore key.

"I'm a popular girl, Walter. Start talking while I still feel generous."

"See, the thing is . . ." He sighed. "I kinda forgot what he said."

Her jaw dropped. "You . . . forgot?"

"There was a lot going on, lady. I was sure them Nazis was fittin' to kill me. All I could think about was how I was going to get out of there alive."

Flak coughed. "Doesn't that just figure? Knight's down and it's all for nothing."

Ramona rubbed her scalp. "Not for nothing. Pensive

can dig through and get those memories. Just takes time."

Slycke cringed. "I'm gonna get scraped?"

"Yep. If you ask nice, he'll cuddle you afterwards." The phone rang again. She ignored it and instead flicked on her Echo comm unit. "Pensive, we're ready for you."

Ramona crossed the room to where Easy Listener sobbed on the floor. The metahuman's enhanced hearing made him utterly vulnerable to the shock wave–generating armor of Silent Knight. A pang of guilt rose up in her.

"It's all right." She got an arm under him and propped him up. He clung to her like a frightened child. "It's over now."

The buzz of her cell sent a fresh wave of quivers through the crippled old man. She dug it out of her jacket pocket to silence it—and blinked. The number was familiar, terribly familiar.

"We just wanted to be left alone," Easy Listener whimpered. "We wouldn't hurt anyone. You didn't have to bring an army."

Army? "Just us, old-timer."

He shook his head. "So many troops to arrest an old man. It's not fair."

"I told you, there's only—" Ramona stopped. There was something horribly wrong. Why hadn't Pensive confirmed her orders? And the persistent caller, who kept calling back, avoiding voice mail...

She gasped and flipped the cell phone open to answer. "Benjamin!"

There was nothing neutral about Benjamin Franklin Hotline's voice. "I told you to be there before six."

"We were. Slycke's right here, under arrest."

"Ramona." He spoke her name with disturbing urgency. "That wasn't the reason." He paused. "You're not my only client."

"What do you mean?"

"I—get out of there right now. I can't tell you more without violating client confidentiality."

Ramona looked up at the tableau of the secured metacrooks and the wounded Silent Knight. "Who's out there, Benjamin?"

"Just go. Use the back door." The line went dead.

"Damn." The comm line was silent as well, hissing like it had on the day of the invasion.

Flak gave her a concerned look over Musclehead's shoulder. "What's wrong?"

"Not sure." She turned to Easy Listener. "What do you hear?"

"Ringing..." He shook his head to clear it. "And footsteps, dozens. An engine, unfamiliar. Someone being strangled. Guns—rifles. Machines." Easy Listener paled further. "They're not Echo, are they?"

"No," Ramona said. "I don't think so."

"They're speaking...it's German. I can't understand what they're saying."

"I can guess." She retrieved her sidearm and slapped in a fresh cartridge. "We're already acquainted."

Southwind gave a laugh. "Speak of the devil! I was in the mood for some payback. What should I do with Mr. Exxon Valdez here?"

"Put me down," Slycke snarled.

"Hold onto him. That intel is still our primary objective."

But Southwind shook his head. "Can't do that and defend you."

Easy Listener had climbed back into his chair. "They're advancing. They're on my porch! Oh, Lord, protect us..."

The Nazis had the building surrounded. Benjamin Franklin Hotline told her to use the back door. Was it too late?

Ramona knelt by Silent Knight and Belladonna. "Can he move?"

"Not really," the healer said. "Not without support, which would require Flak or Southwind."

"Then we leave him." The words sounded foreign as soon as she spoke them. "To cover our retreat."

"Retreat?" Flak had released Musclehead, who rubbed his arms. "You're joking, right?"

"No. Think of this as a football game with Slycke as the ball. Our team's goal is to get him to safety, no matter what it takes."

"We should stand and fight," Belladonna said.

"Damn straight," Flak said. "We got the firepower."

"I want blood. They have to pay." Southwind said.

Ramona stood and faced them all. Her spine tingled. "No. I give the orders. We run. Now."

A buzz issued from Silent Knight's speaker grill. "Orders confirmed. I will provide covering fire." The mechanical quality of the synthesized voice didn't hide the finality in the statement. "Commence retreat at Detective Ferrari's command."

Belladonna clenched her fists. "This isn't right. My patient—"

The building shuddered from an impact on the roof. Plaster dust shook down from the ceiling. "No more time. Let's go."

"What about these clowns?" Flak gestured at

Musclehead and the cuffed Twinkletoes, who still sat with his legs outstretched.

Ramona aimed her gun and fired two rounds. Twinkletoes flinched. The bullets shattered the chain of the handcuffs.

"Evacuate them. Southwind, keep Slycke secure."

"Ain't no more need for that," Slycke said. "Jus' lemme go, I'll run plenty fast on my own."

Ramona ignored him. "Which way to the back door?"

Twinkletoes was on his feet and standing at the far door in an instant. "Over here."

"Carry the old man as far as you can when we break through their lines," Ramona told him.

Southwind raised a hand. "Wait a second, ma'am. I can fly us out of here in a snap."

"And when a stray shot hits you? We drop out of the sky and splat. No, we need to move on our own feet."

Easy Listener cried out and covered his head. Ramona jerked around to watch him. What had he heard?

"Down!" Flak shouted.

The ceiling over the old man and Twinkletoes collapsed. Beams slammed into the floor, and drywall fell in sheets, released from decades of failing support. A metallic claw the size of a man forced its way through the rubble and grasped the metahuman speedster. Talons the length of a man's arm pierced his chest. He died without being able to scream.

The wall nearest Ramona caved inwards. A huge, gleaming metal shape wedged through the opening, weaving from side to side. Though the lines were stylized and sleek, there was no question that the shape took the form of an eagle's head. Between its bulbous glass eyes, a swastika stood out in relief.

The robotic eagle fixed both eyes on Slycke.

The Echo metahumans wasted no time. Flak leapt forward to throw his arms around the eagle's head. The eagle dashed him against the floor and ceiling, but Flak's skin had the tensile strength of steel, and the thrashing took far more toll on the house. The eagle plunged into the room and headed straight for Slycke, still suspended in the air.

Belladonna seized Ramona's arm. "Let's go, let's go!" They ran across the center of the room, ducking as the second, airborne eagle tore through the rest of ceiling with a blood-curdling, half-organic hunting call. Its wingtips battered the rafters; antigravity engines glowed orange along the length of its pinions. Ramona swerved to avoid the buffeting wing and stumbled. A claw, already coated with Twinkletoes' blood, reached out for her.

Thunder resounded in the room. Silent Knight's armor had been absorbing all the sound in the room to convert it to concussive energy. The cacophony from the destruction of the ceiling gave him a spike in power, and he released it at the eagle. Shards of metal feathers exploded from its chest, showering Ramona. Instinctively she covered her head with her arms—but with only a nanoweave vest to protect her, the shrapnel tore through her jacket and into her arms.

Belladonna dragged her to the wall, just under the shuttered window; she tore open the seams of Ramona's sleeves to reveal bloody flesh. Belladonna plucked out the largest of the fragments as Ramona gasped in pain. Then warmth flooded from the healer's fingers into Ramona's arms.

"Can you move your arms?"

"I think so."

Slycke's cries cut through the cacophony of collapsing ceilings. The gunmetal eagle dragged Flak along as it snapped at Slycke as though he were bait hanging from a hook. Southwind yanked him back and forth to keep him from being sliced in half.

The blue girl's face was resolute. "That thing is going to kill our target. You were right about the intel."

Ramona shook her head, dislodging tears of pain. "That was all talk. I never meant for anyone to die just so I could question him."

Belladonna grabbed her arm. "Listen—I can read minds, too. I'm not as good as Pensive, but I can do it if I can get a hand on Slycke."

"It's—"

"Not my job as DCO. I know. But do we have a choice?" Belladonna's eyes pleaded with her and demanded at the same time.

A rapid-fire popping, followed by the whine of bullets, increased the noise level of the room. Ramona and Belladonna flattened themselves on the ground.

Slycke was a sitting duck.

"It's now or never!" Belladonna shouted.

Ramona reloaded her sidearm. "Go! Go!"

Belladonna bunched her legs under her and ran forward like a dog, using her hands to keep her balance as she hunched over to avoid the volley of bullets from outside. Where the bullets hit the wall, they kicked up dust and splinters; where they hit the eagles, they ricocheted into the floor—or into the occupants. She saw Easy Listener jerking from multiple impacts.

Ramona squeezed the trigger, sending armor-piercing caseless rounds into the tail of the eagle blocking Belladonna's way. The eagle spun, wings sweeping the floor, forcing Belladonna to leap into the air to avoid a devastating swat.

A bullet caught Bella in the thigh. Flipping end over end, she clattered to the floor in a tangle of blue and black.

"Damn it!" Ramona kept firing at the eagle as it advanced on her. The beak opened as if to shriek—and the "tongue" dropped down to reveal a gun barrel. Its focusing tip glowed a wicked azure.

The back door. Ramona was close to it. She dove into the opening as the familiar, teeth-grating whine of the Nazi force beam presaged a blue eruption of energy. The wall where she had been exploded outwards, and behind it, sections of floor, foundation and yard outside.

The robotic eagle's beak clacked and a spent capacitor casing ejected. The gun revved up for another blast.

She got a glimpse of what lurked behind her in the yard: two dozen men in red-and-black uniforms, with white-faced gas masks and coal-black sloping helmets. They fired their rifles into the side of the house.

There was nowhere to go.

The eagle's eye lenses whirred and zoomed in on her, and the monster opened its beak to expose the energy cannon. Desperately, Ramona fired at the blue glow, over and over, as fast as she could. The bullets embedded themselves in the eagle's beak—but for the few that found their way right down the collimator of the force cannon and into the capacitor housing beside it.

In a flash of blue light, the eagle's head swelled and burst; the thing crumbled into the shattered floor with a titanic crash.

Ramona saw Belladonna's head peek over the debris. She was crawling towards Slycke. Ramona tried to move in her direction, but the eagle's energy bolt had opened a hole in the wall that gave the assembled soldiers out front a clear view of the room. Bullets raked across the floor between Ramona and her comrades. She tried to make herself as small as possible and reloaded her gun with her last magazine of armor-piercing rounds.

Flak and Musclehead pounded on the remaining eagle. Foot soldiers poured in from the back door. Those in the vanguard took shots at the two strongmen. The bullets bounced off Flak's invulnerable hide, but Musclehead had no such protection. He cried out as the rounds embedded themselves in his meaty body, mostly in his left side.

The eagle reared up and lunged at him. Caught off guard, he could not dodge the razor-sharp metal beak. It sliced into his shoulder and arm and hauled him into the air. Flak beat uselessly on the robot's neck. In all this chaos, Southwind still held fast to Slycke. His huge black eyes flicked back and forth from target to target. Ramona knew his powers were curtailed by her orders. Meanwhile, as he kept Slycke from harm, he also kept him out of Belladonna's reach.

Ramona reached out with her sidearm and fired blindly. The foot soldiers' cries of surprise and pain were muffled by their gas masks. Those behind her targets returned fire, chewing holes in the drywall as she ducked aside.

The wreckage of the robotic eagle rose into the air. Ramona cursed, appalled. A sick feeling welled up from her stomach: she was going to die.

But the eagle had not come back to life. Instead, it floated towards Belladonna and Slycke.

Ramona felt a tug on her leg. An invisible pull horrifically dragged her out towards the center of the room—into the line of fire.

"Rey, no!"

Gunfire ripped up the floor a yard from her foot. She dropped her sidearm to scrabble at the floorboards. But the force was implacable, irresistible.

A low sound rumbled inside her, gained power, roared into life. The sound was all-encompassing, overwhelming. Silent Knight stood, hands extended, and broadcast a shock wave into the air of the room itself. Bullets lost their trajectories and skittered across the floor, harmless.

Southwind's pull on her increased. She slid under the eagle and rose up until she floated aside Slycke and Belladonna.

A shadow passed over them: the headless eagle enfolded them in its wings.

The space it created was no larger than the back-seat of a sedan, so Slycke's effluvia and Belladonna's blood smeared them all. Belladonna, however, ignored her wound and wrapped her hands around Slycke. He struggled against her until his eyes rolled up into his head.

"Get him," Ramona whispered.

Belladonna's hands roved over his face, almost in an intimate embrace until one of her hands slipped off Slycke's coating entirely. She kept her pressure light, maintaining contact without gripping. Her face screwed up in concentration and her eyes shut tight.

"He's fighting me," she shouted over the roar. "It's not on his surface level, either. He really wasn't paying attention."

"He's expendable. Do what you have to!"

Belladonna cracked her neck, took a deep breath, and bowed her head. Slycke began to jerk as if he had touched a power line. A high-pitched, inhuman wail rose up from his throat.

"Come on, you sick son of a bitch." Belladonna's entire body had tensed up. "Jesus Christ."

"What?"

The healer shook her head as if to clear it. "He's—I got it, by God, I got it."

As if on cue, Southwind released his hold on Slycke, and the metahuman's limp form dropped out of their telekinetically sustained shelter. Silent Knight and Flak took his place. The wings of the robot eagle constricted, and the tail as well, shutting out the light. The four of them pressed together as Southwind released them in order to compress the eagle into a hollow ball of impenetrable metal. The patter of bullets resumed; the soldiers were firing at the former robot eagle.

Belladonna sagged against Ramona. Her blue skin had gone pale. "What's he doing?"

"Something big. Hang on." Flak enveloped Ramona in his arms, Silent Knight did the same for Belladonna.

The ball fell to the floor, then lurched over as a deafening ripping sound enveloped them. The interior of their makeshift shelter was hardly smooth; the metal feathers jabbed at them as they bounced on the inside, like an amusement park ride designed by a sadist. Ramona pressed her head into Flak's chest and let his back and her nanoweave vest absorb the impacts as the ball twirled through the air.

For a pregnant moment, they hung in midair, not from telekinetic force, but in free fall. Then they hit the ground, hard. Flak's head smashed into the eagle's wing and he grunted against an impact that would have split Ramona's skull open.

The ball rolled to a stop against an obstruction. Flak released her. "You all right?"

"Hell of a ride. Thanks."

Flak wedged his hands where the two wings met and flexed. Slowly, painfully, the metal bent, and an opening large enough for them to pass through was created. They emerged into sunlight dappled by the green leaves of the oak tree that had stopped their tumble. In the distance, crashes and gunfire resounded. Ramona shielded her eyes from the sun to get a look at the mansion once occupied by the late Easy Men.

It was virtually scoured from the earth. Any recognizable structure from two-thirds of it was gone. Beams and roofing and wiring were twisting away, only to be slammed together, like fistfuls of modeling clay in the hands of a petulant child and torn apart again.

And then the remaining wing of the mansion rose into the air, and came crashing down atop the rest, compressing it all down to a height of mere feet. A spindly figure hovered in the air above it: Southwind, freed of his obligation to protect Slycke or the rest of the team. He had turned the mansion into a weapon, and left nothing to doubt or mercy. Blue energy beams lashed out at him from the trees nearby, but he was in full battle rage now, the pain of the loss of his lover channeled into unholy destruction.

A blast of displaced wind washed over them.

"Good God," Ramona said. "I doubt Southwind left any survivors, but the after-action team should be on its way. I had no idea he was capable of that."

Flak helped Belladonna to her feet. "He may not be. That expenditure could kill him. I don't think he cares."

"I hope it was worth it." Ramona met Belladonna's eyes. "Well? Is it?"

The blue girl looked immeasurably old in that moment. What Belladonna had seen in the vile depths of Walter Slycke's mind, Ramona could only guess. She put a comforting hand on the girl's arm.

Belladonna hung her head. "I don't know. It's—it's weird, a non sequitur. Maybe you know more than I do."

"It's all we have, right now." She squeezed. "Thank you."

"All in a day's work for a DCO." Belladonna managed a wry almost-smile.

The blades of the Echo helicopter beat the air above them. As columns of dust kicked up around them, Ramona let herself close her eyes and think about nothing at all.

INTERLUDE

Bottom feeders.

You get them in every disaster. We got them now, in spades, the "smart guys" that make a very high profit off the misery of others. The PMCs were some of those. Private military companies were basically highly organized, heavily funded mercenaries with as much money sunk in their legal, PR and packaging departments as they had in their bullets and fatigues. The aftermath of the Invasion created a feeding frenzy among them. They took contracts, they heavily recruited to fill those contracts, and anyplace where the law was not there to step hard on them immediately, they took the law into their own hands and became judge, jury and on-the-spot executioner. The ones who'd bought politicians ahead of time got the fattest gigs first, but everyone in the biz got a slice of the terror pie. Life on the ground was great for a merc. They had systems worked out where as long as your CO filed the right papers, you could shoot, confiscate, or "secure" whatever you wanted. PMCs became the elite looters of the aftermath, "securing" valuables and supplies, and guarding them in the most luxurious "command posts" they could take over, like million-dollar condos.

Their highest-paid members were the guys who wrote the after-action reports, spun to always make it the other guy's fault. On the ground, people knew. But up where the money was, far from shunning them, anyone that had anything to lose and wasn't thinking about scruples lined up to hire them. Frightened people do that, and then they have the illusion that everything is all right again.

I expect the Thulians are laughing about that.

CHAPTER TWELVE

Karma Chameleon

CODY MARTIN & MERCEDES LACKEY

Payback was hell.

John Murdock had spent the last five years of his life thinking about no one and nothing but himself. Now it seemed that every responsibility he had shrugged off in those years was coming back on him.

Once upon a time, before the Program, he'd have pitched in here without a second thought. That person, *that* Johnny Murdock, seemed like a stranger to him now. Someone out of a book or a movie, someone he couldn't possibly be.

Hell, maybe it was just karma catching up to him.

He was living better than he had in years, though that wouldn't normally have been saying much. That was just the material side of it, though. The people here, beyond all reason and expectation, had welcomed him. Trusted him.

Maybe that was what had gotten to him—the trust. It wasn't something he had given or received for far too long, and he ached for it somewhere deep inside of himself. But at the same time, he hated the broken-record feeling of playing through the paranoia over and over again.

So instead he tried to think about what needed doing. Right now what needed to get done were the community gardens. Not pretty ones, but working ones. Grocery deliveries were still sporadic, and half the people here that had once had jobs were either unable to get to them, or else the job was under a pile of rubble. People were going to need to eat. Gardens would provide some of that. And besides what Hog Farm brought in, John had managed to find seeds in some of the most unlikely places: the wreck of a hardware store here, an abandoned grocery there, even an old five-and-dime that had been nearly moribund by the look of it before the invasion.

On the plus side, no landlords had shown up looking for the monthly rent checks, and the city seemed to have forgotten—maybe fearing riots—that utilities were supposed to be paid for.

This neighborhood was old enough that the houses had yards, even if some were the size of postage stamps. But a tiny yard could still support a garden, and could even provide food enough for two households, with skill and a little good luck, and there were the bigger, community gardens Hog Farm helped put in. People without yards helped out those people who planted, if for no other reason than they hoped to get some of the bounty. There was a more subtle effect from the planting, though. Planting a garden is a way of acknowledging that, yes, there *will* be a future. People who have given up don't garden. People with a will to survive get their hands dirty, and nurture.

An old Southern tradition returned, too. There

was a time, long before satellite TV and cable, when evenings would be spent on porches or stoops, with rocking chairs and sun-brewed tea, and everyone in a neighborhood would walk along and visit with each other. Now this was resumed, at first, as a way of making sure gardens wouldn't be disturbed, but each night the "patrols" got more relaxed, and the vigilance let down. The gang members split off in ones and twos and stayed to talk with their elders. Before long, even a couple of the street toughs might be spotted kicking some debris out of the way for an old couple strolling from home to home.

John was busy hammering together a set of scavenged two-by-fours for a mulch bed when one of the neighborhood kids came running up to him. He set down the power drill he was working with, wiping his hands on an already dirty T-shirt. "What's the rush, kid? Y'wanna try your hand at this?"

"Nuh-uh, Mister John." The youth gulped for breath, hands on his knees. "I came over here to tell you . . . there was a guy at your place. He's asking around for you. Some dude in a suit."

"Suit?" John's heart felt like it froze in place. *The Program. They're here!* After a few moments of sheer panic, John started breathing again, relaxing his hands so that they weren't balled up into white-knuckled fists. Then his reason came back. Time to think, to work an out for this. "Did he ask for me by name? Does he know I'm here right now?"

"Nuh-uh. He just said that he was looking for the 'meta' that was looking after our 'hood. What do you think he wants?"

John shook his head. "Dunno, kid. But I aim to find

out. Stay here; Jonas looks like he needs a hand with those bags of soil. Why don't ya give him a hand?" He patted the kid on the shoulder, doing his very best to walk calmly; he didn't want to spook any of the people at the garden, some of whom had overheard his conversation with the boy and had clearly taken an interest. Once he was a block away, edging against one of the destruction corridors, he started running. His mind was racing with strategies, possibilities, escape plans; how he would get out of the city, out of the country—off of the planet if it were only possible—this wasn't just for him. If it was the Program, everyone here was in danger.

Who was it? Why did they want him? Should he just abandon everything and start running now? It would've been smarter to go in the exact opposite direction than the one he was heading. But John couldn't shake the thought that whoever was looking for him might lean on the residents of the neighborhood to try to find him. If he could have just had the trouble all for himself, he would have taken it readily; he wasn't prepared to set up folks that were depending on him for more pain than they had already gone through.

He had the distinct impression when the kid said "suit" he wasn't talking about a three-piece and tie. Armor maybe. Or the whole package, like that Silent Knight Echo OpThree. Had Echo sent someone else after him now? In less than five minutes he had arrived; edging to the corner of a building and peeking out around it, John was somewhat surprised at what he saw.

It wasn't armor. In fact, the guy looked like a used-car salesman. What John's old man used to call "the Sears Sucker Suit." Polyester, the kind of thing that you couldn't destroy with a nuke. Blue, because that was supposed to be somehow less intimidating than black. He was middle-aged, and it showed on his form; a spare tire was definitely growing around his midsection. He stood there, hands clasped behind his back, staring up at John's old industrial building as if waiting for him to appear in one of the windows. *Well, this is...different. What the hell does this guy want?* Waiting a few heartbeats to collect himself, John finally strode out from around the corner, making a beeline for the suit. His training still kept him on his toes; he was careful to approach the stranger from his right side, which would probably be the hand he used to go for a weapon since most people were right-handed; coming at him in that way would mean that the muzzle or whatever dangerous bit this guy could pull would have to travel in a longer arc in order to get a bead on John.

The stranger looked over to John as if pleasantly surprised. John came to a stop about fifteen feet away, taking the chance to be the first to speak. "So, you're lookin' for me. Who are ya, an' whaddya want? I've got stuff to do."

"The name's Chuck Smith," the man said, with a professional snake-oil smile. He looked down, kicking a piece of concrete rubble absentmindedly. He took a couple of steps past the debris towards John. "I think you might be interested in a proposition from my firm."

John eyed him sourly. "What firm, an' what're ya offering? If you were able to find me, you probably already know that I'm fairly set as it is, an' I don't like much in the way of annoyances."

The man rubbed the back of his head, and shifted his weight towards John. "Ah. You had a visit from Echo, I gather." The man chuckled, and rocked forward a little on his toes. He took another step forward, close enough now for John to notice that he was wearing some sort of light body armor under his hideous suit. Superaramid maybe, the next gen from the old flak jackets. "Tesla's Nanny Squad. Well, they have their hands full these days, and they're pretty short of personnel. You can rest assured that unlike them, we don't bite off more than we can chew."

"You still haven't told me who this 'we' is." The stranger fished in his jacket as John tensed, watching him through narrowed eyes. But all that came out was a card. The man handed it to him.

It was a much more polished piece of presentation than the rep was. Not just a business card, this was a tiny CD. Slip it in a computer and it would probably give you a slick PowerPoint pitch. *Blacksnake Security Services*, it said in flowing script. *Professional Protection Guaranteed.*

"Blacksnake. That PMC that got famous over in the Sandbox. You're mercs." John had never had too much of a taste for merc work; there were some reputable companies, but for the most part they were like Blacksnake. Most private military companies concerned themselves with private security, through personal bodyguard work and protecting key sites for their employers. Others focused on fulfilling roles that underequipped and corrupt militaries in third-world countries couldn't provide, and some rarely filled humanitarian roles.

However, Blacksnake, and the companies like them, went deeper than that; assassination—never directly traced back to them, naturally—and assisting in coups weren't out of their scope. John lowered the card, looking at Chuck. "So, whaddya want with me?"

"We're recruiting. We heard about some of your work here, and we figured you could do better than this—with us." Smith glanced up at the abandoned building, with a little smile playing on his lips. "We've even got a dental plan. I know what you're thinking. We couldn't possibly want you. Well, under most circumstances, that would be true. We don't know anything about you, except that your actions tend to indicate you've got some training in . . . how to put this? . . . our area of interest. And without references, that would normally not be enough to get you a look-over, much less a pitch. But"—Smith raised a finger—"you're a meta. And we're prepared to waive a lot of things to recruit a meta."

Why, 'cause there seem to be fewer of us lately?

John hesitated a moment before replying. "No, thanks. I'll figure out something on my own. If you'll kindly get outta my neighborhood, we'll call it a day. An' don't be stopping by with any more offers; I'm not interested."

The man looked ostentatiously hurt. "You haven't heard the offer yet. That's a bit of an unfriendly attitude, if you don't mind my saying so."

"Don't much care what your offer is. I don't need whatever you can offer." John crossed his arms in front of his chest with finality, settling the discussion.

Smith made a sour face. "I was really hoping that you wouldn't take that tone with me. You know, Echo is limited by how much they can push you. We aren't. And since you invited Echo out of this neighborhood, that could technically mean we could take it under our jurisdiction. It's a fact, ever since the invasion, people get rather nervous about having loose metas around, answering to no one, operating on their own. I wouldn't doubt that somewhere there's a file on you, and a bounty with that file. Maybe even at Echo. And among other things, we collect bounties." He sighed heavily. "Don't make me do something we'll both regret."

John arched an eyebrow, uncrossing his arms. He straightened up to his full height, easily half a foot over Smith's. He ignited a jet of flame in his right hand, letting it sit there idly at his side. "I'm already regrettin' you coming here. Don't make it any worse for yourself. Now, get."

John had expected him to try to negotiate, or even to try to come off as a hard-ass with some sort of "We'll get you!" line. But he didn't. Instead, he moved in on John, and moved far quicker than his frumpy appearance had led John to believe he possibly *could* move.

It was only after Chuck had gut-punched John—*hard*—that he realized that he had allowed the Blacksnake representative to get within arm's reach. John staggered, stumbling backwards on the uneven ground. His flame extinguished, he wrapped his arms around his aching midsection as he widened his stance to catch himself. Looking up as he sucked in breath, John saw Chuck unbuttoning the front of his jacket, revealing a pulsating device on his belt. Iridescent armor gleamed dully under his shirt; even though John had glimpsed it earlier on, he hadn't recognized it for what it was: some sort of mecha-armor, not superaramid.

His mistake. This was going to be a fight.

Not wasting a moment, John snapped into action. His enhancements made him faster than any normal man. Chuck was caught off-guard by the unexpected movement, and John had a clean shot at disabling his attacker. He clamped his left hand around his opponent's shoulder—why was he so damned slippery?—and prepared to step into Chuck to plant an elbow through his throat; it was a killing move, and would have crushed the man's trachea and maybe even his spine, with John's enhanced strength. Then there was more pain, as John's elbow smashed into the air less than a centimeter from Smith's throat.

In another snap-moment, John was being kneed and hit simultaneously; he reacted, blocking the blows, but was still driven back.

What the hell was that?

His elbow throbbed; he had no doubt it would have snapped from the force of his blow, if it had been *only* bone. *"That"* had to be some sort of force-field armor.

"Not friendly, John. Yes, we know your name, your first name anyway. Not friendly at—" John was already on top of Chuck again, lashing out with fists, elbows, feet and knees. He tried to grapple with the other man, but couldn't find purchase; he couldn't grab onto his clothing, hair, or even his limbs without receiving a flurry of return blows. John's body was rocked by the strikes and his vision blurred. As he knew all too well, getting hit wasn't like it was in the movies; getting punched and kicked *hurt*, knocked the air out of him, dizzied him, and made it hurt to block or return those blows.

Ducking under a swing and redirecting a vicious kick by twisting out of the way and slapping it with the flat of his right hand, John dropped to the ground. He arced his leg hard into Chuck's rear foot, where all of his opponent's weight was resting. Smith's legs went out from under him; whatever sort of force field he had on, it didn't make him completely invulnerable. As soon as Chuck was flat on his back, John was on top of him, trying to put the other man into a hold so that he could get at the device on his belt.

More blows came from Chuck, aimed at John's face and midsection. His ribs creaked, and he had several cuts opening on his brow, cheek, chin, and lips. John knew that he couldn't take too much more of this sort of punishment. He needed to end this fight, and fast. Smith managed to snake an arm out from under John's hold, and used it to grapple John closely. There was a sharp *whump* accompanied by a flash of light, and John was skidding across the ground, his skin tearing open on gravel and broken glass. His back slammed against a curb, stopping him instantly. Stars were swimming in front of his eyes, but he jumped to his feet out of reflex. Chuck was still climbing up from the ground; he was fast, but he wasn't the most nimble person. John relaxed, letting his control wane for a moment. Twin lances of blindingly-white flame sprang from his outstretched hands, flying towards Chuck. Both jets of fire rebounded off of the force field at obtuse angles, cutting jagged swaths through whatever they impacted with. Chuck, finally back on his feet, looked worried, but continued to move towards John. John responded with more fire; surrounded his attacker in it completely, firing arm-thick bolts of plasma, igniting the asphalt beneath his feet. None of it got through, and Chuck kept advancing.

John continued blasting and moving, never allowing himself to get cornered; if he got within arm's reach of Smith again, he might not be able to recover in time. His shin was bruising terribly from where he had kicked the force field with it, and he was starting to limp. His ribs told him that they didn't want him to breathe anymore, and the blood trickling into his eyes made it hard to see.

Sick an' tired of this shit.

John feinted to his left, then back to his right before charging at Chuck head-on. He fired a wide burst of flame at his opponent's face, obscuring his vision; Chuck threw his hands up in front of his face and stumbled backwards, instinctually flinching away from the attack. John closed in with his opponent, and scrambled for the techy-looking belt, which he could only assume and hope controlled the force fields; if he could disable it, he was sure that he could make quick work of this bastard.

His fingers scratched at the invisible wall just a centimeter above the device, unable to penetrate; John's control on his fires lapsed, and Chuck was able to see again. He grabbed John by the back of his neck and his jeans; John could see some sort of hydraulic joints ripping through the elbows, shoulders, and knees of Chuck's suit as he hefted John above his head, and then threw. John hit the brick wall beside the entrance of his home fifteen feet above the ground, crushing several of its bricks and knocking a good many others loose before falling back to earth with a sickening thump.

Everything went black for what seemed like an eternity, give or take a few millennia. When he came to, he knew that he was still alive, at least somewhat; Smith was talking again.

"—sure is nifty, isn't it? See, these are the advantages of working with Blacksnake; you get all of the best toys. This servomotor exoskeleton gives me the strength of twenty men; slow and somewhat ungainly, but very fine for power work, don't you think?" John didn't want to move; he could hardly breathe, and his vision was dark around the edges if you didn't count the stars swarming in front of his eyes. He was done, and done for. He couldn't defend himself effectively anymore, and this smarmy and smug middle-management flunky was going to be the end of him. "The real shame is that it didn't have to be like this." Chuck paced slowly towards where John was lying, not in a great hurry to finish off his opponent. "I would offer you a second chance, but I have an appointment downtown. I've got to pick up a new suit before then, so I'll make this quick. Open or closed casket, John?"

"Fer me or you?" John croaked out, blood seeping from his mouth. It clicked for him right as he finished delivering what he thought were going to be his last words, again. He knew what to do. Smith smiled, raising a foot to crush the life out of John—

—and then the air inside of his protective force field ignited into plasma, which in turn ignited his clothing, skin, and what little hair he had in the first place. Chuck couldn't scream, because all of the air in his lungs was on fire, and the lungs themselves were seared in an instant. John lay there watching as Chuck Smith did an odd sort of dance, cooked alive silently in his own force field. For one moment, the memory of the kid in New York, ramping up until he was nothing but a man-shaped thing too white-hot to look at, flashed across his memory. After a few seconds the Blacksnake recruiter fell backwards, and not even smoke came from his body; there was only a wispy veil of combustion, inside which polyester, skin and exoskeleton crisped. Then, whatever device that had been powering his force field malfunctioned and died. There was an instant of charred corpse against the ground, its mouth wide open, and then with a *whumpf,* it flashed over from its own intense heat and burned openly.

John didn't have the strength or the willpower to stand. He crawled over the rubble and grit, crawled up the stairs to his flat, and then crawled into bed. After that, the world stopped for John Murdock as unconsciousness took over.

Seraphym watched the man below her crawling towards the entrance of his building. It would be a long crawl up, with no working elevators. Solemnly, she sensed the terrible pain he was in, how he had been reduced to mere animal instincts. Only once had there been any kind of moment of *feeling* in this fight, and it had not been for the man who had called himself "Chuck Smith," and who was, in fact, actually Roger McSkye, a senior recruiting agent for Black-snake, operating under the code name "Hardbody."

No, John Murdock had felt nothing for this man, even at the moment that John was killing him. When someone became an opponent for John, an attacker, a threat, they ceased to be human. The brief rush of emotion had come with the memory of that poor child in New York: guilt, anger, bewilderment and anguish that John had been unable to help him. And that had been over in a moment.

John Murdock was a brutal and dispassionate fighter, divorced emotionally from the killing and the need to kill. He had begun the fight with what should have been a murderous blow. He had ended it with another.

But she sensed a terrible void in him, and mourning, far past conscious thought, that this was what he had become. He recognized what he was, and hated it. This, perhaps, was the root of his self-hatred. Somehow . . . somehow he had to come out of this. Somehow he had to heal, or be healed, if he was to grow, to become . . . whatever it was that was on the other side of that blank spot in the futures.

There were other futures where, presumably, he did not change. Sera could only see them now as they turned up from the man's maddening blind spot, because now they could not happen. One suddenly appeared and ended here; Blacksnake would send another operative, and John would die. One, already aborted and withering, and seen like a glimpsed reflection in glass—he had accepted the offer and gone on to join the mercenaries. That one ended when he was sent to kill *her* and she showed him the inside of his own mind. Where that would have led, she could not see, for already that future was crumbling, back to the origin points of passing moments. There were those where he ran, those where he joined Echo and was then forcibly reclaimed by his Program, others where he became a kind of half recluse in this building, emerging only at night, to scour the neighborhood for things to kill.

But most of those were withering too. He was already changing. He could not stop the change. That was just as well; those futures all ended in apocalypse, the thing she had been sent to prevent.

He had managed to get the door to his apartment open now, and crawl inside. She considered this. Considered helping him. Animals, wounded near to death, would crawl off alone to heal or die. Which would he do now?

She opened her mind a little and let other thoughts brush against hers. The child. The grocer. The old woman who was knitting John socks from yarn saved from ruined sweaters, who fed him soup and thought about him as a kind of surrogate grandchild. Those would do.

Gently she suggested that something was wrong. John had not been seen for hours. Someone should look in on him.

Satisfied that the suggestion had settled into their minds, she sighed and turned her thoughts further outward.

There. Another one to save.

She was away in a flash of fire.

John was angry. He was actually waking up, which wasn't precisely what he had expected to happen. And waking up carried with it all of the burdens of being conscious and alive after the fight with Chuck Smith. Namely, various types and degrees of pain. It took him a long time to be able to pry his swollen eyes open, widening them until the thin slivers of light leaking through became smeared and over-bright shapes. His head pounded as if Smith was still hammering on it, his mouth was as dry as sandpaper, and his entire body felt as if it had been passed underneath a steamroller.

He'd felt worse. But not much worse. And not often.

Eventually, his vision focused again after much effort. He made out the ceiling of the room that he usually slept in, with peeling paint and water stains from leaks in the roof. With Herculean effort he was able to turn his head to the right, seeing Jonas the shopkeeper snoozing quietly in a battered lawn chair. The TV was playing silently, and there were a few bags of groceries littered around the room. Looking down at himself, and immediately regretting doing so, John saw that his midsection was completely bandaged, as well as most of his arms and what he could see of his legs. Straining to reach up with his hand, he felt his own face; more bandages, sticky and itchy against his pulped and ruined skin.

With a start, Jonas woke up, blinking several times as he looked about the dirty and dim room. Spying John and seeing that he was awake, he smiled kindly, his yellowed teeth gleaming in the single lightbulb's glare. "I was wondering when you would wake up. I was starting to get tired of feeding you and changing your bandages, kid. Figured I'd let the cockroaches and rats take over for me, in a bit. I don't need to ask, but how're ya feeling?"

"Like hammered shit. You?" John managed to prop himself up on an elbow, a feat in and of itself considering how badly damaged his arms were.

"I'm dandy. Couple folks are looking after the store while I've been up here babysitting your sorry rear. Some of the younger fellas that you were working with took over keeping the 'hood in check. They're not bad kids, once they have something to put their minds to." Jonas passed his hand over his mostly-gray salt-and-pepper hair. "Kind of funny; I used to watch a lot of nature shows, and I always figured they were like those young bucks butting heads over girls and territory. Turns out I was right. Now that they *can* do just that, and get praised for it, they've just settled right down."

John nodded. He wasn't terribly sure as to what to say next. "Thanks," he mumbled, "for keepin' me breathin'. I'll actually start buyin' some of the junk ya have at the store now, maybe."

It wasn't much, but Jonas recognized it for the compliment and sincere thanks that it was. "Anytime, fella. I figure that you'll live, for now. Who was that guy that you had it out with? There wasn't much left of him when Toby came to fetch me. To be honest, there wasn't much left of you, either." John was silent, looking off into a corner instead of meeting Jonas's gaze. After a few long moments, Jonas spoke again. "Fair enough. Talkers are usually *only* talk when it comes to that sort of thing, anyways." He sighed, standing up with an effort. "Now that it looks like you'll at least live for a little while longer, I've gotta get back to the store. I'll have one of the kids come up here tomorrow to check on you." Jonas rubbed his apparently-arthritic hands and looked down at John. "We moved the remains of that guy you fought. Didn't seem like the body oughta stay near where you live. We put it in an old fridge and it kinda got lost somewhere." Jonas looked troubled by that, but then stepped to the door. "You heal pretty quick, so it shouldn't be all that long before you start pitching people out of windows. 'Defenestration,' that's called. There's a word for you. Make you a Scrabble champ." Still quiet, John nodded, and the conversation ended. Jonas left the building, and left John with his thoughts.

And, the same as every night when "it" happened or that he bothered to think about it, the shakes came again.

It was all about what he had become. Conditioned to fight effectively, to kill reflexively when his mind and all of the things that should have made him a man, made him human, told him not to, John was a dispassionate predator. Distance helped; targets at the end of a rifle scope were just empty uniforms that needed to be filled with neat holes. Once you got closer, it got harder. You could see human expression, how old the "target" was, if he had looked like someone you had known in the "real world" back home. Most of the time, working with a unit of like-minded asskickers, the responsibility was diffused. You didn't precisely *know*, truly know, who had fired the fatal shot. In the latter part of John's career, that had changed; all of the killing was up close and extremely personal; you knew where the rounds went when you sent them downrange, and there was a high level of aggression there. Knife kills, with a long blade or bayonet slipped into someone's kidney from behind—since slitting throats was a terrible idea; John had known too many that had cut their own hands doing it, instead of "getting it right"—were the worst. You could feel exactly what you were doing to the person. You could feel the heat from their body, their sweat evaporating into the air, the breath leave them as they slumped to the ground. The paradox was that the easier it got, the worse it felt.

"Back home" became more and more remote, something that had little relevance to who and what you were now, and what you might find yourself becoming. Back home, they didn't understand. They lived shallow, easy lives where no one ever had to think about killing, and dying was only something that happened by accident, or at the end of an illness or long life. Death was something easily meted out by Hollywood, racked up on console games by thumb actions, or it happened off-screen in slaughterhouses. After a while John realized that it was only the men he'd worked and trained with, his buddies, who understood. But even that only helped so much. There was still the guilt, the horrible realization that you've done the worst thing possible to another being of your species. And then when you had quiet moments to think, you looked at your buddies and you saw one of two things back from them: either equal guilt that made you flinch away and avert your eyes—or utter lack of guilt, which meant they were no longer human. "Two-percenters," those last sort were called—guys that liked to torture small animals in their spare time because it was cheap and easy practice. Two-percenters were few and far between, and John honestly, earnestly hoped he wasn't drifting in that direction. Despite his stern exterior and professional cool, they scared John. It nagged at him that he had shared beers with them, and often. They wore the same uniform, ate the same MREs, and stood watch while he slept. He shook to wonder how far down their road he had already gone, and to realize he could not take that measure. He took it as a bad sign that he simply couldn't tell.

It always took a few hours for him to get himself

under control. Alcohol didn't help much, but it was something to steady him once he was done sweating and convulsing uncontrollably. Gingerly changing into a fresh shirt and grabbing a beer out of a case that Jonas had generously left for him, aching with every move, John headed out to the roof to think. The case of beer made him frown, because a post-disaster area was automatically a destabilized economy. Things were done by sweat, barter or violence now, and that case of beer was a genuine treasure. Yet, it'd been left for him after he'd mercilessly murdered someone. Was it a thank you from the neighborhood, or was it, in fact, a backhanded peace offering to appease his wrath? John found himself hoping the community wouldn't turn on him.

It was a decent Southern night: sticky-hot and clear, with the stars doing their best to shine against the city lights. The air was practically alive with green smells again, thick and pungent. All of the fires since the invasion had gone out, and much of the haze had dispersed, so you could actually see the stars and moon at night. John, no matter all of his public posturing, liked to think of himself as a romantic at heart, despite his failings. Leaning with his forearms against a railing and a precious beer cradled in his hands, John lived in the moment. He wasn't particularly thankful, but he was there, and he was alive, and that's what mattered. For what it was worth.

There was a sound behind him that he couldn't identify. A sighing sound, as if something parted the air gently, and slipped down from the stars. Turning as fast as he could, which was terribly slow in his current condition, John looked to see what had surprised him.

She was just alighting, weightlessly, one foot out-stretched with infinite grace and poise, to touch the rooftop, fire wings extending upwards. Not hammering or fluttering down like a bird. Whatever those "wings" were for, they had nothing to do with how she managed her flight.

The Seraphym.

"Hello, John Murdock." Her voice was a low alto, throaty, with five or six under- and overtones, as if a chorus spoke with her voice.

"You again. The meta with delusions of divinity. Care for a drink? Friend of mine was kind enough to gimme a few cold ones for recuperation purposes." John gestured casually with his beer bottle, despite the pain it caused him to move at all. One must keep up appearances, after all.

Her eyes were the yellow-gold of the heart of a fire, and they had no pupils. The seemingly blind gaze settled on the bottle in his hand. "But it is not cold," she replied. The bottle abruptly chilled in his hand, acquiring a sudden bloom of condensation.

"Is now," John said matter-of-factly, taking a long pull from the bottle. "Thanks, by the way. You're full of surprises."

"Am I?" She tilted her head to the side, looking oddly birdlike. But not a pretty little songbird, no matter how beautiful she was. This was a falcon gaze, the look of eagles, sizing up a lesser animal. "And yet you strive so hard to seem unsurprised by anything."

"Yeah, well, I'm a jerk. What's new?"

"Perhaps you can tell me. It is all old to me. The same cycle, endlessly repeating."

John chuckled mirthlessly. "Sister, it's all always

been the same play. Don't mean it hurts any less with each iteration." John took another long drink from his bottle. "Men proving that they're men, society humming right along, the best and the brightest runnin' with the flow, an' the rest of us stuck with the bill."

"The sun striking warm on a winter afternoon. The pure scent of the first honeysuckle in spring. A child's laugh. A lover's kiss. Joy, John Murdock."

"Sorry, but I'm feeling morbid. Trifles, to those of us that've taken everythin' an' lost it all in the same act. Poetry...folks, the boy wants to be a poet." John laughed again, mostly amused with himself.

"So be a poet."

"There's no money in it."

"But much joy. Food for the soul."

John sighed. "Even in Atlanta, soul food ain't enough. Joy doesn't pay the bills. Blood an' sweat, however, do."

"You can do both." She waved a hand dismissively. "One does not negate having the other. Millennia of artists have proved that. And millennia of dreamers, philosophers, mystics. You think they did not toil and sweat? Your self-imposed limitations are crutches, John Murdock. You think they support you. You can walk with them. But you cannot run, nor fly, with crutches."

John paused for a moment, leaning back against the railing on his elbows. "Y'know," he said, mock-seriously, "If you keep callin' me John Murdock, you're just my middle name away from soundin' like my mother. 'Sides. Killin' is different. Spendin' the blood of others is different. An' there ain't no good to come of it."

Again, that eagle look. "Your soul is sick. Surfeited and sick with death." Where anyone else he knew would have looked away at that moment, somehow those fierce eyes bored into his. "Death is what it is. Not an ending. Only a changing. The question becomes whether you have the right to be the instrument of that change."

"Forgive me if I'm skeptical. I've been too busy workin' at my profession to be ponderin' the philosophical implications." John grimaced, chugging the rest of his beer. He looked at his empty bottle in confusion, then turned to the supposed angel in his presence. "Can y'do anything about this?" he said, holding up his bottle. "Gettin' sloshed is a lot harder with runs to the fridge." She blinked once, and the bottle in his hand chilled again, growing heavy. He nodded, drinking from the now-full bottle again. "Much obliged."

"You . . . intrigue me." A ripple passed through the fire of her wings. "The depth of your despair is a challenge." Another ripple. "It was Pride that created the Fallen, but it is Despair that keeps them in hell. I should not like to see you in a hell of your own making, John Murdock."

John looked at her soberly, still leaning against the railing. "An' why precisely do you give a damn, miss?"

She hesitated. It was not the sort of hesitation that usually came in a conversation. It felt for a moment as if everything around him was holding its breath, waiting to hear her answer. It felt . . . portentous.

"Because . . . everything depends on it." Her wings shuddered open wide, and her entire body took on a look of aliveness, of anticipation, and perhaps, of fear.

"Well, gee."

He got no chance to say anything more.

"I speak too much," she cried, and in a burst of

flame, arrowed up into the sky like a shooting star in reverse.

Watching her fading into a speck against the night sky, and then vanishing, John was left alone with his thoughts. "That was strange," he said to no one but himself. He was too tired to care terribly much, to be honest. He'd somehow accepted that meta's presence, despite the fact that she preached to him as much as any church's soup-kitchen Bible-thumper, and despite her having violated one of the few places where he felt a modicum of safety. She was nuts, that much he was certain of. But he had never seen anything like her, at all, ever. Too damned weird.

Not wanting to think anymore, John took one last look at the sky, wondering if she'd be back again. Before he went inside, he desperately hoped for her sake, and his own, that she wouldn't.

CHAPTER THIRTEEN

Blackbird Fly

MERCEDES LACKEY & DENNIS LEE

Greymalkin rubbed up against Vickie's leg, purring. She scratched his ears as she stared at the blinking cursor. At this point, she had made contact with every magician on her extensive list. Some few had replied, most with extreme caution. A handful had indicated they would consider signing up with Echo. The rest would either answer her, or not. And until she started getting definitive answers, she was stalled.

There were not enough metas. The mages were afraid, all but the scant handful that were passing themselves off as metas—or who, like her, were both meta and mage. And they should be afraid; in the past, the Nazis of the Third Reich had more than dabbled in the occult, they had made themselves masters of it. There was no telling if this new lot still had that mastery. If they did—magicians were in danger. The use of magic was an inexact science. It was all a matter of knowledge and training and will, and there were always X factors that could skew things, the Heisenberg Uncertainty Principle of the Unseen.

On the other hand, Vickie had seen and felt nothing yet to indicate that the Nazis had even the remotest knowledge of magic now. And if that was true, then magic and mages could be what tipped the balance, exploiting a hole in their strategy they didn't know they had.

Again, she heard her new friend Bella's voice in her mind. *Start small. Meet people a few at a time. And get yourself in shape. They offer to train all of us in freerunning—Le Parkour—Echo OpOnes and Echo SupportOps especially. Just like they offer to train us in first aid, paramedic training, hand to hand and firearms. That way even the ones with no powers or tiny powers can escape if they're trapped, even if they don't have a ton of athletic ability. And the ones that do, they're like monkeys on steroids. They can get across a town faster than anyone without a chopper when there's gridlock. Go to the Parkour classes. That's a start.*

Well, she'd looked up Parkour. She'd downloaded a ton of video. It didn't look that different from some of her early physical training. She didn't need to go to the classes, face all those people...but she could use the Parkour course at the Echo campus. She could practice on her own. Maybe she'd meet one or two people there at a time. That would be doable.

She shut down the computer, and went after her sweats, ignoring the armor on the stand. It wasn't time yet for that.

As always, she left the light off in the bathroom, changing in the comforting darkness. She did it all by feel: wrapping wrists and ankles for extra support; adding socks; long, lightweight sweat pants and a long-sleeved shirt with a hood; gloves—this time with traction palms. She was as ready as she was ever going to be.

Grey gave an approving flick of his tail as she snagged her Echo-logo vest that marked her as an OpOne with a right to be on the campus and carried an RFID tag sewn inside. She pulled it on over her shirt as she walked to her car.

The drive was one she had made only once before, when she'd gone to meet with Bella and that Russian woman. She forced herself to be calm. She told herself that the course would be empty. It was the middle of the day, so who would be out there training or warming up?

And after passing the gates unchallenged thanks to her ID, and passing the buildings still being reconstructed, she parked her econobox in a lot with only a scattering of vehicles and found that the course was, indeed, empty. She assumed it had always looked like this, and it was unlikely the attackers had bothered doing anything to a place that had already looked like a war zone. Building façades with wrought iron and steel balconies and windows faced reproduction ruins; from what she had seen on the videos, this place was a freerunner's idea of heaven. Everything here was designed to be climbed, jumped, or otherwise traversed.

Once, she would have thrown herself joyously into the challenge.

Now, she stood there staring at it, her palms sweating.

Start slow. No one said you had to be one of those amazing French monkeys the first day. And warm up before you try anything. Then follow the Parkour creed: move forward. Always forward.

Forty-five minutes later, she was sweating, shaking with pain, and ready to cry with frustration. It wasn't just that she was out of shape. It was that her body didn't do what it used to. Scar tissue pulled and hurt as if it was ripping open, and she had scarred tendons in her ankles and wrists as well as scarred skin. Her balance was unreliable, thrown off again and again by unexpected pain. *No!* her muscles would scream, often right in the middle of something, and she'd fall, saved only because she still knew how to fall, thank the gods. Tuck in her head, arms pulled in and hands protected, twist so she'd roll diagonally across her back from shoulder to rump, scrubbing off momentum steadily instead of suddenly.

And then, when she was most unbalanced, mentally and physically, flailing with heart and soul, came another push.

"Yer doin' that all wrong, ya know."

Fear stabbed her, and she whirled.

A tall man, meta tall, which meant he towered over her and made her feel like a child. Bare chest, black pants, black boots, some sort of red scarf wrapped around face and head swathing his shoulders, matching red wrappings around his wrists. A memory that did not fail her, although everything else did, identified him from all the Echo files she had studied, committing to memory all the faces of the metas that survived. Fear had driven that close study. Fear and paranoia. *You might have to work with them. Know everything about them so they can't hurt you.*

Memory put a name to the not-face, the costume, the narrowed eyes that were all that was visible beneath that hood and wrapping.

Red Djinni.

And fear rose up to choke her, for she had no ammunition, no information. His file was mostly barren of everything but speculation.

"I suppose you can do better?" she said, the words coming out harsh and grating. Drive him away with them. Make him not want to share the course with a virago. That was all she could think of to do.

"You're damn right I can," he replied, with an undertone of a sneer. "Come on. Show me what you've got."

All right. She'd meant to come out here and maybe encounter one or two other people. Granted one of them wasn't supposed to be Red Djinni, but... she set off at a run and made the first set of obstacles.

He was ahead of her, moving at blinding speed, with extra double and triple somersaults, flips, even backflips. It made her angry, as muscles cramped and burned, everything tightened and pulled, like worms of fire under her skin. He waited for her at the first checkpoint. "Holding back?" he mocked.

"Just... getting started..." she said through gritted teeth, fighting pain, fighting to stay balanced, fighting to keep from running away. He shot off ahead of her again, traversing things she hadn't even realized were obstacles, with the careless nonchalance of a gibbon. She pushed herself harder.

"Yer fallin' behind, darlin'," he mocked at the second checkpoint.

"I'm not your darlin'," she snapped. Bad enough that he was doing this, after seeing what a fumbling infant she was at this. Worse to rub it in like this, to humiliate her. The anger was almost the equal of the fear, and she pushed herself harder still and felt all her muscles trembling with reaction and pain, her stomach in cold knots, her eyes stinging. She was *trying*, dammit! Why was he making a fool out of her for *trying*?

He was off again, making it all look as easy as breathing; she was half blind with pain and unshed tears as he waited at the third and final checkpoint. "You should try doin' this with a Nazi on yer tail," he goaded. "Now that's some motivation."

"I did, thanks," she panted, stumbling to the end of the course, where she leaned against the wall, not out of breath, but gasping with so much pain that even her fear was temporarily gone.

And then, a new voice behind her made her freeze with the start of an attack.

"Enough with the horseplay, Djinni. We've got a job to do. I sent you over here to assess the new recruit, not show off for her."

Another male voice, deep, authoritative, unamused. Djinni came down out of the tops of one of the building façades in a series of extra-spectacular flips, landing in front of them. "What horseplay, Bull?" he asked, a glint of challenge in his eye and more than a hint of mockery in his voice. "Just working out. That a crime?"

The voice behind her snorted, and the owner of it stepped around her to stand almost toe to toe with Djinni. He was a head taller than the Djinni, with long white-blond hair in a tight ponytail, chiseled features, and the usual sculptured body of most of the metas she was familiar with. She felt like a deformed dwarf, and shrank inside herself. Perfection. They were perfection. And she was a ruin...

"Assessment?" The second man's tone was brisk and impersonal.

Djinni's casual air of superiority vanished, and the laughter disappeared from his eyes. When he spoke, his tone matched Bull's. It was cold and professional and unmasked. "She is physically unable to perform at our level, Bull. She's got some fire, but she's using most of it to keep from bolting. I recommend against. Put her in the field on our retrievals, and we'll spend half our time watching out for her."

The brutally accurate picture made her cringe and shrink even smaller. Two strangers, two strange men, looming over her—it was pushing her fear. Hard. Add to it what they were saying...

"Operative Nagy, I presume?" the newcomer said, deliberately turning away from Djinni to look courteously at her. He pronounced it "naggy."

"Nahzh," she managed to get out, correcting his mispronunciation. "Vic. Nagy."

They both stiffened a little, then—she saw it, she was good at reading body language—forced themselves to relax. They'd reacted to her name. Her first name. Not in recognition of her, personally, it was more like a wince in reaction to the name itself. As if the name was painful, and they were wincing away from the pain.

And neither of them had noticed the other doing it.

"Operative Nagy," the man said, with the correct pronunciation. "Tentatively OpOne, active. You're listed as a magician?"

She nodded stiffly. Djinni snorted.

"Then I've asked Echo to assign you to my team for a retrieval. I'm callsign Bulwark, Echo OpTwo. We're going after someone who's being protected, I am told, by another magician, and I need a magician to counter him. Fighting fire with fire, so to speak."

He could not have chosen a worse simile, given that she was already on the edge of a panic attack. It was her turn to be engulfed in memory.

Fire . . . the flames roared up around her and the pain, the pain, she was going to die . . . She couldn't breathe for a moment. Couldn't think. Couldn't speak. Fear held her and shook her like a dog shakes a rag toy, when a spark of brightness, of more fire, up in the heavens behind the two men made her glance up. And with the look, somehow, she *made contact.*

She couldn't have said how. She wasn't a psion. Yet she felt something touch her mind, assess her with compassion, and reach out to her. And *that voice,* that she had heard once before, echoed in her mind, washed over her, through her, mind and spirit; another fire, but one that countered the fear and the pain for just a moment. This was more like a caress, or like a mother's embrace, that only *manifested* as firelike, but couldn't possibly harm.

Peace. Be still.

It was only a moment, just long enough for the tiny glint of flame to wink out again, but it was enough, enough to break her out of the attack, and though she was still stiff with fear, she could, at least, speak again. "I—I'm not supposed to be doing fieldwork yet—" she stammered. Hadn't he seen for himself? Hadn't he heard the Djinni? She wasn't ready. She burned with shame. Would she *ever* be ready?

"You are the only Echo magician in Atlanta," Bulwark replied. "I'm afraid you'll have to make an exception for this retrieval. You've been assigned to work with me on this. We leave as soon as you're ready. We'll be going to New Orleans."

His tone left absolutely no doubt in her mind that if she did not go with him voluntarily, he was perfectly prepared to force her. She went unbalanced for a moment, her vision briefly graying out. She scrambled for a way to get away from them long enough to get some control back. Maybe to get away? If she could lose them long enough... "I-I need to get back to my apartment. Leave my car. Change. Pack?"

He nodded. "That would be wise. We may be gone a few days. Red Djinni and I will follow you in an Echo vehicle."

To make sure she went. There would be no escaping into the maze of Atlanta. No hiding in her apartment. She didn't even try to protest; she sensed it would be useless. Instead she turned and stumbled a little back to the parking lot, fumbling her keys out of her pocket.

Behind her, not even trying to lower his voice or disguise the contempt in it, she heard the Djinni say, "Jesus, Bull! What're you thinking, hauling *that* along with us?"

"We need a mage," Bulwark said calmly.

Djinni snorted again. "What's she gonna do, pull a rabbit out of a hat to distract Tomb until I can pin him down? When are you going to stop insisting on bringing dead weight on these jobs? She's *useless*, Bull! She won't stand—"

By then she had reached the shelter of her car, gotten inside and slammed the door on the last of whatever it was that the Djinni was saying. As she pulled out of the lot, hot, angry tears burned down her face. *Useless.* Of course she was useless. The Djinni had hit the bull's-eye. She was useless. To them. To anyone. To herself. Useless, hideous, worthless . . . she cried, hopelessly, all the way home.

They pulled in to park behind her, but didn't get out of their vehicle. It looked as if they were still arguing. That was fine. She didn't want them in there with her, in her sanctuary, violating it. She didn't want the Djinni to have the satisfaction of seeing her in tears. She ran up the stairs and fumbled the door open, slammed it behind her, and wondered, for a moment, if she could just lock up again and pretend she didn't hear them out there, hear the phone, hear her Echo radio.

But no. No, she had to go through with this. If she didn't, they'd come after her anyway. And she had to go through with this because maybe, maybe, she might be able to do something. She had a responsibility. She had to try.

The panic attack ebbed, and with the easing of fear came the expected aftermath. Her gorge rose, nausea overcoming her.

She ran for the dark bathroom, threw up in the toilet, stripped off the soaking-wet sweats, and ran a brief shower. They could wait for that. She didn't want to be in a closed car stinking of sweat and vomit.

She used half a bottle of mouthwash and scrubbed every inch of herself furiously, using amber-scented soap and shampoo to eradicate the last of the stench, rubbing her burnt skin with the amber-scented lotion that was the only thing that helped. Then she re-dressed from the skin out in cotton underwear, black socks, black cotton knit trousers, black turtlenecked, long-sleeved T-shirt, black gloves, boots. She pulled the suitcase out of the storage closet, and packed more of the same.

She paused for a moment, then added her lightweight armor to it. Not the heavier battle suit on the stand, but the chain mail equivalent. She could manage that. And she might need it. The mail, made of tiny black metal plates of an alloy that would surely puzzle the Echo scientists sorely, would stop bullets as well as the Echo nanoweave. She'd proved that before. And in New Orleans, in the wake of the Invasion . . . she would need something that could stop a bullet. Black-handled athame went into the sheath in her boot. The techno-mage's road kit, unused for so very long, went into her laptop bag. She scooped up the contents of her bathroom shelf and dumped them on top of the armor, and stuck a sample-sized bottle of mouthwash in a pocket just in case she had another attack.

She turned to find Grey sitting behind her, looking at her with bemusement. <*A trip?*>

"Fieldwork." She went to the kitchen and made sure the connections to his refrigerated watering fountain were still solid. "You've got two weeks of kibble in the dispenser and I just cleaned your box—"

<*Please. If I need to go, I'll walk through the walls. If you are going to be gone for two weeks, I do not want to use the box. Is the cable bill paid?*>

"Yes." She unplugged her keyboard and plugged in the one with the mousepad and the oversized keys. Ironically, Grey had trouble using a mouse. "There, you can surf too. I'll be checking my email."

They both paused and stared at each other. She was marginally calm, and emotionally exhausted, as she always was in the wake of a panic attack. This state of false quiet would hold, she hoped, at least until they were on the plane. Grey did not ask "Will you be all right?" or even "What the hell do you think you're doing?" Instead he said, *<If you need me, summon me. Good luck.>*

Slinging her laptop bag over her shoulder, and grabbing the suitcase, she went out the door.

Before she could change her mind and hide in the back of the closet.

The vehicle was exactly like the one that Vickie had driven when she showed the Russian around; broadcast-powered and silent, and as sleek as something out of a fifties science fiction movie. Vickie pitched her suitcase in the trunk with their gear, and her laptop bag into the back seat, which she had all to herself. Bulwark drove, the Djinni sat silently beside him, in the kind of stony silence that suggested they had been shouting at each other at the tops of their lungs before she left the apartment building. Bulwark did all the talking on the way to the airstrip.

"As you know, New Orleans was hit hard last year by Hurricane Irena, and the invasion finished what Irena started," he said, in that matter-of-fact voice she remembered from the agents who had run FBI briefings when she'd assisted her parents as a teenager. That was supposed to be against the rules, of course, but when you were a member of the metahuman Paranormal Division, otherwise known as the Spook Squad, rules got broken. A lot. Bulwark hadn't been in the Bureau, but he was ex-military, and a lot of the buzz-cuts in the Bureau were too. Jarheads, mostly. She had him pegged as an ex-Marine, though that detail wasn't in his file. Probably, being a meta, he'd been in one of the meta Marine squads that officially didn't exist. Hell, he probably knew Semper Fu. "There's not a lot of detail on what actually happened, but·the end result is that the city government is fundamentally gone, and the city is being run by the Krewes now."

Djinni glanced at him, jarred out of his silence. "The wha—?"

"Social organizations, or they were," Bulwark answered Djinni smoothly, without missing a beat. "Originally founded for the purpose of running the Mardi Gras parades."

"Hold up, yer sayin' the guys that toss beads and build floats are runnin' the damn city?" Djinni sounded incredulous, and Vickie didn't blame him.

"You have to be a big man in the area to get invited into a Krewe," she said softly, looking steadfastly at her hands. "They don't let just anyone in. Before the invasion, these guys financed the parades, and that doesn't come cheap. They have warehouses, businesses, a lot of them are restaurant owners so they have food—and some of them are supposed to have ties to organized crime."

"So when all hell broke loose and the city government collapsed, the Krewes had local organization and resources. They took over, and what was left of the police mostly defected to them." Bulwark sounded mildly approving of what Vickie had contributed. "Now the city is divided up by parish, and each parish is being run by a different Krewe. There's some gang warfare going on, too, because the remains of the out-of-town gangs didn't exactly have the same borders drawn up that the Krewes did. We're going into a hot situation. I have a local contact, but I don't know how much help she is going to be."

Djinni muttered something Vickie couldn't hear.

"Some of the Krewes are..." she swallowed. "They're into voudoun."

Djinni groaned. "That would be why we have you along, I suppose," he said sarcastically. "To protect us from zombies." He shook his head. "Hell, I've seen plenty of zombie movies. Just give me a shotgun, a flamethrower and some grenades. We don't need an amateur getting in the way. And besides that, Tomb never had anything to do with hocus-pocus."

"Tomb didn't, but his brother is a prominent voudoun priest," Bulwark retorted, as Vickie burned with mingled anger and embarrassment. "And when Tomb got out of prison, he went to his brother, who is protecting him. We will need Operative Nagy to deal with the brother while you get to Tomb."

The Djinni shook his head again, and lapsed into a sullen silence that lasted the rest of the way to the airstrip.

She got out of the car first, and found herself unexpectedly struggling with her suitcase, which had gotten wedged in by the men's gear. With a growl of impatience, Djinni reached for it at the same time that Bulwark did, and for the first time since she had come out of the building, both were close enough to get a hint of the faint amber scent she had showered in and smoothed on her scarred and welted skin.

That was when it happened again. Both of them winced, and this time, looked quickly at her. Their pupils dilated for a fraction of a second. Bulwark's breath caught in his throat, and the Djinni went very still.

It was only a moment. Then things went back

to normal as the Djinni wrenched her bag out and shoved it at her, and Bulwark extracted several heavy duffels in a methodical manner. Neither of the men had noticed that the other had reacted to the same breath of fragrance, but Vickie had, and they had reacted exactly the same way. Mentally she filed that away as something to be looked into later, and dragged her bag to the plane. It was going to be a long trip.

"So Echo is sending agents to fetch Tomb. How very amusing." The impeccably dressed black man sounded exactly like the actor Geoffery Holder, if anyone in the room was old enough to remember what those cultured and faintly sinister tones sounded like.

"I thought you didn't care 'bout Tomb Stone," the bearer of that information ventured, as Le Fevre's two muscle-boys nodded gravely. The muscle-boys were sweating. Hardly surprising under the circumstances, but Bocor Le Fevre was pleased to see it. Let them take note of the hazards of failure.

"And I do not. Tomb Stone's metahuman talents are no use to me. But his brother will protect him, and when he moves to protect Tomb, he will leave his flank unguarded. In fact"—the man steepled his fingers together—"it would not surprise me in the least if Jacob Stone thought that the Djinni was here, not on behalf of Echo, but on behalf of some new gang." His teeth gleamed whitely in the darkness, and caught the light radiating from the well-dressed creature crouched over its prey in the center of the room. The creature's face was an approximation of a black man's, but with gashlike features, and its suit was of a 1920s cut with lapels edged in feathers and long white ribbons. "I believe that just might pry the Stone brothers out of their lair. Why don't you run off, there's a good fellow, and spread that particular bit of misinformation for me?"

The djab in the suit made a mock bow to Bocor Le Fevre. "You keep your bargain, I will keep mine." The djab returned to his meal, the no-longer-screaming body of Le Fevre's former bodyguard, who had failed to keep the men of the Kronus Krewe out of the Django warehouse that was Le Fevre's headquarters. There was no blood, of course, and there were no outward marks on the body, but what the djabs did as they feasted on life-force was far more painful than any physical torture, and could be far more prolonged. Le Fevre had silenced the screams as soon as they began, for they annoyed him after a time, but the meal's bulging eyes and expression of ultimate horror were enough to let the current bodyguards know just how terrible it was to be turned over to one of the Bocor's allies as a meal.

The Bocor bowed back. "When we have Jacob Stone, you may eat him."

The spirit radiated an unhealthy, greenish light for a moment. "I look forward to that hour."

Le Fevre thought for a moment. "And while you are at it . . . bring me the links to those spirits of the Red Djinni's enemies that are within my reach. I want to find his weaknesses."

"That is easily done," the djab chuckled. "The Djinni has many dead enemies, and they would tell you these things for nothing. You have but to summon them. I will get you names."

Le Fevre laughed, as the djab faded away, off

to possess as many people as he could to spread the disinformation that the Red Djinni was forming a new gang, and was here to recruit Tomb Stone, whether Stone wanted to come or not. The djab's meal writhed and mewled, more than half mad now. Le Fevre beckoned to his bodyguards and gestured towards the man that had brought word from the leaky information sieve that passed for Echo HQ in New Orleans these days. "Take that away and put it in my workroom," he said, with a faint smile. "My ally will want it when he gets back."

The men shuddered, and complied.

The Echo craft was eerily silent. There was no roar of jet engines outside the fuselage, which made the sullen quietude inside the craft that much more unnerving. There were only four sets of seats here, as the rest of the craft was given over to cargo space—two pairs of seats facing each other on either side of a narrow aisle. The Red Djinni had the left-hand four all to himself; he had jammed himself into the corner of the window seat on the front-facing bulkhead and brooded, legs thrust aggressively out into the space between the seats, effectively taking up as much of the space as possible. His arms were crossed over his chest, and he had not once removed his signature scarf, so all that could be seen of his face were his eyes, glaring sullenly. Bulwark and Vickie perforce had the other four seats. He took the front-facing pair; she got stuck with the rear-facing ones. Then again, motion sickness was the least of her worries. The way that the Djinni was glaring at her, you would have thought that she had mortally insulted him. And as for

Bulwark, he had gotten even more reserved, if that was possible. She still couldn't figure out what she had done to either of them to make them act this way.

"This meta we're after—Tomb—" she said finally, just to break the silence. "Why is he called that?"

Bulwark shrugged. "You ought to ask Djinni about that. He's the one that worked with the man."

The Djinni grunted. Bulwark gave him a sardonic glance. "Be nice. Tell the lady."

"She's your pigeon. You tell her."

Bulwark rolled his eyes. "You know how it is. A lot of metas like their nicknames or aliases to be bad puns on their powers. His real last name is Stone, and he plays dead."

Her brow creased, but Djinni interrupted impatiently. "He doesn't just *play* dead, he *is* dead. No pulse, no breathing, uses no oxygen, the whole nine yards. You can seal him inside an airtight container, fold him up however you want him before he stiffens up, and ship him inside any place you want to get into. Then when you're ready, he comes back to life and lets you in."

She felt her eyes widen. "A self-induced hibernation without a cryogenic chamber?"

The Djinni shrugged. "Damned if I know. *He* always said he was dead. He didn't bleed either. You could stab him and he wouldn't feel it, or bleed more than a couple drops. The only thing he didn't do that a dead man would was rot."

"But how did he know when to wake up?" Of all the strange metahuman powers she had ever heard of, this was one of the strangest. But she could think of a thousand ways he could be useful... and certainly he must have been invaluable to a professional thief.

"Beats me. He would only say 'the loas tell me,' whatever the hell that means."

She blinked, her ever-present fear ebbing with something this fascinating to think about. She turned to Bulwark. "You did say his brother is a voudoun houngan, right? Or is he a bocor?"

"So I've been told. I'm not sure what that means. I don't know the difference." Bulwark eyed her with speculation.

"A houngan is a kind of priest, in a religion that is as much magic as mysticism. A houngan is...oh, this is oversimplifying by a huge margin, but he's a 'white' magician in the popular parlance, though that is a dangerous term to apply to voudoun." She bit her lip. "Forgive me if I assume too much, but I suppose you don't know much about the magical, nonstandard religions. All right: take it that voudoun is a religion in which guilt and sin are minimized or absent altogether, and you might sum up the philosophy as 'if you aren't harming anyone or scaring the horses, do what you want, and if someone hurts you, or tries to, give as good as you get.'"

Djinni cackled nastily. "Sounds like my kinda church!"

Bulwark gave him a withering glance. "I'm sure."

Vickie shrugged. "It's not Christian. It borrows heavily from the trappings of Catholicism, but that was largely so that the African slaves that practiced it could continue to wear their emblems and signs and have their religious objects without having to hide them. Santeria, which is associated with Hispanic-dominated Mesoamerican descendants, does the same. However, in keeping with a lot of primal religions, the practitioners of both voudoun and santeria openly use magic."

"Yeah, right." The Djinni's eyes were sardonic. "To delude the rubes in the pews, no doubt."

At that moment, she badly wanted to perform some small bit of magery, just to wipe that hidden smirk off his face. Three things stopped her. One, discipline—in the hard school in which she had learned you did not do magic just to show off, for magic was fueled to a greater or lesser extent by a mage's own power, and what you wasted in display was power you might need in the next moment for something important. Two—until she did something that could not be ascribed to a metahuman ability, she had no way to prove she was a mage and not a meta. And three—he wasn't the one who had dragged her out on this job. The person who had, Bulwark, already believed. After this, it was unlikely she would ever see the Djinni again, or so she devoutly hoped. Trying to convince him was a waste of time and energy.

So she just continued with her explanation. "Now, it *is* a religion, which means there is a mystic, occult component to it. In this case, a good half of what gets done on behalf of the voudoun practitioner is done, not by the magician himself, but by the loas, greater and lesser. The lesser ones are simple spirits of the dead—ghosts, but with a kick, since belief in them gives them power and energy and that enables them to act in the physical world. The greater..." she hesitated, "...well, the greater are the gods and goddesses of voudoun. Except that these gods and goddesses come and take over the bodies of the worshipers. It's called 'being ridden,' and it's a great honor. The lesser loas can also ride the worshipers but can't do the sorts of things the deities can."

Bulwark's brow wrinkled. "You mean demonic possession?"

She shook her head violently. "They aren't demons, and it's voluntary, at least for the most part, although on occasion a 'good' loa might take over someone who is in need of a lesson and administer a spiritual reprimand and punishment. Anyway, that's where the magic and the mysticism overlap. Contacting the dead or the—otherworldly—isn't a metahuman ability like psionics, and it isn't strictly magic either. It's a third thing." *Like having an angel talk to you.* She took a deep breath. At least Djinni had shut up, and Bulwark seemed to be listening, even if this must be sounding like something so far out of his experience that it amounted to a totally alien culture and mindset. "That's the—for lack of a better term—'good' voudoun. There's a black magic voudoun too. Those practitioners are called 'bocor,' and they are all about power. Whatever stands between them and what they want gets flattened, period. So you can see, it makes a big difference whether Tomb Stone's brother is a houngan or a bocor."

She didn't go into the other intriguing aspect of this—that Tomb's power was certainly metahuman, but it was clear he shared some of his brother's mystic ability too, if it was true that the loas told him when to "wake up."

"The counterpart to the houngan's loas are the bocor's djabs," she continued. "For all intents and purposes, you might as well call them demons. And if Stone's brother is a bocor, *that* is what we will be dealing with."

Djinni rolled his eyes, and shook his head, and his

hard tone made it clear he thought she was a fraud, and if he had his way, he'd throw her out the plane door and let her apport herself home. "Lady, I don't believe in magic, or pixie dust, demons, ghosts, or elves."

Was she mistaken, or was there a trace of regret in that last?

He flexed his fingers, and made a fist. "Whatever mumbo-jumbo this guy is pulling on the rubes in New Orleans, he's not gonna be pulling it on me. So you do your hand-waving for Bull since he wants it, if you can manage to stay on your feet long enough, and stay outta my way. I'll handle Tomb Stone, and his brother too. You're about as much use to me as a librarian."

She flushed with anger and shame, and turned away, staring out of the window. She wanted to give him a snappy retort—the old Vickie would have—but the words got stuck in her throat. Instead she hunched her shoulders and fought down the tears of frustration and pain. He'd gone beyond being rude. Now he was deliberately being cruel.

"Ignore him," Bulwark said, with a hard edge to his words. "You don't answer to him, you answer to me."

She ducked her head as a kind of answer; that seemed to satisfy him, and he left her alone, taking out a sheaf of papers to study. But the Djinni kept giving her *looks* that felt like barbs, and she flushed uncomfortably, and finally she undid her seatbelt and headed for the lav. As she did so, a breath of the amber scent she found so comforting followed her, and once again, she saw both men react strongly to it, their pupils dilating. The Djinni stiffened all over for a moment, and if his glare had been a bullet, she'd have been dead.

Safe in the privacy of the lav, with the door locked, it suddenly hit her. Both had reacted to her scent. Both had reacted to her name. Now, she had never to her certain knowledge met either of them, she doubted either of them would react that way to a man, so it had to be that they were each reminded of some other *woman* named Vic. *Two* women, named Vic, who both favored amber as a scent, was well within the realms of coincidence. But three? Three in the limited circles of metahumans? Amber was not a common scent; it had been popular a few years ago when she picked up on it, but since then she'd had to order it specially.

Scent was a potent trigger of memory. And she would bet her last dollar that they were reacting to the memory of the *same* woman. Not just any woman, but one that meant a *lot* to both of them. Djinni, especially... he'd started acting like a jerk right after he heard her name. And once he'd had her scent? He'd turned cruel. As if he thought she was somehow purposefully trying to impersonate this woman, who-ever she was. With a reaction that strong, it hadn't just been friendship between them. It was harder to tell with Bulwark, but the fact that he reacted at all tended to make her think the same.

She would bet her last penny that neither one of them had any idea that the other was holding the memories of the same person, too. And if either of them figured *that* out...

Wonderful. As if this wasn't already a fun-filled excursion...

The stress built, and she threw up in the toilet. Again. When the spasm was over, she flushed it and clung to the sink for a long time, weak and shaking, before fishing the bottle of mouthwash out of her pocket and using it.

Now they would both probably think she was bulimic.

It just got better and better.

Echo had taken over one of the older French Quarter hotels for crew quarters, and it was still worse for wear from the hurricane. The hurricane and the invasion had hit the Big Easy with a one-two punch from which it would probably never recover. There were more National Guard, Blacksnake, insurance adjusters and journalists than tourists on the streets, and most of the hotels were three-fourths empty. Small wonder Echo had been able to take over this hotel. The room Vickie got was tiny, but at least it had a working shower and she didn't have to share it with anyone. She took down the mirror in the bedroom and put it behind the dresser, taped a towel over the one in the bathroom, showered and changed again, and washed her own clothing out in the sink, hanging it to dry in the shower stall. No way in New Orleans was she going to allow *anything* personal of hers to leave the room in the hands of a stranger. She left orders with the staff that her room was strictly off-limits to maid service, and put magical wards around it to ensure no one could get in—or if they could, at least she would know that they had.

And as for ordinary access, she had ways of dealing with that, too. The hotel might have been old, but it used mag-strip key cards. With a feeling of weary amusement, she unpacked her laptop and her road kit, and after a half hour of hacking the hotel computer system, made certain no one could get into her room with any key card *but* hers. The Echo people here had left some gaping holes in their security, relying on the hotel computer to control access to the rooms like that. She was only a midlevel hacker, after all, when you discounted what she could do with a magic interface. She made another mental note to leave things in better shape before she went home.

She looked with longing at her antianxiety meds, but didn't take any. They interfered with her ability to use magic, and to see the otherwise unseen. She'd have to tough this one out. But at least now she knew why Djinni was being an asshat, and as always, knowledge gave her a kind of defense. Maybe even a touch of sympathy. Whatever had happened, it was pretty clear Djinni and this woman had not parted company amicably, and he was still raw over it.

Bulwark's contact was a woman named Mel, who tended bar in the Quarter. They found her chewing out a pair of men in Blacksnake uniforms, which brought a smile to Bulwark's face, and when she had thrown them out and turned her attention to them, Bulwark had gotten down to the business of asking questions. Unfortunately, there hadn't been a lot that Mel could tell them. The best she could do was to send them to two little shops, off the tourist maps, where the local practitioners got their supplies. Careful inquiries there yielded nothing, although at Bulwark's insistence, it was Vickie doing the asking, and not either of the two men. In keeping with the way a local would, she left her cell phone number on a piece of paper—not a card—to be passed on to Jacob Stone, but she rather doubted anything would come of it. It was not as bad as it could have been.

Bulwark's presence kept pretty much everyone at a respectful distance. But she was still cold and shaking when they returned to HQ.

Meanwhile, Djinni was off on his own trail of inquiry, which she presumed to be among the criminal element. Until he came back, *she* did what she did best—research, via her cell modem and her laptop. Her road kit, assembled before her interesting times, held ziplocked bags of carefully coiled jumpers, probes, specialty tools and splicers, soldering gear, clips and patch cables, crossovers, quasilegal tone generators, and even an acoustic coupler powered by a 9-volt battery. There's no school like old school, her old code-wizard pals would say. She still had a certain number of contacts and favors owed at the FBI, which meant that a lot of information she might not otherwise be able to "see" was available, if you were clever enough. When Djinni turned up again, his manner was still sullen, so she guessed he hadn't had much success. Fortunately, she had.

They retired to the suite Bulwark shared with Djinni. Until this moment, she had done nothing an Echo detective with an understanding of the occult underground couldn't have done. But the sooner they found Tomb, the sooner she could get home, away from both of them, and hide in her sanctuary again. So it was time to do what she was here to do, whether Bulwark knew he needed this or not.

"I can find Tomb for you," she said in a flat voice, before Bulwark could start in on some new plan to hit the streets, which was the last thing she wanted to do. "But I need something of his. A signature would do. I did some research; he had a bank account at the Gulf Coast Bank and Trust. His signature card should still be on file in the French Quarter branch."

Djinni stared at her blankly; Bulwark, speculatively. Neither said anything, as her nerves stretched and frayed. "I'm not sure I understand what you want us to do," Bulwark finally said.

"Get me the signature card!" she snapped. "Get that, and I can find him!"

"But it's after-hours—" Bulwark began.

Her temper disintegrated. "And *he* is a professional thief!" she hissed, pointing at a startled Djinni. "How hard can it be to get a signature card out of an unsecured area in a small branch bank?"

"Why don't you just magic it out?" the Djinni sneered.

A vein in her temple started to throb, and she clutched the table as a wave of nausea assaulted her. "Because there are rules to how this works, and I can't," she replied through clenched teeth. "I don't do breaking and entering. You do. Just get me the damned card."

And with that, without another word, she shoved herself violently out of her chair and staggered out the door and down the corridor to her own room. She managed to get there without throwing up for a third time, and she sat in the bottom of the shower with hot water drenching her until she was sure she wasn't going to. Then she wrapped herself in the hotel robe and shivered under the covers until she was sure she wasn't going to have a crying jag. When the knock came at the door, she nearly jumped out of her skin.

"It's Bulwark," came the voice, before, shaking with reaction, she could ask who it was. "I have the card."

It took a moment before she could answer. "Shove it under the door," she said in a choked voice.

There was a soft sound of paper over carpet. When she peeked out from under the bedspread it was there, next to the door. She closed her eyes, and took long, deep breaths. Then she got up and went to work. And when she was done, she dressed in her black coat of mail, her heavy leather combat pants and boots, picked up her kit, and headed for the suite.

The arguing was audible halfway down the hall. She almost turned back around and went back to her room, but—*the sooner we get this guy, the sooner I can go home.* That was enough to keep her going. She longed for her sanctuary as saints were said to long for heaven. The door to the suite wasn't quite shut, so she shoved it open with her foot since both hands were full of laptop and mage kit. Harder than she intended to, as it turned out, or else it wasn't as jammed against the carpet as the one in her room. It slammed open against the wall, effectively putting an end to the argument and putting her full in the glare of Djinni's outraged stare, and Bulwark's frustrated one.

"Fat Markey's Bar, on Peachtree between Wayon and Beau Soi," she said.

"What?" Djinni demanded, as Bulwark said, at the same time, "Tomb's in a bar?"

"I told you. I found him. That's the good news. The bad news is that his brother almost certainly knows I was looking for him and he's probably on his way to warn him or protect him or both." The wards on Tomb Stone were very good, and she had been in a hurry. She had likely tweaked them. Not enough so that Jacob Stone would know who had been looking, but enough for him to know that *someone* had been.

"Let's move." Bulwark was on his feet and reaching for his kit, as Djinni impaled him with a glare.

"You *believe* this crap?" he shouted in outrage. "You're going to send us out on a wild goose chase into the middle of gang territory because some bulimic tea-leaf reader says our man's in a—"

Nerve and temper snapped at the same time, and temper won. "*Shut the hell up!*" she shrieked, almost losing the grip on her laptop. "I don't answer to *you*. I answer to *him!* And I want to go *home!*" The last came out in a wail, and tears of anger streamed unheeded down her cheeks. "I don't care what you think! What I do follows laws and logic, and works, and I will be *damned* if I let the target get away and end up here for weeks because *you* are too fricking stubborn to believe someone who has done this all her life *and done it for the FBI* is a useless crackpot!"

Her voice spiraled upwards with each word until it cracked on the last one.

Absolute silence. Both men stared at her with eyes gone wide, and a little shocked looking.

"Now *get* your gear and get the car and get *in* the car, because we have maybe twenty minutes to get to him before his brother does!"

"Yes, ma'am," said Bulwark, and he did a quick pat-over of his equipment.

Between the welter of emotion and all the stress, Vickie went a little blank for a moment, because the next thing she really knew, she and her kit and laptop were in the front seat next to Bulwark, with the Djinni in the back. Her laptop was open and running on the cell modem. The GPS rig was giving him directions to the bar, while the cantrip packet linked via a USB cable to her dowsing program was giving her a steady blip, still, on the dot that was the bar. She may have blanked, but it seemed she had been giving the men sensible answers, because her awareness picked up in the middle of one.

". . . agion. That means that anything that has been in contact with someone before is always in contact with him. Of course, that can wear away—if something passes through enough hands, it's like a scent that wears off. In fact, that's a good analogy, because if you know what you're doing, or you know someone who knows, you can 'wash' that scent right off of things. That's why mages are more careful about Contagion than serial killers are about leaving their DNA lying around." She took a deep breath, blinked, and kept on. "That's why I went for the bank signature card. Not too many people handled it, it's *old,* and I was gambling that Jacob completely forgot about it. And I was right. This"—she pointed to the cantrip packet, in the center of which was the card, folded in an intricate pattern—"works just like an antenna for my dowsing program."

"Wait, wait, you use a program?" The Djinni sounded a little dazed.

"I'm a techno-shaman. It's what I do." Her head was pounding now. Her stomach was in knots. "A lot of great magicians were the rock-star scientists of their day. Wizards and witches using magic in the old days were like modern researchers discovering how stuff all around us works. What looks like quaint bone-rattling to you now was the CSI of its day. And it still works. Some of it gets updated though. Almost all my investigative magic interfaces in some way with modern technology. That's why the FBI still uses me. Like they did before..." She gulped, as the old pain threatened to engulf her, and she fought her way through it. "...before I got... hurt. With the things I do, people like me, we don't... we don't heal up like other people do. Some things just don't get better. Our wounds are more like soul damage or brain damage than..." She took another deep breath to steady herself. "It doesn't matter right now. What matters is those—"

Scattered red and green dots were moving on the blue one that was their target. "The red ones are djabs. The green ones are loas. There's either one or two voudoun workers out there, heavily cloaked, and I can't tell if it's a bocor that can control both djabs and loas or a bocor and a houngan, but in either case, we are going to reach Tomb about the same time they do."

She heard the sound of—something odd—going on in the back seat. "Then let the games begin," said the Red Djinni, with grim elation. "It's about frickin' time."

"You let me handle the spirits," she said sharply. "You take them on *only* if they possess someone."

"Hey, the spooks are your problem, darlin', just like you say."

She kept her eyes on her laptop screen. They were almost there...and so were the spirits.

Bulwark spoke as the bar sign came in sight. "Djinni, go in the bar and try to talk to Tomb. I'll go around the back in case he tries to make a break that way. Nagy, do..." She glanced at Bulwark, who shrugged helplessly. "Do whatever it is you do."

She shut the laptop and shoved it under the seat. It was not going to help her now. Now... it was time for old-fashioned combat magic. She hoped she would not have to call on Gaiaic magic too; it was crude stuff, good for use in the open, between two large opposing forces, but woefully unsuited for use inside a building—unless you wanted to bring the building down.

She and Djinni flung themselves out of the car as Bulwark slowed it, but didn't stop. With a shriek of tires, he spun it around the corner, heading for the alley behind the bar. Djinni bounded inside. Vickie pulled her atheme from her boot and followed. She stopped at the door, called up energies from the Earth, and sketched a series of lines and glyphs in the doorway with her knife. They hung there, glowing, for just a moment. If Djinni had been looking at them, he would have actually seen them. He wasn't, of course. He was peering into the darkness of the bar as the jukebox wailed Patsy Cline's "Crazy."

When he saw who he was looking for, he straightened up from his crouch, and strolled in a leisurely fashion to the sole occupant of the farthest table. The jukebox chose that moment to quit, and the Djinni's voice, though soft, seemed very loud in the silence. "Hey, Tomb."

Tomb Stone looked up.

That was when all hell broke loose.

Tomb threw his table at the Djinni, and made a break for the back door. Djinni vaulted the obstacle and went after him. The front door was assaulted by half a dozen men, of whom four crossed the threshold and dropped like someone had smacked them with a two-by-four as the spirits controlling them were stopped by Vickie's protections, but two more stumbled through and kept coming. One lurched for Stone. The other grabbed a chair and threw it at Djinni, and a bizarre sound like a half-dozen wet switchblades came from the red-wrapped man's direction.

What the—

Vickie didn't wait to figure it out. She yelled. Djinni turned in time to see the attacker, and that was when she saw what she must have *heard*. The Djinni's hands had sprouted long, sharp claws on the end of every finger. He slashed before she could warn him that the person the spirit was riding was probably innocent—then, as the claws hit, she saw what he had probably already seen, the gang tats on the man's biceps, neck and bald head.

No, he was certainly not innocent.

The man screamed—and the djab burst out of his open mouth, just as another man—and something else—made it through the front door.

This man was bare-chested and tattooed too, but no street gang had ever invented these tattoos. Vickie's guess as to the identity of the man was confirmed when Tomb shouted his brother's name, and scrambled to his side. Jacob Stone and his giant companion stepped to protect Tomb and to face down Red Djinni.

"You—" said the magician, coldly. "You are a murderer and a thief. You stink of the blood of the innocent. You are lawful prey."

Djinni sneered and crouched.

Wait, wait—blood of the innocent? Lawful prey?

Vickie had no time to think about that, for the strange-looking creature at Jacob's side lunged for Djinni. It was crudely man-shaped, a thing that looked as if it had been constructed from a mishmash of found swamp objects. Twine and wire bound together cypress knees, Spanish moss, bits of boat and trolling motor, planks and fishing poles, rope, and more. It may not have been fast, but there was no doubt that it could hit like a tank. It shattered the nearest table with a fist instead of shoving it away, creating a spray of splinters rather than just breaking it. That was when Vickie knew with despair that she was going to have to wreck the bar.

She called the Earth, and the Earth answered.

New Orleans was built on swampland, so what came to her call this time was not an upthrust of rock, bursting through the floor of the barroom, but a geyser of mud. It knocked the magician off his feet. It plastered his creation to the ceiling; then when Vickie released the Earth again, dropped it into the hole she had created. It thrashed. She told the muck to become a sucking mire. It thrashed more, and the more it thrashed, the more it sank, as Jacob Stone cursed and looked wildly about for the magician that had entrapped his magic-born servant.

But now the bar had been invaded by the next wave. One lot assailed the front door and about two in every six made it inside. More were trying to come in through the back. With one eye on the thing sinking into the pit she had created, Vickie cast a wary eye at the back, which was being blocked by Bulwark. There was a glossy bubble around him, just filling the space in the doorway, though the wood of the doorframe bulged and was creaking a bit. Men ridden by spirits pounded on the bubble with fists, bits of wood, and machetes, none of which got through, though they were inflicting plenty of injury on themselves and their fellows as their blows rebounded uncontrollably. Djinni was piled on by three men, each wielding machetes in one hand and chair legs in the other. But that was, by far and away, not the worst of the assault.

That, only two people in the bar could see.

The air was aswirl with spirits, and Vickie had her hands full fending them off Djinni and Bulwark. Bulwark's bubble did nothing to keep them out. Djab, they had to be—she could see that when they *did* manage to get through, and raked their long talons over one or the other of the men, a spark of life-force drained away at the touch. Or rather, drained from Djinni—they tried the same trick with Bulwark, but he was protected in some additional way. They screamed in silent protest, but mostly they couldn't get through to drain him.

You are lawful prey. Was that it? Had the Red Djinni's past finally come back around on him? On rare occasion, houngan *did* call djab, when the target was a murderer, rapist, or some other violent criminal... lawful prey. Maybe Bulwark was "innocent" enough to gain some protection from that alone.

But Djinni clearly was more than they had reckoned with. He hardly seemed to notice the drain. He fought like a berserker, going down under a pile of assailants, then throwing them off and going after *them* in turn. But the spirits riding them were as fast and as cunning as he was; they might not be able to do much damage to him, but he was having a hard time laying so much as a claw on them.

With a kind of muffled wail, the last of the construct vanished into the mud. Vickie drove the water out of the mud pit, trapping the thing. That was when Jacob

Stone, face twisted with fury, finally found his rival mage and locked eyes with her, and she felt the fear rise up in her and choke off her breath. No, not just fear, it was her fears personified, made real and solid, a clutching hand at her throat.

She couldn't breathe.

Her protections on Bulwark and Djinni failed. Djinni went down under an avalanche of bodies, physical and ghostly. One spirit inside the bubble managed to get enough power to manifest physically for a moment, and used that moment to bring two translucent hands down on Bulwark's head, knocking him out cold. The bubble failed as he crumpled, and the men who had been struggling to get in through the back now came pouring inside.

Her lungs were burning. She struggled against the fear, the thing that was cutting off her air, and her vision started to fail. Jacob Stone stared triumphantly into her eyes and grinned.

And a spirit materialized out of the back bar and engulfed him. He screamed, the cry of a man who sees his own death coming and is helpless to stop it. The choking hand of fear let Vickie go.

Experience and intuition directed her. *Not one, but two . . . bocor and houngan, and we're being used . . .*

Operating on instinct alone, she gulped in air, stumbled across the bar and slashed her atheme across the back of the thing that was killing Jacob Stone. She did it in no particular pattern, but the thing howled and pulled away, leaving Stone half conscious, but still alive.

That was when the Djinni erupted from beneath his pile of assailants with what looked like a two-by-four in his hands. He spun in a furious circle, and a moment later, stood panting, bleeding from dozens of stabs and slashes, his signature shoulder wrappings torn half off, exposing an ugly, strangely wrinkled-and-scarred mass of tissue at his neck. He was battered, but alive, eyes furious.

Staring at the thing that had attacked Jacob Stone. He could *see* it!

It must have drained enough life-force from Stone to be able to manifest in the real world. It stared back at him for a moment, then shimmered as all the other spirits in the bar became very, very still. The humans still being ridden dropped to the ground as their riders let go of their "mounts" to lend what must have been their leader additional strength. Whoever this djab answered to, it was not Jacob Stone.

It shimmered again, became amorphous . . . and then . . . where the spirit had been, was a woman.

A meta, that much was obvious from the costume. And stunning, absolutely stunning. She had a face that could have graced a magazine cover, and the body of a goddess. Even among metas, who so often seemed to have a heightened physical presence, she was beautiful. The fury drained from Djinni's eyes in an instant, and he began to tremble, visibly. The lovely woman held out her hands to him, her expression half promise, half pleading. He took a single, stumbling step towards her.

Epiphany whacked Vickie in the face. *That's her. That's the other Vic.* And this woman had to be dead, or the djab could not have assumed her form. There were rules to these things . . .

Djinni took another step towards the vision, eyes glazing over. Vickie watched as life-force began flowing from him to her. The creature smiled. *Will. He has one of the strongest wills I've ever seen. Will is magic. As long as he fights her, the djab can't drain him. But if he gives it to her—*

And a red rage took hold of Vickie.

"Get off him, you bitch!" She wanted to scream it, but all she could do was choke it out. She called up every last vestige of magical energy inside her, everything she could gather from the Earth Her Mother, and threw it, not at the creature, but at Red Djinni. *"Djinni, you asshat, wake up! Vic is* dead *and that is not her!"* She put all the force of will and power she could into her words, rendering them into an impromptu spell, and punctuated her shriek with a beer bottle that hit him in the shoulder. Then, as the Djinni started back for a moment, some of the dazed look leaving his eyes, she remembered something else.

Salt. Blessed salt. The one universal component for dispersing ghosts. And djab were nothing more than very, very powerful spirits of the dead. She spotted her kit on the floor within reach, mud-spattered but intact. Closer still were the remains of the bar, and despite the mud spatters everywhere, the bowls of bar peanuts and pretzels were within even easier reach. Bar snacks were always heavily salted, to encourage more drinking. She grabbed every bowl she could reach, and chucked them at the powerful djab, which roared a bone-chilling howl. The disruption of its manifestation was palpable, and Vickie used that moment to retrieve her bag. She broke its zipper in a frenzy, and pulled out the stapled paper bag of blessed salt. Tearing that open, she hurled it in an arc, and sprayed the creature with the contents.

It screamed, as did every other spirit in the bar. The form of the lovely metahuman woman melted away and reshaped itself into that of the hideous djab, and it flung itself on Vickie, still very, very much in the physical plane. Once again, she found herself fighting for her life, as the creature slashed at her mail with claws as long and wicked as the Djinni's. They caught and penetrated the mail, and the links joining the plates gave. The djab ripped a gash in it, slashing the shirt underneath, exposing the mass of hideous burn scars that laced her from neck to toes. She managed to kick it off with a surge of power; it lunged for her again as she looked up at it, rage gone, so terrified she had been reduced to nothing but incoherent whimpers.

Which was when Jacob Stone, with a roar, stood up and called upon the god Ogun to "ride" him. And Vickie blacked out.

She came to lying on a bed. Not hers, not her hotel room; this room had the preternaturally neat look of one inhabited by—

"—a classic case of leaping before we looked," said Bulwark in the other room.

"Ah, you are awake." Jacob Stone had a Jamaican accent, not a New Orleans one. "I told them to leave us alone in here, that you would be fine."

"Fine is relative," she croaked. Then she remembered, and her hands clutched frantically at the blankets. "Did anyone see?" she choked out, panic rising to engulf her. "Did anyone—"

"Only me, I think. I served as your nurse." He patted her hand reassuringly. "I have in my time seen much worse, but my loas told me that you do not wish any eyes to fall on you. So I covered you, I carried you myself, I put you here with my own hands. And here—" he gestured at the hotel bathrobe lying at the foot of the bed. "You can put that on, if you are ready to go to your room. I could not enter it, nor could Bulwark, nor the staff." He chuckled. "They are most vexed. That is clever work."

She was going hot and cold with shame. "There was a bocor—"

"Who used us against each other, yes," said the elder Stone. "Adolphe Le Fevre." Stone's long face looked sour. "He has been a thorn in my side since the invasion. He is under the impression that I want what he wants."

In the other room, Djinni was laughing, as was a stranger. "Tomb, I thought we taught you better. And you *believed* those jackasses? Why would I telegraph my moves that way?"

"If you had simply waited until you knew we were in the city and put a tail on us, you would have seen we were coming from here," Bulwark said mildly. "We weren't trying to hide our movements."

"Ah well, my brother would say, 'The guilty man flees where none pursueth.'" There was a sigh. "Here I was, tryin' to stay straight, an' you show up, Red. An' people are tellin' me you're startin' up a new gang—"

"Control of this parish?" Vickie hazarded. Stone nodded. "As my brother said, just now. He cannot imagine that I only wish to be left in peace to heal and help those who come to me." He shook his head. "This is not my city, and I am not needed in Kingston. I can go anywhere. I told my brother as much, so we will both join your Echo. There is a greater enemy to be countered than Le Fevre." He got up from the chair beside the bed. "There is your kit, there is your computer, and there is what is left of the metal shirt. I think it can be repaired."

"It can—" She was, once again, too exhausted for a panic attack. All she wanted now was to get herself and her stuff back to her room, cocoon herself in clothing again, and go home.

"Then I will join the others. I think you should too, once you are composed." He gave her a measured look. "I think it would be courtesy, at least." He left, closing the door behind him. She pulled her aching body out of the bed, muffled herself in the bathrobe, and grabbed her gear. All four of the men in the other room looked up as she opened the bedroom door.

"When you're cleaned up, come back here, Op Nagy," Bulwark said, formal, but friendly. "I've got a food delivery coming."

"Yeah, Tomb told us not to order from the kitchen; it stinks," the Djinni said.

The other Stone, whom she had barely gotten a glimpse of until now, spread his hands wide. "What can I say? They brought their own cook. To New Orleans? A crime."

She ducked her head and scuttled off to her room. Once inside, she put down her things and sat on the bed with her face in her hands. Her throat ached, and in fact, she hurt all over, more than the usual ongoing pain; there were taped-up tears through the scars from the djab's talon slashes, and probably huge bruises under the scars, and the scars hurt and hurt . . .

It was the touch of magic, she realized. She'd been

warned about that. She went to the bathroom and slathered on her lotion, defiantly. To hell with them. She hurt, and they could just get over their fricking reflexive reactions to her perfume.

And then, she realized, she was officially off-duty now. It was over. With a feeling of release, she grabbed her meds and swallowed down a pain pill and an antianxiety pill, dry. By the time she was dressed and, she supposed, looking fit to be in company, they had started to work. She rejoined the others. The food had arrived, and for the first time since this had started, she felt like eating.

They had saved a chair for her, placed a little apart from the rest, placed a little in shadow. Whose work had that been? Jacob Stone's probably. She took the plate he passed over to her, already laden with red beans and rice, crawfish pie, and jambalaya, and met his eyes. They were kind eyes. She managed to smile.

"Good job, team," Bulwark said, raising a glass of beer. "Tom, Jacob, I'm glad we sorted things out. Nagy, I'm going to recommend upgrading you to OpTwo. Good work."

"OpTwo?" Djinni objected. "Bull, she might not be as useless as I thought, but c'mon..."

Vic, who felt the angry flush in her cheeks once more, thought of any number of retorts but paused instead. The Djinni's tone, while still snarky and caustic, had softened somewhat. Moreover, something had softened *between* them, though Vickie couldn't figure why *he* would have let up any on her. But as for her...that glimpse of his neck, and of his naked soul when he thought he was looking at a lost love...she couldn't be angry with him right now. Maybe it was the drugs, maybe it was because she was too tired, but probably not. If she was hurting, and walking wounded, well, so was he.

"Useful enough to save *your* sorry ass, Red," Bulwark observed, and before Djinni could react to that, continued. "If it hadn't been for that tracing she did, you'd still be hunting."

Red considered that. "Point." He turned and gave her the briefest of nods, perhaps the closest thing to an apology he could manage. "Guess you psions have your uses."

"Magic," Bulwark corrected. "And she did a good job in the bar too, even if we are going to have to pay for her wrecking it."

He said nothing about the illusion of the other Vic. So he didn't know... and if Djinni remembered, he wasn't saying. Better if he didn't remember.

"That didn't go as badly as it could have," the Djinni muttered. "You might even say we won."

"Well, that did not go as well as it could have," Le Fevre mused aloud. His chief djab was not happy, but it could not deny that it had not done what it had been tasked to do. He had placated it with permitting it to feed on some of those others who had failed him. It would take some time before it undertook any great tasks for him again, but he could make do with lesser spirits.

Meanwhile, the Stones, elder and younger, were leaving. The Echo mage, the only other possible person who could oppose his rise to power here, was leaving. That left the field open to him. Unlike some others of his kind, Le Fevre was not interested in pursuing personal vendettas. There was only so much magic to be used, and why would anyone of sense use it to get revenge instead of power?

So...

"In fact," he observed to the empty room, "I would say I won."

CHAPTER FOURTEEN

A Hard Rain Is Gonna Fall

CODY MARTIN & MERCEDES LACKEY

Most of the time, Atlanta was so humid it felt like you could almost cut the air. Today there was no "almost" about it. The air was supersaturated, and the black clouds slowly rolling towards the city promised that it wouldn't be long before the place was under what some of the locals were calling a "toad-strangler."

Those clouds weren't quiet either; there was enough lightning and thunder off on the horizon that John Murdock was fighting to sleep through the midmorning, if not the afternoon. "Working" all night, in addition with the handyman stuff he did during the day, took its toll. Nightmares didn't help much, either. Metas usually needed less sleep than normals, but John actually dreaded the few hours of sleep he got.

When he finally did manage to rouse himself from bed, it wasn't even dark yet, aside from the clouds blocking out the sun. His squat was muggier than usual, leaving John's clothes soaked with sweat. It'd be worse once he got outside, of course; he could only hope that the storms would have a nice accompanying breeze to keep him cool while he did his errands and made his rounds in the 'hood, and maybe the rain would provide a free full body shower. Absolutely nobody's hygiene in his neighborhood was great since he'd arrived, but then again, whose ever was after a disaster? It didn't matter who you were, smelling April fresh wasn't a huge priority when your main priorities were, oh, food, shelter, and a lack of bullet wounds.

It hardly seemed fair. The weather reporter on the tube was getting positively frantic with his flash flood warnings, and John had to wonder how all the folks in their tents and temporary shelters were going to weather this one.

Well, at least his people would be all right.

His people. Damndest thing, but that was the most honest way to describe the situation. He was responsible for them, now. This wasn't to say that the 'hood was helpless; everyone had banded together a lot since the attacks, and had become fairly self-reliant. But John was still a big part of their protection and aid, and they used him like the resource he had become.

Jonas seemed to think that he should just settle down into the position of local sheriff and get over it. He just couldn't do it. He'd never been a fan of the police, and was even less of one now. And yet, he couldn't *not* do it either, at least in deed if not in badge.

John privately dreaded the day when things got back to "normal," and someone official decided to poke around. Or worse, to offer him a job. But hell, that was gonna be a long time coming; things just weren't stable enough yet for these folks to take care of themselves.

He steadfastly refused to listen to the little voice in his head that asked "And what if they never are?"

Shaking his head to clear out that troublesome line of thinking, John got himself cleaned up to walk his territory. The little voice in his head gave a last sardonic snicker and receded into the dark depths of his brain. Rain or shine, someone had to check on things. Bad guys didn't stop for flash flood warnings.

But the moment he left his door, his clothing was plastered flat to his body by the pounding rain in seconds. If there had been wind, he would have suspected a hurricane, the rain was coming down that hard. *"Neither snow, nor rain, nor heat, nor gloom of night stays these couriers from the swift completion of their appointed rounds."* Pulling the collar of his jacket up higher, he trudged off through the flooded streets. The worst part about hard rains like this one was that all the trash and filth came up with the deluge, clogging everything. Garbage floated up from the storm sewers, got spread out from trash piles, and got washed down off roofs. Add to that, the dust and powdered brick and wreckage . . . Yep, the garbage was hitting the streets. Usually in more ways than one.

Tonight was no different. John was only a few minutes into his walk when he saw quite the scene unfolding. Underneath one of the few working streetlights in this part of town, two people were fighting. Scratch that; one person was beating the ever-living crap out of another. The storefront that they were brawling near had been smashed in; bits of glass glittered in the lamplight and a few boxes were scattered into the street.

That store had only just reopened too. Cracking his knuckles and shrugging off his sopping wet jacket, John started off at a clumsy jog to reach the pair. "Hey! Knock it off, both of ya!" No guns were in evidence, not even knives. This looked like a garden-variety drunken brawl, or a couple of crooks getting into an argument over the spoils of their latest heist. John was a few paces from the stronger-looking one when it happened.

He felt a sharp pain in his left bicep; a needle dart of some sort was sticking out of it. Immediately, he began to stumble, finally splashing down on his hands and knees. The world swam in front of him, the dirty runoff water and rubble blurring. John's head began to feel very heavy, and his breathing was slowing down.

Poison . . . tranquilizer . . . something. Straining, he managed to turn his head to his left flank; three men carrying assault rifles and dressed in non-descript, black military uniforms—"ninja suits," the kind of stuff you saw in mall-ninja magazines and *Soldier of Fortune*—quickly closed in on him, setting up a perimeter. Looking over to his right, he saw three others doing the same. The two bruisers that had been fighting when he showed up had stopped; the smaller one was shivering in a pile under the lamp, and the tougher one was walking very calmly towards John. He shrugged off a dirty trenchcoat, revealing a similar get-up as the other men; the sole difference was the pair of swords that hung on his belt, one long and one short.

The man had a swagger, a self-assuredness that set John's teeth on edge. *He's a smug bastard.* Feeling his anger rising that he'd been stupid enough to walk into the trap, John's vision began to clear, strength returning to his limbs. He didn't let on, though; he kept his breathing erratic, and acted as if his every move pained him. Finally, he looked up at the tough brawler; he assumed that the one with the swords was in charge. "Who . . . are you?" he choked out.

The leader ignored him. "Secure the package. We're leaving as soon as I tie up the last loose end." The leader turned to face the shaking man on the ground; John caught a glimpse of an insignia stamped onto the sheath of the longer sword. It was a single snake coiled caduceuslike around a sword. The sword was silver, the background red. The snake was black.

Son of a... Blacksnake.

The team closed in around him; they figured that he was beaten, and had already slung their rifles. John acted; he splashed hard to his left, flinging gobs of water and trashy muck into the eyes of the nearest merc. In an instant, he was on his feet, lunging right; a flash of hands, and he shattered the collarbone of one of the commandos, ripping his rifle away and snapping its sling. There was no time to bring the rifle to his shoulder, so by its barrel and flash suppressor John swung it in a wide arc, pivoting on his back foot. The butt of the stock connected with the blinded merc's temple, and there was a sickening crack; from the stock splintering or the man's skull, John didn't know, and didn't care.

"The package" must be him; for some reason they wanted him alive for now. But he wouldn't stay that way for long, no matter what the reason was that they were taking him. There was no way out of this except over bodies.

He hefted the rifle and swung it backhanded, aiming low and to his right; one of the commandos had taken a step forward and tried to grab his shoulder. The rifle fractured his target's knee, sending a cruel shard of bone to protrude through his battle-dress uniform pants; the merc screamed, crumpling lopsidedly to the ground as his leg collapsed. John jumped

over him, the rifle clattering to the ground as he was
reaching for the merc with the shattered collarbone.
He grabbed the back of the man's ski-masked head,
then hooked his thumb; a split second later he had
jabbed his hand forward, puncturing the mercenary's
eye and ripping it out. Drenched with rain, John's
hands were already slippery; the fluids and blood that
gushed over his thumb made no difference as he let
go and moved on to the next target. The man's scream
spiraled upwards into a whistling shriek, then stopped
as he passed out cold from the pain and dropped into
the gutter. One more on the right side; the man had
cleared his pistol from the holster on his thigh sub-
load, and was racking the slide. *Stupid. Didn't keep
a round in the chamber? Gonna cost ya.* John turned
his body so that it was parallel to the pistol, and then
quickly stepped next to it. Gripping the merc's wrist
with his left hand and the semiauto's barrel with his
right, John twisted the pistol sharply so that it was
perpendicular to him but still pointed in a "safe"
direction. The merc's fingers snapped, bent outward
from his palm. Completing the movement and sliding
behind his opponent, John placed the disabled man
in between himself and the remaining mercenaries.

No time to wrench the gun free and ready it, John
drew his own pistol from the back of his waistband.
Suppressed rifle fire sent supersonic cracks shrieking
into the rainy night; the muzzle flash and report was
muted, but they weren't using subsonic rounds. A
moment later the crack and flash was uncannily echoed
by a nearby lightning strike and simultaneous *boom* of
thunder. Rounds impacted with John's hostage, and the
man's body went limp; John watched as the top of his

head exploded into a mist of blood, bone, and brain matter. Falling backwards, John cleared the "target box" and began firing; no time for looking down the sights, he relied totally on point shooting. He killed one for sure, and wounded the last remaining commando. Rolling the body to the side, John got up into a crouch; he ejected the expended magazine for his pistol and loaded a fresh one, thumbing the slide release to chamber a new round. Another lightning strike and explosion of thunder lit up the street.

The injured merc was on his back, pistol in hand. John's mind barked a harsh laugh, reminded of something he was asked once a long time ago. *"Are you injured, or just hurt?"* He shot the last merc twice in the face. John didn't want to have to worry about someone reporting back; killing these losers would keep him from having to kill more second-rate mall ninjas, or so he hoped.

Standing up to his full height, he walked around the irregular circle of dead and dying, and finished the job by shooting each in the head. More lightning cracked, punctuating and covering his shots. If anyone had heard this, and he frankly doubted they did or cared, by the time the storm was over there would be no signs of the slaughter.

John ejected the magazine from his pistol, examining the back of it; he still had two rounds, plus one in the chamber. He hadn't brought a third and fourth magazine; he didn't think he'd need them tonight, since he hadn't fired his pistol since starting these "patrols." Slamming the magazine back home, John looked over to where the streetlamp was still blazing its sickly yellow light. The Blacksnake team leader, the one with the swords, was standing calmly. His palms were resting on the pommels of the still-sheathed swords. *Guess this guy never heard of what happens to folks that brings knives to gunfights.*

"If I were you, John Mur—" John raised his pistol and fired twice at the merc leader. *Talkers. They're always talkers, for some reason.* Just as John was sighting his follow-up shot, something flat and shiny was flying towards him; before he could react—which was saying something with his reflexes—his pistol was knocked from his grip and into the darkness, his hand cut on the back. John's gaze was just returning to the merc when he felt the first cut; a tickling slash across the ribs. Enough to draw blood, but not enough to nick organs. John hadn't noticed the merc leader taking the sword out of its sheath, but he sure noticed how sharp it was.

"Shit!"

The leader was on him again. John lashed out, leading in with a strong jab followed by several kicks; the surviving merc easily dodged all of John's attacks, parrying with the flat of his blade or simply evading. John realized that his opponent was toying with him; he was keeping John at sword's length, trying to tire him out.

John made a gamble. He turned his back to the mercenary, and knelt down. Over the sound of the pouring rain, John thought he heard a whisper of words with the curiously toneless quality of a voice over a radio. The leader paused for half of a heartbeat, and then surged forward. John twisted around, bringing his right hand slashing upward in an uppercut. He was clutching a chunk of concrete, and hit the merc squarely under the chin, staggering him. John threw the piece of debris as hard as he could at the mercenary, who turned to have it strike him in the shoulder, twisting around and bringing his sword up into a high-ready position. *Serious for ya now, ain't it?*

John didn't have time to twist out of the way, or slap the blade aside. Lightning flashed, thunder boomed, and John felt a dull thud as the blade of the longer sword plunged into his side. The mercenary was up close to John, their eyes locked together. Still smug, still cool and collected. *Damn it, they sent someone like me after me,* John thought. With a grunt, John smashed his head forward once, twice, three times; his opponent's nose cracked and started to spew blood through the ski mask. John locked his arms together and smashed them downward, breaking the leader's grip on his sword. Stepping back, turning, and then launching himself backwards, John cried out in pain as he impacted the dazed mercenary. He swayed on his feet, and then fell forward, twisting in time so that he didn't land on the handle of the sword. The merc had a hole in the front of his uniform, displaying pale flesh that was just as quickly flooded with blood; his hands were on his short sword, the blade already halfway out of his sheath. Then, the man's eyes rolled into the back of his head, and he collapsed, dead.

With a gasp of agony and curses muttered through clenched teeth, John pulled the sword out of his side, bringing it out as straight as his shaking hands could manage. It cut through the water, disappearing as soon as he dropped it. Had it hit anything vital? He couldn't tell. His augmentations shut out most of the pain, flooding him with the endorphins that were supposed to keep him fighting long after everyone else had dropped.

This time he didn't have to fake the pain; he looked down at himself, and he knew it was bad. Worse than it felt, probably. And he had a limited amount of time here, buoyed up by adrenaline and endorphins, with extra control from his implants, to get done what needed to be done. And just as he thought that, the implants kicked in, numbing him down to the bearable level. He got to his feet, methodically going through the bodies and collecting all of their equipment, even down to their boots. It wasn't surprising that they weren't carrying anything that could be used to identify them. Well, except for the emblem on the sheath of the longer of the two swords, a bit of vanity that the dead merc would probably have paid for eventually if John's bill hadn't come in first.

Once he was done, he had amassed a nice-sized pile of tactical gear, rifles, and boots, all soaking wet. *Now to the other business.* Slowly, John began clearing away some rubble from across the shop; once he was done, he dragged each of the bodies to the pit he had created, and then closed it with as much broken concrete and bricks as he could stand to; the pain was finally getting past his reserves of strength. His purpose in throwing the bodies under a destroyed building was twofold. First, no one would really pay that much attention to some bodies in rubble; disaster-relief services were still uncovering people from the invasion. After tonight's rain and a few days in the heat, he seriously doubted that anyone would care to examine them too closely, either. At most, they'd call it a dump site for a gang hit. Second, Blacksnake would be wondering what had happened to their team. If they had bodies, they'd know exactly what happened. Making those people disappear, however, would *scare* someone. No one would know what had happened. No one would know if the "disappeared" people might show up again. Had it been John? Had it been the Nazis? Had it been Echo? No way to tell. Knowing was good; not knowing was terrifying. And it just might be enough to keep him from having to kill more merc goons.

He'd need someone to help stitch him up and to carry the gear back to his place in the morning. He could have done both himself, but he was honestly too screwed up at the moment to want to. He'd have to take the rifles and sidearms with him tonight, though; wouldn't do to have some kid find them after the storm cleared up. Lugging the rifles and pistols in his arms, John finally remembered the one man still alive, aside from himself. The stranger was still on the ground under the lamp, shaking almost to the point where it looked like he was going into convulsions. John staggered over to him, weaving a little from side to side. "What's your story?" John barked.

"H-hired m-m-me. B-bait for you." The man recoiled from John like a wounded animal shrinking away from a predator. "G-gonna k-k-k-kill me?"

John looked at him thoughtfully. "Naw. I'll leave ya for someone else to deal with; I'm done for tonight. Get outta this neighborhood, an' you'll live awhile longer." Without another word, John continued to bleed and slog his way back home, disappearing into the rain. He might be closer to dying than living. *C'est la guerre.*

Jonathon Frieze liked his job. What was more, he was good at it. Tonight was a pisser of a night, but he was getting paid; it sure beat a cubicle.

Their job was to bag and tag a meta that BS wanted alive; he couldn't fathom why, but he didn't really get paid to worry about such things, either. The team for the job was assembled locally, pulling a number of different guys from security jobs at corporate headquarters and government institutions; the operation leader was called in from out of town, and brought a weird ninja guy with him to lead the team. After everyone was briefed on the target's location, abilities, and likely avenues of retreat, the op leader sent them out to take care of business. A stealthed chopper ride later, and they were set.

Frieze hated having to climb the water tower in this rain, but it was his preplanned spot to set up his lurch. The thirty-pound rifle that he was lugging with him wasn't helping things; not only was it a load to tote, but he was the tallest and most conductive thing for at least a couple dozen blocks. He just hoped there was a lightning rod somewhere nearby so he didn't end up a crispy critter.

His rifle deployed, his body settled into a semicomfortable prone position, and his comm gear doublechecked, all he had to do was keep his eyes peeled and wait. The trap they had set up was pretty decent; there's not much arguing a person can do when he's subject to tranquilizers and a half-dozen assault rifles. There were some pretty tough metas out there, resilient ones that could shrug off bullets and even bombs or worse, but they were a rarity. And most of them were already with Echo or Blacksnake or in jail. Or were super-Nazis. This joe was none of the above. If things went south, Frieze had a friend in Mister .50 BMG. It was a heavy round, normally reserved for antimateriel roles, but the head honchos didn't want to take any chances. If Dead is Good, then Really Damn Dead is better.

Frieze did his little squirm exercises, as regular as clockwork, as all good snipers do. When the rain started up, he clicked his scope one notch to compensate for drag. Eventually, he saw the package; walking down the street on the outside of the neighborhood he inhabited, just like their intelligence had indicated. He notified the team leader using their op order. "Deliberate, stage left. Package. Unarmed. Approaching from the east. Forty meters, slowly." All he received was a cold double click on the comm in acknowledgement. He watched their target through his rifle scope; the rifle's kit was monstrous-looking, but had nifty things like Generation IV night vision. It wasn't perfect, especially at these ranges, but it was better than using moonlight. He saw the target, sopping wet, move in closer. Saw the teams close after he had fallen to his knees, and then—the comms exploded in chatter. In an instant, the man was on his feet, moving like a blur; within seconds, several of the retrieval team members were down, some undoubtedly dead. Frieze bunched up on his rifle stock, settling it into his shoulder. Things had *definitely* gone south.

But he hadn't gotten the go code yet. He had to follow procedure; clicking his comm over to the leader channel, he radioed back to base about the "rapidly deteriorating situation" and how chances for success were diminishing. Within seconds, he had a kill order authorized; he relayed this to the team leader, lining up his shot without missing a beat. He already had the range dialed in. "Got him. Stand by." *Center of mass, center of mass, center of mass . . .*

gotcha! Jonathon Frieze's finger slowly tightened on the feather-light trigger...

Seraphym was all but invisible in the pouring rain, with her fires dimmed down to next to nothing. Navigating the blind spot around the life of John Murdock had brought her here. She periodically dashed off to save or help those that the Infinite wanted her to—the mortals who would be critical in protecting their world—but on the way back from the most recent one, it occurred to her that she might learn more about John Murdock's future by staying near him and seeing what, and who, he affected. She decided that unless the Infinite advised otherwise, his vicinity could be as much of a home base as she had so far.

She hovered, without a wingbeat, above and north of a water tower set atop of the roof of an industrial building, not thirty feet from a man stretched out prone on the roof of the tower. The man had a huge rifle propped up and aimed below him.

He was dressed in a mottled dark gray that blended into the gray metal of the roof, but he could have been dressed in scarlet and not have been seen in this weather. Between the rapidly closing dusk and the rain... he, too, was all but invisible.

A mortal would have frowned or sighed. Seraphym did neither. A quick brush of the mind, a search in him, revealed details about his life. Knowing the darkness of the souls of so many that had joined Blacksnake, she was neither surprised nor disappointed. They had made their choices. This man had made the choices that brought him here. And those choices had summoned her.

She had sensed this moment in the futures, and had

waited until he was fully preoccupied with his target
before igniting her fires and dropping down between
him and his target, silent as a raindrop.

Frieze went mind-blank with utter terror, a blur of
fire in his scope, and a terrible fire in his mind.

You are a wicked man, Jonathon Frieze, something
said in his brain, which was nothing but the truth. The
choices that led him here had uniformly been bad,
beginning with the wanton slaughter of wildlife with a
BB gun at age five, an adolescence and adulthood of
torturing animals and his fellow humans, the decisions
to murder, and ending on this rooftop, a contract killer
in the employ of Blacksnake.

But, as was predictably the case, he had rational-
ized all those choices. He told himself that he'd *had*
no choice, for those situations he could not rationalize.
In his own mind, he was justified, a hero.

But now he could not rationalize that anymore.
That fire that caught around his vision and then felt
like it seared into his skull, lit up everything in his
mind equally. The tricks and deceptions were as plain
as the choices he had made, and their results. Nothing
that helped him cope in years past worked anymore.
Suppressed memories were as plain as ink on paper.
Painful realities that had been drugged or drunk away
were clearly defined. The truth was burning his mind.

He recoiled, letting go of his rifle. Scrabbling away
on his belly, he was desperate to get as much distance
as possible between him and the terrible weight on his
mind. Without realizing it until it was too late, Frieze
went over the edge of the water tower, whimpering
pitifully as he plummeted to the rooftop, and then

got up and staggered to fall off the building to the asphalt below.

Seraphym watched as the sniper followed the rifle over the side of the tower.

Felt his life end with a wet, muffled crunch on the pavement below.

And that too, was his choice.

She banked her fires, bowed her head, and sank down to the rooftop, giving over a moment to mourn, for the death was also hers.

That was her choice.

John's gray shirt was soaked with blood from the stab through his abdomen. He was bleeding out, with blood flowing freely from the entrance and exit wounds. The sword hadn't hit a vein or an artery, but it didn't need to. You could bleed to death just as efficiently from an injury like this one. He had used up his "blow-out kit" to try to stop the bleeding; these emergency medical kits were normally used on gunshot wounds, though. He was dying, and he knew it. His heartbeat was speeding up, and he was getting dizzier and weaker with every step in the driving rain.

The circumstances being what they were, John couldn't help but to think back on his life, to growing up in Virginia, his parents, school and friends. He'd had friends once. And a life. Graduating college and joining the military, with his retired Army father and stay-at-home mother proud to see him in uniform. Basic, Rangers, and then later being lucky and skilled enough to make it into the famed Delta Force. Several tours of duty, some in the Middle East and South America...

and then the Program. The changes there, and . . . *her.*
Escape, and then five years on the run from everything
and nothing, but mostly himself. And here he was. With
nothing much to show, nothing much accomplished, and
all of it ending in a rain-drenched street.

Well, that wasn't true. He had genuinely helped
some people: the people back at the bar when all of
this started, some scattered and lucky souls he had
found in the rescue work of picking through wreckage,
and the people of his neighborhood, his adopted "territory." There were also the people he had killed and
maimed—no small number, in the last few months.
He didn't enjoy killing, but he didn't do it casually
either. The lives saved and the lives taken all added
up. *A good tally for just one dumb jerk. A good ratio.*

John was starting to gasp for breath: "air hunger,"
since there wasn't enough of his blood to carry oxygen
away from his lungs. He didn't have much longer, but
his feet continued to carry him onwards. Those implants:
they'd keep him walking after he was dead, maybe.
John Murdock, Zombie. *Braaaaaiiiinssss.* The hilarity
of it was too much, and started him laughing. He didn't
have the breath to do it, but he laughed anyways, which
gave way to hiccups. He laughed even harder, and must
have been a terrible sight. Except there was no one
out here to see it. *If a dying man gets the hiccups in a
toad-strangler rain, does anyone hear it?*

He was stumbling more than walking, now. He had
a general idea of where he was going, but was getting
to the point where he was past caring. Sitting down
and resting seemed like an increasingly good idea.
But he was stubborn; he knew that if he stopped
now, he'd never get up again. So, he kept walking.

After what seemed like forever and then some, he reached his destination. It was a worn-down office building with an adjacent warehouse on the edges of the factory district. The door for the office building had been replaced with a sturdy metal one that looked like it belonged in a bank vault. Over the top of the door was a red star with Cyrillic letters in gold in the middle of it, the letters looking like CCCP. That wasn't what they were, of course, the letters really stood for esses, not cees, but ninety-nine rubes out of a hundred wouldn't know that.

John staggered up the concrete steps, almost slipping and ending his comedy right there. He made it to the door, one hand clutched at his side as he slammed a free fist against the heavy portal. The last of his strength used up, John fell to his knees, hand still holding his injured side.

"Keep your shirt on!" came a muffled voice from within—good English? It puzzled him. There were several banging and clunking sounds, a curse, and the door was hauled open with a harsh scrape. John was bathed in light and warmth from within, and he squinted up at the female silhouetted by the glare.

"Jeebus Cluny Frog!" said the woman, who dropped to her knees beside him. She knocked his clutching hand aside, slapped her own where his hand been and bellowed at the same time. *"SOVIE!"*

John chose that time to slip into unconsciousness. *Good ratio...for one guy...*

To say CCCP had welcomed Bella's help was simplifying the situation. Red Saviour seemed to have a certain amount of respect for her, possibly because Bella stood right up to her, but Red Saviour was not going to admit that CCCP needed help from anyone. Not even from Moscow, let alone a *nekulturny* capitalist.

Sovie—Soviette, the CCCP's official doctor in residence—had been only too happy to have her, and welcomed her with open arms and an amazingly generous nature. CCCP had opened a free clinic along with their soup kitchen—both of which were understaffed—and even if Bella had not been a healer, she still would have been a translator and an extra pair of hands. As it was, she was working from the time she hit their door to the time she walked out of it.

Even now, in this deluge of a rainstorm. She was setting up first aid kits at all the doors, and jump bags too—because if an emergency came up, you might not have the time to run up the stairs to the third-floor infirmary. She was right beside the front door, double-checking the contents of both, when the hammering started.

After practically jumping out of her skin, her main reaction was of annoyance. What idiot would be out there in this weather? The locals all knew to come to the free clinic entrance around the side. Surely it wasn't another snoop from City Hall, not after Saviour had run the last one off with a crowbar.

"Keep your shirt on!" she shouted, irritated, as the pounding continued. With a curse, she began wrestling with the half-dozen door locks, some of which seemed to date from the time of the Caesars. Finally she got the last of them unlocked, and hauled the heavy door open, wincing as it scraped the concrete floor.

The light from behind her poured out over the man, half kneeling, half falling over at her feet. She didn't need the red-stained rain pooling around him to tell her he was hurt, and hurt badly. Her own senses screamed it.

Shocked, she dropped to her knees beside him, pulled his clutching hand from the wound in his side, and felt her energies being *sucked* away from her into that terrible injury.

"*SOVIE!*" she bellowed, knowing that the man was near death, just by the way her power was pouring into him, and that if he *could* be saved, whoever he was, no way she could do it alone—

But then something made her tear her eyes away from her patient and look up.

Just in time to see the fire-wreathed figure touching lightly down in the street, wings of flame outstretched on either side of her. Just in time to feel the touch on her own mind, and—

—fire exploded behind her eyes.

It was like turning on a water fountain to get a drink, and having a fire hose open up in your face.

If she'd had any thoughts, they were completely washed away in the flood of . . . what the angel was. There was only this that was at all coherent: *Heal him. Save him.*

And managing to isolate and grasp a tiny, tiny thread of energy, tiny in relation to what *She* was, though easily a hundred times the strength of what Bella and Sovie combined could do, she did just that.

The angel nodded, as Bella mended tiny capillaries, knitted up muscle, stopped the bleeding, kick-started the man's own body into replacing the lost blood at

an accelerated pace. She felt the heartbeat falter a
moment, then skip two beats, got ready to kick-start
that too, but then it resumed beating on its own,
steady and strong.

It is well. Keep him there. Keep him safe.

The overwhelming Presence left her mind. The
angel arrowed upwards and was gone into the dark
of the night. Bella was left alone in the rain, kneeling
over the previously-dying man, wondering what the
hell had hit her.

"*Blin!*" said Soviette behind her. "Who this is—no,
never minding. We must get him upstairs. Who and
what and why and how can being wait." And it was her
turn to bellow, this time for the CCCP's all-purpose
workhorse, Chug, as Bella tried to catch her breath.

And then came another touch on her mind.

We must talk, you and I.

When John Murdock woke up, he initially panicked;
he didn't feel any real pain, which wasn't a good sign.
After what had happened to him, not feeling pain
probably meant that he was dead or close enough. He
could sense that he was still breathing, and could hear
someone else's heartbeat and the other little noises
of life nearby. With immense effort, he cracked his
eyes open.

He was looking at the ceiling: an old-fashioned,
embossed-tin ceiling that probably dated to the turn
of the previous century. Someone had slapped a fresh
coat of thick institutional-green paint on it. Some other
wag had mounted a poster in the middle of it, of a
Herculean woman holding a Soviet banner. He didn't
recognize her; she had bobbed hair but it was shorter

than the woman he'd seen on the television and the costume was white with a red star on the chest.

"You are wakink?" The soft, pleasant voice made him turn his head slightly to see the original subject of the picture on the poster coming to the side of the bed.

She was stunningly beautiful, in the top-model-beautiful way that most metahuman women were. But a kind expression in her blue eyes softened what could have been cold beauty. Her black hair was cut in the same bob as the woman on the poster, but she was wearing a doctor's smock and there was a stethoscope around her neck. Upon seeing her, John groaned as if in pain.

"You are beink still hurt?" the woman asked, frowning slightly.

"Naw. I just realized I'm in hell."

"*Shto?*" Her frown turned to puzzlement.

"This has gotta be hell. There aren't any pretty gals in heaven."

She stared at him for a long moment, then shook her head. "If is beink *Amerikanski* funny, am not gettink it."

With an effort, John propped himself up on his elbows; his wound didn't hurt, but he was still fatigued beyond belief. He imagined that between his own implants and the half-dozen IVs running into him that he must be pretty well medicated at the moment. "Don't worry 'bout it. If I'm not in hell, where am I?"

"Is beink infirmary of headquarters of *Super-Sobratiye Sovetskikh Revolutzionerov*," the woman replied, holding her head up with a flash of pride in her eyes.

"So, looks like I stumbled to the right place. This is the CCCP's HQ."

"*Da*, is beink—what you call CCCP incorrectly. And

why you are beink fall on our doorstep, Comrade—?"
She arched an eyebrow, inviting a name and a reason for
being there. "I am beink Doctor Jadwiga Pavlova Tiko-
nov, but am mostly beink known by callsign Soviette."

John regarded her coolly, sizing her up for a few long
moments before speaking. "Murdock. John Murdock,
pleased t'meetcha. To answer your question," he looked
down at his side, then back to her, "I got into a bit of
trouble." He tried to stand up then, and immediately
regretted the decision; he swayed in place before the
Russian woman steadied him. As resilient as he was, his
body just had not caught up with the damage that had
been done to it yet. He *had* lost a lot of blood; it was
a miracle that he was still alive and breathing.

John extended his hand. "Thanks, Jadwiga."

She didn't seem to notice his hand, so he dropped it
quickly to his side. In fact, she pushed him rather insis-
tently back down onto the bed. She was a lot stronger
than she looked. "Is not to be thankink me, Comrade
Murdock. Was *Amerikanski* Comrade Bella Dawn is
findink you like drowning cat on doorstep." Jadwiga's
smile was rueful. "She is leavink me werry little to do."

"*Sestra,* is drowned cat ready for interrogation?" The
woman that stalked through the open door *was* one he
recognized. This was Red Saviour II, the redoubtable
leader of this group, just as beautiful as Soviette, but
with none of the softness. She looked down at John
with her hands on her hips. "So, Comrade—"

"Murdock," Jadwiga supplied.

"Murdock. Why is it you are here in my headquarters and not in decadent *Amerikanski* hospital,
eating popsicles?"

"To be honest, I'm not sure why I stumbled over

to y'all. I was pretty out of it. Guess it has somethin' to do with the sorta negative attention that ninja stab wounds get from the cops at regular hospitals. Plus, I don't have the sorta cash to throw away on a hospital." He shrugged and tried some flattery. "Heard from some folks that I know that y'all ran a free clinic. An' that you were Reds, so y'all can't be *completely* bad."

"He is dressed like sturdy worker, Commissar," Soviette put in. "Perhaps enemy of the people ambushed him."

"Bah." Before John or the doctor could stop her, she peeled off the gauze and peered at his wound. "Enemy of the peoples are carrying katanas now? Did you not pay your sushi chef, John Murdock?"

"'Tis a scratch.' Like I said, I got into some trouble."

"These hands, they are laborer's hands," Jadwiga added.

Saviour frowned fiercely. The tattoo on his hand was an ouroboros: a snake swallowing its own tail. It was wrapped around the number 155, and done in bold, black ink. "This tattoo and these scars—are *nyet* what I see on common laborer, *sestra*—" And then she switched to Russian, and continued her sentence, speaking urgently and with some apparent recognition of what John's scars might mean. The doctor kept shaking her head, causing Saviour's frown to deepen.

She glanced suspiciously at John, then tapped the tattoo. She switched to English. "And what is beink this?" Jadwiga tried to shush the Commissar, but she stared at John, still expecting an answer.

John looked down at his hand and the symmetrical scars that covered most of his body before replying, deadpan, "Birthmark."

"Ho, ho," Saviour said flatly. "Is beink *Amerikanski* comedian. Is *nyet* so funny. I am needink to know what has been dropped on my door. Jadwiga is soft heart of us. I am iron fist."

John shrugged. "To be accurate, I didn't exactly force my way inside."

"Yes? And are you viper in fruit basket?" Saviour's eyes brightened with anger. "I have obligation to protect the comrades, John Murdock. I have seen scars like these before, and am *nyet* to be lied to."

"He cannot leave, Natalya," Soviette put in firmly. "And at the moment, he is *nyet* threat, either." John allowed wisdom to prevail, and kept silent. If they had examined him while he was out, they both probably already knew that that statement was false.

Saviour turned her attention back to him. "Why here, *Amerikanski*? Are you here from CIA? FBI? NSA?"

"Not exactly my sort of crowd anymore. I'm an anarchist."

"Nat." It was a new voice from the door, one somewhere between a soprano and a contralto, a speaking voice that promised it belonged to a singer. "Chill. The Hog Farmers vouch for him." The young woman in the paramedic outfit that stood in the doorway was also—clearly—a metahuman. There just were not a lot of blue-skinned, blue-haired people around that weren't metas. "Besides, I got a decent read on him. He's no threat." At Saviour's skeptical glance, the young woman sighed. "Come on, Nat, what can the CIA find out here that you wouldn't just tell them?"

Red Saviour gave the newcomer a look that would have burned a lesser being where she stood. "You scanned him."

"*Da,* I scanned him." The blue woman added something. "*On ne sostoit v pravitelstvennoi organizatcii nikakogo tipa.*" It was in Russian. Finally Red Saviour nodded.

"He can stay for now. But when he is healed—"

"When I'm healed, I'm outta here." Scanned? What was the medic talking about? Unless—John got chills down his spine. Was she a telepath? Had she read his mind? Weren't there supposed to be protocols about that?

"Out of here—maybe. We will see." Saviour raked them both with her eyes, then shrugged and strode out. The blue medic nodded at Soviette.

"Get some rest, doll. I'll take over the infirmary for now."

The Russian didn't protest, which might have demonstrated her level of weariness. She gave the blue medic an affectionate arm-pat as she passed, and a moment later they were alone.

John started to get up. He wasn't quite sure what he was going to do, but one thing for sure was that he didn't want to be two seconds more in a room with the kind of telepath that would read his mind as ruthlessly as this woman implied she had.

He tried to get up, that is. This woman was also stronger than she looked. Or he was weaker than he thought. She gently but firmly shoved him back down on the bed and held him there.

"Since I just lied my ass off for you, buddy, the least you can do is glue *your* ass to this bed and heal," she said, more good humor showing in her eyes than appeared in her voice. "I'm Bella. I *am* a telepath and an empath and I did *not* scan you, or at least, no more than I can help. But I needed to give Nat a reason to keep you here, and I don't think she would have accepted the one I got."

John was having the feeling that events were rushing past him faster than he could keep up with them. All he could think of to do was to ask the question that occurred to him with her last sentence. "An' what would that reason be?"

"That an angel told me to heal you, save you, keep you here and keep you safe." The absolutely sober expression she wore made the words hit him like a gut punch.

This Bella—she had seen the angel too? And talked to her? But if another person had seen her, did that make her—*real?*

"It doesn't take a rocket scientist to figure out you're in trouble, laddie-buck," the medic continued. "The angel seemed to think you'd fit in with this motley crew here. Now, Nat and Sovie both reacted to those scars of yours, as if they had seen something like them. Add to that you survived a gut stab that would have put John Q. Public on a slab, that you have been keeping a profile so low you're looking up at ants' bellies, and that someone seriously wanted you out of the way, I can add two and two as well as anyone. Scars plus all the rest of it says *high dollar implants* to me, and that says *government program.* The fact that you aren't running around either with Echo or some Army goon squad tells me you've escaped them, and you don't want them to know you're still around."

He was ice-cold inside. Even if she hadn't read his mind, she was good. Smart. He was in no shape to kill her and run; he didn't *want* to kill her anyway, and he couldn't run right now...

So he just kept quiet.

"Here's my point, cowboy," she continued quietly. "Someone out there, someone absolutely extraordinary, wants you as alive as whoever you were running from wanted you dead. And if I were to assess your situation, there is one thing that stands out. I don't think you can run and bury yourself again. So that means you have two choices. You can get friends and allies, or you can run and die like a lone wolf—a '*nekulturny* running dog,' as the parlance around here goes." She shrugged, but her eyes were compassionate and understanding. "There would be worse people you could take up with than CCCP. They share a lot of points of philosophy with you, if you are what you say you are. And they are extraordinarily loyal to their own." Now she took her hand away. "So for right now I am going to leave you and let you think that over. I need to—make a quick inventory of the supplies."

He nodded although he got a sense that she was going to do more than that. And when she left him alone with his thoughts, he found himself turning what she had said over and over and finding very few flaws in it.

And that... was terrifying.

CHAPTER FIFTEEN

When Push Comes To Shove

MERCEDES LACKEY, STEVE LIBBEY
& CODY MARTIN

"... so I'm not exactly persona non grata, but I am also not the most welcome face at Echo right now," Belladonna shrugged.

"For doing what needed to be done?" Saviour snorted. "This is sounding familiar to me."

Bella kept any comments to herself. "Well, they can't fire me, not when they're sending out recruiters to pull in petty metacriminals and giving them a chance to reform, redeem themselves, and join the happy family. We're stuck with each other."

Bella was loitering here for a reason, hoping to be able to bring up the subject of John Murdock. She'd been visited by the enigmatic Seraphym twice now since the man had dragged himself to the CCCP headquarters. Both times Seraphym had made it emphatically clear that John was somehow important, that he was in danger still... and that he needed to be with CCCP. Why? Well, angels weren't prone to giving reasons. *And you know, you just don't march*

535

up to one and demand an explanation either. Well, Saviour might, but . . .

A man's gruff voice interrupted. "So, where's the chow hall in this joint? Hospital food ain't my normal board."

Well, speak of the devil, just the subject I wanted to bring up. Bella looked up to see Murdock standing in the doorframe. He looked groggy, clutching bandages at his side and rubbing sand out of his eyes. "Anyone there? I heard talkin'."

"We are in meeting. You are leaving room now." Red Saviour's tone was dismissive, and brooked no dissent.

"Thanks for the hospitality, but I'm not really feelin' up to taking orders. Didn't mean to interrupt anything."

"Commissar, *I* asked him to talk to you. Murdock, a little respect for the Commissar, *if* you please." Bella tried to radiate calm, the way Jadwiga did.

Red Saviour shrugged and fastened a glare on Murdock. "Very well, you are talking to me."

He shrugged as well, still holding his side. "Well, chow hall seems to be out of the question. With your leave, I'd like to get my stuff and scoot, unless there's any more business for me here."

Bella cast her eyes up to the ceiling. "Give me strength," she muttered. She turned towards Saviour, her expression now one of respectful conciliation. "Commissar, with all due respect . . . you're undermanned here and the only 'trusty native guide' you have is me. And I belong to Echo. I suggest you consider offering Murdock a place here, with the CCCP, as an ally at least. Someone with eyes on the street." There was a faint look of distaste on Murdock's face when she mentioned Echo. *Good.*

Then Bella turned to Murdock. She raised one eyebrow. "You think like these people. You have a lot in common. I suggest you consider hooking up here. Take advantage of common goals."

John looked plainly skeptical, but held his tongue. Red Saviour's face took on the identical expression. She folded her arms and scowled deeper.

"You ask me for very much trust, Comrade Bella. CCCP is Russian organization, led by Russian, for Russians. And Moscow has promised me sturdy Russian backup as soon as paperwork clears"—she waved a hand in the air—"which, I am admitting, could be next year."

"Which means you need people now, Saviour. *Especially* given what we have just been discussing." Bella's expression turned grim. "Neither you nor I think that the frickin' Space Nazis got scared and ran away. Three pop-ups say otherwise." *And I haven't told you everything yet . . .*

"*Da.* The lessons of Great Patriotic War are not so quickly forgotten in my country as they are here. This is why all-powerful Supernaut force guards Mother Russia." She snorted in contempt. "Meanwhile, I am running *nekulturny* soup kitchen for homeless capitalists." The Commissar leaned forward. "Comrade Murdock. What can you offer me to justify my trust? I am wanting to hear from your mouth, not blue girl's."

"Largely depends, for starters, on whatcha need, and second, what you folks can provide for me and mine."

"Yours? You are having family? No pets, no childrens, that is rule."

"No family; folks died in this last attack, as far as I know. I'm watching a neighborhood that's sorta isolated from the rest of the city. If I'm gonna sign on with y'all, I'm gonna need assurances that they won't be left out in the cold."

"You walked here; it can't be that far. Whose store centers it?" Bella, having worked with the Hog Farmers, knew most of the cut-off areas like the back of her hand.

"The one at the corner of Elm and Lee. Run by an old fella named Jonas. He's been the one that's been helping me organize the neighborhood, get folks working together to pull through this mess."

Bella turned to the map pinned on the office wall and tapped her finger on an area that had been outlined in pale pink marker. "Here, Saviour. That one of yours?"

"I have made overtures to locals, but I am, as you say, small staffed. I cannot send Chug out to do, er, sane human being's work. He frightens children." Red Saviour pursed her lips. "He frightens armies, too. But let us ask him in person. Chug!" Her shout made the room jump. "*Davay, davay!*"

As if he had been eavesdropping, the stony creature lumbered into the room, brushing both shoulders against the doorframe. "Hullo, Commissar."

Red Saviour snapped her fingers at him as if she were summoning a dog to her side. In Russian, she said, "This American is interested in staying with us. Do you like him?"

Chug fidgeted. "I dunno."

"Take a long look at him," she continued. "Do you think he could be your friend? Perhaps join you at the park for a stroll with the squirrels?"

"I like the squirrels," Chug said, perking up. "I think they would like him, too."

"Aha." Red Saviour switched to English. "You have passed the squirrel test, comrade. Do not ask what that means. I want you to brief me on situation in College Park."

John scratched his head, sighing. He walked in front of the map, making a V with his fingers around the pin Bella had placed in it. "The Park got cut off from the surrounding area by two destruction corridors that followed a couple of roads on the periphery. Power is still out in about a quarter of it, so folks have jury-rigged it or have generators going. Clean water is being brought in where city water ain't workin', and some of the hydrants still work, but it's a hassle. There's a community garden that we've started up, but it'll take some time before it produces even a percentage of what folks need, and there are a couple dozen lawn gardens. We got the street toughs wrangled into protecting most of those. Everything else is being given on good faith by the stores in the area, by what Hog Farm is bringing in, or what's been scavenged. It's in bad shape, but the folks are making do as best they can with what they have." He turned back to face Saviour. "Crime isn't a real problem, but it won't stay that way."

"No incursions by the Rebs?" A slow, devious smile had begun to spread on Red Saviour's face.

"None so far. Small-time crap by local thugs looking to take advantage . . . and a few high-paid outsiders. Anybody that's caused trouble hasn't lasted long enough to keep on causin' trouble."

Red Saviour stepped up to the map. She traced a line from the destruction corridors to Echo headquarters, then to her own. "I am sensing power vacuum.

Reb activity in our district has escalated in last two weeks, with more extortings and hate attackings. This, I am thinking, is being prelude to push into new territory. Right in backyard of Echo but they are doing nothing because Rebs are not metahuman."

"Scum are scum, but Echo has their set of priorities. Poor folks don't necessarily rate all that high."

She nodded. "We can prepare them for siege. People's Blade is knowing these streets well enough. Perhaps you will show me yours?"

"That's workable. Do ya really think that the Rebs would push towards my neighborhood that soon? What kinda numbers are we talking about?"

"I believe Americans are capable of all manners of idiocy, at all scales." At that moment, Red Saviour looked just like a frowny, crotchety old man. "Our best guess, two hundred foot soldiers."

John shook his head. "Way outta my league, especially if they're armed the way rumors paint them to be. So, what's the deal? I show ya the situation, and we go from there?"

"You show me situation, *da*. Then I decide what we shall do, and then we are executing plan." She rolled her eyes. "I am sure I am receiving many advices from American comrades."

"You can cut down on how much unsolicited interference you get by deciding now on who you talk to, Commissar," Bella pointed out.

"*Shto?* I am not understanding you."

"You can say 'I only interface via blue girl' and make it stick. That controls what they can get out of you and I control what you get out of them, including grief. You take Murdock here for your community interface; Murdock, you do the same. They never get a chance to try and pull anything out of you, because he's your face-man."

Red Saviour barked out a laugh. "And I thought Americans were simple-minded. This is being as convoluted as Moscow bureaucracy. Is first time I have felt at home in overheated hellhole." She reached into her pocket for a *Proletarskie* cigarette and lit up. Great, pungent clouds of tobacco smoke wafted to the ceiling. "This is plan I can follow. Comrade Murdock, does it meet with your approval?"

"Ain't any harm in it, so far as I can see. It'll work." He didn't sound completely convinced, but appeared willing enough to go along and agree for the moment.

"Can we go to the park now?" Chug, forgotten until this moment, spoke up in Russian.

Bella's face softened; she looked almost angelic. "I'll take you, Chug," she replied in the same language. "The nice man is hurt and needs to lie down. Later today, I promise."

"*Nyet,* I forbid it." Red Saviour brushed Bella's offer aside with a wave of her cigarette. "He is no dog to walk around in grass. Chug can lift city bus—then eat it. Let Soviette accompany him."

If Saviour intended to offend her, she didn't succeed; Bella laughed. "And who do you think Jadwiga's had in charge of him for the last four days? I'm only a medic, I can't do surgery or prescribe. I haven't taken him as far as the park yet, but he's been doing a helluva job on urban renewal at my direction."

"I am fearing babysitting bill from Echo. Are you not having job? But very well." The Commissar's harsh expression mellowed. "And *spasibo.*"

Bella kept her grin strictly internal. As she had suspected, Saviour had a soft spot for the strange, childlike creature. There was a story there...one day, she'd get it out of Jadwiga. "No babysitting bill, and no, I am still doing my Echo shifts. But since the invasion I only seem to need about three hours of sleep in twenty-four. What am I supposed to do, play video games?"

John interrupted. "Well, this has been enlightening, but I figure that I'm going to go pass out again for a while. Better on a hospital bed than the floor." He nodded to Chug. "Nice meeting ya...Chug's his name, right? Right. Wake me up when we're headin' out to survey the neighborhood." With that he shambled back toward the infirmary.

Bella withdrew and put in a call to Vickie. It was short but sweet. "All right. All the ducks are in a row. Send that email, then get down here. The only way she'll believe it, and respect us, is if we are right here to deal with her when she gets it."

There were few places Red Saviour could escape the cacophony of Hensel's construction workers. Hammering, bricks crashing down, the scream of steel being cut, and men shouting orders and retorts. The union men had made themselves at home in the CCCP headquarters. Some gave her and her comrades curious looks, as if they were the interlopers. The noise upset Chug in particular, who had curled himself into a nook in the basement like a hibernating bear.

Red Saviour had no such luxury. Matters had to be conducted. And besides, she was about to do some shouting herself. That intruding little capitalist sorcerer girl had sent her an email that made her blood boil. And now Red Saviour Senior was about to get it in the teeth. She growled as she accessed the secure voice connection to Moscow.

"No kindly greetings for your father, my Wolfling? Would you like to hear about my new girlfriend? You'd like her: she collects pistols." Nikolai Shostakovich took on the usual bantering tone that he knew infuriated his daughter.

"I don't care if you are dating the Premier's concubine herself. You have *lied to me*." Natalya had started out loud and ended in a shout. It was a good thing this conversation was in Russian, otherwise people in Peachtree Square would be talking about it in fifteen minutes.

She could almost hear his expansive shrug. "It is a politician's job to lie. What lie in particular bothers you?"

"This packet you sent me. It is full of nonsense culled from a child's primer on the Great Patriotic War. Did you think I paid no attention in school?"

"You were more interested in fisticuffs. But I thought the refresher would be helpful. You have much on your plate."

"Don't patronize me. You and Uncle Boryets have your tricks and I see through them: unload a ream of useless information so that I will lose interest in the matter and busy myself with petty thieves. Meanwhile, I am getting better intelligence from *nekulturny* models and the heir to Rasputin!"

There was a surprised pause. When her father resumed, his voice was not so smooth, not so controlled. "You...have something to do with a sorcerer?"

"As little as possible, but apparently she is more useful to me than my own flesh and blood. What do you know about the death of Hitler? What do you know about the way the Nazi metas disappeared? What do you *really* know about the Thule Society?"

"I know what you know. Hitler put a bullet into his head."

"Then I know that you are a liar." There. It was out. The first time she had ever dared say that to her father's face. She felt a fire burning deep in her gut and had to clamp down her powers as her fists flared briefly.

Yet Nikolai didn't rise to the challenge. In fact, he spoke in slow, kindly tones: "Something is upsetting you. Perhaps we should discuss this another time."

"Don't you dare end this call until you have told me the truth."

Nikolai sighed. "It's ancient history. Let it be."

"Swastikas trampled through Red Square. That wasn't ancient. What are you withholding, Papa? Why?"

"It was good to talk to you, Natalya." He let the statement hang, the implication obvious. "I'm leaving the office now." The line went dead.

Natalya looked down at the computer screen. The cursor blinked at the end of the line, an email to the secure account that the magician should in no way have had access to. That she could . . . told Saviour that she was going to be even more useful than the Russian had thought. But the contents . . .

Thule Society infiltrated Nazi metas circa 1942 and probably directed the course of the war from that point. Hitler assassinated by Ubermensch, witnessed by Himmler. Source: Rheinhold Karl Fritz, former SS commander, also known in occult circles as "Black

Flame," secretly a member of Himmler's inner circle of occultists in opposition to the Thulians. According to Fritz, Red Saviour was not only aware of this, but enabled the assassination, as coordinated by Himmler. Fritz suggests Ubermensch then removed Himmler and brought in a Thulian psionicist to orchestrate suicides and wipe memories. My further intel suggests this has relevance to the current incursion.

Minutes passed, as weighty as hours, but her father did not call back. She tried to envision how her father, always a devoted patriot, could be party to any intrigue involving his dire enemies, the enemies of her people, but the concept was too appalling and abstract. Natalya had always thought of Nazi Germany as a monolithic monster, united in hateful purpose. How could Hitler's own followers turn so dramatically against him at such a crucial time? This was as if FDR had been cut down by Yankee Doodle. Or the Emperor of Japan by Divine Wind.

The sorcerer feared Red Saviour, this she knew. Could she be attempting to undermine the solidarity of the CCCP by driving a wedge to divide its very heart in two?

She glared at the phone. "Come on, old man. Don't make me wait."

"NAT!" The bellow was not from the person she wanted to speak to right now.

"Go away! I am working."

"This won't wait." The blue girl marched into Natalya's office with that very sorcerer in tow. The sorcerer did not look happy to be there.

"You!" Red Saviour leapt to her feet, eliciting a satisfying cringe from Vickie. "Not satisfied to slander my father by email? Now you trespass in my head-quarters?"

The girl was clutching a sheaf of papers to her chest; she closed her eyes and thrust them at Saviour.

"Oh, now you make your accusations with paper. My father is hero of Soviet Union—the Motherland. You have very much nerve to claim he colluded with Nazis."

"He stopped the war," Vickie squeaked.

"The Russian people stopped the war . . . with help from some allies. Wars are fought by nations, not by individuals."

"No, he stopped the war *right then*. Before Hitler could use his A-bomb on Moscow." Vickie's eyes were still squeezed shut. And she said something in Russian that could only have been a direct quote from her father. It had all the right phrasing, all the right nuances.

And the right pragmatic feeling to it. *"Esli ti vibiraesh mezdu adom ili diavolom, diavol—luchshii vibor."*

When you face hell or the devil, the devil is a better option.

Red Saviour gawked at her. "Where did you learn these things?"

The papers in Vickie's hand shook so hard they rattled. "It's in there. My secret sources. Occultists, magicians, on both sides of the former Iron Curtain. It never was more than a Paper Curtain for us. But . . . as Fritz said, it all seemed to be ancient history, hardly worth believing, not worth talking about . . . until swastikas poured out of the sky. And he already told all this to Echo, who patted him on the head and told him to go away."

Natalya took the papers from Vickie's hands and set them on her desk. "I'll read them later."

"Echo's been holding out on you, Nat," said Bella. "Vickie's dug up a lot. It's not just Red Saviour Senior who's been keeping you in the dark. And, oh, it gets better, Nat." Natalya could not help but see that Bella was not at all intimidated by Saviour's fuming anger. "And I will bet a cookie that rat bastard Tesla has not bothered to tell you *this* part."

"*Shto?*" Saviour's eyes glittered. "There is more than my father allying himself with Nazis?"

"*Da*, and this is as recent as the headlines. Show her, Vic."

The sorceress shoved more papers at her. Photographs of someone taking the armor off one of the troopers. Natalya's eyes widened, and her jaw dropped a little.

"This is—shopping photos, surely—"

Bella snarled. "No. It's real. About a third of those damn goose-stepping bastards are, were, *aliens*. As in, yes, not from this world. I know. I *saw* them. Without the suits. At Groom Lake. I just didn't have the proof to show you." Her lips twisted. "That would be why they tried to retrieve every suit and body they could and attempted to incinerate the rest. Now put that together with the Thulians infesting the Nazis in 1942 and what do you get? Explains the house painter's A-bomb very nicely, doesn't it? And it also explains fricking spaceships full of *Schutzstaffle*."

With a practiced motion, Red Saviour extracted a cigarette from her pocket and lit up. She took several long pulls on the foul-smelling import, eyes closed, letting the information sink in. She had seen many bizarre, inexplicable things in her life, enough to eschew paranoiac explanations over common sense. Yet her father's evasive behavior on the phone kept her skepticism at bay. The last exhalation was a smoke ring. At last she met both Americans' eyes.

"Let us say that I believe what you have uncovered is being true . . . just for the moment. Why would you share this with me? Surely you are compromising classified information. Does Tesla excite so little loyalty in his employees?"

"My loyalty is to the human race. Which I happen to want to see survive." Bella's eyes actually glowed a little. "Politics and borders be damned. If FDR and Churchill could crawl into bed with that monster Stalin for the same reason, I can sure as hell leak what needs to be leaked to our allies."

Red Saviour felt her stomach churn with outrage. "Stalin? Be careful which lines you are crossing, girl."

Bella gave Vickie a significant look. "About that job. We need to see Tesla now, in the next hour or two at minimum. And we need to get into his appointment calendar without going through his secretary."

Vickie ducked her head. "Right. Uh . . . Commissar? Do you want to watch over my shoulder? It could take . . . a while. Half an hour, maybe. My laptop and stuff are in the medic bay."

"*Nyet*. Report to me when you are finished." The look Saviour shot at her was marginally more friendly. Vickie only hoped that something would happen to turn that I-will-not-kill-you-yet glare into something . . . less lethal.

The Russian turned to Bella. "Now then, comrade. You were comparing me to Stalin?"

❖   ❖   ❖

Telsa was certain that this morning Belladonna and the CCCP virago had not been on his appointment calendar. But suddenly they were in his trailer, crammed between a visit from the FBI liaison and a city planner. With them was a cringing blond girl with her arms full of file folders. She had an Echo uniform, so he didn't give her more than a curious glance before settling on the two attention-grabbers.

Red Saviour wore what must be her dress uniform: a sharp military cut with epaulets and long gloves, and an anachronistic sickle and hammer emblazoned on her sleeve. She smirked at him as a wolf might at its noontime meal.

"Mr. Tesla. So good of you to see me. I cannot fault Southern hospitality." Without being invited, she took a seat. "I am being sure you know your employees who accompany me."

Belladonna grimaced. "For the record, I am an increasingly uncomfortable employee. And right now, you are not gonna like what we have to tell you."

"I can only imagine," Tesla said with a sigh. A gloom settled over him, the inevitability of confrontation.

Red Saviour put out a hand, into which Vickie placed a file folder. The Russian opened it, and after a dramatic pause, read out: "The Thulians are not of this world. We are the pawns of impossible creatures who move us on their chessboard with invisible hands. Tesla must know."

Eisenfaust's last words to Walter Slycke, retrieved by Belladonna Blue herself. He strove to control his expression. "That's interesting."

"What's interesting," Bella snapped, "is that you didn't see fit to share it with the leader of the second largest, non-profit metahuman organization on the continent. In your own back yard. Or this—" She took another file from the blonde and slapped it down in front of him, open. It showed an autopsy of one of the aliens extricated from Thule trooper armor. "Or this!" Another file, this one dating back to World War II. He didn't have time for more than a glance before it was the Russian's turn.

"I'm hurt, comrade. So much to learn from each other, yet you never stopped by for tea."

"It appears you have no trouble learning my secrets, Commissar. Should I be upset that you subverted two of my own to steal intel?"

Belladonna flushed a dark blue. "Steal? This is something you should have been sharing in the first place! Jeezus Cluny Frog, haven't you figured out by now that the old rules don't work anymore?" She waved her hand. "Your HQ is toast, two-thirds of your people are dead, and you have no idea where the goons that did it came from or where they went! They damn near got Slycke before we did, we've had three hit squads pop up since, and you can bet your last dime they are going to be back in force!"

Tesla glared at her as she emphasized her tirade with dramatic gestures and made a note to have her fired at once. The last thing he needed was a girl young enough to be his daughter second-guessing what was becoming an increasingly difficult balancing act.

Red Saviour's eyes turned to cold steel as she watched him squirm. "What about the national intelligence agencies? FBI, NSA, CIA. You are keeping them in dark also?"

"We concluded that this intel was not critical to the

current line of investigation to the whereabouts of the Thulian forces. It was the right decision. We didn't want to cloud the water with paranoid chatter." He pointed a finger at the blue girl. "Or, for that matter, get the tabloids in an uproar about ET throwing a *seig heil* at our doorstep. You have a lot of nerve to make that decision for the organization."

Bella glared. "Does *she* look like a tabloid reporter? Wake up, Tesla, this is your ally! Unless you want to alienate her altogether, it's time to play ball. Vic. Lay it on him."

The blonde cleared her throat nervously. "In 1942, Goering was approached by a—creature—who penetrated into his office without passing his guards or his receptionist." As she continued her story, Alex felt the hair on the back of his neck standing up. "...and in order to prevent the detonation of an alien-designed atomic weapon in Moscow, Red Saviour Senior colluded with Ubermensch to arrange for the metahuman to assassinate Hitler and his top officials in their bunker. But then Ubermensch disappeared. And so did most of the other Nazi metahumans. My sources say they were mostly subverted by the aliens we know as the Thule Society. Presumably...they went wherever those ships came from." With a shaking, gloved hand, she put the folder on his desk and looked at the latest Red Saviour, who inclined her head in approval.

Tesla felt his heart sinking as Vickie confirmed what the intelligence agents of Metis had speculated upon for decades.

And in that moment, he realized that he had strayed from the principles on which Echo was founded. Not for the protection of borders, or property, or politics or secret agencies, but rather the protection of people. He had been keeping secrets from the wrong people.

He took a deep breath. "Neu Hyperborea."

The women all stiffened. He leaned forward, hands spread to show that he was ready to talk.

"We know the name of the Thule capital, though not the location. I have agents working to uncover this information right now. You must understand, though, that it is not a simple matter of find the target and pull the trigger. The forces at work here are far, far more complex."

"What is being complex about massacres?" Red Saviour snapped at him. "Those who brought death must meet with the same."

"Shiva is both a creator and a destroyer. When she dances, there's no telling which way the dance will turn."

The Americans blinked at him. Red Saviour began to rise from her seat. "You are mocking me, Tesla, and I am not tolerating it. I will tear down the rest of your campus if you are concealing information that will save lives." Her fists glowed slightly. So did the blue healer's eyes. And . . . the little blonde sprouted a golden aura.

Metahumans did not frighten him. Tesla met her angry glare. "You're in over your head."

"No wonder you and my father got along so well. You are both chauvinist pigs who think you know better than rest of world."

"Your father knows you're unreliable, which is why he palmed you off on us. He expected that you'd amuse yourself with street fights and raids on crack houses. You should stay with what you know."

"Her father is a reactionary old rat bastard who's more interested in chasing women than actually *thinking* about the genie that got out of the bottle!" Belladonna snapped. "For better or worse, *this* Red Saviour has her priorities right!"

"*Da.* And *this* Red Saviour is the one who will be fighting alongside your operatives when next blitz-krieg hits. You cannot choose your allies, comrade. The proletariat must put aside differences to stand together against oppression. If you do not understand that, then you are not worthy of position."

"Fire in the sky..." the blonde murmured, looking a little dazed. She shook her head. "Sir... you have an angel, a real angel, perched on the top of the Suntrust Tower right this minute. Ask any magician. They'll tell you. The Seraphym is no metahuman, and no illusion. She's the real thing. Haven't you thought once about what *that* means? And if you don't believe me, and you won't believe your own Echo mages—ask Mercurye. Or try, anyway. He disappeared shortly after he talked to her. It's in my intel."

Tesla blinked. Who was this woman? She seemed to have the entire Echo database in her head.

Red Saviour's harsh features softened. "So you see, comrade, this war will go on with or without you. I am willing to be your ally—your friend—if you will extend trust to receive trust. Was it not your own George Washington who said, 'United we stand, divided we fall?'"

"I think that was Benjamin Franklin...."

"No, Franklin said, 'We must hang together or surely we will hang separately.'" The blonde seemed to have a good history book in her head too.

"Is not mattering. Sentiment is correct." She offered

a hand to Tesla. "My CCCP is wounded, but it is not broken. I will give you everything I am having to give. Let us face common enemy together." Her eyes blazed with fervor.

Tesla hesitated. "You don't know what you're getting yourself into. You may wish you'd stayed with drug dealers and street thugs."

"Comrade, I survived massacre that now has been named for me. I am afraid of nothing else. What are you afraid of, besides failure?"

He grasped her hand. An uncertain grin spread across his face. "Point taken." Then he turned to the two Echo operatives. "I'll have to upgrade both of your clearances...hell, what you're about to see and hear doesn't even have a clearance. I don't think more than three people have ever seen these documents." He headed for the back wall, and a safe.

But that was when a single tone, like a deep, resonating wind chime, sounded from inside his desk. He froze, then shrugged. "Speak of the devil," he said to himself, and returned to the desk, which had been shipped via very special courier indeed when he actually had an office again.

He gave the mouse from his computer three fast clicks and drew an "M" with it. Computer and desktop dropped. The Metis communication device rose to take its place. The mouse had read his fingerprint and DNA of course—it wouldn't do for anyone to be able to get at the device just by an errant mouse click.

Two slender wires extended up, impossibly rigid, with a luminescent aura that stretched between them like slow-motion lightning blasting through the ocean. The crackles resolved into a human face, tanned and handsome and accustomed to petulance. A winged helmet topped blond curls, and the monitor showed the man's bare shoulders. Mercurye peered into the aether.

"Alex?"

"Right here, and with friends. You can speak freely."

"I think I recognize the blue chick. Okay, listen. Things are weird here in Metis, and getting weirder by the minute. I gotta tell you, Alex, there are at least a dozen Echo ops better suited to this spy crap than me."

Tesla couldn't help but smile. "You can't always choose your allies. What have you got for me?"

Red Saviour leaned over. "What is this Metis?"

"Hold on, Rick." Tesla took a deep breath. "Every piece of technology with an Echo stamp originated from Metis—think of it as a family-run business, and we're the official DBA. Metis has been working for world peace behind the scenes since the forties."

"Guess again, chief." Mercurye shook his head woefully. "Business ain't so good."

"What do you mean?"

Mercurye looked over his shoulder in an overt display of paranoia. "Your uncle's running interference for me so we can talk, but I have to make it quick, so listen up." He took a deep breath. "Metis is on the fence with this one. Most of them actually don't want to get involved. They don't want a war on their doorstep."

"War? Is war now?" Red Saviour leaned forward despite Alex's hand on her arm. "What do you know?"

"I can't—damn it, there's no time. Alex, you're on your own. Don't talk to anyone here but Nikola, and don't spill your plans. They won't help, no matter what I tell them. They won't help!"

"What about Marconi? Can't he and Nikola—"

"No good. This place is total Orwell—like some weird soulless utopia for scientists. All they care about is data, and keeping themselves safe." Mercurye's eyes glistened. "Christ, I don't know what to do!"

Alex kept his voice calm. "You're already doing it. Stay there and lobby for us—"

But Mercurye raised his hand for silence—a hand covered with blood. He glanced around and then back to the screen long enough to make contact, with eyes quivering with fear, fear greater than that of individual death: fear of helplessness.

Then in an inhumanly quick flash, he disappeared offscreen. The background, cement laced with pipework, reestablished itself. In seconds, jumpsuit-clad figures with glowing staves dashed past. Alex cut the connection. He sank back into his chair.

"That didn't look good," Belladonna said.

"Excuse me," Red Saviour said. "I am correct in thinking you mentioned names Marconi and Nikola...Tesla?"

"Yes. They're alive, but it doesn't matter." He buried his face in his hands. Everything he had counted on, everything he had thought was in his back pocket, had just been pulled out from under him. There would be no cavalry coming over the hill. Crushing despair pushed him down in his chair.

He couldn't handle this. No way. He was just a CEO, for god's sake! He wasn't a—a general, he couldn't see any way out of this but Armageddon. "Without Metis, we're screwed."

Red Saviour blew air out her lips. "Pssh. Save whining for old ladies. I am not knowing why this Metis is so important to fight against *fashista*, but my plans never included them. Is no different now."

The world was crashing in on him—had been, in fact, since the attack, when he realized that the hidden forces at work had unsheathed their swords. It was the day that he and Metis had feared all along, and yet Metis had decided to withdraw. They were doomed, all of them. Was there any point in dragging this crazed woman down into his personal pit of hopelessness? She would arrive there soon enough on her own. "You don't understand at all," he muttered.

"I don't need to. Is not my job to be hopeless."

"Nor mine, sir." Belladonna's voice possessed a steely grit. "Whatever covert ops you and Metis have been performing to halt this threat doesn't seem to have worked. The Thulians are still out there, ready to strike again. If Echo has to go down in flames fighting them, then that's what we do. Fight until we can't go on."

Red Saviour nodded. "CCCP is no stranger to sacrifice. Is actually in commission." She opened her palm as if cradling an invisible manual. "Your people are ready to give up lives, comrade. Are you ready to lead them?"

Alex blinked at her. "You make it sound easy."

"Dying is no work at all—it finds you. Important thing is what you do before you go down." She slammed the imaginary book shut. "A good leader makes each soldier's sacrifice into a building block for victory." Her lips stretched in a thin smile. "Russians are no strangers to hopeless battles. And yet, we win them."

"Indeed." He sighed. A madwoman was giving him advice, and it actually made sense, which meant his situation was worse than he thought.

And yet—they had hope, hope and determination. For the moment at least, that hope was filtering over to him. He stood on uncertain feet. "I suppose you're right. I was leaning too much on Metis for guidance. I just assumed our interests and theirs had always intersected. I don't see how any war against an organized, heavily-armed metahuman force can be won without Metis's assistance—but now I guess we'll found out."

"We'll do it the way outmanned and outgunned people have always done it, Tesla," Bella said, her eyes blazing blue, her chin up. "Like the Yanks against the Brits in 1776, like the Russians in St. Petersburg against Napoleon, and again in Stalingrad against the Nazis. We'll fight them hard, and we'll fight them smart, we'll make them fight on our ground, and on our terms."

Alex knew better. He really knew better. And yet, at that moment, their determination, their *sureness,* swept him off his feet and, like a wave that buoyed him up rather than crashed down on him, seemed to give him strength. If there was a shore to be carried to—then these two, surely, would bring everyone there.

Belladonna looked like that Rosie the Riveter poster, and Saviour like one of the propaganda pieces on the wall of her own CCCP. They made him believe in them. He felt his own spine straightening with resolve.

"Now you are talking, *tovarisch,*" Red Saviour said, with her own eyes shining. "We win, or we die. Now. Let us be getting all cards on the house."

"Table," Bella murmured.

"Table then." The Russian leaned over Tesla's desk, and he was reminded again of how tall she was. "Now. Tell me what you have not been telling me before." There was cold steel in her voice, and iron in her gaze. "Is time to stop running and take the battle to enemy."

AFTERWORD

That was how we found out about Metis, the Thulians, and the secret cities that had been operating under all our noses for decades.

There were more secrets to come, of course. None of us knew about the March Prophecies yet. And I don't think even knowing about them would have made a bit of difference to Bella and Saviour.

But if we had all known how sorely we would be tested and tried in the weeks to come, would we have still been as determined as we were that day?

I don't know.

But I'd like to think we would. Because the choice really was to fight, or to lay down and die. We could be predators, or we could be prey. It was time for the real fight to begin.

AUTHORS' NOTE

This series owes its existence to the MMORPG, *City of Heroes*, produced by Paragon Studios and NCsoft. The characters began there as the lot of us, separated by the breadth and width of the country, met over our shared enthusiasm for storytelling in the improvised theater of role-playing, and began meshing our characters' lives. The canonical background of the City Of games is so well planned and richly detailed, so well written, it practically demanded that our characters be as well developed and well rounded.

The characters in these books have evolved far past that of course, and into their own story. Some, like Red Djinni, resemble the original only in attitude. But we still play. And we are still creating new characters with new stories to tell. Who knows, one day they might end up in books too.

Meanwhile if you would like a taste, go to www. cityofheroes.com and check out the 14-day free trial offer. Don't be surprised if you get hooked.

The following is an excerpt from:

WORLD DIVIDED

Book Two of the
SECRET WORLD CHRONICLE

Created by Mercedes Lackey & Steve Libbey

Written by
MERCEDES LACKEY

with Cody Martin, Dennis Lee,
& Veronica Giguere

Available from Baen Books
February 2012
hardcover

INTRODUCTION

Victoria Victrix paused for a moment, checked her watch, double-checked her watch against the time on her laptop. Hard to believe she still had almost an hour.

But there was a lot of story to get through before...

Better get back on it.

Her fingers flew over the keyboard. *Still with me, my unknown audience? By this time you've read how it all started for us, how the Invasion arrived all over the world concealed in delivery trucks that disgorged horrors right out of a Hollywood science fiction film. How we learned that the enemy was an old one— because he wore the swastika and was led by Nazi metahumans everyone had thought long dead. How we also learned that not all of our enemies were human.*

How Echo, the organization that until now hadn't needed to worry about anything more organized than a few gangs of four or five metahuman criminals, suddenly found itself facing an army and losing. And how, eventually, the seeds of real organization against the Society of Ultima Thule came to Atlanta, where in Echo's ruined headquarters the repercussions were only just starting to shake out.

And among all those players converging on that Southern City, there were a handful that would make a difference. A handful that could save the world. But first—first, we had to save ourselves.

And there were going to be some we were going to lose. Battles, and people. That's the nature of war.

For this was—is—a war. Make no mistake about it. Even though the enemy had evaporated into nowhere, anyone that had any brains knew that the Thulians would be back.

PROLOGUE

The Invasion provided an unparalleled opportunity for anyone who wanted wealth or power to grab both. There were plenty who did. Politicians began to rise or fall based on their "solutions" or lack of them to the "Nazi Menace," or (more often than not) who or what they chose to point fingers at, agitate about, or scapegoat. It was a free ride for the criminal element. Even—well, especially—the media used the initial Invasion and the subsequent attacks we began to call "Pop-ups" as fodder for their nightly barrage of fear-inducing info-tainment. Shortsighted? Oh hell yes. But it brought in money, and the world over, "follow the money" will never steer you wrong when you are looking for human motive. It's human nature to figure that nothing bad will ever happen to you, because you, of course, are so much smarter, faster, better armed than the poor rubes in the Nightly News body-bags.

But probably the single most self-centered opportunist on the planet was about to take the gloves off and enter the arena. And what was the most dangerous about Dominic Verdigris III was this:

He actually had the brains to pull off just about anything he wanted to. He just had to be motivated enough.

CHAPTER ONE

Dinner Date

MERCEDES LACKEY AND CODY MARTIN

When it all came down to it, Dominic Verdigris III, multi-billionaire, super-genius and all that *and* a bag of chips, was a man who liked to enjoy the simpler things in life.

"I think the shark tank came out beautifully. And ahead of schedule, too!" He folded his arms across his chest, a self-satisfied grin creasing his lips as he glanced at his companion. "Don't you think, Khanjar?"

The stunningly beautiful Eurasian woman in the white silk jumpsuit could have been just about any profession that required amazing good looks. World-class supermodel good looks, almost; save for her being slightly too well-muscled. In fact, she was Verdigris' personal bodyguard, preferred assassin and lover.

"Why a shark tank, Dom?" she asked, her cool tone betraying no emotion whatsoever. "Isn't that a little...over the top? Next thing, you'll want a white angora cat."

"Order one, have it shipped to my New York penthouse." He grinned, the sort of grin that meant he got the joke and didn't want the cat. "But, my dear, being over the top is the point. People, regular people, like to have everything laid out for them in easy to understand bite-sized chunks. They don't like to be ordered or forced to believe something is so, but they like to be led to that belief and have it reinforced according to the way they think the world should be. This all plays into the belief that I'm nothing more than a rich, lovable and eccentric scamp. I intend to keep it that way; everything is so much simpler." He looked back to the shark tank, watching the sleek predators gliding through the water for a moment before turning and walking towards his desk. It was the sort of desk featured in high-end architecture magazines, a long sweep of black plexiglass without even a speck of dust on it, facing the window and the "endless pool" outside. "This lovely villa, for example. I usually prefer something a little simpler, but such extravagant luxury fulfills its purpose. Eccentric billionaire equals brainless twit. But such a nice man."

Khanjar followed him, and took a seat on a butterscotch leather chaise lounge. "Speaking of 'nice man,' you wanted me to remind you about Save the Seals."

He waved his hand. "Oh, of course. Pick a nice round number, six digits, and donate it to them. And at least three other charities or funds that are obscure enough to not be passe, but still do well in opinion polls. I've got the schedule set for when each should be done, so that the PR from one cascades nicely into the next."

"Not Weasel Welfare, then?" Khanjar deadpanned.

"Wouldn't want any of my competitors to get a dime, so no." He laughed at his own joke. "Anything else that needs attending to?"

"There's the meeting and attendant press conference that you're doing with the families of some of your employees that were killed during the Invasion attacks. Scheduled next week, Friday, in California. Everything is already booked."

"Ah, right. I'll put in the paperwork to start a trust for that one office supervisor that died saving some people, include it in the ceremony." He frowned. "Why, whenever things go seriously tits-up, are there always Nazis involved?"

"Speaking of Nazis, what do you want me to do with that Blacksnake assassin we caught in the garden?"

"Him?" The villa's automatic traps had gotten the merc before he'd penetrated too far. "Scrub him of identity, kill him, and dump him once you find out where he came from. Don't bore me with the details unless it's interesting, and try not to have too much fun. If anyone is going to wear you out, it's going to be me."

Khanjar gave him a little bow, and left the room. Verdigris sighed happily; having someone that he could be comfortable with and depend on to make sure things happened his way truly made everything easier and more enjoyable. Still, it was time to work. He settled down at his laptop, calling up several different encrypted emails and communication programs. This was all trivial stuff, no need to wake the desk up for it. Just a few finishing touches were needed for some issues; final orders and pay offs to ensure that a military junta that he was backing would succeed in toppling their country's corrupt government, more bribes to a slew of officials to ensure that the right people would look away when large shipments of drugs were crossing their routes, and that a reporter that had been causing problems for one of his shell companies would meet an unfortunate end. Typing rapid-fire, he was able to finish everything over the course of five minutes. Some of these plots were the result of careful years of planning and dealing, others mere footnotes for other larger schemes. *It's all in the details.*

A thought occurred to him as he finished. Tapping the touch-surface that activated his voice-recorded notes, he said, "Follow-up; need to order more research concerning potential and heretofore unknown Op5 metahuman or metahumans first encountered during the Invasion. Colloquially called 'angels' by mainstream media sources. End note."

The desk alerted him to the fact that it had more camera feeds on the "Mountain Incident," and he spared a moment to watch them. Tesla had bungled that one badly, and he found himself shaking his head over it once again. If there was one thing that Dom knew how to micromanage, it was the perception of his employees. He would never, ever, in a million years, have allowed some petty bureaucrats with an itching outbreak of Not In My Backyard dictate what he did or did not do with any of his employees, even one as problematic as The Mountain.

Hell, given The Mountain's case of profound depression, the disaster that had unfolded when the Governor of Georgia essentially ordered him deported was something even a moron could have predicted. They were all just lucky it hadn't been worse, that The Mountain had killed so few and wrecked so little on his final rampage into the sea. He watched all the camera feeds of the behemoth's walk out into the ocean, correlating them with coordinates and ocean currents from NOA buoys, adding it all to the mix. Everyone assumed The Mountain was dead—drowned, crushed by the depths—

Not bloody likely. So far as Dom had been able to judge, The Mountain didn't breathe and only used air to speak. And he was solid rock; how would the pressure at the bottom of the Marianas Trench bother him? Most likely, he was in a depressive coma down there, like some Japanese movie monster. Dom aimed to retrieve him. Leaving him down there was a waste of an incredible resource, and given his treatment at the hands of Echo and the US Government, it should be no problem whatsoever to recruit him once he was reawakened. Dom already had a staff of six shrinks standing by to turn him into Dom's most loyal employee ever—barring maybe Khanjar.

Khanjar strode back into the room just then, stopping in front of his desk. "Perfect timing, my dear!"

"Dinner will be ready in half an hour. Chef Ausanat also asked me to remind you to stop stealing in there to snatch food and ruin your appetite." Dominic held up his hands in mock innocence. "If you're finished, then the matter in the upper observation room is ready for you to attend to it. Before it starts bleeding on the carpet."

"Right. Let's not delay then, shall we? The carpet up there is worth more than he is." Standing up, Khanjar led him up a flight of metal stairs blended into the wall of the room. The glass door opened soundlessly as they approached, closing behind them. The observation room gave a commanding view of the bay below; from this vantage point, Verdigris could see his own personal yacht at port, as well his sport fishing boat bobbing among the waves. He had loaned it to some of his lower-tier security operatives and engineers for the weekend; they deserved the break. With Verdigris, results counted, and he always made sure to reward those of his people who produced results. Several of the companies he owned openly appeared every year on those "best companies to work for" lists. He rewarded his shadow staff even more generously. The best way to ensure loyalty was to buy it and reward it. If you worked for Dominic Verdigris, and someone tried to bribe you, your best course of action was to report it. You would be rewarded by a bonus of at least twice the size of the bribe, and sometimes a promotion.

This was how Karamjit Bhandari had come to be in Verdigris' observation room. He had been a little too interested in Freshette Filters, LLC, after it had gotten the contract to supply Bombay with a series of new pure water treatment plants when their water infrastructure was destroyed in the Invasion.

Karamjit had never been very imposing before Verdigris' people had gotten hold of him. A typical Bombay specimen of the prosperous sort, he was a little soft around the middle, and just starting to lose his hair. His suit had been very expensive, and nicely tailored to hide that beginning spare tire. Just another CEO in the never ending flood of same that poured out of business schools every year. He would have looked at home at any boardroom table across the globe.

But he was not at a boardroom table. He was hand-cuffed to a steel chair that was itself an artwork—and as a consequence, not very comfortable to sit on. He'd clearly been handled roughly in transport. That lovely suit was abraded and torn, as was his shirt, and his face was bruised and battered.

"Glad to see you made it, Mr. Bhandari. We don't really need to go into how you got here, or what brought you here. You know it, I know it, so on and so forth. It's a really old story; you got greedy. So, I'll cut to the chase." Verdigris held up a small PDA. "This controls several charges that have been placed in your home. Your family is currently asleep, as of about thirty seconds ago. It's a lovely gas, my own invention, there will be no traces that police forensics will find. It'll be enough to keep them asleep until I want, and paralyzed while still experiencing everything when they do wake up." He pursed his lips. "It's not ideal yet, the paralysis is permanent, but I'll work that out later. I'd like you to direct your attention to this screen." He pointed at an LCD monitor positioned on a table in front of Karamjit. Pressing the touch screen, the LCD flared to life, showing a live image of a rather impressive three story home. Activating a function on the PDA caused the house to burst into flame, with gouts of fire spewing out of almost every window. Karamjit started trying to shout and cry through his gag, bucking in his chair against the restraints. "That takes care of the Bhandari clan. You'll be fingered as the one responsible for the arson; a cleverly constructed trail of evidence that hints at your coming psychotic breakdown will make sure of that. It'll also show that you fled the country after raiding your bank accounts, heading for parts unknown and never to be heard from again." Dominic pocketed the

PDA after switching off the LCD monitor, and began to pace in front of Karamjit.

"This could have been avoided quite easily, you know. But, don't worry; your death is rather convenient for me. You are actually doing me a bit of a service, here. Criminals of all stripes have a habit of forgetting loyalties and debts fairly quickly." He paused in front of his victim, who was now sobbing uncontrollably through his gag. "This will be a reminder, not just for your associates, but for everyone; don't fuck with Dominic Verdigris." Khanjar stepped behind Karamjit, and in one smooth motion brought a small kuboton down on the back of his neck with a sickening pop. Karamjit, now limp, went into shock almost immediately, though he retained consciousness. "You're paralyzed now. I think this concludes our business, Mr. Bhandari." Khanjar released the helpless man from his bonds, and shoved him out of the chair. He rolled to the edge off the observation platform, which did not boast anything like a railing. Verdigris did not care for "nanny architecture." If you were too stupid or helpless to avoid falling...too bad, welcome to Darwin's Waiting Room.

Dominic and Khanjar both walked towards the helpless man. The shark tank was directly below. Verdigris smiled; a model of efficiency as ever, Khanjar had applied just the right amount of force to Karamjit when she ejected him from the chair. He dug a toe—elegantly clad in a gorgeous Italian shoe—just under Karamjit's pudgy waist, and shoved. Sometimes it really mattered to add a personal touch when making business decisions.

The former CEO of a company that was shortly

going to be as dead as his family plummeted into the shark tank. The sharks had been primed by a high-tech version of "chumming" that left the water crystal clear. Also Verdigris' invention. On the way to it, he'd come up with a brand new BBQ sauce flavor as well. The sharks reacted to the sudden intrusion with a ravenous feeding frenzy.

Verdigris observed for a few long moments before turning to his confidant and companion. "I'm starting to get hungry. Want to shower, and then we'll work up an appetite together?"

—end excerpt—

from
WORLD DIVIDED: Book 2 of the Secret World Chronicle
available in hardcover,
February 2012, from Baen Books

MERCEDES LACKEY:
MISTRESS OF FANTASY

BARDIC VOICES
The Lark and the Wren
The Robin and the Kestrel
The Eagle and the Nightingales
The Free Bards
Four & Twenty Blackbirds
Bardic Choices: A Cast of Corbies (with Josepha Sherman)

URBAN FANTASIES WITH ROSEMARY EDGHILL
Beyond World's End
Spirits White as Lightning
Mad Maudlin
Bedlam's Edge(ed.)
Music to My Sorrow

This Scepter'd Isle (with Roberta Gellis)
Ill Met by Moonlight (with Roberta Gellis)
And Less Than Kind (with Roberta Gellis)
By Slanderous Tongues (with Roberta Gellis)
Knight of Ghosts and Shadows (with Ellen Guon)
Born to Run (with Larry Dixon)
Wheels of Fire (with Mark Shepherd)
Chrome Circle (with Larry Dixon)
The Chrome Borne (with Larry Dixon)
The Otherworld (with Larry Dixon & Mark Shepherd)

AND MORE!
Werehunter
Fiddler Fair
The Fire Rose
The Wizard of Karres (with Eric Flint & Dave Freer)
The Shadow of the Lion (with Eric Flint & Dave Freer)
This Rough Magic (with Eric Flint & Dave Freer)
Brain Ships (with Anne McCaffrey & Margaret Ball)
The Sword of Knowledge (with C.J. Cherryh Leslie Fish,
& Nancy Asire)

PRAISE FOR LOIS McMASTER BUJOLD

What the critics say:

The Warrior's Apprentice: "Now here's a fun romp through the spaceways—not so much a space opera as space ballet... It has all the 'right stuff.' A lot of thought and thoughtfulness stand behind the all-too-human characters. Enjoy this one, and look forward to the next."   —Dean Lambe, *SF Reviews*

"The pace is breathless, the characterization thoughtful and emotionally powerful, and the author's narrative technique and command of language compelling. Highly recommended." —*Booklist*

Brothers in Arms: "...she gives it a genuine depth of character, while reveling in the wild turnings of her tale... Bujold is as audacious as her favorite hero, and as brilliantly (if sneakily) successful."   —*Locus*

"Miles Vorkosigan is such a great character that I'll read anything Lois wants to write about him... a book to re-read on cold rainy days."   —Robert Coulson, *Comics Buyers Guide*

Borders of Infinity: "Bujold's series hero Miles Vokosigan may be a lord by birth and an admiral by rank, but a bone disease that has left him hobbled and in frequent pain has sensitized him to the suffering of outcasts in her very hierarchical era.... Playing off of Miles's reserve and cleverness, Bujold draws outrageous and outlandish foils to color her high-minded adventures."   —*Publishers Weekly*

Falling Free: "In *Falling Free* Lois McMaster Bujold has written her fourth straight superb novel.... How to break down a talent like Bujold's into analyzable components? Best not to try. Best to say: 'Read, or you will be missing something extraordinary.'"
—Roland Green, *Chicago Sun-Times*

The Vor Game: "The chronicles of Miles Vokosigan are far too witty to be literary junk food, but they rouse the kind of craving that makes popcorn magically vanish during a double feature."   —Faren Miller, *Locus*

MORE PRAISE FOR
LOIS McMASTER BUJOLD

What the readers say:

"My copy of *Shards of Honor* is falling apart I've reread it so often.... I'll read whatever you write. You've certainly proved yourself a grand storyteller.

—Lisa Kolbe, Colorado Springs, CO

"I experience the stories of Miles Vorkosigan as almost viscerally uplifting... But certainly, even the weightiest theme would have less impact than a cinder on snow were it not for a rousing good story, and good story-telling with it. This is the second thing I want to thank you for... I suppose if you boiled down all I've said to its simplest expression, it would be that I immensely enjoy and admire your work. I submit that, as literature, your work raises the overall level of the science fiction genre, and spiritually, you work cannot avoid positively influencing all who read it."

—Glen Stonebreaker, Gaithersburg, MD

"'The Mountains of Mourning' [in *Borders of Infinity*] was one of the best-crafted, and simply best, works I'd ever read. When I finished it, I immediately turned back to the beginning and read it again, and I can't remember the last time I did that."

—Betsy Bizot, Lisle, IL

"I can only hope that you will continue to write, so that I can continue to read (and of course buy) your books, for they make me laugh and cry and think ... rare indeed."

—Steven Knott, Major, USAF

What do you say?

Cordelia's Honor
pb • 0-671-57828-6 • $7.99
Contains *Shards of Honor* and Hugo-award winner *Barrayar* in one volume.

Young Miles
trade pb • 0-671-87782-8 • $17.00
pb • 0-7434-3616-4 • $7.99
Contains *The Warrior's Apprentice*, Hugo-award winner *The Vor Game*, and Hugo-award winner "The Mountains of Mourning" in one volume.

Cetaganda
0-671-87744-5 • $7.99

Miles, Mystery and Mayhem
pb • 0-7434-3618-0 • $7.99
Contains *Cetaganda, Ethan of Athos* and "Labyrinth" in one volume.

Brothers in Arms
pb • 1-4165-5544-7 • $7.99

Miles Errant
trade pb • 0-7434-3558-3 • $15.00
Contains "The Borders of Infinity," *Brothers in Arms* and *Mirror Dance* in one volume.

Mirror Dance
pb • 0-671-87646-5 • $7.99

Memory
pb • 0-671-87845-X • $7.99

Miles in Love
hc • 1-4165-5522-6 • $19.00
trade pb • 1-4165-5547-1 • $14.00
Contains *Komarr*, *A Civil Campaign* and "A Winterfair Gift" in one volume.

Komarr
hc • 0-671-87877-8 • $22.00
pb • 0-671-57808-1 • $7.99

A Civil Campaign
hc • 0-671-57827-8 • $24.00
pb • 0-671-57885-5 • $7.99

Miles, Mutants & Microbes
hc • 1-4165-2141-0 • $18.00
pb • 1-4165-5600-1 • $7.99
Contains *Falling Free* "Labyrinth", and *Diplomatic Immunity* in one volume.

Diplomatic Immunity
hc • 0-7434-3533-8 • $25.00
pb • 0-7434-3612-1 • $7.99

Cryoburn
hc • 978-1-4391-3394-1 • $25.00

Falling Free
pb • 1-4165-5546-3 • $7.99

16th Century Europe...intrigue, knights, courtesans, magic, demons...

Historical Fantasy From Masters of the Genre

The Shadow of the Lion
Mercedes Lackey, Eric Flint & Dave Freer

Venice, 1537. A failed magician, a fugitive orphan, a reluctant prince, a devious courtesan, and a man of faith must make uneasy alliance or the city will be consumed by evil beyond human comprehension.   0-7434-7147-4 • $7.99

This Rough Magic
Mercedes Lackey, Eric Flint & Dave Freer

The demon Chernobog, defeated by the Lion of Venice, besieges the isle of Corfu in order to control the Adriatic. Far from the Lion's help, two knights organize guerrillas, and a young woman uncovers the island's ancient mystic powers. If she can ally with them, she may be able to repel the invaders—but only at a bitter personal price.

0-7434-9909-3 • $7.99

Much Fall of Blood
Mercedes Lackey, Eric Flint & Dave Freer

Two knights on a diplomatic mission are caught in a civil war. One of their few allies is Prince Vlad, grandson of another Vlad—called the Devil by some.

HC 978-1-4391-3351-4 • $27.00
PB 978-1-4391-3416-0 • $7.99
